Widow's Mite
- - -
Who's Afraid?

by Elisabeth Sanxay Holding

Introduction by Gregory Shepard

Stark House Press • Eureka California

WIDOW'S MITE / WHO'S AFRAID?

Published by Stark House Press
1315 H Street
Eureka, CA 95501, USA
griffinskye3@sbcglobal.net
www.starkhousepress.com

WIDOW'S MITE

WHO'S AFAID?

ISBN: 978-1-944520-34-2

Book design by Mark Shepard, SHEPGRAPHICS.COM

First Stark House Press Edition: February 2018

FIRST EDITION

WIDOW'S MITE

Tilly feels like a poor relation. She and her young son certainly wouldn't be living with her cousin Sybil unless they had to. But tonight, as usual, Sybil has had too much to drink, and needs to lie down for a bit before her dinner guests arrive. It falls to Tilly to accompany her upstairs, and naturally Sybil asks for one of her pills. There is only one left, but Tilly dutifully fetches it. After that, Sybil seems to fall asleep almost immediately. How is Tilly to know that the pill contains cyanide? Naturally, the police are suspicious. But how can she confess that she was one who gave it to Sybil when there is no else to protect her son?

WHO'S AFRAID?

It all seemed like an exciting new adventure to Susie Alban, selling Gateway's culture program for Mr. Chiswick. But her first appointment goes sour when the husband of her first contact, hearing the name Chiswick, becomes verbally abusive and slams the door in her face. Later that evening, she comes across the body of the husband on the path to her lodging. The police think that Susie is involved. But this is only the beginning of her problems. Because someone starts shadowing her. Could it be the doctor who befriended her on the train? Or the young student? Or the darkly handsome Mr. Loder? Or even the owner of the lodging house? For whatever reason, one of them wants Susie dead.

Elisabeth Sanxay Holding:
The Revamped Introduction

[Originally published in 2003, re-edited with new material]

"Before the term "roman noir" had even been coined, her specialty was isolated and desperate characters with profoundly poor decision-making skills."—Jake Hinkson, *Criminalelement.com*

We have the Depression to thank for Elisabeth Sanxay Holding's career as a mystery author. Until 1929, she had been writing serious, mainstream novels like *Rosaleen Among the Artists, Angelica, The Unlit Lamp* and *The Shoals of Honour.* She published six novels before the Depression, starting with *Invincible Minnie* in 1920, and ending with *The Silk Purse* in 1928. Early critics noted her expert characterization, and in the *New York Times* review of *The Silk Purse*, the reviewer said: "They are as real a collection of peoples as ever said yes when they wished to heaven they could say no."

So when the Depression hit in 1929 and she was no longer able to sell her mainstream novels, Holding turned to writing mysteries. Or, more properly, suspense novels. Because, simply put, Elisabeth Sanxay Holding is the precursor to the entire women's psychological suspense genre, and authors like Patricia Highsmith and Ruth Rendell owe her a very large debt of gratitude.

Holding was one of the first to write mystery novels that didn't so much ask whodunit, but whydunit? In fact, we know whodunit because it's quite often the main character. It's the "why" that is always the most important part of her books. The psychological underpinnings of her novels form the basis of the mystery. Her characters always act from a very determined point of view. Whether from guilt, discontent, deception, misconception, or even pure altruism, they act out their dramas with very little consideration for other points of view. And therein lies the conflict. They have all got blinders on, seeing just what they want to see, each with their own misguided agenda. They lie when it will get them in the most trouble and tell the truth when it's in their own worst interest. In other words, her characters feel very real to us—we believe in them.

A rich, alcoholic husband grows tired of his well-meaning but lower-class wife. Everything she does irritates him. He decides he must get rid of her but his drinking is making him delusional and easily annoyed. Who can he trust? As he rushes from one hidden bottle, one seedy bar to another, the answer is clearly "no one." When his chauffeur comes to him with a plan to catch his wife with another man, he jumps at it. After all, sooner or later you've got to trust somebody.

This is the basic plot of *The Innocent Mrs. Duff*. What makes the book so compelling is the degree to which Holding gets under the skin of this self-deluded man. She wrote the story in a crisp, staccato style and makes the reader feel every bit of the scheming husband's mounting alcoholic mania. Though casual drinking was more a part of the daily lifestyle in Holding's day, she wasn't afraid to shed some light on its darker aspects. In fact, she had previously explored the theme of the alcoholic male in the *The Obstinate Murderer*—albeit more sympathetically—and clearly knew this personality well.

> *"She doesn't pour it on and make you feel irritated. Her characters are wonderful; and she has a sort of inner calm which I find very attractive. I recommend for your attention, if you have not read them,* Net of Cobwebs, The Innocent Mrs. Duff, The Blank Wall.*"*—Raymond Chandler from a letter to his UK publisher

Chandler makes an excellent point. *The Innocent Mrs. Duff* and *The Blank Wall* (filmed twice, as *The Reckless Moment* in 1949 and *The Deep End* in 2001) are arguably two of her best works, and have almost entirely remained in print since she wrote them. Dell published several of her novels in paperback in the 50's, and Mercury published a few in digest form as well. And back in the 1960's, Ace Books published twelve of her books as Ace Doubles. But until Stark House came along in 2003, she had almost entirely gone out of print. Inexcusable that should happen to an author whom Raymond Chandler called "the top suspense writer of them all" in a letter to his British publisher.

All in all, Holding published eighteen suspense novels in her lifetime, beginning with *Miasma* in 1929, and ending with *Widow's Mite* in 1952. Many of these novels were also serialized in national magazines, and almost all were published in paperback and foreign editions, as well as by mystery book clubs. She also published quite a few short stories in magazines ranging from *McCalls*, *American Magazine* and *Ladies Home Journal* to *Alfred Hitchcock's Mystery Magazine*, *The Saint*, *Ellery Queen's Mystery Magazine* and *The Magazine of Fantasy and Science Fiction*. She even wrote a children's story, *Miss Kelly*, the story of a cat who could understand and speak human, and who comes to the aid of a terrified tiger.

Elisabeth Sanxay was born in Brooklyn in 1889, the descendant of an upper middle-class family, and was educated in a series of private schools, specifically Whitcombe's School, The Packer Institute, Miss Botsford's

School and the Staten Island Academy. She married a British diplomat named George E. Holding in 1913 and together they traveled widely in South America and the Caribbean, settling in Bermuda for awhile where her husband was a government officer. She also raised two daughters, Skeffington and Antonia, the latter of whom married Peter Schwed (until his death in 2003 the executor of Holding's estate and a retired author and publisher with Simon and Schuster).

Holding was thirty-one when her first book was published. Right from the beginning she introduced the theme of discontent that she was to use so often in her mystery books. *Invincible Minnie* starts off slowly—telling at first when it should be showing—but evolves into a fairly lurid tale, the compelling story of a headstrong woman who uses sex to control men and get her way. There's no pat, happy ending either. Minnie runs roughshod over everyone, including her sister and children, and prevails through sheer determination. Holding's lean 40's style was only seen in glimpses in this first effort, but her characterizations were already taking shape in the relentless actions of Minnie and the various people she controlled.

With her second novel, Holding lets the story tell itself, vastly improving over the style of her first book. *Rosaleen Among the Artists,* a bit less melodramatic than *Invincible Minnie,* tells the story of a self-sacrificing young woman struggling to survive and find love in New York City. Though polished off with a sweeter ending, there is much travail as Rosaleen hits rock bottom before finally being united with her soul mate, Mr. Landry. In fact, the two are so matched in the stubbornness with which they hold onto their ideals—tenaciously sacrificing their own happiness at every turn-that they almost wear each other out by the end of the book. Ironically, it is their own principles that almost kill their only chance at love.

In 1929, when the Depression killed her mainstream career, Holding had to do something to help support her two daughters. She could have started writing nice, cozy romantic mysteries. But she just didn't have it in her. The characters she was creating were too contrary, too impulsive—too flawed—and not particularly romantic. They didn't act in their own best interests, holding onto beliefs that invariably precipitated trouble. It's as if they felt compelled to do the very thing that caused the most havoc, even if for all the best reasons.

As a consequence, the mystery novels Holding began to write were dark affairs, having more in common with noir than standard detective fiction. It's easy to understand why she was such a favorite of Chandler's. Murder and mania are always lurking in the wings—and the menace doesn't always exist from the outside, but is quite often found from within. These are characters with something to hide. Sometimes there is a happy ending, sometimes not. Sometimes there is a detective—someone to harry the protagonist into a panic of fear and doubt—but usually not. You might say that Holding's characters are quite often lucky if they can make it to the last page with their health, if not their sanity, intact.

In *The Virgin Huntress* we follow young Monty on V-Day as he meets an older woman, Dona Luisa, and is brought into a world of class and culture he had always dreamed of. He is a charming if somewhat insecure young man, somewhat expedient—perhaps too expedient—in his past dealings with women. In fact, he is constantly nagged by secrets from his past, secrets that begin to fracture him as Dona Luisa's niece Rose begins to pry into his past life. By the end of the short novel, Monty has become completely unraveled, the victim of his own expediency. It's not a pretty portrait.

Another of Holding's favorite themes involves fractious family relationships and domestic disputes. *Dark Power* is a perfect example. In the first chapter we meet a young lady, Diana, who discovers that she is quite penniless and soon to be out on the street. Before this happens, however, she is suddenly rescued by an eccentric uncle she didn't know she had. He happily escorts her back to the family home, where she meets such a thoroughly dysfunctional collection of relatives that by the end of the book she barely makes it out alive.

Holding also loved to examine the way stress works on characters, particularly middle-aged men, and would combine this with her theme of domestic disharmony. *The Innocent Mrs. Duff* is an obvious example, but *The Death Wish* is another in which a man, Mr. Delancey, who had always thought himself happily married, comes to a moment of crisis in which he discovers that he actually hates his wife. She has slowly been emasculating him by controlling his purse strings, but when his best friend reveals a similar domestic situation and announces his plans to kill his own wife, Delancey is plunged into a world of self-doubt. At first he is shocked by his friend's confession, and when the wife of his friend is found drowned, he hopes that it is the accident that it seems to be. But a seed has been planted, and nothing in his formerly phlegmatic life will ever be the same.

Holding's deft hand at characterization makes all these situations ring true, giving them a psychological perspective that not only presents all her characters' foibles sympathetically, but creates the tension that propels her story along as well. Their actions are understandable, given the circumstances, and all the more frustrating because they are so identifiable. In *The Death Wish*, we watch Delancey try to convince himself at first that his wife is simply moody and a bit insecure. He wants to think the best of her. But the reader knows that his wife's insecure nagging is stifling him, her words little barbs that sink in and latch Delancey to her side, subtly but firmly controlling him. We feel his weakness and frustration, his mounting domestic horror, and nothing that proceeds from this realization seems anything less than inevitable. Not even murder.

This is Holding's true forte, that she can make the commonplace, the ordinary, so horrific and so suspenseful. But make no mistake, whether writing about dysfunctional families or failed marriages, her books are full of mystery. In *Lady Killer,* a young recently-wedded ex-model named Honey is on a cruise ship in the Caribbean with her older husband, who is turning out to be a fussy, fault-finding old crab. At the same time that she begins to realize that a life with this man will be completely intolerable, she also becomes aware that the man in the next cabin might possibly be trying to kill his wife. She begins to set about a campaign to protect this poor, plain and unfortunate woman, who doesn't really seem to want her help. In fact, no one on board seems to feel that Honey has any business stirring up trouble.

But the more Honey finds out, the more mysterious her fellow passengers begin to seem to her. Even her own husband begins to seem alien to her. And when she finds a body, even that isn't quite what it seems. But still the little mysteries pile up, and we are swept up in Honey's suspicions and doubts until even we begin to believe, like her, that *no one* is to be trusted.

Miasma presents us with another set of mysteries. A young doctor named Dennison has just about reached the end of his financial resources when he is contacted by a wealthy older doctor in town who wants him to take up residency in his house and assume the care of his patients. All well and good, except that the doctor's young nurse immediately warns Dennison to leave, mysterious patients come and go in the middle of the night, and his predecessor has gone missing. And then there is the weird drug that the older doctor prescribes to certain of his patients, one of whom is now dead from an apparent heart attack. Holding keeps the mysteries coming until both we and Dennison are wondering what the hell is going on here; daring us to put the book down no matter how late it is and how early we have to get up the next morning.

And then there is her Caribbean mystery, *Strange Crime in Bermuda,* a peculiar tale of a missing person on an enclosed island community. Young Hamish is asked to journey to Bermuda at the request of his old friend Malloy, but when he arrives, Malloy sets an appointment to meet him and then fails to show up for their meeting. It soon turns out that no one has seen the man that day, but everyone has a different idea of what of what has happened to him. A sense of confusion and dread sets in as we experience the unfolding events from Hamish's stubborn, narrow point of view. Hamish is continually misled by his various misguided allegiances, until he himself becomes the prime suspect. The resolution is both obvious and unexpected.

Which brings us to the two books herein—*Widow's Mite* and *Who's Afraid?* Holding is a past master at showing how easy it is to lie to the police, and how quickly this lie turns into a maelstrom of doubt and horror for the character who perpetrates it. *Widow's Mite* even goes so far as to start with a dinner party in which one of the guests starts expounding on the essential fault of most mystery novels: the lie. "It never works. If anyone's in any way mixed up in a police case, the only thing to do is to tell the truth about what you know, and tell it quick." When the hostess is found dead, poisoned, this bit of advice is exactly what none of the characters follow, including the protagonist, Tilly.

Tilly thinks that by holding back the information that it was she who accidentally gave the hostess the fatal pill that she will be protecting her young son (the "mite"), who would have no one to look after him if she were taken to jail. But hers is only one justification. Everyone has one, each character thinking that by lying that can protect someone else.

The second novel in this collection, *Who's Afraid?*, offers a more straightforward mystery. A young woman, Susie Alban, comes to a new town to sell a door-to-door charm program called Gateway, but all of her contacts are hostile to her. And someone at the boarding house where she is staying begins shadowing her. Something is terribly amiss, but like oblivious Miss Alban, we haven't a clue what's going on, just that *no one* is quite what they seem. And just to make matters more mysterious, when one of her contacts is found murdered, Susie is, of course, persuaded to lie to the police.

Once again, it starts with a lie. But as Susie quickly discovers: "It was a mistake. It's always a mistake to lie. It always hurts someone; if not other people, then yourself… What a confusing business this is!" Her upbringing dictates that "there shouldn't be any confusion. There ought to be just simply a right thing to do, or a wrong thing." But Holding knows that this is never the case, that it's never that simple. When you start with a lie, there is nowhere to go but south.

There is a reason that Dorothy B. Hughes said that "connoisseurs will continue their rush when each new Holding reaches publication." Her books are, first and foremost, very readable. Not only are they excellent examples of psychological suspense and first rate character studies, they move along at a nice, brisk pace. Holding was never one for overwriting. Her dialog always sounds just right, all the doubtful pauses—the self-serving and self-deceptive lies—in place. We may not always like these characters. Sometimes they can be pretty damn frustrating. But Holding makes us feel compelled to keep reading about them.

Elisabeth Sanxay Holding passed away in 1955 at age 65, and her novels quickly dropped from sight. Until recently, her mystery novels had remained a best-kept secret. But Holding was one of the best, and it is a pleasure to be able to bring her books back into print again, and to see her rediscovered by a new generation of readers. As *New York Times* critic Anthony Boucher wrote back in the 1950s, "she's in a class by herself."

Gregory Shepard
Publisher, Stark House Press
September, 2003/October 2017

"*Holding's name doesn't even appear in many standard reference works ... but remains a writer ripe for rediscovery.*"
—Sergio Angelini, *Tipping My Fedora*

"*A phantasmagoria of despair, distrust and suspicion that consumes protagonist and reader alike.*"
—Ed Gorman, "Elisabeth Sanxay Holding"

"*This is the kind of thing I recommend to a few like myself who find the purest refreshment in hallucinations and horrors, in damnation, dipsomania, and dismay... I have always admired the unusual skill and mischief of Mrs. Holding's writings.*"—Christopher Morley

"*The hallmark of Holding's work was subtle, psychologically nuanced portraits of women making sense of troubled marriages, conflicted relationships with children, or intrigue thrown up by the larger world.*"—Sarah Weinman, *Troubled Daughters, Twisted Wives*

"*Holding was especially intrigued by the phenomenon of middle-aged, educated people under intense stress, and was more concerned with innate justice than the literal letter of the law - and with the uncomfortable zones of grey between good and evil, right and wrong, that characterise much of crime-writing today but were then seen as shocking, if not immoral.*"
—Maxim Jakubowski, "Murders She Wrote," *The Guardian*

"*Her noirish tales are as dark as they can be, with protagonists either swept up by petty human selfishness or as the dealers of the same dark hand.*"—Wes Lubowsky, *Booklist*

"*For subtlety, realistic conviction, incredible economy, she's in a class by herself.*"—Anthony Boucher, *NY Times*

"*If you want to deepen your understanding of noir's roots—and if you want to read some crackerjack storytelling along the way—find your way to Elisabeth Sanxay Holding.*"
—Jake Hinkson, *Criminalelement.com*

Widow's Mite

by Elisabeth Sanxay Holding

CHAPTER ONE

Tilly MacDonald glanced at her wrist watch, and it showed nearly half-past five, the dreaded hour. She was sitting on the grass, in a little glade of silver birch trees, with her small son Robert playing near her with a set of wooden blocks. His dark brows were drawn together; he was growing angry because, on this uneven ground, his buildings kept falling down. The slender trees hid them from view of the house, but Tilly could see it, watch it. She had to do that.

And then her cousin Sibyl Fleming came out onto the terrace, a handsome auburn-haired woman, a little too flamboyant, her slacks and her tight pink jersey very unbecoming to her stout figure and her ruddy face. A maid followed her, with a tray bearing a giant cocktail shaker and a cluster of glasses.

Maybe somebody else is coming, Tilly thought. Oh, if only somebody else will come! For, if nobody came, she would have to go up to the terrace and sit with Sibyl, and it would be miserable. After a drink or two, Sibyl would either cry, about the ingratitude, the treachery, the intrigues against her, or she would become arrogant and domineering. Whatever her mood she did not want to be alone; if no one else came, it had to be Tilly. She and Robert had only been here a week, but already there was a pattern to everything that went on in this house.

Then out sauntered Howard Fleming, Sibyl's husband. If he'll only stay, thought Tilly. Sometimes they would talk for a long time about stocks and bonds and debentures, their broker and their lawyer, whom they distrusted, as they did their doctor. Sometimes they had a neighborhood scandal to dissect.

But this time it was not to be like that. He poured himself a cocktail, and sipped it, standing, a long, lean man, fastidiously dressed, with a disagreeable face, and smooth blond hair which Sibyl, in a rage, had told Tilly was a toupee. Bald as an egg, she had told Tilly. One time, down at the beach, when he was ignoring me *utterly*, and being simply too suave and fascinating to some girl, I simply tweaked it off, and there he was. Everybody simply roared.

Tilly was too far away to hear their words, but from their attitude, the way Sibyl sat up straight in her chair, the way he stared over her head, never looking at her, she knew they were quarreling. In a few moments, Howard set down his empty glass on the table, and strolled back into the house.

I'll have to go, Tilly thought. Sibyl had invited her and Robert to spend the summer, and it had been a godsend; she had sublet their dingy little apartment on Tenth Street; she would have the money coming in, and no expenses here, and she needed money desperately. And it was good for Robert to be in the country.

Her husband Ian had come back uninjured from the war, and, as far as she could see, unaffected by it. He was happy, almost wildly happy, about everything, above all, when he knew they were going to have a child. He, or she, is going to get all the breaks, he had said. Watch my dust. So happy, so gay, so confident. They had had three months of married life when he came back, then he had gone down to Florida to see a millionaire about a "deal." He wouldn't tell her about it. But it's in the bag, sugar, he had said. We'll be on top of the world. She had waited two weeks, alone, in the dingy little apartment, and then she had learned that Ian was dead. He had gone out in a motor-cruiser with his millionaire and a party, and something had happened, an explosion; she had never quite understood. Only that Ian and two other people had been killed. Not the millionaire. He had written Tilly a nice letter, grave and sympathetic, but he had made it clear that Ian had been in charge of the engine, and that the fatal accident had been his fault. Reckless, he had called him. I understand, he had written, that the families of our war-heroes are adequately provided for, but if you should, at any time, be in need of financial assistance, please do not hesitate to call upon me.

All right! Tilly thought. Maybe I'm just a bad manager. For what she got was not "adequate," and as Robert grew older, and went to school and to college, it would be less and less so. I've got to do the best I can with Sibyl, she thought. After all, she isn't *my* cousin, she's Ian's cousin. It's very *nice* of her. If she ever gets furious at me, she'll send us away, and, with the apartment sublet, I don't know where we could go.

"Robert," she said, "you'll play right here till Mommy comes back, won't you?"

"Yes, I *will*, Mommy!" he said, with energy, and he meant it. But he was only five, and the grounds were so large, he always wandered away.

"You promise me you won't go out in the road, or down on the beach?"

"Yes, Mommy."

He was so little, in his shorts and striped jersey, his dark cropped hair, his brilliant, eager eyes, he wanted so to learn about the world he lived in, to look at everything, to feel everything, to try what strength he had. He was affectionate and good, and he meant to do what she told him, but anything would distract him.

She had to go to Sibyl. Ian's ten thousand dollar insurance had dwindled away, during these five years, and when it was all gone.... She rose, a tall girl, broad-shouldered and slender and long-limbed, with a proudly set blond head, clear, fine features, a rich, full mouth, long, brilliant blue eyes.

She was a notable beauty, but she did not know it. She was proud, but it was pride of her Massachusetts family, her college, proud of having been Ian's wife, proud of behaving properly, proud about her little son. She dressed neatly, and that was all, a black faille skirt, a blue bargain blouse too big for her.

As she mounted the steps of the terrace, Sibyl was pouring herself another drink; in silence she poured it, and pushed it across the table to Tilly, and there was an ominous, sullen look on her flushed face.

"Well, no, thanks, Sibyl."

"If you did take a drink now and then," said Sibyl, "you might be a little less gloomy and forbidding. If you'd even smoke a cigarette."

"I'm sorry."

"But there's one thing you've simply *got* to do. I've some people coming in to dinner, and you've got to be decently dressed."

"I have the pretty nylon blouse you gave me."

"*No!*" said Sibyl. "You can *not* come down to dinner in that. You're my cousin's wife, and you're staying with me. I know you like to pose as a poor, forlorn young widow, but it reflects on *me*. Now, when I go upstairs, I want you to come with me, and I'll send for Pauline, and we'll pick out one of my dresses, and she can make any little changes you want."

"But, Sibyl ... Anyhow, Sibyl, there wouldn't be time for her to do any sewing before dinner."

"Really, Tilly, you're so willful and stubborn. You object to *everything*. No wonder people say that Robert's such an unattractive child—"

"*Who said that?*"

"I certainly shan't give you any names, but quantities of people. He's not a bit affectionate and friendly, and he doesn't get on with other children—"

"You mean those horrible Graham children? They're almost the only ones he ever sees here. If there were any nice children for him to play with, you'd see."

Sibyl poured herself another cocktail.

"Well, my dear," she said, "if it's so miserable here for Robert, and if you feel so ill-used—"

No! Tilly thought. She *mustn't* send us away now. The apartment's sublet and we haven't any place to go, and I've got to save money to start Robert in a good school.

"Robert isn't a bit miserable, Sibyl," she said. "He loves the beach, and he loves the gardener's cats. And I don't think I'm ill-used. It's just that I'm—not awfully social."

"I wanted you both to be so happy ...," said Sibyl, with tears flooding her eyes. "When I saw you in that absolute slum in New York, living on that *tiny* insurance Ian left ... How *could* he have left you like that?"

She took a handkerchief out of her purse and dried her eyes, but more tears were flowing.

Tilly was silent for a moment, rigid; she had a queer feeling as if she were somehow holding her heart, to stop it from leaping with pain and anger.

"Well, you know," she said, presently, "Ian was only twenty-three when he went into the Air Force. He hadn't had much time—to make a fortune, or to save a lot. He did—the best he could."

"O God!" said Sibyl. "The ruined lives ...! War *affects* me so—I mean, I suffer so, for others...."

Tilly had heard this before, and she did not feel obliged to listen carefully. She could think, just for a few moments, of her few months of marriage with Ian, and their happiness.

"I've *tried* to do so *much* for you and Robert ...," said Sibyl, pouring herself another drink. "Of course, I have to support Howard *completely* now; he never even *thinks* of trying to earn anything. He *says* he's working on a book, but ... And there's Taylor in school. He never—" She wept again. "He never writes to me—unless he wants—more money."

Taylor Price was her fifteen-year-old son by a former marriage. He was now in boarding school, and, Tilly thought, a very unlikable child.

"I'm going upstairs to rest now," Sibyl said, rising. "*Are* you or are you *not* coming with me to get a dress?"

She was very haughty and cold now, and that was dangerous. She could send us away, Tilly thought; she could even imagine the words. Tilly, I really do *not* see any point in your staying here any longer. You *obviously dislike* me....

"Of course I'm coming," she said. "I'll just run and get Robert and leave him with Gloria."

"My dear," said Sibyl, drying her eyes, "I *think* I've reminded you *many* times before that Gloria is a *cook*, and *not* a nursemaid."

"Oh, she doesn't mind him in the kitchen. She'll give him a bowl of bread and milk—"

"You know *perfectly* well that she won't. She'll fix a whole supper for him—neglecting her own proper work."

But he's only five! Tilly cried to herself. I can't leave him wandering around outdoors alone, when it will soon begin to grow dark. He ought to have his supper at six. He ought to get to bed early....

"I'm going upstairs now," said Sibyl, still cold and haughty. "You can either come up with me, and we'll pick out something decent for you to wear, or you can disgrace me—at my own table."

Sibyl's room was all Sibyl; a wide bed of green lacquer, covered with green taffeta and heaped with pillows, a chaise longue all white, wallpaper with a Chinese design in green and white and brown, a dressing-table with a mirror flanked by lights for various purposes, a jade-green rug, white venetian blinds. It was a large and airy room with the look, the over-elaborate look that Sibyl's clothes had.

Sibyl, a little unsteady on her feet, went over to the big bed, and stretched out on it.

"Ring for Pauline, will you please?" she asked.

Tilly pressed the bell that rang in Pauline's room upstairs, and Pauline was knocking at the door in a surprisingly short time.

"*Entrez!*" called Sibyl, and began at once to talk to Pauline in French, with a hectic fluency. She was extremely pleased with having a French maid, and she took Pauline with her whenever she could; she took her to New York when she went shopping, she took her along when she made weekend visits to friends who had sufficient accommodations, took her to hotels, to doctors' offices, always took her when they made a trip on the cabin cruiser. Certainly Pauline made herself very useful; she gave Sibyl manicures, shampoos, wave-sets; she altered and mended her clothes, and kept them in perfect order; she went on errands, she telephoned to cancel any engagements Sibyl decided not to keep.

She was a stocky little woman, with light hair growing gray, and stout legs with a jerky walk; she was always amiable and obliging, always courteous to Tilly, and a great favorite with Robert. She wanted to teach him French songs, and he liked that. He made little or no attempt to learn them; simply, he liked the way she sang them, with so many gestures. *Les beaux messieurs font comme ça*, she would sing, in her flat and nasal voice, and bend her stiff little body and sweep her arms as if brushing the ground with a cavalier's fine plumed hat.

She listened to Sibyl's torrent of French, with her head politely bent to one side; then she went into the dressing-room, and returned with a black dress. Tilly knew little French, but she understood Sibyl's objection.

"No, madame," said Pauline, in English. "For her, black is best. If you will please put this on, Madame MacDonald."

Tilly put on the dress, and Pauline knelt, rose, went round and round her, putting in pins deftly and very quickly.

"*Bien*, Madame MacDonald," she said. "In one hour I bring it to your room."

"Thank you," Tilly said.

Now I can go and find Robert, she thought. I'll speak to Jenny, and she'll bring him some supper on a tray. I'll give him his bath, and he'll eat, and I'll put him to bed, and read to him, till the last minute. And when she said to him, Robert, darling, Cousin Sibyl wants me now, he would accept that without protest. He knew, in a child's unfathomable way, that Cousin Sibyl had to be obeyed and indulged.

"Will you take a little nap now, Sibyl?" she asked.

"I *need* a nap. Please get one of my pills."

"Couldn't you manage without, Sibyl? I'm sure they're not good for you."

"You don't know anything about it," said Sibyl. "You're so absolutely phlegmatic and unemotional, you simply can't understand high-strung people. People who *suffer*. Please get me my pill and a glass of water, and stop preaching sermons."

Tilly went into the bathroom, and took from the cabinet the long, narrow bottle that always stood in a certain place at the end of a glass shelf.

"There's only this *one* left, Sibyl," she said.

"I'll get more tomorrow," said Sibyl. "Doctor Crowdie never leaves me without them. He knows the frightful state of my nerves."

Tilly put the brilliant yellow capsule and a glass of water on the table.

"Now if you'll *kindly* pull down the venetian blinds," said Sibyl. "And then if you'll *please* go downstairs as soon as you can, to help Howard. The dinner guests will have cocktails until I come."

The venetian blinds were old-fashioned, and Tilly was not very deft with them; one came down lopsided and had to be pulled up again; they both rattled. This always annoyed Sibyl, and Tilly expected a sharp expostulation, or at least a loud, angry sigh. But today she was silent and still. She never goes to sleep as quickly as that, Tilly thought. Maybe she's just furious.

She went over to the bedside and saw that the capsule was gone, and a swallow of water. Sibyl lay with her face buried in the pillow and her knees drawn up, wrinkling the green taffeta spread. But she always lies stretched out, Tilly thought. I don't believe she's asleep.

"Sibyl ...," she said. "Is there anything I can do for you?"

There was no answer. Shall I call Howard? But if she's asleep and he wakes her, they'll have a frightful quarrel, and be nasty to each other all evening. And anyhow, she always does go to sleep soon after she's taken her horrible pill. They must be bad for her, and maybe the effect grows worse and worse. Or maybe she drank more than usual, I don't know....

Then, through the open windows, came the sound of hounds baying, deep and savage. Robert! she thought. She had never heard them before, never seen any here. I've heard frightful stories ..., she thought. I've got to get Robert. Then I'll come back and look at Sibyl.

She tiptoed across the room, and closed the door softly. She ran down the stairs, and it seemed to her that a hound was loping behind her. I'm running away, she thought. Away from Sibyl.

CHAPTER TWO

She ran down the steps of the terrace, with the sense of panic she always had when Robert was not in sight. She would tell him to stay in one place, and he meant to do what she said, but when she was gone, his five-year-old mind forgot; he would see a squirrel run scampering for a tree and he would run after it; he would run after the birds, after some sound he heard, or imagined; best of all, he liked to find a big toad, and he would poke at it cautiously with a twig until it would begin to hop.

"I like toads," he told his mother. "I like them the best of anything. Better than cats or dogs or horses or birds, or anything."

"I don't think they like people," Tilly had answered.

"I don't care," he said. "I like them, and I like frogs, and polliwogs the best."

Such a strange little boy, never lonely, never bored; he lived in a world of his own, of interest, excitement, and tranquil happiness; she had often heard him singing to himself, some formless, tuneless air.

But he could climb the stone wall, and there was the highway, with trucks and cars speeding by; he was so friendly, he might get into a car if a stranger asked him; he might wander all the way to Sibyl's private beach, where the surf came with a deadly undertow.

"Robert!" she called. "Robert!"

He was nowhere in the glade; she ran across the lush grass, and found him sitting under a noble old oak tree with a pile of leaves beside him that he was patiently tearing into shreds; a dark, lean little bullet-headed boy, with almond-shaped deep blue eyes, dressed in dark shorts and a tan jersey.

"Robert, I called you," said Tilly.

"Well ... I thought maybe I answered," he said. "Look, Mommy! These are vallons."

"What are 'vallons,' darling?"

"These!" he said, holding up two lacy fragments of leaves.

"I see! But what *are* they, darling?"

"They're *vallons*," he repeated, loudly and a little severely. "I make them for the birds, and they like them. They make dresses out of them, and nests and—" He thought a moment. "And they make salad," he said.

"It's very nice of you to do all that for the birds," said Tilly. "But now we'll have to hurry back to the house, Robert."

He got up, and took her hand, something he very seldom did. If she took his hand, he would pull it away. He did not want to be caressed or held, even to have his hard little black head stroked. But sometimes he would get up on her lap and put his head on her shoulder; sometimes he would rush at her and seize her round the knees.

He looked up at her now. "You look like a beautiful queen of fairies," he said.

"Thank you, Robert. That makes me very happy."

He still kept her hand, walking beside her.

"A bad, bad boy came," he said. "And he killed a bird and a chipmint."

"Chipmunk. What d'you mean, dear? Did he shoot them?"

"No, he just caught them with a rope, and then he put something in their mouths, like a drop of water, and they died that *minute*. And he said he could do it to me, and I ran away and hid, till he got in a car."

"Robert," she said, "is this—true, darling, or just an interesting story?"

"It's really *truly*," he said, vehemently. "The bird and the chipmint are still right there. And he said he could be the king of the whole world, if he wanted, and I ran away and I climbed up a 'normous tree, and I climbed and I climbed, and I got in a eagle's nest, and he had a gun—"

"What did this boy look like, Robert?"

"He was a 'normous boy, with black hair and black eyes, and I *think*," said Robert, "that he had a black tongue."

"What sort of car did he get into, Robert? A truck? A delivery van? A private car?"

Robert had to think about that. "It was a big, big car," he said. "No. It was a little *tiny* car."

"Show me the dead chipmunk and the bird."

He did not know himself what was truth and what was fantasy; he believed it all.

"Here!" he said, and pulled her by the hand. "He threw them in those bushes."

There was a clump of rhododendron, and Tilly parted the stems, with no expectation of finding anything. But there was a little dead bird there, claws and beak upturned, and near it lay a fat old chipmunk, he too on his back, his short legs curled.

"You—thought this boy killed them, darling?"

"Yes, he did. He had a thing like you put those drops up my nose, and then they died. Quick! Right that minute. Well ..." said Robert, in a calm, philosophical tone, "they didn't mind. And I guess they went up to Heaven."

"Oh, yes!" Tilly said, in haste, and started toward the house. "Robert, don't *ever* go near that boy any more. If you see him, go inside. Keep away from him."

"I will, Mommy," he said, with amiable indifference. They entered the

house, by the back door, into the big kitchen, where Gloria was busy at
the electric range, and Jenny, the housemaid, was arranging cut fruits in
silver cups. Gloria was a stout, gray-haired Irishwoman, fond of the little
boy, and cheerful and rollicking with him. But she was, like many another
good cook, very temperamental, especially after a few drinks, and Tilly was
always a little uneasy for fear that she might grow irritated with the child.

"Do you mind if I take up a bowl of milk and some graham crackers on
a tray, Gloria?" she asked.

"For His Nibs, is it?" Gloria demanded.

"*Yes!*" cried Robert. He liked that name she had for him; he liked her,
and he had no hesitation in asking her for anything. "I don't want *that* supper."

"And you'll not have it," said Gloria. "Jenny'll bring you up a nice, fine
tray."

"With *cake?*"

"Wait and you'll see," said Gloria.

They went out of the kitchen and through the dining room, where the
table was already partly set, glasses and silver glittering in the late sun, into
the hall, and up the broad, winding staircase. Robert went first, as she had
trained him, but his silence she had never taught him, or even suggested.
It seemed to be natural, as if the strange silence of the house affected him.
It was like this almost all day. Gloria very seldom left the kitchen; when
Jenny went up to do the chamber work, she used the closed-in back stairs;
if Sibyl and Howard were at home, they seemed never to move about; Sibyl
would be lying on the chaise longue in the bedroom, reading, or perhaps
talking to some house-guest; Howard was always downstairs, in the library
if it rained, on the terrace in fine weather, sometimes with some man he
had brought home from the Country Club, but usually alone, leaning back
in a chair, looking relaxed, and, Tilly thought, very vacant. Taylor was away
almost all the time, in boarding school, at a summer camp now. A silent
house, a lifeless house, Tilly thought.

Robert had turned the corner of the stairway, and as Tilly followed him,
she thought she saw Sibyl's door close. Howard had gone in there, maybe,
or Pauline. She pushed Robert ahead of her along the hall; she was nervous now about his bath. He had what was called a "youth's bed" in her
room, and they shared a bathroom with any guest who might be next to
them. There might be someone in there now, someone setting her hair, taking ages. Sibyl never told her if anyone were coming.

There was no provision made for the child. It was a big house with several spare rooms and baths, but he had not a corner to play in; Sibyl for-
bade play on the terrace, in any of the rooms downstairs.

"My *dear* Tilly," she had said, often enough, "with *three* servants in the house—of course, it's really not enough, and I always used to have another upstairs girl, but you simply can't *get* them—but anyhow, I honestly *cannot* see what you have to complain about. If you want anything for the child, simply *ask* for it. Only *please* don't let him drag that fire engine thing over your room when there are people downstairs. And please *never* let him sail that airplane thing down the stairs. It might *hurt* someone."

Tilly knocked on the bathroom door, and there was no answer; she tried the knob, and the door was not locked from the inside; she opened the door, cautiously, and there was no one there, and no trace of the things to be expected from a guest of Sibyl's, no lotions, bath-crystals, hair-pins on the floor, cigarette ashes in the wash-basin, perfume heavy in the air. She started a bath running, and then pulled Robert's jersey off, over his head. He could manage all the rest of his dressing and undressing himself, and he was proud of it. He went off, a brown, thin, naked little thing, and just as he left, Pauline knocked on the door with the black dress over her arm.

"Try it!" she said.

"I want to look in on Mrs. Fleming first."

"But I am just there, madame! She is sleeping very nicely."

"You're *sure*, Pauline?"

"But how not, madame? I look at her. It is every day the same, at this hour, only on some days, perhaps more of those cocktails. Now please try this, madame! Ah! ... Madame! Now wait! I have found this silver belt! Only look! *Madame!*"

As Tilly turned to the long mirror in the door, there was another knock on the hall door; it was red-haired Jenny with her sharp nose and her tight lips.

"Gloria told me to bring this up," she said. No "ma'am" for this poor relation; she set the tray down on the table and flounced away, leaving the door wider open.

Pauline closed it.

"Ah! That pig!" she said. "Now, madame, sit down, and I feex your hair."

"Thanks, Pauline, but I—"

"Sit here, madame," said Pauline, and pinned a towel around her shoulders.

She was very quick and deft about the hair-dressing.

"I should like more time," she said. "But already two guests arrive, and Mistaire Fleming is—he does not like to entertain alone, no?"

"I'll have to get Robert out of his bath."

"I will do that, madame. I will give him supper. I will sing to him, I will get him into his bed very happy. Madame, look once more how you are beautiful!"

Tilly looked again in the long mirror; she saw herself, tall and straight, broad-shouldered and slender, long-limbed, her blond hair shining and smooth, in the long, graceful black dress, a wide silver girdle round her waist. She was beautiful, and she knew it, but it caused her little pleasure or interest. Ian was gone, and Robert didn't care.

As she went down the stairs, she heard a sound of voices from the drawing-room. Howard stood behind the portable bar, pouring, and before him stood three guests. There was a very pretty little blond girl, Carola Dexter. There was a vaguely familiar man, the type Howard brought home from the Club, handsome, hearty, ruddy; and there was another man, young, skeleton-thin, with a dark, hollow-cheeked face, and dark, narrow eyes.

"You know Carola Dexter and Dick Cantrell, Tilly," said Howard. "But you haven't met Sam Osborne. This is Sibyl's cousin, Tilly MacDonald."

"Miss MacDonald," Osborne repeated, polite.

"Mrs.," said Howard.

"Howard," Tilly said, very low, "I didn't think Sibyl looked—well."

He gave a little laugh, like a snort.

"I was up there a little while ago," he said. "She's all right." He turned towards his other guests. "Osborne here has been holding forth against detective stories," he said. "He hates 'em."

"I didn't say that," Osborne protested. "Only we used to get such a lot of them in the hospital, with those fool girls in them."

"*What* fool girls, Sammy darling?" Carola asked, looking up at him with her sweet blue eyes.

"Those dim-wits," he said. "The ones that always keep something back from the police or the famous detective. The girls that see a man coming out of the summer-house where the body is found later, and never tell. The girls that see the good-for-nothing nephew sneaking something into Auntie's tea, but never say a word when Auntie drops dead."

"They're trying to protect someone they like, Sammy darling."

"Or themselves," said Cantrell. "Can't blame 'em for *that*. This girl, say, is in love with the murdered woman's husband, and the other fellow has those letters. Tells her he'll show 'em, if she doesn't shut up about seeing him."

"It's all damn nonsense," said Osborne, "and it never works. If anyone's in any way mixed up in a police case, the only thing to do is to tell the truth about what you know, and tell it quick."

"Of course, you *know* so much more about it all, lambie," said Carola. "But, honestly, I can't help believing that sometimes the police do suspect innocent people, and even arrest them."

"They do," said Osborne. "And put them in jail, and electrocute them, and hang them. But not very often."

"Once would be enough for me," said Cantrell, with a loud and jolly laugh. "Believe me, if I'd done anything I thought might make the police suspect me of any sort of crime, I'd never tell 'em one word, if I could keep it hidden."

"You'd be a perfect suspect, Dickie," said Carola. "I mean, so jolly and *un*-suspicious. I'd solve you in the first chapter."

"That's another irritating thing in a lot of those mystery stories," said Osborne. "The writer makes a damned effort to give you the most unlikely criminal. A benevolent old gent in a wheel-chair, an old maid always feeding birds, someone who hasn't any apparent motive. It isn't like that in life."

"Another drink?" asked Howard.

"No, thanks," Osborne answered. "But Mrs. MacDonald—?"

"Never drinks," said Howard. "Never smokes."

Osborne glanced at Tilly, still standing near him.

"But you sit down sometimes, don't you?" he asked, and pushed an armchair forward a little.

"Thanks," she said, with a smile, and he remained beside her.

"Well!" Howard said. "*I'm* going to have another. It may be the one too many, but Sibyl's so late." He glanced at his watch. "Half an hour late! That's not like her. Jenny, run up and ask Mrs. Fleming when she'll be down."

"Yes, sir," said Jenny, and her heels went tapping up the polished stairs.

She came down in a wild rush, sliding, catching herself by the rail; she stumbled over a rug, and fell on her knees before the portable bar.

"Oh, Mr. Fleming! Oh, Mr. Fleming! Oh, Mr.—"

"What's the matter?" cried Howard.

"Oh, go and see! Oh, Mr. Fleming! Her hand—oh! Just as cold as ice! Oh ...!"

"Here! Drink this!" said Howard. "Now go out to the kitchen and— keep quiet."

He poured himself another drink and gulped it down.

"Want me to come with you, Howard?" Cantrell asked.

"Not—n-now," Howard answered. "I'll let you know."

He was certainly drunk. Tilly heard him stumbling slowly up the stairs; his footsteps were heavy overhead. Then there was no sound.

"Well, of course ...," Cantrell said, with a grave and anxious frown, "he probably doesn't want anyone to see her if she's—well—*you* know. Happens to all of us, now and then.... Let her sleep it off, that's the best thing."

No one answered him, and in that silence, Tilly sat forward in her chair, cold with that terror that had come loping after her before. She thought of the little dead chipmunk, and the dead bird, and she rose.

"I'll just run up and see how—Robert's getting along," she said.

Then she sat down again, with a smile she knew was vague and silly.

"Well, no ...," she said, "Pauline's with him. There's really no sense ..."

She ought to be showing some concern about Sibyl. Not Robert.

"Howard's been gone a long time, hasn't he?" she asked.

"Too long," said Osborne.

"I think I'll just run up and see if—there's anything I can do," she said, rising again.

There was no objection, and she went up the stairs. All the doors were closed, and it was dark now; she turned on a switch, and a shaded wall lamp came alight.

I'll look in at Robert first, she thought. No! No, I won't! He might try to make me stay. No! Sibyl first.

She knocked at Sibyl's door, and there was no answer, no sound; she went to Howard's door and knocked, and there was no answer. She went back to Sibyl's door, gave one more knock, and turned the knob. A table lamp was on, mustard yellow with a parchment shade painted with a Chinese scene, giving a soft and mellow light. Sibyl lay stiffly stretched out on the big bed, her eyes staring open, and Howard lay on the floor beside her, face down.

It's ... O God! It's like the chipmunk and the bird.... No, no! Stop! *Do* something.... Wake them up.... O God! I've *got* to see if Robert ... I've *got* to ...

She went down the hall and opened the door without knocking. Robert sat at a small table, dawdling contentedly over his supper, with a queer little silky dog in his lap.

"Ah, madame!" cried Pauline. "Now you discover our secret!"

Tilly stepped back and closed the door without a word. At the head of the stairs she stopped; the stairway seemed a steep and glassy precipice at her feet.

"Mr. Osborne!" she called. "Mr. Cantrell!"

When they came running up, she was still standing there, leaning against the wall.

"There!" she said, pointing to the open door of Sibyl's room. "In there. Both dead. Poisoned."

CHAPTER THREE

"Sit down!" Sam Osborne was saying to her. "*Sit down!*"

"I—no ... I don't want to," she said.

He opened the door of Howard's room, and pulled her in there by the arm, pushed her down into a chair.

"They're both dead," she told him. "Both poisoned."

"Shut up!" he said.

"You mustn't …!" she cried, startled by his loud, rough tone.

"Pull yourself together," he said. "Show a little sense. Don't mention poison again. Remember that."

"But they—are they both—dead?"

"Fleming isn't dead," he said. "Now go and stay with your child until the police come."

"I'd rather not," she said. "There's someone with him—to take care of him. I'd rather—stay alone—for a little while."

"All right. But get this into your head. When the police come, answer their questions truthfully. *And don't do anything else.* Don't tell them any suspicions you may have, any theories. Understand?"

"You're—pretty rude," she said.

"I can be a lot worse than this," he said.

"Are you some kind of policeman?" she asked.

"No," he answered. "Now remember what I've told you. All of it. Answer what you're asked, and nothing else. Keep your theories and opinions to yourself. And try not to tell any lies."

"I'm not in the habit of telling lies," she said, curtly.

"Everybody tells lies to policemen," he said. "Keep to a minimum."

Cantrell had come to the doorway of the room.

"I got hold of Doctor Crowdie," he said. "He told me not to touch Howard, not even get him into bed. He'll be right along."

"Is he going to notify the police?" Osborne asked.

"Wants to see things for himself first."

Osborne went out of the room, and Cantrell sat down heavily on the window-seat and lit a cigarette.

"God!" he said. "You can hardly believe it! Old Howard …"

"But Mr. Osborne says he's not—"

"Doesn't know what he's talking about. I don't like that fellow; never did. He and Sibyl … Well, *you* know. A good many times I felt like telling Howard. Because he never noticed a thing. He's too *decent*."

Tilly got up, holding to the back of the chair for a moment.

"Don't talk about her, now," she said. "Not now."

She went out of the room, and as she went along the hall, the door of her own room opened, and Pauline came out, with the silky little brown dog nestled in one arm. She raised a forefinger to her lips, with a mischievous smile.

"My secret …," she whispered. "Only Robert knows. Madame does not like dogs, but he is here now since a month, and she knows nothing. Sometimes he cries, only so softly—like that, no more. Early in the morning, I take him out, then also in the night. He runs over the grass, he springs in the air. Only look! Eyes like stars, no?"

She parted the little creature's long hair, and two soft, sad, amber eyes looked up at Tilly; the tip of its plumy tail twitched.

"So good!" said Pauline. "I name him Coco. He sleeps always on the foot of my bed—"

She went on, and Tilly stood before her, in a daze. Doesn't she know ...? she thought. Can't she—*feel* it? ...

"Now the little Robert is going to sleep," said Pauline. "He is very content. Perhaps it is better if madame does not enter just now? The dinner is downstairs, is it not?"

The doorbell rang downstairs.

"Some other guest they all awaited," said Pauline.

But this newcomer was not a guest; he was mounting the stairs.

"I must hide Coco!" whispered Pauline, and stepped back into the bedroom, leaving the door a little open.

"The doctor ...?" she said. "But, madame, please! Who is ill?"

"Mrs. Fleming. She's—it's very serious," Tilly said.

"Wait! I put Coco up in my room, and then I return!"

Tilly went into the bedroom then; it was dark and close; for Pauline distrusted too much fresh air. Tilly moved cautiously toward the window, but Robert heard her.

"Mommy?" he said. "Mommy, is everything all right?"

"Yes, dear."

"Will the birds come and get their vallons?"

"If they have time. But they might have to go to a party."

"Mommy! Don't open the window so wide! I don't want the birds to come in here!"

"They *can't*, dear. Not with the screens."

"They can, if they're magic," he said. "Mommy, sit down a little while. Please!"

"If you'll close your eyes and not talk, darling."

"All right!" he agreed, and she drew a chair close to the bed.

And now, in the dark, with the sweet air blowing in, she began to think; the daze, the numbness were lifting, like a fog.

Face it. I know Sibyl is dead. I think she was dead, before I even left the room. But *could* it be that way? So fast? Yes. You hear of things like that, people dropping dead. Strokes. Heart attacks. If I'd got the doctor *then*, perhaps—

But I couldn't do that, without consulting Howard. And he said he'd seen her, just a little while ago, and she was all right. Pauline said she'd just seen her.... Perhaps I should have stayed with her longer, felt her pulse, turned her a little, so that I could see her face.... Only, when I heard those hounds baying.... I've read about children torn to pieces by a pack of dogs. I *had* to see about Robert. But I could have hurried back, much sooner.

Don't be a fool. I'm not guilty of anything, anything at all. If Sibyl had a stroke, or a heart attack, I couldn't know. I'd have done anything I could, if I'd known....

I *didn't* know ... I just felt ... It was simply the way she was lying. And that didn't seem enough reason to disturb her or to bring Howard upstairs. It's so horrible when they fight.

There was a light rap on the door, but it did not disturb the child's calm breathing. She crossed the room on tiptoe, and found Cantrell standing there.

"Howard—," he began.

"Hush!" she whispered, and came out, closing the door behind her. "Robert's just fallen asleep."

Cantrell's mouth was a little open, his blue eyes round and wide; he seemed short of breath as she took his arm and led him a little way down the hall.

"Howard ...," he said again. "Doctor says—Howard will live."

"Sibyl?"

"Dead," Cantrell answered. "Poisoned. Both of them poisoned. Poisoned, in their own house."

"Is the doctor sure ...?"

"He's sure. And the police will be along any minute now. My God! Howard, good old Howard, poisoned, in his own house...."

"It's Sibyl's house," said Tilly.

It seemed to her shocking that he should so carelessly brush aside Sibyl's death, and speak only of Howard, who was recovering.

"How does the doctor think it happened?"

"Doesn't know. Can't imagine. Some damned accident. *My* idea is something got into the bottle of Scotch Sibyl had in the room. I mean, maid spilt some cleaning fluid into it, and didn't want to tell."

"Sibyl didn't drink anything after she came upstairs."

"You couldn't know that. You weren't here all the time."

"But she was asleep when I left her."

"Could have waked up, taken a swig. Then when poor old Howard saw how she looked, he took a drink, to pull himself together. And it knocked him right out. There! That must be the police now."

There were footsteps and voices in the hall below, and Tilly felt afraid of them. They could accuse innocent people; they could do anything.

"Where's Mr. Osborne?" she asked.

"He's been having a hell of a time with Carola," he answered. "She got hysterical, wanted to go home, and Sam wouldn't let her. He said she'd have to stay until the police came; said they'd want to see everyone who'd been in the house while—all this happened. Fact is, he kept her by force; held her by the arm. She fought like a tiger. Kicked him, scratched him—"

He stopped and turned toward the stairs, and Tilly did so, too. Osborne came first, and after him came another young man, tall as he, and lean, but heavier in the shoulders, bigger altogether, big hawk nose, big ears, big dark eyes a little slanted, rather like a figure from an Egyptian frieze. After him came an older man, short, with thin, fair hair and a sharp, anxious face. He was carrying a doctor's bag.

"Where's Doctor Crowdie?" he asked.

Osborne opened Sibyl's door; he followed the doctor and the other tall young man, and closed the door after them. Where shall I go? Tilly thought. What ought I to do?

"I wonder if Carola's still here?" she asked aloud.

"Wouldn't know," said Cantrell. "I shouldn't think they'd bother much with her. She didn't come upstairs at all. Couldn't have poisoned that Scotch."

"I think I'll go down and see," said Tilly.

Then her familiar obsession rose up in her, her irrational, panic fear for Robert. If a policeman came bursting into his room ..., she thought. If they dragged him out of bed, and asked him questions ... I'd better lock him in.

But the bathroom ... Anyone can get in through there. And if I locked that door, Sibyl would be angry. No. Sibyl would never be angry again. For the first time tears came to her eyes, and pity into her heart for that luckless woman. Oh, I'm *sorry*, Sibyl! she said to herself.

Going through the dark bedroom, she locked the bathroom door to the adjoining room; she took the key out of the bedroom door, and locked it from the outside.

"I'm going to wait here, right where I am," said Cantrell. "I want to catch those two medics when they come out, and tell 'em to get that whiskey analyzed."

"But don't you think they'll do that anyhow?"

"I do not," said Cantrell. "I could tell you some things about doctors that might surprise you."

"I'm sure ...," said Tilly, vaguely, and started down the stairs.

There was a uniformed policeman standing in the doorway of the living room, but he glanced at Tilly without interest and she went on past him. Carola was sitting upright on a sofa, her arms folded; her face was tear-stained, raddled, haggard, her blond hair fell limply. Tilly, who had thought of her vaguely as "a girl," saw now that she was a woman very close to middle-age.

"I thought I'd come and talk to you for a while," she said.

"No," said Carola. "I don't want to talk. Let me alone."

It wouldn't somehow be right or fitting to go to the kitchen and talk to Gloria. Or to go up to Pauline on the third floor. I'll go and collect the "vallons," she thought. I'll make up a nice story for Robert about them.

It was night now, and, standing on the terrace, the little glade looked to her black and thick as a forest. There were two police cars in the driveway, and three others; Doctor Crowdie's, she thought, and Cantrell's, and Carola's; only the police cars had parking lights; the others were dark. A dark world; she could not find the "vallons" now. Sibyl, I'm *sorry*, she was saying to herself. I'm sorry.

"Very unusual case, don't you think?" asked Osborne's voice, a little behind her.

"Well, I hadn't thought of it that way."

"Man and his wife both poisoned on the same afternoon. Who d'you think would want to do that?"

"But—it was an accident! It must have been. Mr. Cantrell—"

"I've heard Cantrell's theory. But there's one rather baffling flaw in it. Sibyl's dose was fatal, and Howard's wasn't."

"Then she took more than he did."

"The gimmick is," said Osborne, "that they each got an entirely different poison."

"*What?*" Tilly asked.

"They each got a dose of a different poison," Osborne said. "Sibyl died of hers. She must have been dead for an hour more or less before Howard went up there. Then he falls down, unconscious, as soon as he gets up there. Poisoned. Now, what's *your* theory?"

"I—haven't any," she said.

"Think about it," he said. "And remember what I told you. Don't—"

A young policeman in uniform came out on the terrace.

"Lieutenant Levy wants to see you now," he said.

Think! Tilly told herself. Stop wanting to cry about Sibyl. Stop remembering that dead bird and the dead chipmunk. Stop being one of those emotional idiots Sam Osborne was talking about. Stop worrying about Robert, locked in there alone. You've got to think. Stop being afraid. You haven't done anything wrong.

But she was afraid.

CHAPTER FOUR

Lieutenant Levy was in the library, an impressive room, lined to the ceiling with shelves of books, fine old leatherbound books that Howard's father had left him, along with the best-sellers Sibyl had been buying for twenty years, all intermingled and equally unread now. It was a room Tilly had always admired, for its space and calm dignity, but today Lieutenant Levy had made it sinister.

She gave him the blame, because he was so obviously in charge; a long polished mahogany table had been drawn up to one end of the room, and he sat behind it. Presiding, Tilly thought. A grave young policeman sat beside but a little behind him; Carola sat on a sofa, as she had in the other room; and in armchairs here and there sat Pauline, Gloria, Jenny, and Mr. Cantrell. Tilly sat down beside Carola, Osborne slumped into a chair, with his long legs stretched out.

"I'd like to see you all together at first," Levy said, very amiably. "Then you can check with one another about times, sequences, and so on. While it's fresh in your mind. You'd be surprised, if you knew how quickly a witness forgets. Or remembers things a little wrong. I've already questioned some of you." He paused a moment. "You understand that you are not obliged to answer any of my questions. But I take it for granted that all of you are ready to co-operate with us."

He looked around at them, with a pleasant smile.

"Doctor's ordered Mr. Fleming to stay in bed until tomorrow," he said. "But I had a brief talk with him." He looked at the open notebook before him. "Mr. Fleming states that when he entered Mrs. Fleming's room, he was alarmed by her appearance. He spoke to her, and got no reply. He took her hand, and when he found it cold, he collapsed. Fainted, he said."

He waited a moment.

"The police doctor says he was drugged, probably with chloral hydrates," he said.

He waited again.

"Mrs. Fleming was undoubtedly dead when he entered the room. Both doctors, our police surgeon, and her private physician, agree that Mrs. Fleming died at approximately six-thirty."

No! Tilly thought. No! I was there ...

"Mr. Fleming states that he took no sort of drug, or medicine, to his knowledge. He states that he was in the living room, drinking cocktails with his friends, until approximately eight o'clock. He further stated that it was his wife's habit to retire to her room at six-thirty, and to sleep for an hour, with the aid of a pill prescribed by her personal physician, Doctor Crowdie. Doctor Crowdie states that more than a month ago he had refused to renew her prescription for these pills, and that she could not obtain them without a prescription. Legally."

I gave her that pill, Tilly thought. If he asks me, I'll tell him. I won't be a fool.

"Miss Duval," he said, looking at Pauline, "you say that you entered Mrs. Fleming's room at approximately half-past seven?"

"*Exactly* half-past seven," said Pauline. "Madame gave me that order. I knock. No answer. I enter. Madame! I say. She make no reply. I shake on her shoulder a little, then I say, to myself, *eh, bien!* Today she wish to sleep longer, and I go."

"How did she look to you, Miss Duval?"

"Her face is turned away, and I don't see. Only that she lies there, and does not reply. So I go."

"You didn't think there was anything wrong?"

"And why, monsieur? I think that—but I don't wish to say."

"You'll help us, if you do say, Miss Duval."

Pauline began to cry.

"To me," she said, "Madame Fleming was always the most kind. If now she has gone—I don't *wish* to say—anything."

"Miss Duval, if you feel any affection for Mrs. Fleming," said Levy, "you'll tell us everything you can that might help us clear up her murder."

"Murder?" cried Pauline, in a screech.

"There's no doubt about that," said Levy. "At six-thirty, or close to that, she got a dose of potassium cyanide, and she died in a few seconds."

"Ah ...! *Mon Dieu!*" cried Pauline. "Who does such a thing?"

"Well," Levy said, "there's always the possibility of suicide."

"With her? Never! She liked too much to be alive. Suicide, never!"

"Beside yourself, did anyone, to your knowledge, go into her room?"

"Nobody! But nobody!"

"Mrs. Callaghan?"

Gloria stood up, like a child in school.

"Can you give us any information as to who went upstairs today at six-thirty, or later?"

"I cannot, sir," she said. "I was in the kitchen, and there I stayed."

"Did anyone enter the kitchen?"

"Jenny did," said Gloria. "And she'd a right to, the way she had work to do there."

"Anyone else?"

Gloria's stout, healthy face suddenly became ugly and sullen.

"Mrs. MacDonald and the little boy came in," she said. "Like they did every day. Poor Mrs. MacDonald, she was all the time trying to keep the poor little child out of the way, for there were those in the house couldn't stand the sight of him. He is a fine little feller, but—"

"Thanks," said Levy. "What time did they come in, Mrs. Callaghan?"

"I could not tell you, sir."

"When you're cooking, Mrs. Callaghan, don't you have to time the things? Watch a clock?"

"That's the way I like to do," said Gloria. "But in this house I cannot. I cannot make them a soufflé, or anything like that. Eight o'clock dinner, says she—" She stopped, and crossed herself. "God rest her. It is what she used to say. But it would be eight-thirty, nine o'clock, and them sitting in there with drinks. Drink, drink, drink. And I'd have my good dinner keeping warm, in the oven, it might be, or the double boiler. There was few nights I could serve my dinner right. And with all them drinks, they'd have no interest—"

"Thanks," said Levy. "But about what time did Mrs. MacDonald and her child come into the kitchen?"

"I cannot tell you," said Gloria, "for I did not look at the clock, at all."

"Thanks. Miss Bascom?"

Gloria sat down, and Jenny stood up, angular and severe, in her black uniform, a frilled cap too far forward on her sandy hair.

"Ten minutes to seven, it was, when Mrs. MacDonald and the child come in," she said, in her rasping nasal voice. "It was ten after when I brought up a tray for the child. And Mrs. MacDonald was in the room with him, and Pauline fixing her up in an old dress of Mrs. Fleming's."

"It is *not* old!" cried Pauline. "It is—"

"Thanks," said Levy. "When you took up the tray, Miss Bascom, did you at any time enter Mrs. Fleming's room?"

"I did not," said Jenny. "Why would I? I only went in her room to fix it, and make the bed—when she got out of it. She spent the most of her life lying in that bed. No telephone calls, she wouldn't take them. You darsen't even bring up a telegram. There she'd lie—"

"Thanks," said Levy, but Jenny remained standing, breathing fast, as if the spite and malice were almost beyond restraint.

"Thank you," said Levy, definitely. "Miss Dexter."

"It's *Mrs.* Dexter," said Cantrell.

Carola still sat upright on the sofa, not even glancing at Levy.

"Mrs. Dexter," Levy repeated. "Will you tell me what time you arrived here this afternoon?"

"I don't know," she answered.

"Almost on the dot of six," said Cantrell. "I'm what you might call time-conscious. Always checking. Looking at my watch. Almost on the dot of six she came. I came about five minutes before her, and Howard was here. Mrs. Fleming was out on the terrace then, talking to Mrs. MacDonald. I didn't want to—er—disturb them, and I came in by the side door, and so did Mrs. Dexter."

"Don't *call* me 'Mrs. Dexter'!" said Carola, suddenly. "I don't *want* Richard's name. Call me Miss Allison."

"Miss Allison," said Levy, still polite and patient. "Did you, at any time, go up to Mrs. Fleming's room?"

"No," she said.

"Now, Lieutenant," said Cantrell, "I've told you, and Fleming's told you that Carola—Miss Allison—never left this room from the moment she arrived—"

"Suppose we let Miss Allison answer my questions herself," said Levy. "Miss Allison, why were you so anxious to leave the house without speaking to us?"

"Why *not?*" she cried, leaning forward. "Good God! Sibyl was my friend. We went to school together. When I heard ... I wanted to get away. To get *home*. I *knew*—how miserable she was. I thought—she'd killed herself. I wanted—to go...."

"She never left this room," said Cantrell. "She's had a good deal of trouble lately.... Why don't you let her go?"

"I'm conducting this inquiry, Mr. Cantrell," said Levy, still amiable. "I'm not making any unnecessary trouble for anyone. Miss Allison, did you notice anything out of the way, anything at all extraordinary in Mr. Fleming's behavior this afternoon?"

"No," she said.

"And you state, Mr. Cantrell, that you didn't?"

"I didn't," said Cantrell. "He might have had one over the eight, but—well, he was normal. Perfectly sound."

"And you, Mrs. MacDonald? Did you notice anything peculiar in Mr. Fleming?"

"No," Tilly said.

"I *told* you!" said Cantrell, his face flushed with anger. "I figured out from the start what had happened. And Howard will bear me out. He was all right until he went into her room. There he saw something was wrong, and he ... Well, on the table beside her bed he saw a bottle of whiskey, and a glass half full. He drank what was in the glass, and then he blacked out. It was poison. Same poison that killed poor Sibyl."

There was no glass of whiskey on the table beside Sibyl, Tilly thought. She never took a drink after she went upstairs. And anyhow, she was ... she was asleep.

"It wasn't the same poison, Mr. Cantrell," said Levy.

"*Has* to be," said Cantrell, frowning. "Your doctors haven't had a chance to analyze, and so on."

"They're both fairly well agreed, Mr. Cantrell. Mr. Fleming had had a dose of a certain preparation, often used to induce sleep, but which—" He paused. "Which doesn't mix well with alcohol. However, it wasn't a lethal dose. He might have remained unconscious for some time, but he would—unless complications set in—he would have recovered, even without medical care."

"Well," said Cantrell then, "Sibyl took more of the stuff."

"Mrs. Fleming's death was caused by potassium cyanide," said Levy. "It acts in a matter of seconds."

"Seconds?" Cantrell repeated, startled.

"Our doctor and Doctor Crowdie don't care to be too definite before the autopsy," said Levy, "but they are both fairly certain that Mrs. Fleming was dead at approximately six-thirty."

While I was there in her room, Tilly thought. Alone with her. I gave her that pill.

Levy turned toward her now.

"I understand that you went up to Mrs. Fleming's room with her, a little before seven?" he asked.

"Yes," Tilly answered, "I often did. And this time—today—"

Someone else came into the room, very quietly, even on tiptoe, a soldierly young man in a neat, well-fitting chauffeur's uniform, cap in hand; his light hair, running straight back from his forehead, still showed the marks of a vigorously used wet comb; his manner was correct and amiable but he was no more capable of a respectful look than a brownie; he had a long, sharp nose, merry little gray eyes, a thin mouth, very wide, with curved lines at both corners that gave the effect of a perpetual clown's grin.

"Jensen, sir," he said, with a smart salute. "The chauffeur. I just came on an errand, and there was a cop outside told me to come in here."

"Sit down, Mr. Jensen," said Levy.

"Thank you, sir," said Jensen, "but I'd rather stand up, if it's all right. I do a lot of sitting down, sir," he explained.

"What was your errand, Mr. Jensen?"

"Mrs. Fleming sent me to Stevensport to see a lady—Mrs. Brown—and ask her where I could buy this poison—"

"What!" cried Cantrell.

"Mrs. Brown used this poison, and she said it worked fine. So I went to the drugstore and got some from this fellow that invented it."

"*What!*" Cantrell cried again. "Poison."

He had risen, in his shocked agitation, but Levy seemed in no way excited.

"Weed-killer?" he asked. "Something like that?"

"No, sir. It's called Invisible Fence, and it's to keep out dogs."

"To poison the little dogs?" Pauline demanded.

"No," said Jensen. "They don't eat it. They just don't like the smell of it, and they won't pass it."

"Then why do you say 'poison'?"

"Says 'poison' on the label," Jensen answered. "If taken internally. Only you see, the animals don't eat it. Smells enough. Phew! Phew!"

"You brought this home to Mrs. Fleming?"

Jensen was silent for a moment.

"Yes, sir," and if his face still had its brownie grin, his manner was very sober. "I didn't know all that happened. Mrs. Fleming, she said don't hurry, and I didn't. She said she could sort of smell a dog right in the house, and we'd try the stuff tomorrow. A spray, it is. So I didn't hurry. I stopped at the gas station for a check-up and talk. I stopped at a diner, and I got me some coffee and a cheeseburger. I didn't know a thing that happened here till the gardener told me, down at the gate-house. She's dead, he said. Somebody cut her head off."

"It wasn't exactly that," said Levy. "Where's your Invisible Fence?"

"Left it in the car, sir, in the garage."

"Go and get it," said Levy, "and put it into my car. There's a policeman at the wheel."

"Yes, sir," said Jensen. "Only thing is, the label says 'inflammable.'"

"That's all right," said Levy. "So is my cop. You go and get that stuff shifted. And Mrs. Callaghan and Miss Bascom, you'd better go and get something together for these people to eat."

"It is too late," said Gloria, sternly. "My dinner is spoiled, entirely."

"Give 'em some hot coffee," said Levy. "Open a can of something. Feed them something."

She rose majestically, and Jenny after her; the two women, followed by Jensen, went out of the room.

"I don't want to keep any of you much longer," Levy said. "You're all tired, hungry. All upset. Mrs. MacDonald, you state that you went up to Mrs. Fleming's room before seven?"

"I didn't notice the time, especially," said Tilly. "I usually did go with her. And this time she particularly wanted me to come, and try on a dress." She paused a moment. "This dress," she said.

"How long were you there, Mrs. MacDonald?"

"I didn't notice the time. I pulled down the venetian blinds, as Sibyl— Mrs. Fleming asked me to do. Then I left."

"In what condition was Mrs. Fleming when you left?"

"I thought she was asleep."

"Did she often fall asleep so quickly?"

"I never knew," said Tilly. "She'd lie down and close her eyes, and not speak, and I never knew whether or not she was sleeping. I just knew she wanted to be let alone."

"I understand that you then went into the garden—grounds—estate, to look for your child?"

"Yes, I did."

"And I understand that when you brought the child into the house and left him in your room, you returned to Mrs. Fleming's room. Is that the fact?"

"Yes. I just wanted to see—how she was."

"Why did you do that, Mrs. MacDonald?"

"I wanted to see if she was all right. I often did."

"Why? What did you think might have happened?"

"She—slept so soundly, so very soundly. I was afraid she might fall off the bed. Roll off."

"Had this ever happened?"

"Well ... Yes," she said.

She remembered that she had found Sibyl on the floor, wrapped round and round with the green taffeta spread, sound asleep on the floor. She had called Pauline to help her.

"But no!" Pauline had said. "We place under her some little pillow, and we leave her. She is not hurt; she breathes quietly; she is comfortable. I shall lock the door, I shall sit in here. If anyone knocks, psst! Madame sleeps, I say. In a short time, she wakes, she takes a bath, dresses, she descends, all as usual." And that was how it had been.

Levy was looking down at his notebook, and in the silence, Tilly turned her head away from the sound of Carola's breathing, so quick and gasping. She caught sight of herself then in a mirror across the room, a thin, tall girl leaning back on the sofa, her knees crossed, the long, pleated skirt draped gracefully over her long legs, her blond head set proudly on her long neck, her face enigmatic; no sign or trace of dread or nervousness or tremor. Although she knew very well what was coming, what must come.

"Mrs. MacDonald," said Levy, "while you were in the room with Mrs. Fleming, did you see her take any sort of medicament?"

"No," said Tilly.

"Any pill, powder, even an aspirin?"

"No," Tilly said again.

"Did you see her drink any whiskey? Anything at all?"

"No."

"When you left the room, you state that you believed Mrs. Fleming to be asleep?"

"Yes. I touched her shoulder. I spoke to her, but she didn't answer."

"Do you think it possible that your cousin was feigning sleep, Mrs. Mac-Donald?"

"I don't know."

"Mrs. MacDonald, would it have been possible for any other person to have entered your cousin's room, unobserved, directly after you had left, and persuaded her to take some draft, or pill, something of the sort?"

"I don't know," Tilly said.

"Well, *I* do," said Cantrell. "You couldn't see the stairs where we were having cocktails. Tilly was shut in the room with her child, at the end of the hall. Jenny took the tray up the back stairs. Why, half a dozen people could have gone up there without being seen."

"Thanks, Mr. Cantrell," said Levy. "I shan't keep you any longer, any of you. But—er—of course—"

He left the phrase unfinished, but the meaning was clear enough. But this is going on and on, be sure of that.

CHAPTER FIVE

Levy rose, and with him the young uniformed policeman.

"Now—can I go home?" Carola said.

"Certainly!" said Levy. "You have your car here?"

"No," she said. "I mean—it's here, but there's something the matter with it. Can Jensen drive me home?"

"One of my men will take you home," said Levy.

He took her arm, and led her out onto the terrace. Cantrell, Osborne, Pauline, and Tilly sat where they were, and presently there was the sound of a car starting.

"I think we should eat something," said Cantrell. "Some little thing. Time like this you've got to keep your strength."

"I fix it," said Pauline, hastening out of the room.

Osborne came and sat beside Tilly.

"Congratulations!" he said.

"For what?" she asked.

"For keeping your dignity and your sense," he said. "For doing what I told you. And also," he said, "for looking like a queen."

"Thanks," she said, with a smile. But even in this lovely dress with the wide silver belt, she had no feeling of queenliness, only a sick discomfort. Perhaps that poison—what was it—cyanide something—was in the capsule I gave her? Who else could have got into the room and forced her to take—something? She was asleep. Or ... A matter of seconds. All right! Perhaps she was dead. I didn't know. I couldn't know. The capsule I gave her was exactly like the dozens and dozens of others, little yellow ones. It was in the same bottle; the same drugstore, Dr. Crowdie's prescription.

I couldn't know. But if I'd given her the capsule, and they can't find any other she could have got ... I don't mean they'd have suspected me of murder, but I'd have been—involved, naturally. I'd have had to stay here, and I want to get Robert away, where? I don't know. I'll take all the money I've saved and go to a cheap boarding-house.

"I think I'll go upstairs and open Robert's door," she said. "I left him locked in."

"Couldn't do better than to leave him locked in," said Osborne. "I could think of a lot of good things." His hollow face became alight. "We could have the murderer creeping into the child's room on all fours, to hide the poison cache. We could have a trained hound, very savage, trained to seize the child and carry him off to a cave—"

"Stop!" said Tilly. "You're—brutal."

"Just a test," he said. "You did so well with Levy. I was looking for the weak point. And I've got it."

"What is it?" she asked.

"Your child," he said. "You'd lie, you'd steal, you'd murder for that child."

"You think I've done something like that?" she asked, looking steadily at him.

"Me?" he said, raising his brows in a look of startled innocence. "*I* don't think. I just look around. Just listen. And then—" He paused. "I have extrasensory perception."

"What is that?" she asked.

"I know things," he said. "I see things, hear things—not through my senses."

"What, for instance?" asked Tilly.

"We don't know yet," he said. "It may be an electric current between two minds. It may be something—more than that."

"What more?" asked Tilly.

"There's a great deal we don't know, Mrs. MacDonald. We have strange flashes of intuition, in which we know that someone dear to us is in trouble or danger."

"I don't," said Tilly. "When my husband was killed in the explosion, I was making lemon cookies, and I didn't feel anything wrong."

"We have horrible dreams, of disaster and loss."

"I don't," said Tilly. "I don't have anything but silly dreams—like chipmunks taking away my best tea-cups."

"You're suppressing," said Osborne. "You're frightened, all the time.

About your child. About life, in general. You don't know how you're going to live."

"I don't feel that way," she said.

"You're frightened now," he said.

"No," she said, evenly.

"About your little boy," he said. "About the vallons."

"*What?* How d'you—I mean—what d'you mean?"

He did not answer.

"What are you?" she asked.

"What? What you see here. Any other answer?"

"Yes," she said. "What do you do for a living? That seems to me the best
answer."

"That's damn good!" he said, a light coming into his face. "That's a damn
good way to judge anyone."

"All right. What *do* you do?"

"I'm a famous crook," he said. "I'm a blackmailer, I'm a forger. I'm a
murderer." He smiled a little. "But I'm nice to nice girls. Very nice. What
are you, now? What do *you* do for a living?"

Me? I'm nobody. Nothing. I've never had a job or earned a penny in my
life. I'm not able to support my own child. I'm not a really good housekeeper or cook. I can't sew. I've got friends, and I love them, girls I went
to school with, but they're not important, dazzling people. Just dear and
nice. I've had beaus, the average number, but never anyone like Ian.
Never anyone with such charm and wit; never anyone so handsome and
debonair. Only that little, little time together—and now I haven't anything.
I'm nobody.

No! That's disgusting. That's shocking. I *am* somebody. I'm Robert's
mother, and I was Ian's wife, and I made him happy. I made my parents
happy. I'm not mean or cruel or dishonest, and I'm *not* stupid.

"I'm—me," she said.

"That seems good enough to me," he said. "I knew it, before this, because, you see, I have an extraordinary amount of ESP."

"What's that?"

"Extrasensory perception," he explained. "I see things, hear things,
know things that are happening, or are going to happen, without needing
to use the ordinary five senses."

He was cheerful and easy, but Tilly had a stern look in her eyes.

"For instance," he went on, "if I wanted to, I could see what the set-up
would be in the Kremlin a year from now, and—"

"Then you must know what's happened here tonight," she said. "It does-
n't seem amusing to me. Sorry. Good-night."

"Good-night!" he said. "I think I'll go up, too." As she started up the stairs, he followed her.

Before she was half-way up, she heard Robert's voice, calling her desperately.

"Mommy! Mommy! *Mommy!* Mommy, come and get me!"

She began to run then, up the stairs, along the corridor. She unlocked the door of his room, but it was dark and empty. She closed it and ran to the bathroom, where a line of light shone under the door. He was beating on the door of the next room, which she had left locked; he was barefoot and in his blue pajamas, his dark hair wildly ruffled; there was panic in his eyes.

"Stop now, Robert," she said, drawing him close to her side. "Stop, dear. Here I am."

"They—got in ...," he said. His voice was broken, panting; his face was wet with tears. But he had stopped crying; it seemed to her almost unbearably touching to see his effort to breathe evenly, to recover his baby pride.

"They—got in," he said. "I was asleep, and they got in, and they waked me up and the light wouldn't go on, and I couldn't get out in the hall, and I called you."

"What did you think had got in, darling?"

"I *saw* them, in the dark, flying round and round in the room, and there was—a thing—a sort of cold thing—in my bed. I—called you. Because I couldn't get out.

"What were they, dear?"

"They were birds," he said. "They got in. They wanted to find the vallons."

It was a dream, she thought, with a deep breath of relief. A horrible nightmare.

"They weren't real, darling," she said. "Only in a dream. We'll go and look together."

"No!" he said. "I don't *want* to."

"Come on," she said. "We don't mind things together."

He took her hand then, and they entered the dark bedroom. And something was there; something flying round and round, high up, near the ceiling; one gave a little cheep, a squeak.

"Mommy!" he cried. "What's those birds?"

The bulb had been taken out of his bedside lamp, but the lamp on the chest of drawers came alight. "Mommy! You see! They're—birds with fur! Take 'em away!"

"They're only bats, darling. Perfectly harmless."

"Take 'em away!" he cried.

The screen had been taken out of one window; she took up a newspaper and flapped at the two bats until they flew out, and she closed the window.

"Now they're gone, darling. They—just eat insects. They're perfectly harmless."

"Well, why did they come in *here*, Mommy? Who took my screen away?"

"It fell out, darling. They sometimes do, you know."

"But who locked me all in, Mommy?"

"You're not locked in now, dear little boy. See!"

She opened the door to the hall, and Osborne was standing there, leaning against the wall, hands in his pockets. She pretended not to notice him, and closed the door.

"I saw a man out there!" Robert said. "A *bad* man."

"He's not bad, dear. He's just visiting Cousin Howard. Now we're all right and cozy. You get back into bed, and I'll sit here beside you—"

"No!" he cried. "I *told* you that thing was in my bed!"

"We'll look," she said. "We'll take all the covers off.... See? Like this—see?"

A thin, gray snake slid under the pillow, and for perhaps the first time in her life, Tilly screamed, and fell forward on her knees, half-unconscious, her head swirling.

"Robert ...!" she said. "Robert ... Go away.... Downstairs. Quick!"

With a dream-like effort, she pulled herself to her feet. She looked around the room, and on the bookcase stood a red iron fire engine of Robert's. She took it to the bed, and stood there for a moment. What must I do? she thought. Squash it? Squash—its head? And throw it—out the window? It's—idiotic—to be so—terrified of snakes.... Only—I always was... I can't wait. It might crawl away—and hide.... Go ahead!

She turned the pillow over with a quick flip, and there it lay, not coiled, as she had expected from pictures, but lying stretched straight, like a rope. You must! she told herself. Quick!

A hand reached over her shoulder and snatched up the snake by the tail, whirled it round with a snap, and disappeared into the bathroom. It was Osborne.

"Want to see?" he asked Robert, and the child dropped his mother's hand and ran eagerly after him.

"He's swimming!" he cried.

"It won't be long," Osborne said. "Sometimes you can kill them with a snap—break their necks. But this time I didn't work it. Well, sorry, old boy!"

The water flushed.

"Will he come back?" Robert asked.

"No. Never."

"Well, snakes are awful bad, aren't they?"

"No. There aren't any bad snakes, or animals, or birds, or insects."

"Well, they eat you," said Robert.

"That's not bad, when *they* do it," said Osborne. "The thing is—"

There was a knock on the bedroom door, and Tilly opened it. Jenny stood there, her cap very crooked, her eyes sleepy, her face blotched and cross.

"That Lieutenant Levy, he says he wants to speak to you, ma'am. I said I thought you'd went to bed, but he says sorry, but I want to speak to her a moment. Speak! The way he's been talking ...! You'd think his tongue'd fall out."

"I'll come," said Tilly, and went to the bathroom, where Robert stood looking up into Osborne's face, listening to him, enchanted. "Will you stay with Robert, till I come back?"

"Very glad," he answered, and she went out into the hall where Jenny still waited.

"They took *her* away," Jenny said, very low, as they started down the stairs. "In a kind of long basket, all covered with a sheet. Kind of sagging down, because she was real heavy and—"

"Don't, please!" Tilly interrupted.

This affronted Jenny.

"Well, I thought you'd like to hear, ma'am, with her your husband's cousin, and all."

"Thanks, but not now, Jenny. Thank you."

Levy was alone in the library, except for a uniformed policeman; there was only one green-shaded lamp alight on the desk, and the room looked enormous and black as a cavern. It seemed to her that she could not cross that vast dark space.

"Lieutenant Levy ...," she said. "I—I'm afraid I—can't talk—now. I ... It's been ... I think I'll telephone for a taxi, and take my little boy to the Inn, just for tonight. Then tomorrow morning, as early as you like—"

"Chair, Ryan," said Levy, and the policeman carried a chair to where she stood. She sat down, half the big room distant from Levy. "I'm sorry," he said, in his mild, even voice, "but it wouldn't do for you to leave the house tonight, Mrs. MacDonald."

"But—but *why?* You let Mrs. Dexter go. And Mr. Cantrell. Why not us, my child and I? I—we *can't* sleep here."

"I'm sorry, Mrs. MacDonald. But, you see, we have what seems to us sufficient evidence—at present—that neither Mr. Cantrell nor Mrs. Dexter left the ground floor at any time. They were at all times under observation."

"Well ...?"

"As I understand it, Mrs. MacDonald, you went up to the room of the late Mrs. Fleming?"

"Yes. Yes, I did."

"I understand that the maid, Miss Duval, entered the room while you were there, and that deceased spoke to her. Right?"

"Yes...."

"Did you leave Miss Duval alone in the room, Mrs. MacDonald?"

"No. No, I didn't. She left first."

"The housemaid and Miss Duval state that they both entered deceased's room later in the afternoon. They both state that they spoke to deceased, but receiving no answer, believed her to be asleep. Mrs. MacDonald, to the best of your knowledge and belief, did the late Mrs. Fleming ever speak again to anyone, after you left her room?"

"I don't know. I couldn't hear everything from my room."

"To the best of your knowledge, Mrs. MacDonald, the late Mrs. Fleming never spoke to anyone after you?"

"I don't *know!*"

"To the best of your knowledge, Mrs. MacDonald."

"I never heard her."

"When you left the room, Mrs. MacDonald, was deceased asleep, or did she appear to be asleep?"

"Asleep."

"Was it your impression that deceased had fallen asleep very quickly?"

"Well ... A little. But she often did, for her nap."

"Mrs. MacDonald, you are not obliged to answer this question. But you'll understand it's to your own advantage to co-operate with us, I'm sure."

"I see!" said Tilly.

Oh, God, if I only could see! I haven't told him any lies. Only kept things back from him. I *can't* be put in jail. I haven't done anything wrong. They can't take me away from Robert. But Levy's working around—to something.

He was sitting with his arms spread on the arms of the chair, his broad shoulders a little hunched, head down, his long black lashes lowered. There was nothing hostile in his face, nothing crafty, or cruel. But she was cold with fear of him. This is the moment, she thought. Ian had been what he called "*aficionado,*" loved to see bull-fights, to read books about them. There came always the Moment of Truth when matador and bull faced each other, and one or the other must die. And so, it seemed to her, she and Levy faced each other.

"You were accustomed to go upstairs with the late Mrs. Fleming, when she took her before-dinner nap?"

"Yes."

"And was deceased in the habit of taking any sort of sedatives to induce sleep?"

"Sometimes, yes."

"This afternoon ...," said Levy. "I must ask you again. And please think carefully. Did you see deceased take any sort of pill, capsule, powder? Any sort of medication?"

"No," Tilly answered, readily and evenly.

"You state that deceased was asleep before you left the room?"

"Yes."

"You weren't surprised at her falling asleep so quickly, Mrs. MacDonald?"

"No. It was a hot day, and she'd had some cocktails, and I thought she was—tired."

"Had this ever happened before, Mrs. MacDonald? I mean, had deceased ever fallen asleep so suddenly before?"

"Oh, yes!" said Tilly, almost cheerfully.

"So that you found no cause for alarm?"

"No."

"I see!" said Levy. "Thank you. I won't keep you any longer, Mrs. Mac-Donald."

Then, as she rose: "If anything occurs to you later, Mrs. MacDonald," he said, rising himself, "if you recall anything you may have observed in the late Mrs. Fleming's room, for example, you'll let us know?"

"Oh, yes!"

"Thank you," he said, again.

CHAPTER SIX

Now it was done. The Moment of Truth had come, and she had faced it with a lie.

But I'm not sorry, she thought. If I'd told him I'd given Sibyl that capsule, they'd have gone on and on asking me questions; perhaps they'd have taken me to the police station, or the District Attorney's office, or whatever it is they do, for more questioning. Making me leave Robert here—in this horrible house. I can't leave him. I *won't*.

She found him sitting on his bed, with Osborne beside him, and they were chatting; that was the only word for it, both of them relaxed and enjoying their conversation. Osborne rose, slowly, with a faint sigh.

"Mommy, *you* didn't ever know anything about the lemmings!" said Robert. "The way they run *right into* the ocean, hundreds and hundreds and millions."

"No, I didn't, Robert."

"Sam is very interesting," said Robert.

"Mr. Osborne, dear."

"He said call him Sam."

"Well, good-night," said Osborne, moving toward the doorway where Tilly stood. "By the way, that snake was an absolutely harmless species. Nothing to worry about."

"Thank you," Tilly said, and closed the door after him.

Nothing to worry about. A snake in the child's bed, bats flying about his dark room; the dead chipmunk, the dead bird. Somebody's deliberately trying to frighten him, she thought. Or—harm him? But who? Who could possibly want to do any harm to Robert? If Lieutenant Levy will only, only let us go away tomorrow. I don't know where, but I'll think of something....

She undressed and got into bed; she stretched out her arm to turn off the lamp.

"*No*, Mommy!" cried Robert. "Let's not make it all dark."

"But the light will keep you awake, darling."

"I don't want to go to sleep," he said, and knelt in his bed, across the room from her. "I want to talk to you, Mommy. Mommy, you'd better buy a dog tomorrow, a great, big, *big* dog, and then if that bad boy comes back after my vallons, our dog will chase him, and bite him and bite him...."

She left the light burning, she let Robert go on talking, hearing not his words but the sound of his high little voice, going on and on, in a sort of desperate volubility; he got on his feet and bounced up and down. Let him alone, she thought. It's better for him to wear himself out, and then he'll go to sleep. He's had too much to bear today. The "bad boy," who threatened him, who killed the chipmunk and the bird …

I'll tell Lieutenant Levy about that. Because Robert might be—might really be in danger. There might be some criminally insane boy in the neighborhood…. Why didn't I tell the Lieutenant before?

Because he wanted to talk about Sibyl. And I've forgotten her. I haven't thought of her since I came into this room. Not once. Let me think about her now; that's the least I can do.

"Mommy! Hey, Mommy!"

Robert flounced down in the bed, with his head buried in the pillow, and his rear end elevated.

"I'm a lemming!" he told her. "See? But *I'm* not going to jump in the ocean and get all drownded. I'm going to stay here in the sand. D'you *see*, Mommy?"

"I see, darling," she said.

He went on talking, his voice muffled by the pillow, but he was growing drowsy; in a little while he went to sleep, as often before, in that preposterous attitude.

Now let me think about Sibyl, Tilly thought. She was Ian's cousin—and she did mean to be kind, asking us here for the summer. She did mean to be nice, only ... Well, her life hasn't been happy. Her first marriage was miserable—and she was so romantic about Neville, in the beginning. I don't know whether she was happy with Howard, or not. Sometimes she was furious at him, but other times, lots of other times, she said very nice things about him. Howard's such a comfort to me, she had often said. He's such a thorough *gentleman*, you can always count on him. Especially when we're entertaining.

Of course, Taylor's been a disappointment to her, Tilly thought. He's not a bit affectionate to her. He's got a really hateful manner toward her, scornful and rude. But then, the way she brought him up, one moment simply doting on him, and the next moment flying at him. When he was a little boy, I saw her slap him in the face. Stop! Don't remember things like that about her. Remember how she paid for poor old Uncle Edward in that home for years. Remember ...

Remember the bats. I didn't know they squeaked. Remember the snake.... Robert! Robert! Don't go near your vallons! The snake's underneath them. I can *see* him! But he was going nearer and nearer to the little heap of stripped leaves, and she was far away, on a hilltop, and she could not move. Not one step. *Robert!* she cried, with all her strength. *Raw-bert!* called a jeering voice beside her, and she turned her head to see the Bad Boy. He was as tall as a man, and very bony, but he was dressed like a child, in dark-blue shorts and a middy blouse and a sailor's cap with ribbons streaming down his back. *He* can't hear, he told her. And she could not move; her feet were sunk in clay, in mud, and she was sinking deeper, up to her knees now. Please ...! Please ...! she cried.

Then she opened her eyes, and sat up to look at Robert. He had stretched out now, his face turned sideways on the pillow, tranquilly sleeping. The lamp still burned, but there was a pearly brightness in the sky; the night was over. I'm going to get those poor things, she thought.

She put on her slippers and the rather marvelous negligee that Sibyl had grown tired of and given to her; nile-green chiffon, with long sleeves and a collar buttoned with tiny white pearl flowers; it was far too large for her; she had to hold up the voluminous skirt as she went quietly out of the room, with a bath-towel over her arm.

She had trouble with the bolt on the front door, and when at last she pushed it back, it grated loudly. She stepped out onto the terrace, and for a moment she paused, spellbound by the world she saw. The birds were twittering in the trees, but she saw none flying; the light breeze stirred the delicate flowers planted beside the driveway, pink, yellow, white, so that they looked as if they too were ready to fly, when the sun came. There ought to be music when it comes, she thought; trumpets, and clarions.

Then she remembered her errand, and ran down the steps and across the grass that was wet with dew. I hate doing this, she thought. I hate to pick up those poor dead creatures. But I want to show them to Lieutenant Levy, before ... Before what? Before something eats them. Before someone takes them away.

But they still lay there, side by side, and they were horrible and piteous. Something had been plucking at the bird's feathers, digging into its breast; half of the chipmunk's alert little face was eaten away. With a corner of the towel, she pushed them into the middle of it, rolled the towel, over and over, and picked it up by the ends. If Lieutenant Levy sees this, she thought, if I tell him about the bats. And the snake ... He'll do something to protect Robert.

Then she saw Osborne standing on the terrace, in a belted black shantung dressing-gown over his trousers. He came down the steps and met her as she was crossing the lawn.

"So you're a witch," he said.

"No, I'm not!"

"Has to be so. Who else would be out before sunrise, gathering—I don't know what."

"Some toys Robert had left out all night. I wanted to get them before he waked up. I wanted to see if they were mouldy, or damaged, so that I could fix them up."

"And they were," said Osborne. "They were awful."

"Why do you think so?"

"By the way you carry your bundle. As if it made you sick. Let me take it for you, Mrs. MacDonald."

"No, thank you. Never mind. It's not a bit heavy."

"It's a leprechaun. Dead?"

She smiled, as best she could.

"I'll have to hurry. Because Robert would hate to wake up and find me gone."

She tried to go forward, but he moved to block her way.

"Mrs. MacDonald," he said, "I'd like to help you."

"Thank you," said Tilly, "but I don't need any help."

"Remember the talk we were having yesterday? About detective stories? About how popular it is to have a girl, the heroine, of course, who tries to mislead the police? She doesn't tell them something she knows, or she— shades some fact a little."

"Lies, you mean," said Tilly.

"That's your word, not mine."

"Then you think I've been lying to the police?"

"I didn't say that, either. Only I wanted to advise you—"

"Are you a detective, or a policeman?" she asked again, and she felt her cheeks grow hot. He—*bothers* me, she thought.

"No," he answered. "Just unusually clever. Insight. Perseverance."

"Just what *are* you, Mr. Osborne?"

"I'm an expert, Mrs. MacDonald."

"An expert in what?"

"I don't exactly know, Mrs. MacDonald. But it seems, at the moment, to be the Far East. Japan, China, Korea. I sell articles to newspapers and magazines. Authoritative articles, they're called."

In this pearly light, his dark, bony face had, she thought, a different look, strained, tired, and somehow dangerous. Nothing could stop him, she told herself.

"Have you really been in the Far East?" she asked.

"Eight years," he said. "I was sent over with a zoological expedition, to study the animal life. But that doesn't seem to pay. My articles about animals didn't sell. Except now and then to very choice magazines that paid what you could well call a 'pittance.' But I looked at the people, too, you know, and that's what brings in the shekels. My Life with a Chinese Concubine. Three Months with a Geisha Girl."

"Is that how you lived?" she asked, with distaste.

"No. Very much otherwise," he said. "That's just my wit. But, jester though I may be, please let me give you my word of advice. I've known Levy for a long time, and he's a good deal smarter than you think. He's a bit slow, but that's because he doesn't make snap judgments. And he doesn't make mistakes. When he makes a charge, it sticks. Don't hold out on him, Mrs. MacDonald. Don't—"

"Don't lie to him, you mean?"

"It wouldn't be a good idea."

"Why do you think I have? Why did you come here now?"

"I heard the bolt being drawn on the front door, and I thought I'd take a look."

"I can't see what concern *you* have in this affair," she said, curtly.

"You," said Osborne, and stepped aside.

She went on toward the house, carrying her repellent bundle, and she was startled and very much troubled. Me? she thought. Why did he pick me out as the one who—hasn't told the truth? And why does he care? She ran up the stairs, holding up the voluminous skirt; she opened the bedroom door, and when she saw Robert lying there, still quietly sleeping, she began to cry.

She despised that; she frowned, but she could not stop. She put the bundle on the top shelf of the closet, where Robert could not get at it, and the tears were still raining down her face. She lay down on the bed, still in the green negligee, still crying, and she fell asleep.

"Hi, Mommy!" called Robert.

He was standing beside her, and the sun was shining into the room.

"You look very nice and pretty and like a fairy queen," he said. "Only your face is dirty, Mommy."

"You go and take your shower," she said, "and then I'll have mine."

It was only two days ago that he had learned to turn on the shower for himself, and he was vainglorious about it. She heard the water come pattering down, and he began to sing. "Home on the Range." Singing—in this house ... He doesn't seem to know about Sibyl. Maybe I ought to tell him. But I don't know.... Maybe I'd better wait till he asks.

Sibyl had never come down to breakfast, yet the dining room seemed bleakly empty without her; the whole house seemed empty. If only Lieutenant Levy will let us go today.... Howard will probably want to close the house, anyhow. Perhaps the Lieutenant has found out already who did that horrible thing—put that deadly poison in her capsule. I've given her lots of them, dozens. But I never really looked at the bottle. It was a prescription, but I never looked at the doctor's name, or the name of the drugstore. I'd like one of my yellow goof-balls, she used to say. This looked exactly the same. But if I told Levy I gave her something and never looked at the label, he'd think—I don't know what.

Who did it? Anyone could have got into the bathroom through Howard's room, or her own, when they weren't there. The capsule could have been put there in the morning, when Howard was out riding and Sibyl was asleep. But who would *want* to kill her? I suppose people will say it was Howard, because he wanted her money. But Howard's just not like that. And anyhow, she gave him everything he wanted. He's not a murderer.

Would you know a murderer, if you saw one? Think of all the people in the house yesterday. Not Carola, not Howard, certainly not Mr. Cantrell. Jenny's pretty bad-tempered, but what would she have to gain? Or Jensen? Or Gloria? No.... The only two who look one bit sinister are Pauline and Sam Osborne. It's hard to think of any motive they could have, but they're both more—subtle than the others.

"Well!" said Robert, cheerfully, as he finished his cup of cocoa. "Cousin Sibyl's gone, for ever and ever, I guess."

"Robert! Who told you?"

"Sam did."

"You mustn't call him Sam. Say Mr. Osborne."

"He *said* call him Sam. He said Cousin Sibyl was all dead, and I have to be extra good today and not worry you. So I *will* be. Only after breakfast will you let me go and see if the birds took my vallons?"

"We'll see, later on, dear."

"Good-morning," said Howard, from the doorway. He looked pale and ill, very neat in a dark suit and black tie.

"There's so much to be done ...," he said, still standing in the doorway. "They made the autopsy last night—"

"Robert, run in and see Gloria," said Tilly. But Robert did not move.

"They'll get the reports now, and the District Attorney is allowing us to have the—" He paused. "The ceremony," he said. "Tomorrow. In Brookline. That's what she—what she—what Sibyl always said she wanted. I telephoned the school camp, and they're sending Taylor here, at once. We're leaving—this afternoon. They're sending policemen with us, to be sure we'll all come back. I know Sibyl—would want you to come, Tilly. Pauline says she'll stay and look after Robert."

"Howard, I *couldn't!* I—can't leave Robert...."

"You can bring him, then."

"Howard, he's too little. Howard, I—can't."

"You don't *care* what Sibyl wants?" he asked.

Sibyl doesn't want anything now, or ever any more, Tilly thought. But she would not say that to this stricken and suffering man.

"Howard, I've got to think of my child," she said. "Sibyl would understand that."

"I *want* you to come," he said. "I need you, Tilly."

She was surprised, startled.

"But, Howard ...!"

"I'm alone," he said. "I need you, Tilly."

That was almost too much for Tilly. But still Robert came first.

"I'm so sorry, Howard," she said. "But—"

The doorbell rang, and they were both silent while Jenny went hurrying along the hall. She made no announcement; the two arrivals came at once into the dining room. One of them was Taylor Price, Sibyl's son, a handsome, dark boy, very tall for his sixteen years, and with him was a short, stocky little man with a high crest of gray hair.

"Mr. Fleming?" he said. "My name is Abbott. The school—the camp— sent me to bring Taylor here. We—er—it's a rule.... We don't care to—er— have our boys travel alone."

"He's the one!" cried Robert, springing up, and oversetting his chair. "He's the one!" he cried again, pointing at Taylor. "He's the bad big boy that killed the bird and the chipmink—and the little lemming."

CHAPTER SEVEN

Robert, with his black brows drawn together, was pointing his forefinger straight at Taylor. But Taylor glanced at him with scornful indifference, and the pompous young man who had accompanied him, and Howard, too, paid no attention to the child.

"*He's* the bad big boy that killed the—"

"Hush, darling!" Tilly said to him, in a whisper so serious that it impressed him; he let his accusing finger drop.

"Taylor, m' boy ...," Howard said. His mouth twitched; he blinked his eyes rapidly. "I know—you must believe that I know ... The shock—the—the—all of it."

"Oh, thanks!" said Taylor.

Well, at least you can't call him a hypocrite, thought Tilly. He doesn't even pretend to care about Sibyl—his own mother. I never liked him, even when he was little, and I certainly don't think he's improved.

"Er—my name is Abbott, sir," said the pompous young man.

"*Wilfred* Abbott," said Taylor.

"Sit down, Mr. Abbott," said Howard.

"Thank you, Mr. Fleming, but I won't intrude on you—at this time of—this time. I came, because Mr. Bailey has, as you no doubt know, a strict regulation about any of the boys from the school, or from our summer camp, traveling alone. So I was glad—" He stopped a moment, his sun-browned face turned a deep red. "I—er—that was certainly not the word I intended, sir.... I volunteered to come with Taylor, because I had had the—privilege of meeting the—meeting Mrs. Fleming on two or three occasions at the school. I've engaged a room at the little inn here, and I'll be waiting there.... Any time.... Anything."

"But he is the boy that camed yesterday," said Robert, suddenly. The conversation, the atmosphere, the entire lack of attention he was getting bored him, and made him rebellious.

"Er—may I ask ...?" said Abbott. "Er—madam—"

"Tilly, Mr. Abbott. Mr. Abbott, Mrs. MacDonald."

Abbott made a clumsy bow, like a youth in a dancing school.

"Mrs. MacDonald, do I understand that the—your son? Thank you! That your son is saying he saw Taylor here yesterday?"

"Did, too, see him," said Robert. "And he—"

"It's quite impossible, Mrs. MacDonald. The boys never leave the camp unattended, and you may be sure that any long absence on Taylor's part would have been noticed and checked."

"I see!" said Tilly, politely. "Now, Robert, you've finished your breakfast, and we'll go out in the sunshine."

"Just a moment, Tilly," said Howard. "This is—I'll have to explain ... They made the—the autopsy last night, and, although they're waiting for—for some sort of reports from the laboratory, the Medical officer is—he feels definite. In any case, Levy's given us all permission to take a train to Boston at noon. For the—the ceremony. He won't let us drive there, and there'll be plainclothesmen on the train, but—in any case—"

"But—but—but ...," said Robert, softly.

"In any case, it's ... That's where Sibyl would want—to rest."

"Is Cousin Sibyl going in the train?" Robert asked, with interest. "Are you going to sit her up and—?"

"Hush, Robert!" said Tilly, sternly. "Yes, Howard?"

"We'll be back tomorrow morning. And you can safely leave Robert in Pauline's charge."

"Howard, I can't!" she cried. "I'm sorry, but—really I don't want to leave him."

"Tilly, I consider it would be—*most* unsuitable to take the child with us. He—I'm sorry to say this, but he's not a—a very well-behaved child. I don't blame you, Tilly. No woman alone can bring up a boy."

"Mrs. MacDonald," said Abbott, "I'd be very pleased to undertake the lad's care, while you're absent. I—naturally, I've had considerable experience with boys. We can go swimming, rowing, a ramble through the woods."

"No," said Robert. "I'd rather stay with Sam."

He really was behaving badly this morning, but, Tilly thought, it was the atmosphere of the house, it was Howard's nervous stammer, it was, beyond anything else, his belief that Taylor was the "bad, big boy" of yesterday.

"Sam?" said Howard, with a frown of surprise. "Does he mean Osborne? Well, Mr. Osborne's coming with us. Naturally. I've known him and his family for twenty, thirty years. And now he's—" He stopped short. "He's helping me with—some work." He paused again. "If Mr. Abbott will be good enough to stay here, in the house, and there'll be Pauline and the two maids—"

"I want to stay with my mother!" Robert cried. "There was a snake in my bed—"

"Hush!" Tilly said, again. "I can't leave him, Howard. Really I can't."

"I think," said Howard, deliberately and sternly, "that in view of the circumstances, it's your duty to come with us, Tilly. Even if it's simply to—to—keep up appearances. I mean, everyone knows she was Ian's cousin, you and your child were guests. Everyone would consider it—well, to say the least, unfeeling of you. I mean—pay your last respects. Not much to ask."

It really isn't much, Tilly said to herself. It really would look heartless—and queer, if I don't go. Only I won't leave Robert in this house.

"All right, Howard," she said. "But I'd rather Robert went to the Inn with Mr. Abbott. It would be a little change for him."

"A change?" Howard repeated. "I can't see why the child should need a change."

"I *want* him to go to the Inn!" said Tilly, so vehemently that Howard's brows twitched in surprise, and a certain alarm.

"Now, now!" he said. "You're—overwrought, Tilly. You must—" He frowned, thinking of what it was she must do. "A little brandy," he said.

"At breakfast time!" she cried. "It's a horrible idea!"

She knew very well that she was speaking too loudly. I don't care! she thought. I'd like to stamp my foot. I'd like to—yell.

"What's more," she said, "*I'm* going to take him to the Inn, before we leave."

"But Tilly ...! Mr. Abbott will—"

"I'm going with him *myself*. I will! I'm going to get his room there—and everything. I will!"

"Why not?" said Osborne's slow, almost languid voice from the doorway. "You and Mr. Abbott and Robert and I can stroll down there now, and get the kid settled. It's a nice place, Robert. You'll like it. They have a little dock there, and boats, and maybe Mr. Abbott will take you out rowing."

"I will, indeed!" said Abbott, earnestly.

"Then I'll pack his bag," said Tilly.

"Pauline can do that," said Osborne. "The chauffeur can take it later, in the car."

"I want *all* my things!" said Robert. "I want my express wagon, and my blocks, and—and *everything*."

"You'll get 'em," said Osborne. "Ready, Mrs. MacDonald?"

"You mean—*now?* This moment?"

"Why not?" Osborne asked.

Tilly looked at him for a moment.

"All right!" she said. "I'll be back in a very little while, Howard."

"I beg of you not to let anything delay you," said Howard. "We leave the house at eleven-thirty, sharp. It's been—it's very complicated. Railway tickets, hotel reservations, and then ... Fortunately, I have a half-brother living in Boston. I got him on the telephone, and he's being most helpful. Getting in touch with Sibyl's people, arranging for the—ceremony. Her family plot. The music. He—"

"I won't be late, Howard," said Tilly.

It was ill-mannered, and perhaps even unkind to interrupt him. But I couldn't listen to him for one single second longer, she thought.

They went out of the house, into a sparkling morning with a steady breeze.

"Can I just go and look at my vallons?" Robert asked.

He had suddenly grown quiet, almost meek. When she said they had no time to stop now, he accepted it without protest.

The Seafarers' Inn was an old-fashioned wooden building, set flush with the road; on one side was a well-kept lawn, with wrought-iron chairs and tables, shaded by fine old trees, and in back there was a little sun-bleached dock on a quiet inlet from the sea.

"But if Robert went out of the front door, he'd be right in the road, with all the traffic!" said Tilly.

"Mrs. MacDonald," said Abbott, a little hurt, a little offended. "I'm accustomed to taking charge of groups of boys, and you can be assured—"

"Yes!" said Osborne. "Go ahead and be assured, Tilly. Abbott will look after your kid."

The landlady was an odd-looking woman, with dyed black hair and a fretful face; she was very stout, but her legs were very thin, and in the rear, just below what waist she had, was a great protuberance, which gave her the look of some sort of fantastic wading-bird.

"I'd like my little boy to have a room connecting with Mr. Abbott's," Tilly said.

"We don't *have* no connecting rooms any more," said the landlady. "And we're not going to, neither. We had 'em, and it led to immoralness. And that's something I won't put up with."

"Well, a room and bath, as near Mr. Abbott—"

"No baths," said the landlady. "Except there's an accommodation on every floor, and a bathtub, too. But if you want any hot water for a tub bath, it's thirty-five cents, because of how prices have went up. In *my* day, we kept ourselves real clean and neat, without no bathtubs and hot water. And no connecting rooms."

"But you see," said Tilly, "my son's only five. And I have to go to a funeral in Boston."

"Mrs. Fleming's?" asked the landlady. "My, that's a dreadful thing. But the way those society people carry on ... Only five? He's real tall. Well, I brought up six of my own, and I guess I can look after him."

She looked at Robert, and her fretful face was completely changed; it had a look of tenderness and compassion. She opened the door of a clean, sparsely-furnished little room, and turned to Robert. "Now, if you'll be real good," she said, "I'll bring my radio up here. But eight o'clock, it goes off, and out goes your light. That agreed, young feller?"

"Yes, ma'am," said Robert, obviously delighted by the prospect of a room alone, a radio under his own control.

"I like kids," said the landlady. "You don't have to worry about him. My! That was a terrible thing, about poor Mrs. Fleming. Suicide, do you think?"

"I don't know anything about it," said Tilly. "But please don't let my little boy hear any talk—"

"He'll get his meals up in his own room," said the landlady, "or else outdoors with that teacher feller. But I'll see he doesn't get downstairs with those society people that got yachts and drink till they're blue in the face. No. Don't you worry."

"No, don't," said Osborne. "Come along now, Tilly. Your child's in good hands."

Robert kissed her good-bye, absent-mindedly.

"I'd like to go out in a rowboat," he said. "And maybe I could catch a lot of fishes."

"Maybe you could," said Tilly. "Well ... See you tomorrow, darling. And you'll be good, and do whatever Mr. Abbott says, won't you?"

"Ah reckon so," said Robert, still absent-minded.

"Better come along, Mrs. MacDonald," said Osborne. "You don't want to be late."

She set off with him along the road that was so commonplace, so much at variance with Sibyl's luxurious estate. There was a filling-station, a diner, a beer-garden; there was a stream of cars going to the public beach, most of them filled with the sort of people Sibyl couldn't endure. She had had built a graceful but forbidding iron fence, tall and spiked, all along her grounds, to keep her safe....

"Look, will you?" said Osborne.

They had come to the entrance of the driveway, and in front of the house seven cars were parked.

"The cortege," said Osborne. "It's going to be a fine, first-class production. It's pathetic, in a way. I don't think there's one soul on God's earth who'll miss her," he said.

"But—Howard ...?" Tilly said, and it was only half a question.

"He was born to be a widower," said Osborne. "He'll go every year to put flowers on her grave. He'll have a big framed picture of her in his room, and he'll carry a small one in his pocket. He'll—"

"Stop!" said Tilly. "It's—horrible. Anyhow, maybe Taylor cares more than anyone realizes."

"Maybe he does," said Osborne. "Nice idea. And maybe Sibyl cared more for Taylor than I ever realized."

"I think it's a great mistake to be cynical," said Tilly.

"Much less painful than being gullible," said Osborne. "You don't get hurt so often. Or so badly."

"Do you mean you think *I'm* 'gullible'?"

"Let's call it 'trusting.' Innocent. Artless."

"And in just what way?" she demanded, and she was angry now.

"You've been living in a house with a murderer," said Osborne. "And you're not even very curious to know who the murderer is. I don't think you care, particularly. You have a sort of no-use-crying-over-spilt-milk attitude about the whole thing. Sibyl was murdered. Too bad. But nothing can bring her back, so why not drop all this upsetting business about investigating, and so on."

"You mean I ought to be thinking about justice, and vengeance, and so on, all the time?"

"No," he said. "Let's use a word I'm sure will appeal to you. Let's say 'duty.'

"Duty—to Sibyl? To the State? To—?"

"No. Just to your fellow-creatures. If anyone commits a murder, and gets away with it, he—or she—is always likely to do it again. Anyhow, he—or she—remains a person who's capable of murder. Not a good idea, to leave a killer loose in the world."

"You're talking as if *I* knew who did it. As if *I* could help."

"Maybe you could help," he said. "Anyhow, you don't need to hinder. Levy's a good man, intelligent, honest. And very, very persevering. The chances are that he'll get the murderer—in the end. But I'd say, the sooner the better. Before anything else happens."

"Naturally," said Tilly, cold and curt.

"All right. Then tell Levy everything. Tell him the truth."

"Are you implying that I haven't? That I'm a liar?"

She looked straight at him.

Her dark eyes were blazing; there was a hot color in her cheeks. But Osborne looked back at her, with no sign of contrition.

"A very nice one," he said. "You mean well."

In her anger, she walked faster, and Osborne let her draw ahead of him. She had been brought up to look upon a quarrel as ill-bred, and disgraceful. Keep your temper, she had been taught, and she was doing that. But it was like something churning inside her, and it came into her mind that maybe it would be better to let it out, to tell Osborne what she thought of him. Impertinent. Meddlesome. *Odious.* Calling me a liar. Practically accusing me of protecting a murderer. Odious. Impertinent.

She went up the steps to the terrace, and Jenny opened the door.

"Lieutenant Levy says he wants to see you, ma'am, and Mr. Osborne, too. In the library, right away, he says," she said, in a tone of spiteful triumph.

Tilly's anger was in an instant smothered by cold dread and dismay, like a fire quenched by icy rain. She was afraid of Levy, as she had never before in her life been afraid of anyone.

CHAPTER EIGHT

If he's found out that I did give Sibyl that capsule ..., she thought. It'll be worse now, after I've lied about it. Because I did tell him a lie. Suppose he arrests me? Takes me away for questioning, or whatever they do? What will happen to Robert? That Mr. Abbott *seems* very nice, and trustworthy, but, after all, I don't really know him.

As they went down the hall, she saw four or five people in the drawing-room, all silent, sitting erect in their chairs, the women in black. They went on, to the library, where Levy sat behind the desk, holding a letter-scale between his two big hands. Wasn't there an Egyptian god that weighed souls? Tilly asked herself. That's what he looks like.

He put down the scale and rose when they entered, and he seemed toweringly tall. Howard was sitting on a sofa beside Taylor; Carola was here, and Dick Cantrell, and Pauline, wearing a black hat tilted raffishly to one side, very incongruous with her pale, displeased face.

"I shan't detain you now," said Levy. "But there are a few things ..."

His voice, as usual, was quiet, but not mild now. "You understand," he said, "that this is a very unusual privilege. To allow all the persons who were in this house at the time of Mrs. Fleming's death to leave not only the premises but the state. However, at the request of the Governor, the District Attorney has given his consent. But—"

He paused, he bent his head, and pushed the letter-scale back and forth.

"You will be accompanied by four members of our force, three men and one woman. In plainclothes. They have their instructions, and they will do nothing to embarrass or inconvenience. *But—*" He paused. "Any attempt to evade their supervision, or to hamper them in any way whatever, by any person or persons, will result in immediate arrest."

"Me, too?" asked Taylor, with a look of bright interest.

Levy ignored him.

"The funeral is to take place at eleven o'clock tomorrow morning," he went on. "This, too, is very unusual in a case like this, but the County Medical Officer, as well as Doctor Crowdie and the laboratory experts, are all completely agreed upon the cause of death, and so on. After the funeral, you'll take a train leaving at approximately one o'clock, and change at

Grand Central for a train that will bring you here. I shall want to see all of you as soon as you return. Is that clear?"

"Very clear," said Cantrell, earnestly. "Very fair. I think I can say that we all appreciate—"

"We'll have to leave at once," Howard interrupted, looking at his watch.

Everyone rose, and they filed out into the hall. Howard nodded at the silent group in the drawing-room, and they too rose, and joined the rest. Howard brought a small notebook out of his pocket, and read aloud from it. Second car, Cantrell, Mr. and Mrs. Berkley, and Eloise. As their names were called, each of them moved forward, down the steps, and into one of the cars.

"Tilly," said Howard, "you'll be in the first car, with Carola and Taylor and myself."

The cars all started. But where's Sibyl? Tilly thought. She had imagined that the cortege would be led by a hearse, but there was none; nor, as far as she could tell, any police cars. The police must have been just put in with other people, she thought. Perhaps they'll get clues from things they hear....

"Sit up straight, Taylor," said Howard, severely.

But Taylor remained as he was, slouched down on the folding seat, his knees crossed, almost level with his chin.

"Why?" he asked.

"It's not respectful, to loll that way."

"Respectful to whom?" Taylor asked.

"To your mother. Sit up straight."

"Oh, she won't mind," said Taylor.

"*Sit up!*" said Howard, more loudly.

"Oh, don't!" said Carola. "Please don't. We shouldn't think of anything now—but Sibyl—and our memories."

Tears were running down her cheeks, but they did not disfigure her. She's really very, very pretty, Tilly thought. And maybe she's nice. Maybe she's sincere. I don't know. She paid no more attention to Tilly now than she had ever done in the past; she was polite enough, but completely indifferent. She leaned forward now, and took Taylor's hand.

"Oh, Taylor!" she said. "If you only knew how your mother used to talk about you. We met—you know—on board a ship—going to France. We'd both just got our divorces—and it's such a miserable feeling. We both felt the same ... I mean—just after a divorce—you have that feeling that you haven't—any *home*. It's so terribly forlorn.... We used to talk about— where we'd live when we went home.... And Sibyl used to say—any place would be like a home to her, as long as she had her Boykins there. That's what she used to call—Ouch! Taylor! You're hurting me!"

"Am I?" Taylor asked, raising his brows, with a look of innocent surprise.

"You simply *crushed* my hand!"

"I don't realize my own strength," said Taylor.

"Apologize to Mrs. Dexter, at once!" said Howard.

"I apologize, Mrs. Dexter," said Taylor. "Where was I when my mother went to Paris?"

"Where ...?" Carola said, at a loss. "Some place where you were happy and well looked after. I can't quite remember the *name* of—whoever it was."

"I can," said Taylor. "Her name was Molly Monaghan, and she'd been one of my mother's servants. She lived in a dirty little house, with three dirty kids of her own, and she and her husband were drunk all the time. But my mother said Molly was 'devoted,' and—"

"That'll do, Taylor," said Howard.

"Yes, sir," said Taylor, with exaggerated respect. "She said it would be a 'home atmosphere.'"

They reached the railway station, just before the train arrived; they all got on board. Such a lot of us! Tilly thought. There was no parlor car, so they sat where they could; some of them went into the smoker; Tilly sat down beside a woman who belonged to their party, but whom Tilly had either never met or had forgotten, a thin and dour woman in a black hat and a black suit too heavy for this weather. Could she be the policewoman? Tilly asked herself.

They all got out at Grand Central; they followed Howard across the great rotunda, all keeping rather close together, in a sort of swarm. There were parlor-car reservations for them on this train, and they settled themselves, a little more relaxed; some of them talked in low voices. I don't want to talk, Tilly thought. Not to anyone. Not to the people she knew, and any of the strangers might belong to the police. And you might say something, just some little thing, that would give you away.

I've got to stop being so nervous and—frightened, she thought. I'm not a criminal. I haven't done anything so terrible. Except to tell Lieutenant Levy that I didn't give Sibyl a capsule, or see her take one. I'm pretty sure it's not perjury, unless you've taken an oath. I don't think they could do anything to me for that.

Except suspect me. Except suspect and disbelieve everything I say. Except think I know other things.... But what good would it have done, if I had told him I gave Sibyl the capsule? I didn't know it was poison, and I'm sure Sibyl didn't know, either. I don't know how a poisoned capsule got there. I can't even imagine who'd put it there. The people in the house when it happened were Howard, and Carola, and Mr. Cantrell, and myself, and the servants. Oh, and Sam Osborne. And how did *he* know I'd told a lie to Lieutenant Levy?

Did he *see* me? she thought. If he'd been in Howard's room, and opened the bathroom door even a crack, he could have seen me. And has he told Lieutenant Levy that he saw me?

I don't think he'd do that. I don't know why, but I just don't think he would. Maybe nobody will ever find out that I gave her that capsule. Oh, if only it would be like that, and I could take Robert and get away....

She was growing a little drowsy, and it would, she thought, be a blessed thing if she could sleep through even a little part of this interminable journey. She took off her hat, and leaned back; she closed her eyes.

"Dare to be true. Nothing can need a lie.
The sin that needs it most grows two thereby."

That was her grandmother speaking.

"Oh, what a tangled web we weave
When first we practice to deceive."

Lying is a sin. And be sure thy sin will find thee out. You'll have to be punished for your sin. But not yet. Please, please, not yet. Wait till Robert's grown up. He's only five. Please wait....

It was growing dark when they reached Boston, and, in the Back Bay station, Howard addressed the little swarm.

"I did the best I could, with the hotel," he said. "But there's some sort of convention here, and I couldn't manage as I wanted. I'm afraid some of you will have to share bathrooms. I've arranged that dinner shall be sent up to all of you. Unless, of course, you prefer to go down to the public restaurant. Breakfast will be served in your rooms at nine o'clock, and we'll assemble in the lobby at ten-thirty. I most earnestly request that *no one* be late."

Tilly was young, and healthy, and she was hungry. As soon as she got into her room, she called room service, and ordered clam chowder, and fried chicken with two vegetables, and peach ice-cream. Robert would love this, she thought. All right. He'll have plenty of dinners like this. I'll see him to-morrow, and maybe the next day they'll let us go.

Go where? The couple who are subletting our apartment won't be gone until the first of October, and it's only early in July now. I haven't enough money to pay for us in a hotel.

Her dinner came up then, on a wheeled table, and it was delicious. It does you good to eat, she thought. She telephoned to the desk for an evening newspaper; she undressed, and in Sibyl's marvelous negligee, she lay down on the bed to read.

But almost at once the bathroom door opened, and Carola came into her room, barefoot, in a pale yellow, lace-trimmed slip. She was crying again, and there was a strong smell of liquor about her.

"I've *got* to talk ...," she said. "I've *got* to talk—to someone. Sibyl ... Sibyl and I saw each other—every day. I *hate* the country—but I got Ricky to buy me that house there, *only* because I'd be near Sibyl. The alimony Ricky sends me is so *miserly*, I don't know how to live on it. I only have one servant, and she's horrible. Only a cheap little car, a thousand years old, and no chauffeur. And there's Ricky, absolutely *rolling* in money ..."

She sat down in an armchair, crossing her bare knees.

"I haven't *anyone*," she said. "I'm all alone. If I had a child, like yours ..."

Leave Robert out of this! Tilly thought.

"My parents are dead, and I never had any brothers or sisters. I haven't *anyone*.... If I'd had a child ... Only, Sibyl said it was the most *awful* experience. She said that when she came out of the ether, and they showed her the baby, she screamed, and then she fainted. She said the baby was so hideous and weird, all red and wrinkled, and his mouth open, like a fish. Anyhow, Neville—that was her first husband, you know—Neville was *cruel* to her. I don't think she ever got over the shock of the whole thing. She did admit that Howard was wonderfully kind to her, but she never quite realized how understanding and wonderful he was to her."

Tilly was, by training and by nature, courteous and long-suffering. She let this most unwelcome visitor go on and on, because she could see how genuinely wretched and disturbed Carola was. But it was hard, very hard.

"I'm not going to this—funeral tomorrow," Carola said. "I couldn't take it."

"But, Carola—," Tilly said, and it was the first time she had used Mrs. Dexter's first name. "If you don't go, the police might—"

"The *police!*" said Carola, with infinite scorn. "Everybody *knows* it was suicide."

"I don't think so," said Tilly.

"Well, *I* do," said Carola. "I *know* she wanted to die. She told me so."

But people like Sibyl—and like you—are always saying that, Tilly thought. Always saying, when the least thing goes wrong, I wish I was dead. In her fatigue, her dread, she scarcely heard Carola any more, but from time to time she glanced at her, with great compassion. She looked lovely in her lemon-colored slip, her blond hair loose on her shoulders, but she looked forlorn; she was too thin. She hasn't anything, Tilly thought. And I've got Robert. My son. My son child. My own darling, my life. Perhaps he'll be— a famous naturalist....

He was. She saw him standing on a platform, tall, lean, dark, entirely at ease, giving a lecture. The true significance of vallons, he said, lies—

"*Tilly!*" cried Carola. "Are you asleep?"

"No," Tilly answered, rousing herself with an effort. "But I am pretty tired, Carola."

Carola sprang to her feet.

"Oh, you're tired, are you?" she said. "A hell of a lot *you've* got to be tired about. You simply lived there, sponging on Sibyl, you and your child. You gave her all kinds of dope. You were cold—and horrible to her. She told me so. You worked on Howard; Sibyl told me so. You felt sure Howard would look after you, and that brat of yours. You *knew* you could get more out of Howard than you could from Sibyl. If it *was* murder—" She paused a moment, looking at Tilly with her eyes narrowed. "If it *was* murder," she said, "*you* did it."

She went out then, through the connecting bathroom, slamming the door behind her.

I'm going to sleep, Tilly told herself. I don't care what Carola said. I'm going to sleep, and tomorrow I'll get back to Robert.

She did get to sleep, so suddenly that she did not wash, or brush her teeth, or go through any of her usual routine. When she waked, the lamp on the bedside table was still lighted, she was still wearing Sibyl's negligee. And someone was knocking at the door. She got up, unsteady with drowsiness, and opened the door, and it was a waiter with her breakfast. If you can eat, Tilly told herself, and if you can sleep, you can get through almost anything.

It was a good breakfast, and she did eat, leisurely. She took a bath, and dressed, and she was down in the lobby well before ten-thirty. Howard was there, and Cantrell, and Osborne, and many of the group that she did not know. Funny, she thought, some of them must be Ian's relatives, too. She was suddenly glad that there hadn't been, in the few short months of her marriage, a chance to meet them. Ian had never talked about them. Sibyl was the only one she had known. Tilly waited, until she saw Howard glance at his watch; then she went up to Osborne.

"Carola ...," she said. "Mrs. Dexter ... Do you think I'd better go upstairs and see if she's ready?"

"She's not coming with us," said Osborne. "She's too high-strung. That's all right with Howard."

The whole thing was much less of an ordeal than Tilly had expected. They all went, again in a cortege of cars, to the funeral parlor, where there were many other people waiting for them; they all went to look at Sibyl, and, in a frilled white negligee, she looked calm, even majestic, handsomer than ever Tilly had seen her in life.

"Beautiful," said Cantrell, beside her. "At peace now—after all the storms of life."

His eyes were misty with tears; many in the assemblage were crying; one or two sobbed loudly. But Tilly had no tears; she felt nothing but an affectionate regret. Poor Sibyl! she thought. I'm sorry.

But her thoughts were all fixed upon Robert now. She listened with respectful attention while the clergyman read the service; she listened to his eulogy of Sibyl. A noble and generous woman ..., he said. Our hearts go out in sympathy to her husband, and her son....

She glanced at Taylor and she found him looking at her, his eyes narrowed, and a faint smile on his face so malicious that it startled her. Never mind! she told herself. It's over now. I'll get Robert, and we'll go away.

When the service was over, there was another of those mass movements, like a swarm, a crowd of people moving along together in silence. Howard took her arm and stopped in the wide tiled hall.

"I'm not even able to go to the cemetery," he said. "Levy insisted upon my taking this train. But thank God, Sibyl had relations and old friends here in Boston who will go. Who will take my wreath...?"

Carola was waiting for them at the station, pale, but very chic and charming in her black linen suit. She sat next to Tilly in the parlor-car; from time to time she cried a little; from time to time she talked to Tilly, in a friendly, almost intimate way. Has she forgotten? Tilly thought. Forgotten that last night she accused me of murdering Sibyl?

Let it go. I'll see Robert in a few hours, she thought, and we'll get away. It's over. If Lieutenant Levy has found out that I gave Sibyl the capsule, I'll admit it. It can't make any difference. He can find out for himself that I couldn't possibly have got that poison—cyanide potassium—something like that. He couldn't dream up any motive for me. No. It's over. I don't care how poor we are. I'll take Robert away—somewhere. Maybe I could be a housekeeper—or a cook—and keep him with me. No. It's over.

They all got out at Grand Central; they all went in a swarm after Howard to the local train; they all got out at the station, where a line of cars waited for them.

"Tilly," Howard said, "you'll come with Taylor, and Carola, and myself. This way."

"Just a moment, please," said Lieutenant Levy.

He wore a uniform now, dark-gray, with a broad black belt.

"I'd like to see Mrs. MacDonald in my office first," he said.

"Look here!" Howard began.

"I'll see you presently, Mr. Fleming. At your house. This way, Mrs. Mac-Donald."

She went with him, to a coupe driven by a policeman in uniform; she got in beside Levy.

"What is it *now?*" she asked.

"I'll have to—get some information from you, Mrs. MacDonald," he said. "We'll wait until we get to my office."

I'm riding in a police car, thought Tilly, dazed. What does it mean?

"Are you—is it going to be long, Lieutenant?" she asked.

"I don't know, Mrs. MacDonald."

"Then couldn't we stop at the Inn, and get my little boy?"

"Not just now, Mrs. MacDonald."

"But—why are you taking me away like this? Aren't you supposed to tell me? Or—or have a warrant, or something?"

"You're not under arrest, Mrs. MacDonald. There are some questions I want answered, that's all."

"But why just me? I do want to get my little boy. Can't you please—?"

The car stopped then, before a big, old-fashioned wooden house on a side street in the town. It had a veranda, a neat lawn in front; it could have been anyone's home. Except that at the entrance to the steps there were two green lights, clear in the dusk, illuminating a sign over the doorway. Horton County Police Station.

"I don't want to go—in here!" she said.

"I'm sorry," said Levy.

He helped her out of the car, and kept her arm in a firm hold. They mounted the steps to the veranda, and a policeman in uniform opened the door. They entered a bleak, bare room, where a burly, red-faced policeman sat at a desk, speaking on the telephone; on a bench against the wall sat two policemen, who rose as Levy entered. They passed through this room, down a narrow hall, and he opened the door of another room, closing it as she entered.

The first thing she noticed was a sickly stench of corruption, overlaid with the smell of some drug or antiseptic. And on the desk, on thickly-folded paper, lay the dead bird and the dead chipmunk, decomposed into wretched little heaps.

"I found these yesterday on the shelf of the closet in your room, Mrs. MacDonald," he said. "The Medical Officer is making further tests, but he says he is quite sure they were killed by potassium cyanide. Can you explain their presence in your room, Mrs. MacDonald?"

"No," Tilly said.

Because if I tell him the truth, he'll get Robert into it. Without any warning. Without me. I was going to tell him, but I wanted to talk to Robert first. Because Robert can't just answer questions, from a stranger. He's so little, he doesn't really know the difference between the truth, and the things he makes up. He'd be worried and confused, and heaven knows what he'd say.

She remembered how he had pointed at Taylor, and said he was the bad big boy who had killed those little creatures. He believed it, too, but it wasn't so. Taylor had been in the school camp with Mr. Abbott.

"Someone must have put them in my room, while I was away."

"That's not possible, Mrs. MacDonald. I had men stationed in the house. The only person who entered your room—besides myself—during your absence was Miss Duval."

"Oh, not Pauline!"

"She was in your room. She packed a bag for your son. But one of my men was in the room with her all the time."

"Someone put them there the day before, when I was downstairs, or out of the house."

"You must have opened that closet several times during the day, Mrs. MacDonald. Do you wish to state that you never noticed that good-sized bundle on the shelf?"

She was silent for a time, sitting in a chair, facing Levy behind his desk. The smell of corruption seemed to grow heavier, smothering. The bird and the chipmunk were almost shapeless now, as if they were melting.

This is a serious, a horrible thing, she thought. And I'm making it worse, by lying. I'm making myself worse, by lying, and I'm making myself contemptible and shameful. How can I bring up Robert to be honorable and decent, if I'm a liar?

She looked up at Levy. It was a shock, to see his face so stern, but she was not to be deflected now.

"No ...," she said. "I haven't been telling you the truth."

"I knew that," he said.

CHAPTER NINE

"I did give Mrs. Fleming a capsule," she said. "She asked me to bring it, and I did."

"Approximately how many capsules were left in the bottle after you gave this one to Mrs. Fleming?"

"It was the only one left."

"And you replaced this empty bottle in the cabinet?"

"I don't remember. Maybe I just took the capsule and brought it to her. I don't remember."

"What was the label on the bottle?"

"I didn't look. Sibyl—Mrs. Fleming   told me there was only one left."

"If you didn't look at the label, how did you know this capsule was what

Mrs. Fleming wanted?"

"Because it looked just like the others."

"You'd given her other capsules?"

"Yes, and I'd seen her get the bottle and take them herself."

"What was your reason for not telling me this when I first asked you, Mrs. MacDonald?"

"I thought maybe I'd be taken away, and questioned, and I didn't want to leave my little boy."

"How long did you remain in the room, after you had given Mrs. Fleming the capsule?"

"Only a little while. I just pulled down the venetian blinds."

"Five minutes?"

"I don't know. One of the blinds stuck a little. It could have been five minutes, but certainly not more."

"Did you look at Mrs. Fleming, before you left the room?"

"Well, yes. Yes, I did."

"Did you notice anything unusual about her appearance?"

"Well, I just thought she'd gone to sleep very quickly."

"If you were in the room for five minutes, or less, Mrs. Fleming was undoubtedly dead when you left. You had no suspicion of that?"

"No, I didn't! I didn't!"

"Why did you return to the room shortly afterward?"

"But I told you. Sibyl had gone to sleep—I mean that! I thought—so very quickly, it—worried me a little."

"And when you saw her this second time?"

"I thought she was still asleep."

"Did you put the flask of whiskey on the table beside Mrs. Fleming's bed?"

"No. I don't remember its being there when I first left her."

"And when you returned?"

"I didn't notice any flask there."

"And when Mrs. Fleming was late in coming down to dinner, were you alarmed?"

"No, I wasn't. It had happened before."

"I see!" he said, and was silent for a moment. "And these?" he said, with a loose-wristed, back-hand gesture toward the dead creatures on the desk. "How did they get into your closet, Mrs. MacDonald?"

"I put them there. The day before yesterday, I went out into the grounds, to bring my little boy in for his supper. He was playing there, sitting under a tree. And he showed me these two dead things. He told me a 'big bad boy' had come, and threatened him, and killed the poor little creatures."

"Why did you bring them into the house, Mrs. MacDonald?"

"I did that early yesterday morning. Because I wanted to show them to you. Because something very horrible happened that night."

"What happened, Mrs. MacDonald?"

"The screen was out of our bedroom window, and there were bats flying around in the room. And—there was a snake in my little boy's bed."

"What did you do then, Mrs. MacDonald?"

"Mr. Osborne was in the hall, and he came in and killed the snake."

"I see!" said Levy.

It was clear now to Tilly that he did not believe her, Perhaps not a word that she had said. It's too late, she thought. If I'd told him everything, from the beginning—

"We'll have to ask your child if he can identify these animals," said Levy.

"Oh, no! Oh, please, *please* don't drag Robert into this! I beg you!"

"He's not going to be frightened or hurt in any way. What's more, nothing he says will be taken too seriously. But I want his story, for what it's worth."

"No, please! He'll only tell you what he told me. This big boy killed the little creatures with a syringe, Robert said, but it might have been a needle, a hypodermic needle.... He's so young—he wouldn't know...."

"They weren't killed by injections, Mrs. MacDonald. They swallowed potassium cyanide—no doubt by force. It's a thing that even a very young child could do."

"*Oh, God!*" cried Tilly. For a moment there was a whirling blackness; she could not see, could not hear.

"Mrs. MacDonald! Drink this!"

Levy was holding a small glass before her.

"What—what is it?" she asked.

"It's Scotch."

"No. No, thank you. No ... I never—no, thank you."

"Mrs. MacDonald, we've sent for your son—"

"Oh, no! Oh, please don't!"

He took her arm and pulled her up; he led her to a divan covered with dark leather. "Lie down!" he said, and put a big, hard leather cushion under her head. "Mrs. MacDonald," he said, standing beside her, "it's necessary to go through with this. It's—unfortunate, if anyone has to be hurt. But you must bear in mind that Mrs. Fleming was murdered."

"No—," Tilly said. "No. You can't—be sure."

"We're very sure, Mrs. MacDonald."

He crossed the room, with his limber stride, and opened the door.

"Miss Duval," he said, and Pauline entered.

"Madame!" she cried. "You are ill? Madame—so pale—"

"All right," said Levy. "We'll look after Mrs. MacDonald. Sit down, Miss

Duval."

But Pauline remained at Tilly's side; she stroked her forehead, she pushed her hair back from her temple.

"Miss Duval," said Levy. "*Sit down.*"

She could not mistake that tone, and she moved away, to take the chair before the desk which Levy had indicated. Levy had already seated himself.

"Miss Duval. On the day of Mrs. Fleming's death, did you see any yellow capsules in her bathroom cabinet?"

"Monsieur," said Pauline, earnestly, "I cannot say. The maid—that Jenny—she was the one who attended to the bathroom. Me, I open the little cabinet only if there is something to put away. Perhaps Mr. Fleming's razor, perhaps tooth-paste, anything I find not in order. About that day I could not tell you. I was in a hurry; I did not look. But on other days ..."

"Go on," said Levy.

"Other days, many, many other days, I see these capsules. The label says Doctor Crowdie and Beale's Pharmacy. It says cannot be renewed or a copy given."

"Have you seen any of the capsules recently?"

"Monsieur, it is so difficult to say, when you are accustomed to see something. I don't know what day, but I know it was a long time."

"A week?"

"Oh, I think not a week. Maybe three days—four days. You understand, monsieur, I *cannot* say. Because one day is not so different from another."

"I understand. Miss Duval, are you prepared to sign a statement that you have several times within the past three months seen these yellow capsules in the bathroom cabinet?"

"Yes!"

"Within the last week?"

She bit her lip, and frowned, and was silent for a moment.

"Yes, monsieur," she said. "It must be so. Because almost every day, when I go up before dinner to help madame to dress, there is something I put away in the cabinet. And always I look at that bottle. Because I think it is very bad, those pills. Sometimes it is full, sometimes half-full. But never do I see it empty."

"And you can't suggest anyone who might have removed the bottle, after Mrs. Fleming—"

"No, monsieur. But I have thought—"

"What have you thought?"

"Monsieur, I have seen nothing, heard nothing. It is only a thought."

"I'd like to hear it, Miss Duval."

"Don't you think, monsieur, that perhaps Doctor Crowdie himself may drop the bottle into his pocket? If he did not wish anyone to know that he is giving these bad pills?"

"That's not at all likely, Miss Duval," said Levy. "Crowdie's a reputable doctor; he wouldn't prescribe anything he thought would discredit him. In the second place, we've questioned Beale and everyone employed by him for the last year. He's willing to take an oath that no one in this house has brought him a prescription for any sort of narcotic for three months, and that his stock hadn't been tampered with. They're kept locked. Miss Duval, did anyone in the house go frequently to Beale's, or the other local drugstores?"

"Me, I have been in there. As to the others, how shall I know, monsieur, where they went when they left the house?"

"No. Of course not."

He had taken up the letter-weight again, and was looking at it with deep attention.

"Miss Duval," he said, "I understand that every week Jensen went in to New York, and brought back a supply of drugs for anyone here who'd asked him—"

"Who tells you this?" Pauline cried, her eyes flashing, her voice louder. "He does not bring 'drugs.' He is very kind, very obliging. He's very good. Madame permitted him to visit his aged father every week, and near the subway station is a large shop, where he would buy for us tooth-powder, a lotion, a cold cream, aspirin, things like that, *very* much cheaper than we can buy here. But not drugs. He is a very good young man. He is always kind to my little Coco, and Coco she is devoted to him. And, monsieur, that is always a sign. The dogs know who is good."

"Well ...," said Levy, with a shadow of a smile. "I've met some pretty bad characters whose dogs were fond of them."

"Jensen is very *good*. He is honest, he is kind—"

"I see! Now, one more question, Miss Duval. Have you ever known of anyone, either living in this house, or coming here as a visitor, who has ever attempted to frighten or to hurt Mrs. MacDonald's child?"

"The little Robert?" Pauline asked, startled.

"No!" said Tilly.

"Just a moment, Mrs. MacDonald. Now, if you'll answer my question, Miss Duval—"

"But nobody!" Pauline said. "Everybody here—" She paused for a moment. "If anyone has done such a thing, it is that Jenny," she said. "I *know* it is she has told you that poor Jensen brings us 'drugs.' One day she steps on the foot of my little dog, and she cries, and what does Jenny do? Laugh, laugh, laugh! She is cruel! She is bad—"

"I see!" said Levy. "Have you ever heard her threaten the child? Ever seen her hurt or frighten him?"

"I have seen this, no. But I tell you she is capable of—"

"Thank you, Miss Duval."

There was a knock on the door, and a policeman entered and went up to the desk and spoke to Levy, too low for Tilly to hear.

"All right. Bring him in," said Levy. "That's all for the present, Miss Duval. Thanks."

She moved toward the door, with obvious reluctance, and before she reached it, Robert entered, alone.

"Ah, *mon petite!*" cried Pauline. "You are well?"

She put her hand on his round little head, but he drew away from her. He glanced at his mother, but he did not smile or speak. The policeman followed Pauline into the hall, closing the door after them, and Robert stood, very straight, in the middle of the long room.

"Sit down," said Levy, pointing at a chair before the desk near Tilly's. But Robert clasped his hands behind his back and stood where he was.

"I'd like very much to hear about this boy who came the other day," said Levy.

"He camed," said Robert, briefly.

"What did he do when he came?"

"He killed lots and lots and lots—of lemmings."

"Lemons?" Levy asked.

"*Lemmings,*" Robert repeated, loudly and angrily.

"How did he kill them?"

"With a little tiny, tiny, *tiny* gun."

"Did you know this boy?"

"No. But he was *bad.*"

Levy rose and crossed the room, and opened the door. "Price!" he said, and Taylor entered.

"Yes!" said Robert, and as Taylor advanced, Robert moved, a littler nearer to Tilly; he gave her a quick sidelong glance, unsmiling, unfriendly. But he wants to be sure I'm here, she thought. Oh, *why* don't they let him alone? What's the use in asking him questions? He's so little ... He doesn't remember. He imagines things, makes them up, and then he believes them. He's afraid of Taylor. He's a little afraid of Lieutenant Levy, too, sitting there at the desk, in uniform, asking him questions. Oh, poor little thing! He doesn't know what it's all about.

"Yeah ...," Taylor said, and sat down on the arm of a chair. "The kid told me that, too. He told me he saw me, the morning of the day my mother died, and I was killing lemmings." He smiled, sneeringly. "Shooting them. I told him there weren't any lemmings in this part of the world. And I told him I wasn't here, anyhow. I was away, in camp. Mr. Abbott can tell you that."

"Now, Robert," said Levy, and he spoke gently to the child. "When you saw this boy, how was he dressed?"

Robert looked around the room, and Tilly could see that he was trying, not to remember, but to think of something, anything, that he would find dramatic. "Like that!" he said, pointing to a framed photograph on a table, of a Scot in a kilt.

"Did you see any of these dead—animals?"

"Yes, I did! I did see them!"

"Come up to the desk, now," said Levy, "and tell me if you think these are the dead animals you saw."

"Oh, no!" cried Tilly. "Please no!"

"I'm sorry," said Levy. "But it's necessary."

She had not noticed that the dead creatures were covered with a newspaper now. They must, she thought, have been so covered when Pauline came in, or Pauline would have made some remark. No, Pauline would have screamed.

"*Please* don't!" she entreated, remembering the condition of the creatures.

But Robert wanted to see them, and as he approached the desk, Levy lifted the newspaper, and a sickly smell arose. Robert stood looking at them, his lips parted, his eyes wide.

"No!" he cried, almost in a scream. "No, no! They're not! They're not!"

He backed away, and ran to Tilly; he put his arms round her neck, and with his little hard head against her shoulder, he began to cry. He very seldom cried, and he had never cried like this before, frantically, with wrenching sobs.

"It's *not*—my lemming ...! Take it *away!*"

Levy wrapped the dead creatures in the newspaper and put them on the floor under the desk.

"They're gone now, Robert," he said. "Nothing to cry about. Can't you quiet him, Mrs. MacDonald?"

"No," said Tilly, holding him close to her.

Levy rose and went over to him; he patted Robert on the shoulder.

"Come now! Come!" he said. "You're not a baby. You're a big boy. You can help your mother a great deal, if you'll just answer a few questions. You want to help her, don't you?"

"No!" Robert cried. "Go away!"

"Just tell me what you saw in your room the other night. Was there a snake there?"

"*No!* Mommy! Mommy! Make him—go away!"

"What's the use?" asked Taylor. "The kid's an awful liar. He's been brought up on fairy tales."

"Shut up!" said Tilly, perhaps for the first time in her life.

"He saw lemmings, that weren't there. And he saw me, when I wasn't there. He could easily see a snake in his room that wasn't there."

"Mr. Osborne saw—that," said Tilly.

"Oh, Sam Osborne would see anything you told him to see," said Taylor.

"Shut up!" said Tilly, again.

"Keep out of this, Taylor," said Levy. "When I want to hear from you, I'll tell you.

Taylor shrugged his shoulders and leaned his head back against the wall. But there was no need for him to say any more. The harm was done. Tilly could see how fantastic her story must seem to Levy, and now Sam Osborne's confirmation would be suspect.

"I won't keep you any longer now, Mrs. MacDonald," said Levy, and she rose and picked up the wildly sobbing child.

Now I'm completely discredited, she told herself. I don't know what will happen now.

CHAPTER TEN

They went out, hand in hand, into the corridor brightly lit by unshaded electric bulbs. Robert held her hand tight; his tears had stopped, but from time to time he gave a sob that was like a gasp.

He's had too much to stand, Tilly thought. Ever since that day—it seems so long ago—the day the boy came while he was making his vallons. The day Sibyl died ... He says Taylor is the boy, but it can't be that way, if Taylor was in the camp, with Mr. Abbott. Then who was it?

A maniac. Some unknown, horrible, dangerous creature who had killed Sibyl, had killed the bird and the chipmunk, who had put the snake in Robert's bed. Someone unknown ...

They went into the room, where the policeman sat at the desk, and another policeman sat on the bench against the wall. Here, too, it was brightly, even glaringly lit, and as they went out of the building, the darkness surprised Tilly; the green lights on either side of the entrance shone out on an empty street, lined with trees, the branches tossing wildly in the wind.

"Mommy, where are we going?" Robert asked.

"We're going home, darling."

"Back to Cousin Sibyl's house?"

"Yes. We'll walk a little way and see if we can find a taxi."

"No! I don't *want* to go back there!"

"It's only for a little while, dear."

"No! No, Mommy, I *won't* go back in that room!"

"I'll stay with you, Robert. I won't leave you alone."

"No!" he cried, clutching her skirt, trying to hold her back. "No, Mommy! Go in another house!"

It was beginning to rain, a faint drizzle that pattered on the leaves, and, standing there with her child, Tilly felt that they were utterly forlorn and lonely, facing a dark and rainy world. *I* don't want to go back to Sibyl's house, any more than Robert does, she thought. But we have to.

A taxi stopped before the police station, and a man got out, slamming the door behind him. Even in the dark, Tilly recognized that angular figure, that easy stride. But Robert was indifferent.

"Mommy!" he said, still dragging at her skirt. "Mommy! What did that policeman have in there, all wrapped up in a newspaper?"

"A little bird and a chipmunk, dear. The same ones you saw, beside the tree ..."

"No. You're a liar!"

"That's not a nice thing to say, Robert. You wouldn't like me to say it to you."

"They smelled," he said, and began to cry again. "And they looked ... Mommy! Why did they look that funny way?"

Osborne had come up the steps, and stood beside her. But Robert must be answered.

"Because they were dead, darling."

"Why does it make 'em look so funny—to be dead?"

It was Tilly's conviction that questions like these from a child must be answered as clearly and honestly as possible. She came of an outspoken, even blunt family; she tried never to be evasive with her child. But this was hard; hard to talk of death to this little creature at the beginning of life.

"You see," she said, "they were getting ready to go down into the earth. And down there, they'd help the trees and the grass and the flowers to grow."

He was silent for a moment.

"Did Cousin Sibyl look funny like that?" he asked.

"No. She looked very nice, Robert. Very handsome and—happy."

"Did she like to be all dead?"

"Yes," said Tilly. She felt tired to the point of exhaustion, yet it seemed to her necessary to go on, to explain, if she could, the meaning of this new and overwhelming reality her child had been forced to meet. "You see," she said, "the things we love in Cousin Sibyl—in everybody—don't get dead. The kind, good things. They go on."

"*I* don't love Cousin Sibyl," said Robert. "I think she's an old bad bastard."

"Robert!"

"She's an old bad *bastard*," said Robert.

"That's a very naughty thing to say," Tilly told him, and that was just what he wanted. He repeated his phrase; he wanted to be naughty, to shock her, to defy her and all the new, strange, frightening world that was closing in on him.

"It's silly," said Osborne.

At the sound of his voice, the child gave a start; his hand grasped Tilly's convulsively.

"Sam ...?" he said. "How did you get here?"

"I'm always here, when needed," Osborne answered, in a tone Tilly found irritatingly smug and boastful. "You're hungry, aren't you, Robert?"

"No!" said Robert.

"We're all hungry," said Osborne. "We'll get in that taxi, and we'll go to the Inn, and eat a good dinner."

"Thanks," said Tilly, "but I think we'd better go home."

"And where's 'home'?" Osborne asked.

"Oh, don't *bother* me," she cried.

"I'm not going to," he said. "Come on!"

He picked up the child, and Tilly followed him down the steps; the driver opened the door and she got into the cab.

"Cigarette?" Osborne asked.

"Thanks. I don't smoke."

"Well, if you'll permit me ...," he said, and lit a cigarette for himself; in the little flare of the match his bony, dark face had a smile like a cat's. Or a devil's, Tilly thought.

"Carola's been talking," he went on. "She's been telling all and sundry— including Levy—that Sibyl treated you shamefully, and you had to stand it, because you were penniless."

"I'm *not*."

"I'm telling you what Carola's saying. She says nobody could blame you for wanting Sibyl dead. She says you knew you were going to inherit a handsome sum of money from her—"

"I don't know anything of the sort!"

"Well, I hope to God you don't," said Osborne. "Motive. Opportunity. Obstructing the police in the performance of their duty. Why the hell did you leave those things in your room?"

"I forgot them, that's why. I took them in there, because I wanted to show them to Lieutenant Levy. I thought it might be an important—clue, if they'd been poisoned, too."

"They are, all right." The cigarette glowed red as he drew on it. "The lawyer's coming tomorrow morning to read the will, and then we'll see."

"See what?" Tilly demanded, coldly.

"Motive."

"It's preposterous!" Tilly cried. "Nobody could think I'd do a thing like that."

"But why not you?"

"I'm not—well, I'm not—like that."

"Maternal love ...," said Osborne, thoughtfully. "One of the fiercest passions. You wanted money for your child, and she wouldn't help you out with his education. She treated you very badly, and you hated her—"

"That's a lie!"

"That's a big liar," said Robert, with satisfaction.

"How can you say things like that?" Tilly cried. "How can you think things like that about me?"

"I'm not giving you my personal opinion," said Osborne. "What I think doesn't matter. I'm simply showing you what could look like a very plausible theory."

"And Howard? Am I supposed to have poisoned him, too?"

"Oh, that is a side issue."

"I can see that. Nobody seems to care about that. And why?"

"Howard looks like an after-thought. And he's still alive."

"And where was I supposed to get these deadly poisons?"

Osborne threw his cigarette out of the cab window, and turning her head, Tilly saw the ghostly outline of the spiked fence, like silver in the rainy night. They were driving by Sibyl's place now.

"They're holding Jensen," he said.

"You mean—he's been arrested?"

"For further questioning. Y' see, both Pauline and Jenny are ready to swear that they've seen these yellow capsules in Sibyl's bathroom cabinet right along, for weeks and weeks. Well, Doctor Crowdie says he hasn't given her a prescription for Nembutal since May, and it's not renewable. The local druggist is a cautious old guy. The police are satisfied that he didn't sell her any on the side. So Levy did some ferreting. Servants, guests, nobody knew anything about those capsules. Then it came to light that Jensen had opened a savings bank account in New York early in June—"

"How did it 'come to light'?"

"The cook—what's her name—"

"Gloria."

"Gloria," he repeated. "Gloria says she found a bankbook on the kitchen floor. Jensen had left his jacket hanging there, and she thought the book must have fallen out of his pocket. Anyhow, she looked in, just to be sure, and it was for an account in the name of Richard Peters. A deposit every week, always in cash; a balance of three hundred and twenty dollars since the early part of June. She says she put the book into a pocket of Jensen's coat, and there was never a word out of him about it."

"She was probably snooping in his pockets."

"Very likely. Anyhow, she said she never asked him any questions about it, because she was afraid to."

"Why?"

"Well, in the first place, he was one of them foreigners, and you could never tell what they'd be up to, with the plots and plans they've got, to be blowing up the country, God help us. And then he'd a way of looking at you, you'd think he was laughing to himself at you."

"How do *you* know all these things?"

"I've been a-ferreting myself. I'm the one who got that story out of Gloria."

The taxi stopped before the Inn; Osborne paid the driver, and got out, and Tilly followed him, holding Robert's hand. Mrs. Raeburn, the landlady, opened the door for them.

"I'm real pleased to see you," she said. "It's late, but I kept everything nice and hot. And I've got something special for the little boy."

"What?" Robert asked.

"You eat your meat and vegetables, and you'll see," said Mrs. Raeburn.

She led them to the dining room where there was a small table laid for three.

"Sit right down and make yourselves at home," she said. "And if you hear any noises, don't be bothered. There's some of those summer visitors in the bar…. I declare to goodness, sometimes I think to myself I'd rather do without this money than put up with 'em, and the noise and trouble they make. But my nephew, he tends the bar and he looks after them. He won't stand any nonsense from them. You've had enough, he'll say, if it's a millionaire he's speaking to. You'll get no more drinks here."

She went off to the kitchen then, and Robert got up on the chair where a telephone book had been laid for him to sit on.

"You must have told Mrs. Raeburn we were coming," Tilly said.

"I did," said Osborne.

A sudden irritation rose in Tilly; she wanted to fly at him, to accuse him of being unbearably sure of himself, pleased with himself. But she repressed this, and was silent until her dinner was set before her, a plate of roast duckling and green peas and sweet potatoes; she began to eat with an unexpected appetite, and the irritation vanished.

"What did Jensen say about the bank account?" she asked.

"Oh, he admitted that he'd opened it, and had made the deposits. Said he had done it for someone else. They're still trying to make him tell who the 'someone else' is, but I don't think they'll succeed. There's no charge against him, no tie-up with the murder, or the pills. He's very amiable and reasonable, but he refuses to give any information about 'Richard Peters,' or how he got all that cash. Of course, it smells like blackmail but—"

Mrs. Raeburn came in from the kitchen, with lemon pie and coffee for Tilly and Osborne, and for Robert a glass of milk and three little gingerbread men, with eyes made of raisins.

"Are they to eat?" he asked.

"Yes, indeedy!" said Mrs. Raeburn. "I made them just special for you. Here! Take a bite!"

"And drink your milk with it, dear," said Tilly.

Osborne lit a cigarette, ignoring the pie and the coffee.

"I'm telling you all I know about the case," he said.

"Well, thank you ...," Tilly said, hesitant, a little doubtful.

"And there's a purpose in it," said Osborne.

"What purpose?"

"If you know anything, if you have any information, even any suspicion, tell Levy. And for God's sake, don't wait."

"I have told him everything. I told him I brought Sibyl a capsule."

"You told him too late. Pauline told him that before they came out here, while they were in New York, Sibyl always lay down on the bed for that pre-dinner nap, and told her to bring a capsule. All right. That was Sibyl's habit. Pauline wasn't with Sibyl that afternoon, and you were. What's more, it's pretty well established that Sibyl was dead when you left her room."

"*I* didn't know! How could I know?"

"You didn't look at her? Didn't see anything unusual about her?"

Tilly was silent for a long moment.

"I didn't know—Sibyl was dead," she said.

She took a sip of coffee, and then she raised her eyes to Osborne's face.

"I did think she looked—queer," she said. "But I didn't know—I *couldn't* know it was—anything like that."

Or did I really know—and not *want* to know? Did I—just leave her there, and hurry off to Robert?

"Could she have been saved, if—the doctor had come sooner?" she asked.

"No. With a dose like that, it's a matter of seconds. Don't get your New England conscience working on that. Nothing could have saved her. The thing—"

Robert jumped down from his chair with a thud, and went to Tilly's side.

"I want to go to bed," he said. "I want to go upstairs. *Now!*"

"Why, I declare!" said Mrs. Raeburn, from the doorway. "You haven't eaten up even one of your little men! Finish him up, and drink your milk, that's a good boy."

The gingerbread head with its big black raisin eyes lay on his plate; Mrs. Raeburn picked it up and held it out to him.

"Eat it up, now," she said, coaxingly.

"No!" cried Robert, and his voice rose, almost to a scream. "*No!* Take it away!"

Osborne took the cookie from Mrs. Raeburn's hand; he pulled out the raisin eyes.

"It's nothing but a piece of cookie," he said, casually. "Mind if I try a bite?"

Robert did not answer, but Osborne took a bite, and laid the fragment on the child's plate. And it was not a little dark-eyed head any more. Robert moved nearer to look at it.

"Let's go," said Osborne to Tilly. "Taxi there, Mrs. Raeburn?"

"It just came," she said, a little stiffly. "I've made these cookies for plenty of other children, and I never yet saw one of 'em take on like that."

"He's over-tired," Tilly explained. "Otherwise, he'd have been delighted with them. It was very kind of you to make them, Mrs. Raeburn."

"Well ...," said Mrs. Raeburn, mollified. "I did hear that they'd taken the poor little object down to the police station, whatever for I can't imagine. But I heard Mr. Cantrell telling that Mrs. Dexter about it, in the bar. It's a shame, Mr. Cantrell said. Oh, I don't know, says Mrs. Dexter. Children see a lot more than people imagine."

"So they do," Osborne agreed. "Come on, Robert."

"Come where?"

"In the taxi," Osborne answered, and picked him up, over his shoulder.

"I'll take him now," said Tilly, when they were in the cab.

"Better let him alone. He's half-asleep already."

It was a short drive, too short; the taxi went on through the steady rain, at a moderate speed, but inexorably. Back to that house.

"Then you think that I might—get into trouble?" Tilly asked.

"You're in trouble right now," said Osborne. "I don't mean that you're likely to go to the electric chair, or even to jail. But you've given the impression that you know more than you've told. That you're holding out on Levy. And if you're down in Sibyl's will for something handsome ..."

"Then what?"

"Then there will be a lot of questions. A lot of worry and bother. And every answer you give will be suspect, because you started off with a lie."

"You're odious when you talk like that!" said Tilly.

"So be it," said Osborne, with a sigh.

The taxi turned into the drive, and the house loomed before them, dark and strange.

"But why aren't there any lights?" cried Tilly. "It's not late. It can't be much after nine."

"Howard's idea," Osborne answered. "He ordered all the shades pulled down yesterday, after we left for Boston. I don't know how long etiquette requires them to stay down, but *he'll* know. Anyhow, Pauline and Gloria and Jenny all approve of it, highly."

The taxi stopped, and as Osborne leaned forward to pay the fare, a new thought came to Tilly.

"You've been very nice," she said. "I'm afraid it's been a great expense to you, these taxis and the dinner.... I—thanks."

"*De nada,*" said Osborne.

He got out, still carrying Robert, sound asleep now; he rang the bell and when Jenny opened the door, he went on past her and started up the stairs.

"Tilly ...," said Howard's voice, very low. He came out of the drawing-room and came to her side. "Chet Price is here. The lawyer. We'll have to have the reading rather earlier than I wanted tomorrow morning, but Chet has to get back to town. Nine-thirty. Please don't be late."

"I'm never late," she said, in a tone so curt that Howard frowned in surprise.

She went up the stairs, hot with resentment; the door of her room was open, and Robert lay on his bed, sound asleep, while Osborne was taking off his shoes.

"I'll finish, thanks," said Tilly, in the same curt tone. "Good-night."

She locked the door directly he had gone, and set to work on Robert. He was limp as a rag-doll, but heavy and hot; it was a struggle to get his jersey off over his head, to get his arms into his pajama sleeves. She tucked the sheet tightly over him, and went into the bathroom for a shower.

She got into her own bed, doubling the pillow under her head; she left the lamp burning. I'm not going to sleep yet, she thought. I've got to think things out. If there's anything I didn't tell Lieutenant Levy ...? Anything I noticed ...?

But the *idea* of Howard saying "Please don't be late"! I'm *never* late. For years and years, on my school reports—it was Tardy: no times. I'm never late. It was very provoking of Howard.... Entirely uncalled for....

Robert was shaking her shoulder.

"Mommy! Wake up, Mommy! Someone's knocking on the door!"

She opened her eyes and sat up straight. "Madame! Is me, Pauline. It is after nine, madame, and I bring you some coffee."

She got up to unlock the door, stumbling a little from drowsiness.

"*After* nine ...?" she asked.

"A little moment only, madame. Ten minutes, perhaps fifteen. I bring you some good hot coffee."

"Oh, Pauline, thank you! But I haven't time. Pauline, will you please dress Robert, and give him something to eat?"

She began to dress herself in frantic haste. A black skirt, and a white blouse.... I'll be late.... Oh, never mind my hair! I'll be late....

CHAPTER ELEVEN

She was late. The people assembled in the library were obviously waiting for her: Howard, Taylor, and Carola, two unknown women in black. Behind the desk where Levy had sat there was now a thin-necked, narrow-shouldered man with pince-nez on his long nose, and beneath them a tiny mouth pursed up in a querulous pout.

"Is everyone present now?" he asked. "Miss Duval?"

"She'll be here in a moment," said Howard, taking Tilly's arm and leading her to a chair.

"Mr. Osborne?"

"*Osborne?*" Howard repeated, startled.

"Samuel Osborne," repeated the man behind the desk, irritably. "I was under the impression, Howard, that I gave you a list last night."

"You did, Chet," said Howard. "But I'm afraid I didn't read it very carefully. I thought I knew pretty well who was wanted. I'll get Osborne at once."

As Howard went out of the room, Pauline came hurrying in; she stopped by Tilly and bent over to whisper.

"The little one now eats his breakfast with Gloria, madame."

Howard came back, with Osborne; they all sat down, they all looked at Mr. Price behind the desk.

Mr. Price picked up a long document and looked at it with a frown. Then he raised his brows, and that started the pince-nez sliding down his long nose; he pushed them back, and cleared his throat with a sound like a growl.

"Yes," he said, and growled again. "'I, Sibyl Fleming, being in my right mind ... do declare this to be my last will and testament.... My beloved son, Taylor—, the sum of one hundred thousand dollars, to be held in trust for him until he shall have reached the age of twenty-one years... '"

But what a lot! thought Tilly. I didn't imagine she had so much.

"'My cousin Josephine Evans, of Boston, the sum of five thousand dollars, also my Georgian tea-set and tray ... My cousins Marian and Genevieve Stockley, of Boston, jointly the sum of five thousand dollars ... To Robert MacDonald, son of my cousin Ian MacDonald and Mathilda

MacDonald, of New York City, the sum of five thousand dollars, to be held in trust until he shall have reached the age of twenty-one years ... ' "

Sixteen years! Tilly thought. He needs it *now*....

"'To my cousin-in-law Mathilda MacDonald, of New York City, the sum of five hundred dollars, also my garnet earrings and necklace—'"

Tilly's eyes filled with tears. Sibyl thought I'd like them, because they've been in Ian's family so long, she thought.

"'To my friend Samuel Osborne, my library ... To Pauline Duval, of New York City, in recognition of her loyal service, the entire contents of my wardrobe, including my mink coat and my platinum fox wrap ... To my beloved friend Carola Dexter, my opal ring—'"

"No!" cried Carola.

"Hush!" said Howard, sternly.

Mr. Price growled again, and went on reading.

"'To my beloved husband, Howard Fleming, the entire residue of my estate including my house in Swallow Cliff and all the contents thereof, also my holdings, stocks, and debentures—'"

On and on he went; Tilly sat watching him, but not listening any more, until he had finished.

"Sam," said Howard, in a low, grave voice, "will you drive Mr. Price to the station? He's in something of a hurry."

"Sure," said Osborne. "And the two ladies—?"

"Well—er ..." Howard said. "That is—unless they'd care to stay to lunch...?"

There was a courteous murmur from one of the ladies in black.

"Oh, thank you, Howard, but I really think we'd better be getting home now...."

"I see!" said Howard. "Then ... if you're ready ..."

Mr. Price rose and moved toward the door, but Carola sprang to her feet and caught him by the sleeve.

"I want that taken *out* of the will!" she said. "I won't *have* that opal ring! Please cross it out of the will before you go."

Mr. Price looked down at her with a sort of shiver of disgust.

"That's quite impossible, madam," he said. "The will must be offered for probate—"

"But now—this moment—I own that ring, don't I? Well, I *won't* own it! It means the most horrible bad luck, and Sibyl *knew* it. She tried—"

"Carola!" said Howard. "Get hold of yourself!"

"No! Sibyl tried to give it to me, ages ago. But I wouldn't take it. She inherited it from somebody, and she was terrified of it. She never wore it. She *knew*—"

"Madam ...!" said Mr. Price, trying to draw away from her. But she still clutched his sleeve.

"It means a horrible death!" she went on. "Sibyl *told* me so. And now—
it's mine. I won't—"

Howard took her wrist and detached her clutching fingers.

"Sit down!" he said, sternly, and pushed her down into an armchair.
"Now, then, Osborne ...?"

With polite nudges he formed the two ladies and the lawyer into a small
procession, which followed Osborne into the hall, and he brought up the
rear. Pauline sat stiffly on the edge of the sofa; Carola had turned, her face
buried in her folded arms against the high back of the chair; she was sobbing, forlornly. But Tilly watched her with no feeling of pity. Like a child,
she thought. Or like a doll, with all that long blond hair. Utterly irresponsible and self-centered. And dangerous.

Pauline rose, with a loud sigh, and went over to Carola.

"Madame would like a cup of coffee?" she asked.

"No!"

"A cup of tea? That is good for the nerves."

"*No!* Let me alone!"

Pauline shrugged her shoulders, and thrust out her underlip in a scornful smile, and turned to Tilly.

"Madame, if you will go into the dining room ...? Your breakfast is
ready."

"Where's Robert, Pauline?"

"Robert? He is in the kitchen, Madame. Gloria is most good, today. She
lets him fill the salt-shakers, and other things to amuse him."

When Tilly went into the dining room, no one was there. I'm glad, she
thought. If I can just have a cup of coffee before I have to talk to anyone,
or listen to anyone ... But that's contemptible, to depend upon coffee. Or
any stimulant. Maybe I ought to take a glass of milk instead.

But when Jenny set a steaming cup of coffee before her, she began at once
to sip it. Now that Lieutenant Levy knows I'm not inheriting a lot of money
from Sibyl, she thought, perhaps he'll—

Howard entered the room, and sat down at the head of the table.

"Thankful for a quiet moment," he said, somberly. "This strain ... I want
to discuss things with you, Tilly. Tell you my little idea."

"Yes, Howard," she said, politely.

"Of course," he went on, "it's impossible for you to stay here any
longer. We have to think of appearances, Tilly," he said.

"Yes ... of course," Tilly said, only half listening.

"This is my idea, Tilly. You know the gardener's cottage, at the end of
the drive? It hasn't been in use for some two or three years. We haven't had
a resident gardener. Only a man who comes in every day, and occasion-

ally a helper."

"I see," said Tilly.

You have to be patient with Howard, she told herself. He can't help being so roundabout and tedious.

"My first thought was the Inn here," he went on, "But Lieutenant Levy prefers you to stay here until he's finished his—his investigation. And, at the rate he's proceeding, it seems likely to take God knows how long. I can't see that he's accomplished anything whatever. Except to cause a completely unnecessary—" He paused for a word. "Complication," he said. "Embarrassment. These newspaper men ... I've managed to keep them off the premises, but they've taken snaps.... It's—"

He paused.

"I don't like that fellow," he said. "That Levy. Sibyl's—Sibyl's—"He could not get the word out. "What happened was an accident, pure and simple."

Tilly glanced away from him. Sibyl took cyanide—by accident? And where did she get it? And what about *you? You* were poisoned, too. Unconscious. Was that an "accident," too?

For the first time, she began to think and to wonder about Howard's mishap. It had been, she thought, most strangely ignored. Yet the two poisonings must belong together, she thought. There couldn't be two murderers here. They ought to look for someone with a motive for killing both Sibyl and Howard. And that couldn't be me. Then who?

"This was my idea," said Howard. "It's obviously—I mean, you can't—you wouldn't wish to stay here. Gossip—and so on ... The gardener's cottage is in excellent condition. My idea is that you should move in there—live there, with Pauline to look after you. I've sent her down there now, with a man from the village to help her—shift furniture—put up curtains—and so forth. She'll cook for you—do the marketing. I—naturally, I'll defray all expenses."

"Thank you, Howard," said Tilly, absently.

What does "defray" really mean? she thought. "Fray" means to tear and frazzle things. Then how do you de-fray things?

"I think you'll be comfortable there, Tilly. If there's anything you want—?"

"Thank you, Howard," she said, with more warmth. "You're very kind."

He pushed back his chair and rose.

"Not at all," he said. "I'm only too glad to help, Tilly. And—" He paused again. "I feel it's what Sibyl would want," he said. "I'll come back presently, and we'll inspect the cottage."

Tilly went on with her breakfast, glad to be alone. I want to think, she told herself. Only I seem very stupid today.... Why doesn't anyone seem to take any interest in Howard's being poisoned?

"Mrs. MacDonald?" said a voice, another portentous voice. It was young Abbott, the schoolmaster, standing in the doorway. "May I speak to you for a few moments, in confidence?"

"Why, of course!" said Tilly, suppressing a sigh.

He came into the long room, and stood close beside her chair.

"I'm in a dilemma," he said. "It's entirely my own fault. I don't know now what steps I should take, and you're a New Englander, like myself, Mrs. MacDonald. You're the only person here I can speak to. I—need advice."

Well, don't ask me, Tilly thought. I'm a fool. Sam Osborne will tell you so.

"I suppose you've heard about the Lambson School?" Abbott asked.

"Well, nothing except that Sibyl said it was very good." And fabulously expensive, Sibyl had said.

"It's unique," said Abbott. "People come from all over to study Doctor Lambson's method for dealing with problem children. He accepts them from the age of two up to twenty. Of course, he has different houses, different routines for the various age-groups, but the method is the same. A continuous psychoanalysis—without the patient's knowledge—until total recall is achieved. The results are extraordinary. For instance, we had one boy who had been an arsonist for seven years. He had started at least—"

Jenny came in, with a plate of bacon and eggs for Tilly.

"You *had* your breakfast, Mr. Abbott," she said, in the special tone of annoyed defiance she used for Tilly and all others who were not genuine guests.

"Yes. Yes," he assured her, too eagerly, and Jenny retired.

"Of course," Abbott went on, still standing close to Tilly, and speaking in a loud tone, "this method necessitates a very large staff. Doctor Lambson interviews each boy once a week, and he requires a detailed report from each boy's supervisor. As a rule, each supervisor has three boys in his charge; never more than three. Taylor was in my charge. I—I blame myself."

"Sit down, Mr. Abbott," said Tilly, sorry for his obvious misery.

"No, thanks," he said. "No. I blame myself. I failed with Taylor, from the beginning. I realized that it would be a difficult case. You know, of course, that he had been dismissed from several schools and camps in the past—"

"No, I didn't. What for?"

"He's almost completely non-co-operative," said Abbott. "I was never able to make a report of any value to Doctor Lambson. I could never get the boy to talk of his childhood, his relations with his parents, and so on.

Doctor Lambson himself found a most serious block in the boy's mind, erected, of course, to conceal from the conscious some profound psychic trauma."

"I'm afraid I don't understand much about all that," said Tilly. "Does it mean that Taylor was unmanageable?"

Abbott's hand grasped the back of the chair before him; his earnest young face looked desperate.

"It means that *I* failed!" he said. "At the camp, I was in sole charge of Taylor. I thought I'd made some progress. I thought I'd got him interested in lepidoptery and—"

Jenny came in again.

"More coffee, ma'am?" she asked.

"No, thank you," said Tilly, and Jenny left them.

"I'll—come to the point," said Abbott. "The boy got away. He took the car which was there for my use, when necessary, and he left the camp early in the morning."

"What morning?"

"The morning of the—tragedy," Abbott answered. "He left this note in the garage. I kept it. I—have it here."

He brought a folded sheet of writing-paper from his pocket, and opened it to show one line in a small but clear hand.

Back to dinner, so take it easy. Taylor, the problem child.

"He came back about eight," Abbott went on. "I'd made up my mind that if he hadn't returned, I'd telephone Doctor Lambson. I—I admit I should have done so before. As soon as I missed him. But I—No. I shan't make any specious excuses. I—" He swallowed. "I was afraid of losing my job," he said. "I didn't report his absence."

"Could he have come here?" Tilly asked.

"Easily."

They were both silent for a time.

"I—haven't reported the matter to the Police Lieutenant," Abbott said. "I told the boy I might feel obliged to do so—and he was—as usual—defiant and—jeering. I don't know ... I think I can honestly assure you I'm not thinking of my job, in this connection. It's a—a question of where my duty lies."

The knuckles of his broad, short hand grasping the chair had whitened; he was looking at Tilly with a scowl.

"I don't *know* ...," he said, raising his voice. "There's my duty—as a citizen.... But, after all—fifteen ... I mean—I don't *know*. I don't know if he should be held responsible. At fifteen."

"Mr. Abbott ...! But if he did come here, I think Lieutenant Levy ought to know. He might have seen something—he might have information that would be helpful."

"He had access to a small store of cyanide," said Abbott.

Tilly pushed back her chair and rose, and Jenny entered the room.

"Have you finished, ma'am?" she asked.

"No!" said Tilly, sharply. "I'll ring when I'm ready."

"It's so late—"

"I'll ring," said Tilly, and Jenny once more left them.

"I don't know where else we could go to talk," Tilly explained to Abbott. "I don't know who's in the house now, or where anyone is. How could Taylor get—that?"

"I had some, at the camp. Crystals from which I made a solution for my collection of lepidoptera. I—I kept it under lock and key. But—locks can be tampered with."

"Did you look to see if it was gone?"

"I opened the locked compartment to get out my money, when we were leaving to come here," Abbott answered. "I glanced, you might say automatically, at the bottle of crystals. It was in its usual place."

"But—empty?"

"No," he answered. "But—I shouldn't be able to state—with any accuracy—whether or not some of the contents had been removed. I mean—it's difficult to remember just how full a bottle was.... I mean—I *should* have known. But I don't. I knew, too, that the boy was—was extremely hostile toward his mother at the time. She had written again, in answer to some letter of his, to say his allowance was stopped until he wrote an apology. Doctor Lambson wrote to Mrs. Fleming, advising her against this course of action, at the present time, but he got no reply. I—perhaps I did wrong, but on two or three occasions, I lent the boy small sums, for some legitimate expense. Underwater goggles, for instance, and—"

"But you don't *know* that he ever opened your locked—whatever it was?"

"Compartment," said Abbott. "No. I have no evidence, Mrs. Mac-Donald. But ... The day before the tragedy, the boy asked me for ten dollars, giving a reason which I didn't find acceptable. I refused. And—there was a ten-dollar bill missing from my wallet in that compartment, Mrs. MacDonald."

Tilly realized that she was standing just as Abbott stood, gripping the back of her chair.

"I don't *know* ...," he said. "Whatever has happened, I hold myself responsible. Wholly responsible. Fifteen ... In my charge ..." He raised his heavy glance to look straight at Tilly. "I don't *know*," he said. "I don't know whether or not I should report this to the police. You—have a child of your own. I—I should like your advice, Mrs. MacDonald."

"No!" Tilly cried, backing away from him.

"I ask you for your advice, Mrs. MacDonald," he said, loudly.

"No ... Wait ...," Tilly said.

"There's nothing to wait for, Mrs. MacDonald," said Abbott.

CHAPTER TWELVE

Oh, wait! she cried, but only within herself. I'd like to—think. I'd like to ask Sam Osborne....

"There's a man in jail already," Abbott went on. "Jensen, the chauffeur. Suspected of complicity in the crime. Perhaps if I gave the police my story, it would clear him. But—I don't know. I've tried to think the thing out. To decide where my chief responsibility lies. The boy was in my charge...."

"Do you think he did—do you think he *could* do—such a thing?"

"I don't *know!*" cried Abbott, almost in a shout.

"But you've seen him—you've been with him for days—"

"I'm not a trained psychiatrist, Mrs. MacDonald. I don't pretend to understand the mental processes of that boy. He's by far the most difficult charge I've had. But Doctor Lambson has accomplished most remarkable results in other cases.... If the boy could remain in his care for another year—or possibly two ... There might be a complete change of personality. A complete readjustment. Even a partial recall of some earlier psychic trauma—"

"Yes," said Tilly, curtly. "I'm afraid I can't give you any advice, Mr. Abbott. You'll have to do whatever you think best."

She wanted to get away from him and from his talk. This isn't my responsibility, she told herself. I'm not going to advise him, or anybody else.

"If you don't mind," she said. "I think I'll get Robert—"

She turned toward the door. But she could not go; she could not leave this room; she could not leave Abbott. The Moment of Truth, she was saying to herself. Face it. Every time it comes, face it.

"I think you should tell Lieutenant Levy," she said.

"But the thing is—a police interrogation might do the boy untold harm—set him back—"

"There's no use worrying about what *might* happen," said Tilly. "That's just thinking that the end justifies the means. And it doesn't. Nobody can see what the end of anything is going to be. All you can do is tell the truth."

"But, Mrs. MacDonald ... My responsibility toward the boy—"

"You're not responsible for him," said Tilly. "And if you think he's capable of such an unspeakably horrible—crime, you ought to help to see him shut up where he can't do any more harm."

"But prolonged psychiatric treatment—"

"I don't believe in psychiatry," said Tilly.

"What!" cried Abbott. "*What!*"

"I've read in the newspapers, dozens of times, about people discharged as normal from mental institutions who came out and committed murders, or set fire to buildings, or did whatever horrible things they'd done before. I don't care why people commit atrocious crimes, any more than I'd care *why* a rattlesnake bit me. Most people don't commit crimes. And they're the ones I care about."

"Mrs. MacDonald! The boy is only fifteen—"

"You asked for my advice," said Tilly, "and you got it. Tell Lieutenant Levy the whole thing." Now she could go. She opened the swing-door to the pantry and went through it to the kitchen.

"But isn't Robert here?" she asked Gloria.

"No, ma'am. Pauline, she took him out, down to the gate house, she said."

The old, unreasoning panic rose in Tilly again. Pauline's so foreign, she thought. She might give Robert something to eat that would make him sick. Or even a glass of wine. I'll have to hurry....

But that scene with Abbott had changed something within her. No, she told herself. I'm not going to be like this. I'm not going to hurry. Not going to be so frightened about Robert all the time. It's bad for him, and bad for me. I'm not going to be that sort of mother. Suspecting everyone ...

She went out of the back door, and strolled, deliberately slow, along the side of the house. Of course, I can't be easy, she thought, until I know who put those things into Robert's room, who killed those animals.

Until I know who killed Sibyl. Why don't I think more about that? Once we know that, everything will be different. Taylor? No! I can't believe it! I don't really know him, and I never liked him, but I can't think he's a monster. His own mother ... Unless it was an accident. Unless he didn't know that cyanide was so deadly. Sam Osborne said that the snake in Robert's bed was harmless. Perhaps it was all Taylor's idea of a joke, a cruel, insane joke.

She started across the lawn, still sauntering.

"Tilly!" called Howard's voice. "Where are you off to?"

Turning, she saw him on the terrace, with Cantrell and Osborne.

"I'm just going down to the cottage to get Robert," she answered.

"Please *don't*," said Howard. "I don't want you to go there until it's all in order. Then we'll make a little tour of inspection, after lunch."

She felt sure, from his tone, that he was planning a surprise to please her, and it seemed to her unkind and ungrateful to thwart him.

"I won't go inside, Howard," she said. "I'll just get Robert—"

"That's not necessary," said Howard. "There's an extension telephone to the cottage. You can call, and tell Pauline to send him along."

"All right," said Tilly, but very reluctantly.

"I'll get the cottage for you," he said, and held open the screen door for her. He went to the seldom-used telephone that stood on a table behind the stairway; he pressed some little buttons.

"There you are!" he said, and pulled back the chair for her. "That's the extension to the cottage."

"Hello?" Tilly said, holding the receiver to her ear. "Hello? *Hello?*"

She waited; she spoke again; she waited.

"Howard!" she said. "There's no answer."

But Howard did not answer, either, and turning her head, she saw that he had gone. I'm going to get Robert! she cried to herself, and hurried out to the terrace. The three men were all turned away from her, watching the drive, and Pauline and Robert were running toward them, hand in hand.

"Monsieur!" she cried. "What tragedy ...! Monsieur!"

She was out of breath, tears running down her face, but Robert showed no sign of distress; he pulled his hand away from hers, and mounted the steps to the terrace, in a sturdy, manful way. Pauline seemed unable to make this effort; she stood in the drive, looking up at them, clasping her hands before her.

"Monsieur! Such tragedy! Monsieur, such crime! Such *wickedness!* Monsieur!"

"What's happened, Pauline?" asked Howard.

"A crime! A wickedness, without compare! He is *dead! Killed! Murdered!*"

Howard went down to her, took her arm, and led her up the steps.

"Sit down!" he said. "Come now, Pauline! Try to calm yourself. Try to tell me—"

Sitting forward, on the edge of a wicker chair, she seized Howard's coat sleeve, looking up at him, her face distorted.

"Monsieur! He must be punished! He must suffer! He's a monster!"

Osborne had gone into the house through one of the French windows; he came back now with a small glass in his hand.

"Brandy," he said. "Best thing, Pauline."

"Ah ...! *Ça-y-est, Monsieur!*" she said, with a sob. "*Monsieur, je vous remercie, mais beaucoup.*"

She took a sip, another one, and Tilly watched her, with cold dread in her heart. Murder? Murder again? In this sweet summer morning? It's like a fog, she thought. Like a miasma, creeping along the ground toward us.

Pauline took another sip, and turned toward Howard.

"*Monsieur,*" she said. "*Pardonnez-moi, je vous prie.... Mais—je suis ab-solument—*"

"In English, please," said Howard.

"I tell you *all,* Monsieur," she said, still weeping, but more calmly. "Very well! I go to the cottage, I take with me little Robert, and in my arms I carry—" A sob interrupted her. "I carry—my little Coco. This morning he is quiet, very quiet; he looks up at me with one eye closed."

She made a hideous face, one eye closed, her tongue out.

"He is telling me this way—*maman,* I wish only to sleep. I say *no, bébé!* I put him down on the grass. I say, now run a little. Do some little exercise. For the liver. Then I enter the house with little Robert. There is there already a young man from the village. Italian. *Il s'appelle Pietro. On ne peut pas senter trop de confiance—*"

"English, please," said Howard. "Drink your brandy, Pauline."

"Thank you, monsieur." She took another sip. "Very well, I do not trust the Italian always. One remembers, in the war—"

"Yes, yes!" said Howard.

"But this one, this Pietro, he is not lazy. He is working hard, and I too begin to work. The little Robert, he runs from one to the other. Please bring me that curtain rod! Ah! Thank you! He is very happy. He is helping. Is it not so, Robert?"

Robert was not attending to her, he was sitting on the broad stone coping, busy with some string and a top he had taken from his pocket.

"Very well," Pauline went on. "We are working, then. The door opens. No ring. No knock. There he stands!"

She was obliged to rise to demonstrate this arrival.

"There he stands!"

"*Who?*" Howard asked.

"It is that Taylor!" she answered. "There he stands!" She sat down again. "I say to him, Have the goodness to get out, at once. He answers, in French, *Me voici. Je suis venu—*"

"English!" said Howard, frowning.

"Very well, monsieur. He speaks French very well, that one. He has the clever mind of the criminal. I say to him—Go! In this house you do not plant a foot. He laughs." She gave a short, sinister laugh. "Hah! I have things here, he says. I shall take them away. I say, You shall take nothing from this house until Mr. Fleming shall be here. He laughs. Is it so? he asks. I take what I like. Then he goes to the stair. This I must not permit. I am forced to cry to Pietro, Stop him! He is a thief!"

"Pauline!" said Howard, shocked.

"Monsieur, it is the truth. I never tell this before, but now ... Monsieur, it was in New York, in the apartment. You are out, Madame is asleep. Me, I am going to the kitchen. I pass down the corridor. I look into the salon, and there I see him. He is holding Madame's purse, open, in his hands. He is taking out money. *Alors*, I cry, What are you taking? He turns. He sees me. *Ta guale!* he says."

"What's that?" Howard asked, frowning again.

"It is a rudeness, Monsieur. Be quiet, it means. Shut up! Put back your *maman's* money, I say. He puts it into his pocket. I shall tell madame! I say. *Bien!* he says. I shall tell her *you* took it. I shall tell her I have many times seen you take her money, sometimes a little pin, a bracelet. I say, Very well, my brave young man, we shall see!"

"You told her ...?"

"Monsieur, I cannot. Madame is already so sad, so troubled about that boy. I tell myself, if she will miss the money, if she will think that the cook, that myself, that some person is a thief, then I must tell. But madame—" She paused. "Madame is not careful of money. She gets into a taxi, for example. She opens her purse. Ah! But I have nothing here! I thought I had some sum of money, but I am mistaken."

"Yes," said Howard. "Go on, please."

"Pietro assists me, and we oblige him to leave the cottage. We sometimes have to employ ourselves, and—" She sobbed again, and finished the brandy. "I do not forgive myself! I forget the little Coco. Then, suddenly, I remember. What he is doing? I ask myself. For he wished always to be at my side. I open the door. I call him. Nothing. I go out. I call. There— by a bush —I find him. Dead. Murdered!"

"I see!" said Howard, with a sigh of relief. "You mean—that is the mur- der ...?"

"My little Coco! I have no husband, no little children, my parents are dead! I am exile, in a foreign land, and I have only my little Coco!"

"I'm very sorry," said Howard.

"I run to the policeman—"

"What policeman?"

"Monsieur, there is always a policeman here now, in your gardens, per- haps more than one. How do I know? I tell this policeman. I bring him to see my little Coco—"

"He's dead, Mommy," said Robert, glancing up. "But I didn't care."

"Hush!" cried Pauline. "You must not say that!"

"I don't care," Robert repeated. "I looked at him, and I touched him, too, and I didn't care."

"Hush!" cried Pauline. "You are cruel!"

"Never mind that now," said Howard, with severity. "We'll look into this, Pauline. Perhaps your dog was—er—ill. Natural causes—"

"He is murdered!" cried Pauline. "And it is that Taylor who does it! Monsieur! Save for this, I could never, never speak. But now ...! He has this poison that kills. Like the poison that has killed madame."

"You have no right to say that," said Cantrell.

"Monsieur! We have all the right to speak the truth. I have telephoned to that Lieutenant—"

"What!" said Howard. "Before you spoke to me?"

"Monsieur, I am so agitated.... I tell him my little Coco is killed—as poor madame is killed. And who knows? By the same hand."

"Now, see here!" said Cantrell. "In the first place, the boy wasn't here on the day—on that day. He was in camp. In the second place ... In any case, it's ... It's ... You shouldn't make these—unfounded accusations. It's ..." He paused. "It's *wrong*," he ended.

"Very well, Monsieur," said Pauline. "The Lieutenant is coming. Perhaps he is already arrived in the cottage. He will see for himself—"

"I'll go down there," said Howard.

"Quite right, Fleming," said Cantrell. "Quite right. I'll go along with you."

As soon as the two men had gone down the steps, Tilly rose, and took Robert's hand.

"Come on!" she said. "We'll go upstairs."

And Sam Osborne can cope with Pauline, she thought. I can't stand any more. Carola ... and Pauline ... Crying—being hysterical ... Even Mr. Abbott was so—emotional. If we could only, only get away!

But, going upstairs was not getting away. They had to pass the closed door of Sibyl's room, and it was like walking back into the thick of the stifling fog. She could see that room now, more vividly than when she had been in it. And their own room was no refuge; it had become horrible to her.

"What'll I *do*, Mommy?" Robert demanded.

"Play with your toys, dear."

"I don't want to."

"Well, you'll have to," said Tilly.

"No!" said Robert. "Tell me a story!"

"No!" said his mother. "You're not a baby. You're old enough to amuse yourself for a little while, and let me have a little peace."

"No!" He waited. "No!" he said, again, and when that got no response, he began kicking the leg of the bedside table so hard that the lamp on it teetered dangerously.

"Robert, stop that!" said Tilly, and when he did not stop, she caught him by the shoulder and shook him. He hit out at her wildly, and she grasped both his hands and held them.

"You're a bad little thing!" she said.

"*You're* bad!" he said, struggling to free his hands. "I want to go away. Let me *go!*"

She released him then. Things mustn't be like this, she told herself. Not between Robert and me. I've got to have patience. Only—if we could get away. I don't want to stay in that cottage with Pauline. She was cruel about Taylor. Now when they find out that he wasn't in the camp that day ... Oh, it couldn't be Taylor! Oh, don't let it be Taylor ...!

"Robert, stop that!"

"I want to go out."

"In a little while. Play with your nice fire engine."

Kindly don't let that child drag that fire engine over the floor when I have people here, Sibyl had said. And how few people had come, how limited her life had been.

"Robert, stop that! You hurt my foot."

Don't let it be Taylor. Then who? She closed her eyes for a moment, and it was as if she saw before her a huge sheet of yellow paper, with that list of names typed in a column.

> Alec Jensen
> Jenny
> Gloria
> Pauline
> Mr. Cantrell
> Sam Osborne
> Carola
> Mathilda Smithson MacDonald

And Howard, she thought. But Howard was poisoned, too. Put him down on the list. And which one do you think would commit a murder? Go ahead and think. You'll never get away, you'll never be free, until this is settled. Who do *you* think did it? Who gained by Sibyl's death? Howard. And Taylor. And me, in a way. And Pauline, too, in a way.

But murders aren't always done for gain. They're done from hatred, from fear. Who hated her—that much? Who was afraid of her? Who—?

There was a knock at the door, and Robert jumped up and opened it.

"Lunch is served," said Jenny.

The back of her cap was pinned to her hair, but the front of it reared up, like the crest of an angry bird.

"Mr. Osborne said, serve lunch," she went on. "I'm sure I didn't know *he* was the one to give orders in this house. But he comes marching into the kitchen, and he says serve lunch now."

"Isn't Mr. Fleming here?"

"No. And he didn't leave any orders what time for lunch, or how many.

Only, Mr. Osborne, *he* says—"

"Well, it's time for lunch, isn't it?"

"*Time* for lunch!" cried Jenny. "*I* never heard of any times for anything in this house. Breakfast, and they'd all want trays—ten o'clock, eleven o'-clock. Dinner at eight, she'd say, and then sit out there drinking their cock-tails till near nine, and if you had a date, or wanted to go to the movies—"

"You might remember what's happened," said Tilly sternly. "You might stop thinking about your own grievances and remember—"

"Well, I do!" said Jenny, and her eyes filled with tears. "I'm just as sorry as anyone. But, far as *I* can see, there isn't anyone that's sorry about Alec shut up in jail and maybe be electrocuted."

"Not if he's innocent."

"That won't help him any," said Jenny, sniffling. "Not with all these rich people against him."

"Nonsense!" said Tilly.

"Oh, no, it isn't!" said Jenny. "There's one law for the rich, and one for the poor, and well I know it."

"Come, Robert! We'll get washed for lunch," said Tilly, and Jenny closed the door with a slam.

She's very spiteful and bad-tempered, Tilly thought. But a murderess? I don't think she'd have the brains to plan a thing like that. And I don't think she's the type. Then who? That's for the police to find out. Not me. It's not my responsibility.

Am I my brother's keeper? Yes. Always. No one can escape from that. What other people do will affect my life. And Robert's. No one can be just a spectator. We're *in* this.

She combed Robert's hair, powdered her face, and opened the door. She held out her hand to Robert, but he didn't want it; he ran ahead of her, stamping down the broad stairs. Who's here, in the house? Who are we going to see?

Robert was running along the hall to the dining room, and she hurried after him, with a feeling that in that room there would be someone, or something, startling, confusing, perhaps dreadful.

But there were only Abbott and Sam Osborne standing by the table. Ab-bott drew back her chair, and she sat down. Robert hitched himself up on the chair next to her; the two men sat down, and Jenny came in with cups of jellied madrilène.

"I don't like that," said Robert.

"You mustn't say that. It's rude," said Tilly.

"Why?"

She did not answer, and a complete silence followed. Women are sup-posed to make conversation, Tilly thought. Mother used to tell me that.

She always did. She'd say something cheerful and nice, even if it didn't mean much. I do believe the swallows are getting ready to fly. Well, that means the summer's nearly over. Things like that. She used to sing a song—so sweetly ... "The swallows are getting ready to fly, Wheeling out on a windy sky ..." I wish ...

"We're all very quiet, aren't we?" she said, with a sudden and, she felt, a preposterous gaiety.

"The cat's got my tongue," said Osborne.

Robert looked up, with interest.

"How ...?" he began, when Jenny entered.

"The Lieutenant is here," she answered, "and he says he wants to see Mr. Osborne and Mr. Abbott, but he'll wait till you've et."

"Ask him to come in," said Osborne. He turned to Tilly. "Don't mind, do you?"

"No ..."

Levy came in, looking taller and thinner than ever, in a dark-gray uniform with a wide leather belt. And a gun in that holster, Tilly thought.

"Sit down and have some lunch, will you?" said Osborne.

"No, thanks. I'm here on business, Mr. Osborne. "I'll wait until you've finished your meal—"

"No reason for waiting, Lieutenant. Sit down and have a cup of coffee, and go right ahead with the questions."

"You might prefer to be questioned separately," said Levy.

He looked stern, even ominous today. And Osborne, Tilly thought, was altogether too off-hand.

"Not me!" he said. "I prefer an informal atmosphere. Puts me at ease, and I talk more."

"Mr. Abbott?"

"I—it's—immaterial to me," Abbott answered.

"You understand," said Levy, "that you're not obliged to answer any questions. Anything you say will be taken down in writing.... Beebe!"

A young policeman in uniform came in from the hall, and saluted.

"Sit over by the window," said Levy.

"I wish to God *you'd* sit down, Lieutenant," said Osborne. "If you don't want coffee, what about a cocktail? Glass of sherry?"

"No," said Levy. "Beebe, take this down. Mr. Osborne, from information received I have reason to believe that you were in possession of a certain amount of cyanide of potassium. Do you admit this to be the truth?"

"Yes. That's the truth."

"When did you acquire this cyanide?"

"The day before Mrs. Fleming's death."

"How did you acquire it?"

"I bought it, from a wholesale chemist in New York."

"Did you go to the chemist yourself, to buy this cyanide?"

Osborne brought out a cigarette, and lit it.

"No," he answered. "I gave Jensen the written order. I'm permitted to buy the stuff, for my work."

"What is the nature of your work?"

"Photography is part of it. Travel articles, and so on."

"Where did you keep this cyanide?"

"In the cottage. I had a dark room fitted up there."

"Who else had access to this cyanide?"

"Nobody."

"Do you want to reconsider that answer?"

"No use in that. I had the stuff in a bottle, in a tin box. The tin box was locked, and the bottle hadn't been opened, when I took it out."

"When did you take it out?"

"Early in the morning after Mrs. Fleming's death."

"Why did you remove it?"

"I wanted to get rid of it."

"Why did you wish to get rid of it?"

"Pretty obvious, isn't it?"

"I'd like an explanation," said Levy.

"Very well. If you'd asked me whether I had any cyanide, I'd have told you the truth. But nobody asked me anything. And I didn't feel like sticking my neck out. So I got the stuff, and flushed it down the toilet, and broke the bottle. I wasn't destroying any clues. I wasn't hampering the police. I give you my word—for whatever it's worth to you—that my bottle of cyanide had never been opened."

"Mr. Osborne," said Levy. "I have a statement from the boy, Taylor Price, that he obtained a certain amount of cyanide crystals from the cottage."

"Well, he didn't," said Osborne. "What I had was a solution. There weren't any crystals there."

"The boy is very definite on that point."

"So am I," said Osborne. "I haven't used any cyanide crystals for months."

"You admit that you did have cyanide crystals in your possession?"

"Yes, I did. And I used all I had."

"Can you suggest where the boy might have obtained such crystals, if he did not get them from the cottage?"

"No, I can't."

You're making a bad impression! Tilly cried, in her heart. Don't be so defiant. Don't try to be so nonchalant.

"The boy admits to killing the bird and the chipmunk found in Mrs.

MacDonald's room. He first shot them with a small automatic which was found on his person. They were not dead, and he then forced these cyanide crystals down their throats. He admits to killing Pauline Duval's dog by this method."

"Well?" said Osborne.

Levy looked steadily at him for a moment; then he turned his head.

"Mr. Abbott."

Abbott pushed back his chair, and stood up, very straight.

"Mr. Abbott, you stated that the boy Taylor Price was with you in camp on the day of Mrs. Fleming's death. Are you prepared to reaffirm this statement?"

"No," said Abbott. His lips were trembling; he raised his chin. "No!" he said. "I—lied."

"The boy was here—on these premises—on the day of Mrs. Fleming's death?"

"I don't know. He took my car. He was gone all day. I don't know where he was. He—I—I also feel obliged to add that—that I myself had a bottle of—cyanide solution. Used—in lepidoptery. I—could not state definitely— whether or not the bottle had been tampered with. I—whatever may have happened—I hold myself entirely responsible."

Levy pulled out a chair and sat down on it sideways, "Beebe," he said, "bring the boy in."

Tilly rose, and took Robert's arm.

"Come, Robert," she said.

"I don't *want* to!" he cried. "I want to eat my lunch!"

"You're coming," said Tilly.

She pulled him down from his chair, she dragged him across the dining room, through the swing-door, through the pantry, and into the kitchen.

"Keep him here, Gloria!" she said. "Give him his lunch—anything. But keep him here, will you, until I come for him."

"Indeed, and I have not the time—" Gloria began, indignantly.

"You keep him!" said Tilly. "Don't argue with me. Keep him here, and don't let him out of your sight."

Gloria and Jenny were both looking at her in astonishment.

"Don't gape at me!" she said. "Do as you're told. Look after Robert. He's had enough. He's not going to have any more."

She went back into the dining room, and sat down at the table. Taylor was there now, and Howard, too.

"It's not necessary for you to remain here, Mrs. MacDonald," said Levy.

"I want to stay, thanks," said Tilly.

"Just like Robert," Osborne observed.

Tilly glanced angrily at him, but he was not looking at her. Then she forgot her anger as Levy rose, stood at the end of the table; toweringly tall, he seemed, stern, menacing, with the gun on his hip. Now it's going to start, she thought. Now he knows.

CHAPTER THIRTEEN

"You all understand," he said, "that you have a constitutional right to refuse to answer any questions, if you believe that such answers would tend to degrade or incriminate you. This right, however, does not extend to refusal to answer on any other grounds. Such as a desire to protect any other person or persons."

"You talk like a lawyer," said Taylor, thoughtfully.

"As a matter of fact, I am a lawyer," Levy answered. "Admitted to the bar. But I chose police, in preference. The function of the police, you understand, is not to judge, or to punish. Our function is to protect the public from criminals, and, when possible, to prevent crime."

"You have to do some judging, don't you, before you can arrest anyone?" asked Taylor.

"It's not judging," Levy answered. He spoke to the boy seriously, without condescension. "When we arrest a man, we don't pronounce him guilty. We simply state that we have certain evidences that constitute a case against him. Legally, the man is innocent until he is proved guilty by trial."

"What about someone you *see* committing a crime?"

"Even in such a case, the man taken into custody is entitled to a trial."

"Sure," said Taylor. "Trial with a night stick—or a bullet, if he runs."

"If it seems necessary to the police, for the protection of the public."

"If you see a man running away from the scene of a crime, you can shoot to kill," said Taylor.

"We're obliged to act on the supposition that any person seeking to evade the police, or refusing to stop when ordered to do so, is guilty," said Levy. He paused for a moment. "This applies also to any person or persons who withhold information from the police, or who give false or misleading answers to questions asked them."

"Well, I haven't done that," said Taylor. "I'm a model suspect. I've answered every question you asked, in a fine, honest, manly way. Mr. Samuel Osborne and Mr. Wilfred Abbott both told you lies, but I didn't."

"Come now!" Howard protested, indignantly. "Lieutenant, is it necessary for us to listen to this boy's malicious—malicious—?"

"I'd like the boy to repeat his statements here," said Levy.

"Fine!" said Taylor, and he too rose. "I like attention. Doctor Lambson wrote that to my mother. 'The boy seeks to gain attention, not through accomplishment, or normal competition, but through unacceptable behavior.'"

He was, Tilly thought, a handsome boy, in a way, tall for his age, immaculately well-dressed, in gray flannels and a black shantung shirt, insolent and easy in his bearing. He was clever, and he knew it; he had money behind him, and he was well aware of that, too. Yet, she thought, there was something forlorn about him, something pitiable in his scornful smile, in his slight shoulders, his thin wrists, his long, narrow hands.

"If your mother told you that—" Howard began.

"She didn't," said Taylor. "I found the letter in her desk, and I read it. I don't think she ever read half the stuff old Lambson wrote to her."

"Taylor! That's—outrageous!" cried Howard.

"We'll let that go, for the present, Mr. Fleming," said Levy. "Now, Taylor, if you'll give us a brief summary—"

"'Brief ... " said Taylor. "All right. On the morning of August the twentieth, I rose early. I entered the room in the log cabin occupied by Mr. Wilfred Abbott. He was snoring, loud enough to drown out any little noise I made. I went past his bed, and I took the key out of his pants pocket, where I'd seen him put it, and I unlocked the wall cupboard where he keeps his wallet. I took out ten dollars—"

"That was stealing!" said Abbott.

"Not really," said Taylor. "I knew that if you raised a stink about it, I could get the money from my mother to pay you back. Borrowing, you could call it. Then I locked the cupboard, and put back the key, and I went out to the garage, and borrowed his car."

"The cyanide—?" said Abbott.

"There wasn't any there."

"That is untrue, Taylor. There was a bottle of cyanide in solution—"

"There was a little blue bottle, full of water," said Taylor. "I'd used up the real stuff, a week before, for my experiments."

"Experiments? What do you mean?"

"I used it on toads, frogs, fish, a lot of things I could catch. Then I dissected them. I think I'll study to be a surgeon. I'm a sadist, Doctor Lambson says, and surgery—"

"Suppose we keep to the point ...," said Levy. "You took Mr. Abbott's car, and then?"

"I drove home—if you like to call it that. I was so goddam sick of that damn camp—and Abbott—and Lambson—and the whole damn set-up."

"No profanity!" said Howard.

"None?" said Taylor. "Anyhow, I left a note for Wilfrid—pardon me! For Mr. Abbott, to say I'd be back for dinner. I did that just to keep him quiet, so that he wouldn't tell Lambson, and start Lambson telephoning to my mother. Old Lambson's in a hell of a spot about me. Being a psychiatrist, it's his religion to believe that parents—especially mothers—are responsible for all your faults. But he has to pipe down about that, so that he can get his money out of the parents."

"And your reason for taking Mr. Abbott's car?" said Levy.

"I hoped I'd never go back to the camp," Taylor said. "I thought I'd have a talk with my mother. I'd tried it before, but I thought I'd make one more attempt. I wanted her to send me to an ordinary, first-class prep school—and without her having one of her heart-to-heart talks with the head-master, all about how worried and miserable and disappointed she was about me. But when I got here, I—changed my mind. I knew it wouldn't be any good. I knew she'd only go into her act. 'The child I brought into this world—'"

"And after you got here?" said Levy, inexorable, but with no sign of impatience.

"After I got here, I changed my mind. I didn't want to see her. I thought I'd do some more experiments, so I went to the cottage, and got some cyanide I knew was there—"

"There weren't any cyanide crystals there," said Osborne.

"Well, I got some there," said Taylor. "In an envelope, addressed to you, in the drawer of the desk. And I found an automatic there, too."

"It belonged to—my wife," said Howard. "She'd bought it, before we were married. She had a license for it, obtained in Brookline, after she'd reported an attempt to rob her house there. I—she was—in some ways—timid. But—I managed to get the thing away from her, without her knowledge. I—personally I don't think these things should be left lying around. I—personally, I think they're more of a—a danger than a protection. I shouldn't have left it there in the desk, but the cottage was empty, the windows and the doors were kept locked, and the keys in my possession. They still are. I had no idea that Taylor, or anyone else, could get in there."

"Elementary, my dear Watson," said Taylor. "I'd been getting in there whenever I wanted for the last three years. I got the back-door key off your key-ring—"

"How?"

"Oh, one time when you were ... Well, let's skip it. It was after one of your cocktail parties."

"And after you'd taken the gun and the cyanide?" said Levy.

"I went out of the cottage. I hoped I'd be able to bring down some of the vertebrates to dissect, but I'd never found a gun before, and my shots didn't kill either of the two I aimed at. So I finished them off with cyanide. Being humane, that was. I went to get some lunch in a diner, and when I came back for my subjects, that damn brat was there."

"Taylor!" cried Howard.

"Sorry," said Taylor. "But I can't stand that brat. His mother's always doting on him and—"

"*Taylor!*"

"Anyhow, I gave him a scare then, and a better one later on. I used the gardener's ladder, and I put a couple of bats in his room, and a garter-snake in his bed. I thought maybe Mommy would have a little trouble, laughing that off."

"You stated that on the twentieth of August you did not at any time enter this house. Do you wish to amend that statement?" Levy asked.

"I do not. It happens to be true. And it's also true that I didn't know my mother was dead when I climbed up the ladder. It's also true that I didn't kill her, or have anything to do with her death. I wouldn't think of such a thing." His superior smile turned into a grimace; a muscle in his cheek twitched. "I was brought up to honor my parents," he said. "By the time I was—that brat's age, I was being shuttled from one to the other. My father told me my mother was a bitch, and she told me he was a stinker. And I honored them both such a lot that I believed them both."

"Taylor!" said Howard, again.

"That's my statement," said Taylor. "It's true, all of it. If you don't want to believe it, all right. Go ahead, and do anything you damn please."

"You're certain that the envelope containing cyanide was addressed to Mr. Osborne?"

"Couldn't be more certain."

"What did you do with the envelope?"

"Tore it up. Threw the pieces away."

"Very well," said Levy. "I won't keep you any longer, Taylor."

"May I take him back to the camp now, sir?" asked Abbott.

Levy looked at him. He said, "You can leave the room now, Taylor. Mr. Abbott, too."

"Thank you," said Abbott. "Come along, Taylor."

"Wait!" said Tilly. "If you'll go into the kitchen, Mr. Abbott, Gloria will give you some lunch."

"Thanks," he said. "But I—don't feel particularly hungry, just now."

"I was thinking of Taylor," said Tilly, curtly.

"Oh, yes ... Yes, of course. Then—this way, Taylor, m' boy."

"Go to hell," said Taylor, and walked off, into the hall. Abbott hastened after him.

"Mrs. MacDonald, you needn't wait—"

"Let her stay, if she wants," said Osborne. "I don't mind. I take it you're going to ask about that envelope addressed to me, with cyanide crystals in it. All right. I didn't know it was there. I don't know how it got there."

"Are you prepared to sign a statement to that effect?"

"Yes."

"Have you any suggestions to make as to how this envelope came to be where it was?"

"Well, I have one suggestion," said Osborne. "Or even two. The first is that Taylor didn't find the cyanide in the cottage. The second is that the envelope—if there was any envelope—was not addressed to me."

"You're prepared to deny the boy's allegation?"

"No. I'm not in a position to deny it. Maybe he found just what he said he found. But if he did, I don't know anything about it."

"You admit that you did, at various times, purchase cyanide of potassium?"

"Yes, I did."

"Did you use this cyanide in the cottage, Mr. Osborne? Yes? For what purpose?"

"In connection with my photographic work."

"Is photography your profession, Mr. Osborne? Your means of livelihood?"

"Only partly. I write articles, and so on."

"Are you, at this time, regularly employed in any capacity?"

"I'm a free lance."

"How long have you been an inmate of this house, Mr. Osborne?"

"Well ... On and off, for about three months."

"You have previously stated that you have no fixed residence. Where had you planned to go when you left here, Mr. Osborne?"

"Brazil."

"For what purpose, Mr. Osborne?"

"Write articles. Make photographs."

"Have you ever, at any time, had regular employment, Mr. Osborne?"

"I've had jobs, on and off."

"What was the nature of these jobs?"

"I was a swimming instructor once, at a summer resort. I was a photographer for an advertising agency for a while. I was a steward on a private yacht for over a year. I was a guide in Hong Kong, in Tokyo, in Singapore. I was in the Army nearly four years. In Europe."

"What is your present source of livelihood, Mr. Osborne?"

"I'm doing some writing."

Osborne was answering promptly and readily, and, Tilly thought, truthfully. But it seemed to her that his curt answers were building up a disastrous impression of a drifter, a good-for-nothing, and, more than that, an impression that he was withholding something. Not lying, not evading, but volunteering nothing.

"Mr. Osborne," said Levy, "we can continue this interview in privacy—"

"Not on my account, thanks."

"Very well. From information received, Mr. Osborne, I understand that you have been mailing checks for deposit in a New York bank, with considerable regularity."

"Yes."

"What was the source of this income, Mr. Osborne?"

"Advances. On some work I was doing."

"Mr. Osborne, I understand that these checks were made out to your order, and signed by the late Mrs. Fleming. Do you confirm this?"

"Yes."

"What was the nature of the work for which the late Mrs. Fleming advanced you money at stated intervals?"

"Writing."

"Do you mean that this money was in the nature of a loan?"

"No."

"Mr. Osborne. Did you, at any time, purchase, or cause to be purchased, any barbiturate preparations for the late Mrs. Fleming?"

"I did not."

"Mr. Osborne. With the assistance of the New York City Police Department, we have learned where Jensen bought the supplies of cyanide on your order. We have also learned that at these times, and at other times, Jensen bought—illegally—considerable supplies of a certain barbiturate preparation in capsule form, from an elderly uncle of his, employed in this wholesale chemical company. Jensen refuses to give any information as to his subsequent disposal of these capsules. Have you any comment to make, Mr. Osborne? Any suggestions as to the disposal of these capsules?"

"No. I don't know anything about them. Never knew Jensen got them."

Levy took a small note-book out of his pocket, and began turning the pages. He's not really reading anything in it, Tilly thought. It's just to make a pause. To give Sam Osborne time to think. It's pretty plain what the Lieutenant's leading up to. That Sibyl gave money to Sam Osborne either to get drugs for her, or—what? Because they were lovers? Or—blackmail? He's made himself look like that sort of man, shiftless, a sort of adventurer, who hasn't even any address.

But he's *not* like that. It's not just silly and feminine to think that. I know about people. I've never been swindled by anyone, or very much disappointed in anyone.

"Mr. Osborne," said Levy, "you state that you made use of the cottage for your photographic work. How did you gain entry to the cottage?"

"I lent him my key," said Howard.

"Well, no," said Osborne. "I had a key of my own."

He reached in his trousers pocket and brought out a key ring.

"Here it is," he said. "Want me to take it off the ring?"

"Yes, thanks," said Levy, and Osborne detached a key and handed it to him. "Mr. Fleming!"

Howard gave a violent start. "Yes ...? Yes ...?"

"Mr. Fleming, have you any comment to make on Mr. Osborne's statement?"

"No ...," Howard said. "Except that he—that Osborne—ab-b-bove suspicion. Writing a book with me. Travel book. The money was for research. For his time. All very customary ... Nothing furtive—all aboveboard ... M-m-man of—of—h-honor ... I—I—I—"

"Thank you," said Levy. He closed the little notebook, and put it into his breast pocket, with the key. "One more question, Mr. Fleming, and then I'll be going. I have in my possession a sworn statement made by Mrs. Carola Dexter, in which she affirms that, in the presence of a witness, you declared that you wanted to marry again—if you could get rid of your wife. Do you confirm this, Mr. Fleming?"

"D-d-damn ...!" Howard cried. He tried to rise, but he sank down into the chair again. "*Lie!*" he shouted, and fell forward, slamming his forehead on the table.

"He's hurt himself!" cried Tilly, springing to her feet.

Neither Levy nor Osborne even glanced at her, or at Howard.

"Is it all right to ask who the witness was?" said Osborne.

"Quite all right. Mrs. Dexter gave me the name of Richard Cantrell as witness."

"What does Cantrell say?"

"Mr. Cantrell," said Levy, "doesn't remember anything—about anything." He moved toward the door. "Nobody in this case remembers anything. Nobody knows anything. It's a big help."

CHAPTER FOURTEEN

Howard slid sideways from his chair, and fell to the floor with a soft thud. Tilly ran to him, and knelt by his side, saw his face white as chalk, his eyes closed.

"He's hurt himself," said Tilly. "Will you call up the doctor?"

"He's only passed out," said Osborne, looking down at Howard. "He'll be all right."

"You don't know. He struck his head hard on the table. He may have hurt himself seriously. If you won't call the doctor, I will."

"Take it a little easy," said Osborne. "Give him ten minutes, even five, if you'd rather. The only doctor I know of here is Crowdie," he said. "And I don't think we'd better send for him."

"Why not?"

"Howard wouldn't like it."

"*Why not?* D'you have to be so cryptic and all-knowing, like a great detective?"

"That's not how I feel, right now," said Osborne. "I feel like the biggest damn fool there ever was."

"All right. Why wouldn't Howard want Doctor Crowdie? He's been their doctor for years."

"I might as well tell you," said Osborne. "It's no secret. The police know it. And you'd probably hear about it, anyhow, before long."

"Tell me."

"I was in Howard's room when Crowdie and the police doctor were working on him. I heard what Crowdie said, and so did Howard. Crowdie told Levy he believed Howard had taken the chloral hydrate himself. He said he'd been called in twice before, to treat Howard for the same condition. He said that last summer, when Howard had stopped drinking, he'd prescribed chloral hydrate, to help him sleep. Said he warned Howard that the stuff was dynamite, if he took it along with alcohol. But Howard started drinking again, and one night, when he couldn't sleep, he took a dose of the stuff, and knocked himself out. He swore he didn't have any chloral hydrate, and you can't get it without a prescription. But he did get more— or he had some left, because he knocked himself out again, when they first came out here. And this time they found an almost empty bottle of it under Howard's bed. No label on it. Howard said he'd taken off the label; said it was the original bottle Crowdie had prescribed. He said he hadn't taken it—knowingly. He said that when he saw Sibyl, he thought she was ill, and he drank the whiskey that was already poured out, in a glass on the table beside her. Said he was shocked by the way Sibyl looked, and wanted to brace himself up."

"Well, why couldn't it have been that way?"

"Because you said there wasn't a glass of whiskey on the table when you left the room. And there's one thing very certain. Sibyl didn't get up and pour herself a drink after you'd gone."

Tilly was silent for a moment.

"Then someone else did it ...?" she said, half-questioningly.

"Sure. Someone else who knew Howard would be the one to find Sibyl dead. Knew he'd drink the glass of whiskey; and doped it with enough chloral hydrate to knock him out. But not a lethal dose."

Tilly stood looking down at Howard on the floor, his feet on the big cushion, his face so white.

"It could have been that way," she said.

"Sure," said Osborne, and he, too, was looking down at Howard.

"Can't you stop being mysterious?" Tilly demanded. "Can't you say what you think?"

"No. I can't. What I think isn't evidence, and anyhow maybe I don't know what I think. Only ... Howard's a good egg, after his fashion. But he's got what you might call a low breaking-point. And he's had to stand all the things a stuffed shirt can't stand. Disorder, confusion, crazy extravagances, crazy quarrels with neighbors, servants, tradespeople. One time when they were having a dinner-party, all the oyster forks had disappeared, at the last moment. He was absolutely sunk."

"I can't think that's very tragic," said Tilly.

"It was—for him. In the first place, it was a humiliation he never got over, to see their guests eating oysters with big forks. In the second place, the missing oyster forks couldn't be found, and Sibyl accused a maid they had of stealing them, and the maid got a lawyer and they had to pay her to keep the case out of court. Months later the forks turned up. In a suit case of Sibyl's. She— He's coming to, poor devil."

Howard's eyes fluttered, opened, closed again; be gave a long sigh, like a groan.

"Take it easy, old man!" said Osborne, and going to the sideboard he poured a drink from a decanter. Kneeling beside Howard, he raised his shoulders. "Just drink this down," he said.

"It's—brandy, Sam!" Howard protested.

"Good for you," said Osborne, and Howard drained the little glass.

"Better?" Osborne asked. "Now I'll help you upstairs, and you can rest for a while."

"Thank you," he said. "I—in a few moments—I promised Tilly—that little tour of inspection—and the cottage."

"You'd better lie down, Howard," she said. "There's no hurry. I'll wait."

"Well, no," said Howard. "You might want some changes made, Tilly, and this man I've got there is leaving at four. I—think I can make it now."

"Howard, please don't! Please rest first."

With Osborne's help, Howard got up. But he still held to Osborne's arm; he was still white, his blue eyes looked dim.

"In a few moments—," he said. "The man's leaving at four. You may want changes made, Tilly."

"I'll go along with her," said Osborne. "I'll help you upstairs now, Howard, and you can rest."

"I—think I'd rather rest down here," Howard said. "In the—the library, I think."

Osborne helped him out of the room, and Tilly stood, motionless, until Osborne returned.

"Do you mean you think—it was *Howard?*" she demanded.

"No," he answered. "I don't think anything. Come on! Get Robert, and we'll go along."

"I don't really care how things are arranged in the cottage," said Tilly. "Pauline's there. She'll—"

"Please don't argue," said Osborne. "Just get Robert and come along."

"But I don't want to."

"Look here!" he said. "Please don't argue. I'm sick."

"Do you mean ill?" Tilly asked, with a sudden anxiety.

"No. Sick. Come on, please!"

She found Robert lying on his stomach on the kitchen table, drawing on a paper bag with a pencil. He was very troublesome about coming with her.

"I don't *want* to!" he said.

Like me? Tilly thought. Am I childish, and unreasonable, and troublesome?

"Go along with you now!" said Gloria, outraged. "Your poor mother so kind and good to you, and you carrying on like a wild boy."

That seemed to impress him, and he got down from the table.

"I'm not a wild boy," he said, ingratiatingly.

"You are not," said Gloria. "And here is a little cake you can take along with you."

Osborne was waiting on the terrace, smoking a cigarette; they all set off down the drive without a word.

"Where are we going, Mommy?" Robert asked, after a moment.

"To the cottage, darling. Where you went this morning with Pauline."

"Why?"

"We're going to live there. Won't that be nice?"

"Just you and me, Mommy?"

"Yes. And Pauline."

The cottage was before them now, and he stood still.

"I'd like Sam to live there, too," he said.

"Sam would like it, also," said Osborne. "But he can't. It's not protocol."

"I don't *want* to live there!" said Robert. "That bad boy will come and kill me dead."

"That's silly," said his mother. "It's going to be *very* nice and cozy there."

"I don't *like* it!"

Neither do I, thought Tilly. It was a pretty little house, half-timbered, with a pointed roof, a pointed arch over the front door, a little porch with a settle on either side. But the tall trees grew so close to it; it looked dwarfed, unreal, like a witch's cottage in a fairy forest.

"Tilly," said Osborne, "you'll be all right there. Levy'll keep an eye on you, and so will I."

He took her hand, and she was comforted and pleased by his warm, steady clasp.

"I wish Pauline wasn't quite so temperamental," she said.

"Probably does her good," said Osborne. "I've often thought that if I would yell, and kick, even faint, I'd be a happier man. And I might gain some weight."

"You are rather thin," said Tilly.

"Very thin. Lonely. Homeless."

"Haven't you any—family?"

"Only a couple of parents, and two brothers, and a sister. All married. Including my parents."

They went on, hand in hand, and Robert came behind them, scuffing up the gravel.

"You talked to me," said Tilly. "You were quite eloquent about my telling everything to the police ..."

"Meaning I didn't do it myself? I've answered every question they've asked, truthfully."

"That's quibbling," said Tilly.

"I know it," he said. "But, just the same, the advice I gave you was absolutely sound. Hew to the line—let the chips fall where they will."

"My grandfather used to say that," said Tilly. "When I was a little girl, I had a sort of picture in my mind of a man up in a tree, sawing off a branch, and the chips were falling down and getting into the eyes of the people underneath."

"You can get more chips in more people's eyes, if you just go hacking around any old how."

"I don't know—," Tilly began, but she stopped, and drew her hand away from Osborne's, at the sound from inside the cottage. Carola's voice, very high, very clear.

"You're a cruel, wicked liar, Dick Cantrell!"

"Nothing of the sort," Cantrell responded. His voice, too, was loud, but resonant and steady. "When the question was put to me, I answered truthfully. I certainly do *not* remember Howard's saying what you quoted him as saying."

"Then you were drunk."

"I'm never drunk," said Cantrell, sternly. "And you know it."

"You were right there when Howard said he wanted to get rid of Sibyl."

"He said nothing of the sort. Sibyl had threatened to leave him—by no means for the first time—and he said that if she did leave him—permanently—if she wanted a divorce, he would marry again."

"Marry *me*."

"Carola, your name was not mentioned."

"It *was*, you old liar."

"Carola, it was extremely foolish and improvident of you to tell that story to the police. Don't you realize that you were providing them with a motive?"

"What do y' mean—motive?" Carola demanded, scornfully.

"I mean," said Cantrell, "a motive for killing Sibyl."

"They wouldn't think that about *me*," said Carola. "Nobody would—but *you*."

"I don't think we ought to listen—," Tilly began.

"Keep still!" said Osborne.

"I know you helped me out," Carola was saying. "But I *offered* to pay you back. I *tried* to pay you back, and you wouldn't *take* the money."

"I told you I wouldn't accept it, Carola. I told you—I tried to warn you against your method of getting money."

"What did you expect me to do? Starve to death? Go around in rags?"

"You're not penniless, Carola. Wait! I admit your income—your alimony—is inadequate to your scale of living. But you could either go to work—"

"Doing what? Go on the streets?"

"You could either go to work," said Cantrell, "or you could live in a very much less expensive way."

"Certainly! I could live in a furnished room in a slum. Never see anybody. Never go anywhere. Never have any decent clothes."

"That would be infinitely preferable to what you have been doing, Carola. I've already pointed out to you that you would be sent to prison if your illegal traffic in drugs—"

"They—they're *not* drugs. They're just sleeping pills. I take them myself. I'd go mad if I didn't."

"They are drugs. And traffic in them is not only illegal but dangerous. There have been many, very many cases of suicide by barbiturates."

"If people want to commit suicide, that's their responsibility. Not my headache."

"Try to think how you'd feel if you knew you had provided—for money—the means for committing suicide."

"I wouldn't feel anything at all," said Carola. "I don't think suicide is one bit wrong. I think people have a right to kill themselves if they want to. Anyhow, nobody's going to find out about my selling those capsules—unless *you* tell them. Jensen won't tell. He made a good profit himself—out of me. I don't know whether he really bought them, or just stole them, but anyhow he made me pay plenty. And he wants to keep on, when he gets out of jail."

"I hear this," said another voice, Pauline's voice, and she too spoke loudly and with that note of hysteria Tilly had learned to dread. Sibyl, Carola, Jenny, Taylor, Abbott, even Howard ... The voices of people who had lost control, who were possessed. "Do not be afraid, madame, but that *I* shall tell the police. It is for *you* that that fine young man is in the cell of a prison. It is *you* who have led him into wickedness. You who—"

"Oh, shut up!" said Carola.

"I? I shut up?"

"Never mind, now, Pauline," said Cantrell. "Don't say anything more. And don't speak to the police, or anyone else about this until I've talked it over with you. If Mrs. MacDonald agrees, I'll come back later for that fine French dinner you promised me. Now I'm going to drive Mrs. Dexter home."

"No, you're not!" said Carola. "I came here to have a few words with that kept woman of Howard's, and I'm going to wait until she comes."

"You're not," said Cantrell. "You're coming with me now—if I have to carry you out to my car."

"I won't!" There was a moment's silence. "Stop!" Carola shrieked.

"Is he going to kill her dead?" Robert asked.

"No," said Tilly. "No, darling. Sam, go and see—"

The front door of the cottage opened and Cantrell came out, with Carola over his shoulder, struggling frantically.

"Sam!" cried Tilly. "Stop him!"

"Not me," said Osborne, and as Tilly moved forward, he caught her by the arm. "Keep out of this, Tilly."

"No! But his face ...! He looks so—furious! Sam, suppose be hurts her! Suppose he—"

"I don't care if he strangles her," said Osborne.

Cantrell had gone through the gateway into the road with his burden; they were out of sight, and Carola shrieked again.

"Help! *Help!*"

Then there was silence, and then the sound of an engine starting.

"Is she all dead now?" Robert asked, with interest.

"No, darling," Tilly answered, mechanically. She I looked up at Osborne. "She called for help—"

"That's the best thing she does," said Osborne. "She's been to Howard, God knows how many times, yelling for help. Money to pay 'the doctor.' To pay her servants, her taxes. Her fines for speeding. She tried to nick me once for twenty-five dollars, but she didn't get it. To Cantrell and to

Howard, and probably a lot of other people, she's always and forever a Morrowly of Pelham, so she has to have servants, and cars, and what they call 'decent' clothes. But I don't seem to be impressed. Did you happen to hear what she called you?"

"I don't care. It was horrible to see him drag her away like that. To hear her screaming for help."

"You heard what Cantrell was saying to her. You know now that she's been supplying—God knows who—with these capsules."

"I want a pony," said Robert.

"Not just now, dear."

"Yes! Now! Cousin Howard *said* he'd buy me a pony. I want it now!"

"Well, you can't have it now. Come! We're going into the house now. Do you want to come in, Mr. Osborne?"

"The name is Sam. Do you want me to come in?"

She hesitated for a moment. "Well ... yes," she said.

She rang the bell, and Pauline, in a green overall, a blue ribbon tied over her hair and under her chin, opened the door at once.

"*Mais, s'il vous plait, regardez donc, madame!*" she cried. "*Ce jeune Pietro, il a tant travaillé, c'est presque impossible! Et tant de goût! Regardez, je vous prie, ce qu'on a fait ici....*"

She went on, in a rapid French which Tilly did not understand, and with an enthusiasm Tilly did not share. The windows of the little sitting-room were heavily curtained in dark green rep, there was a green carpet on the floor; there was, in Tilly's opinion, far too much furniture here, and too heavy for the room.

"She wants you to go upstairs with her and see what Pietro's doing," said Osborne.

Reluctantly Tilly went up the steep, narrow stairway, and found Pietro fastening a valance of wood covered with chintz on the mantelpiece of a small bedroom.

"Your room, madame!" said Pauline. "All is comfortable for you, no?"

"Oh, very!" said Tilly. "You've done wonders," she said, politely, to the young Italian.

Then Pauline led her to see Robert's room, smaller than her own, furnished with a white iron bed, a big old-fashioned chest of drawers, two rush-bottomed chairs, a marble-topped pedestal table, a dark red carpet, dark red curtains, dark red bedspread. The trees shut out the light; a branch was brushing back and forth across the screen.

"Red is cheerful," Pauline said.

"Yes, it is," Tilly agreed. "I'll have to go downstairs now, Pauline. Mr. Osborne's waiting."

"He will wait, madame," said Pauline, with a meaningful smile. "You must, please, see the bathroom. See if all pleases you."

"Very nice," Tilly said, looking at the dim and narrow little bathroom with a chipped old tub standing on curly legs. "Very nice, Pauline. Now I'll really have to go down—"

"But a moment, madame! I show you my room. And, madame, two things, if you please."

She had opened the door of another room, small, narrow, dim and crowded, like the others. "Madame permits that I keep here my little dog?" she asked.

Tilly looked at her in amazement that was almost terror.

"I have, as you see, a little basket for him," said Pauline. "I keep him here, that he will not disturb you."

"But, Pauline, I thought—"

Tears came into Pauline's eyes. "Madame, please ... I do not speak of my little one who has gone. I cannot. But Mr. Cantrell—but what kindness! This morning he takes me in his auto to this place—what is it?—many little dogs. Ah, yes! This kennels. He tells me, regard these little dogs. Choose which you will. I see one—so small—a little nose of black velvet ... *Bien, alors!* says Mr. Cantrell. I buy this little one. He is yours. But let him remain here with his mother one more week. Then, if madame permits ...?"

"Yes, certainly."

"And, madame, do you permit that Mr. Cantrell shall dine here tonight? I should not have asked him this, before your permission, but, madame, when he buys for me this little dog, I am so pleased, so thankful, that I do not think."

"Why, yes, that'll be all right, Pauline," said Tilly. "Now I'll have to go downstairs."

"You understand, madame, I have all materials in the house. Mr. Fleming has said to me, order what you will. Me, I like *much* better to go myself to the market. There I see. There I choose. Today this is good, the other is not good. I look. I say yes, or I say no. But there is no auto so this morning I telephone. Everything is now arrived. Milk, grain, oranges, for Robert—"

"That's fine!" said Tilly.

I can't listen to her for one single instant longer, she thought. Is she going to keep on like this, talking and talking and talking, all the time we're here? "That's fine, Pauline," she said again, and turned away to the staircase. All the time we're here? And how long will that be? Weeks? It's very kind and thoughtful of Howard, but I don't *like* this cottage. I—really hate it.

The somber, crowded little sitting-room was empty; the sound of Robert's voice led her to the kitchen, where she found the child with Pietro, and, to her surprise, Howard. He was still pale; his eyes still had a look of dimness, but he was neat, business-like, talking to Pietro.

"You say you've fixed the sink yourself? Then I'll call up the plumber, and tell him not to come. Now, if you have time to take a look at the cellar ... I think there's a lot of rubbish down there, old furniture, and so on."

"Yes, sir," said Pietro. "I'll run down there now. And what about these pictures, sir?"

He was holding out a sheaf of large, glossy photographs.

"Rubbish!" said Howard, loudly. "Burn them up."

"Some of them are real pretty," said Pietro. "I'd like to take 'em home, if you don't mind."

"I'll—glance over them," said Howard, and took them from Pietro's hand.

Robert was trying to wind an old window-shade back on its roller; nobody had noticed Tilly, and she now retreated, letting the swing-door close silently. I don't want to talk, she thought. And I don't want to hear anyone else talking. I suppose Sam got tired of waiting. But he'll come back.

I'm tired, she thought. I'd like to lie down in my room for a few moments. But not with Pauline up there. In one corner of the sitting-room there was an ungainly old spring-rocker upholstered in brown; she sat down in it, and it was very comfortable; it was very pleasant to rock gently, with almost no effort, so good to be quiet, to be alone....

The swing-door opened, and in came Howard.

"Oh, Tilly?" he said. "Is everything satisfactory?"

"Everything is fine, thank you, Howard."

"Good! I'll have to go back to the house now, Tilly. See this investment counselor fellow. But if it suits you, what about my coming back here to dinner? The house—it's natural, I suppose—it gets on my nerves."

"I'd love it, Howard," Tilly answered. "But, you see, Pauline asked Mr. Cantrell to dinner here."

"What!" cried Howard. "Pauline ...? Tilly, surely you don't allow your servant to issue invitations?"

I wish I was Robert, Tilly thought. Then I just wouldn't answer at all. And if Howard said it was very rude and naughty not to answer, I shouldn't care.

"It's something rather special," she said, and because she could not be Robert, she went on, to tell about Cantrell and the little dog.

"Very kind of him," said Howard. "Most generous. Well, then, suppose I come, too? Unless—" He gave a smile that was surprisingly roguish; dimples came in his pale cheeks. "Unless it's a case of two's company, eh?"

"Oh, no! I'd love you to come."

"Cantrell's an eligible bachelor, you know."

She made herself smile.

"I *want* you to come, Howard."

"Thank you! I accept with pleasure," he said.

Tilly went to the door with him, and when he had gone, she returned to the spring-rocker. I want to be alone, just for a little while, she thought. I want to be quiet. The rocker squeaked softly, the trees rustled outside, Robert was talking to Pietro in the kitchen; Pauline was trotting about upstairs. But it was quiet in this corner. Forget Carola's frantic screaming; forget Howard stuttering ... Howard fainting; forget Taylor.

Taylor was the worst, she thought. He's only fifteen—and he's so bitter, so warped, so dreadfully lonely. Only fifteen ... What will happen to him now? Will Howard look after him? What will become of him? What—?

Robert came into the room, and the spring-rocker enchanted him; he sat on one arm of it.

"Go faster!" he commanded.

"I don't want to, Robert. I want to rest."

"Why?"

"Because I do."

"You're unreasonable," said Robert.

Tilly suppressed a smile at the unexpected word.

"Maybe I am," she said. "But I do want to rest for a little while, Robert. Why don't you go up and help Pauline?"

He thought that over, and then, to her relief, he turned away toward the stairs. I can't talk, she thought. I don't want to listen to anyone talking, not even Robert. I wish Howard and Mr. Cantrell weren't coming to dinner. I wish I could go upstairs and lie down—but with Pauline there ... It's coming to an end, Sam said. Lieutenant Levy knows who killed Sibyl. He'll arrest someone—and someone will scream.... Like Carola. It was so horrible to see her struggling like that, to hear her screaming like that ... To hear Robert crying so, when he saw the poor little dead things ... To hear Pauline, when she was telling about Taylor ...

Horrible voices, screaming, accusing, hating, terrified ... But if it's coming to an end, Robert and I can get away. Only where? I've let the apartment till the first of October, and if we board somewhere, it will cost so much. I've got to get Robert a new winter coat. He couldn't begin to get into his old one. And I want to start him in a good school next year. I don't know when I'll get that five hundred dollars from Sibyl—

And I don't care. I won't care. I won't even think about it. It's sordid and hateful to think about it, when Sibyl's dead. Murdered. That's what I ought to think about. About justice. About—

The front door of the cottage opened with a slam, and Tilly sprang to her feet. The wind ...? she thought. But there was no wind; only a light breeze. Before she had crossed the room, Carola had entered. Her white blouse was torn and dirty, her face was smudged, her blond hair tangled.

"Now!" she said. "*Now* you're going to get what's coming to you, you damn smug little bitch! You're going to be arrested, any minute. You'll be in jail tonight. And you'll end up in the electric chair!"

"What are you talking about?"

"You'll find out soon enough, you hussy! Dick Cantrell dragged me into his car. He dragged me along the ground by my feet—"

"He didn't."

"Shut up! He did! He locked me in my room, and he took the key away. He said he was sending a doctor to see me. He said I was going to be put away. Locked up, in some loony-bin, for ever and ever. Not me! I have a telephone in my room and I called up that policeman—what's his name? Levy. I told him how I'd *seen* you kill Sibyl."

"Leave my house," said Tilly. "At once. You've been drinking."

"*Your* house? You'll be in jail tonight, my fine kept woman. I told Levy what I'd seen. I saw you get the package of cyanide from Howard's desk, and I saw you go upstairs to Sibyl's bathroom. I saw you open that capsule and dump out the powder, and fill it up with the cyanide crystals, and put it back in the bottle. I told him I'd swear to it in court. I told him you'd killed Sibyl so that you could marry Howard. But you won't! You're going to die in the electric chair. You're going to be arrested any minute."

"Carola!" said Tilly, in horror. "Try to think what you're saying. Try—"

"Shut up! I got out of my room through the window. I hurt myself. I fell. But I got here ... I got here! I want to *see* you taken off to jail. I want to *see* you strapped down in the electric chair—"

"Madame?" called Pauline, from the stairway. "You wish me to help you? To telephone to the police? To Mr. Fleming?"

"No, thank you. Just keep Robert upstairs," Tilly answered.

Carola's out of her mind with drink, she thought. She's dangerous. She'd say anything, do anything, But I can cope with her.

For the first time in her life, she looked at a fellow-creature as an assailant; she appraised Carola, steadily, without fear. I'm taller than she is. I'm younger and stronger, and I'm in my right senses. If she won't leave, I'll put her out. If I have to, I'll throw her out.

"There!" cried Carola. "I hear a car! Now you'll see! Now you're going to be arrested!"

Levy appeared in the doorway, with the young policeman behind him.

"Here she is!" cried Carola. "The murderess! Arrest her!"

"Just a moment," said Levy, mildly. "We've got to do things in order, Mrs. Dexter."

"I told you I'd swear in court about what I saw. I *told* you—"

"Suppose we sit down for a moment, Mrs. Dexter. Mrs. MacDonald, too."

"Do you mean to say you *believe* what she's said?" Tilly demanded. "Any of it? There's not one word—"

"Just a moment," he said again, with the same mildness. "Now, if you'll both sit down, please ..."

"Why don't you arrest her?" cried Carola. "I've told you what I saw. Take her to jail!"

"Sit down!" said Levy, and, though he did not raise his voice, it was a command. Tilly did sit, on a straight-backed chair against the wall, and, in a moment, Carola flounced down on the sofa. Levy, in his well-cut dark uniform, stood facing them.

"I went to your house, as you requested, Mrs. Dexter," he said. "But you weren't there. The door of your room was locked."

"I got out of the window. I wanted to see her arrested."

"I knocked several times on your door, Mrs. Dexter, and when I got no answer, I unlocked the door. I found a considerable supply of cocaine there, and a syringe. Where did you procure the cocaine, Mrs. Dexter?"

"From a doctor."

"What is the doctor's name, Mrs. Dexter?"

"I don't know. I've forgotten. Just a doctor—somewhere in New York."

"Did you obtain regular supplies of cocaine from this doctor, Mrs. Dexter?"

"No! Drop it. It doesn't matter."

"Did Mr. Cantrell offer, some months ago, to pay your expenses, if you entered a private institution for the treatment of drug addiction?"

"No! He's a liar. I never took it. I got it for somebody else."

"You understand, Mrs. Dexter, that it is a criminal offense to procure cocaine to sell—"

"I didn't sell it. I—gave it away. Drop it!"

"Mrs. Dexter, I have received information that for the past six months you have been purchasing large supplies of barbiturate capsules, which you resold at a profit to—"

"Who told you that? It's a lie!"

"Mrs. Dexter, I have the names of two persons in this community who state that they have bought such capsules from you."

"Drop it!"

"Mrs. Dexter, I suggest that you undertook this illegal traffic in barbiturates in order to secure money for cocaine."

"*Drop it!*" she cried, almost in a scream. "I'm not going to talk about it. I won't answer any questions about it."

"This is a very serious charge, Mrs. Dexter."

"Drop it, I tell you! Don't bother me so."

"You wish to state that you saw Mrs. MacDonald take a package of cyanide crystals from Mr. Fleming's desk?"

"What?" she said. "Oh, that? Yes, I did."

"Where were you when you saw this, Mrs. Dexter?"

"Me? I was in the hall."

"Will you describe the package?"

"It was a little envelope. Of cyanide crystals."

"How did you know what was in the envelope, Mrs. Dexter?"

"Because—I did know."

"You stated that subsequently you saw Mrs. MacDonald filling a capsule with cyanide in the late Mrs. Fleming's bathroom. Where were you when you saw this?"

"Oh ... In the hall."

"At what time did you see this?"

"In—the morning."

"How long after you allege to have seen Mrs. MacDonald take the envelope from the library?"

"I don't ... Just a few moments."

"Did you follow Mrs. MacDonald upstairs?"

"Yes. I did! I was afraid she was going to kill Sibyl. I knew she wanted to, and I knew why. I knew—"

"Very well. What did you do, Mrs. Dexter, after you had seen Mrs. MacDonald fill this capsule with what you believed to be a fatal poison?"

Sweat was glistening on Carola's face; her lips were parted; her eyes were fixed on Levy's face, with a dreadful intensity.

"You're just trying to ... You're trying to ... Drop it! Let me alone!"

"What did you do, Mrs. Dexter, after you had seen Mrs. MacDonald preparing the capsule?" Levy asked, still mild, still patient.

And, Tilly thought, cruel as a cat with a mouse. He had already entangled Carola in her own lies, and Carola was half-aware of this. She was confused, frightened, helpless.

"Did you inform the late Mrs. Fleming of what you had seen?"

"I—wrote her a note."

"I see," said Levy. "How did you deliver this note, Mrs. Dexter?"

"I pushed it under her door."

"Did you knock at the door, Mrs. Dexter?"

"No. I thought she'd probably be asleep."

"You state that you believed the late Mrs. Fleming to have been in imminent danger. After pushing this note under her door, what further steps did you take to warn her, Mrs. Dexter?"

"I—" Carola began, and stopped, and a change came over her. She looked, Tilly thought, like a sleepwalker suddenly awake on the verge of an abyss, aware of the pit before her, rocked by a gale of wind.

"I didn't write any note," she said.

"How did you warn the late Mrs. Fleming?"

"I didn't warn her," Carola said. "You see, I wasn't sure." She spoke now with a sort of dull cautiousness. "You see, I didn't think Tilly would dare to do that. I thought she'd taken the cyanide to commit suicide with."

"You state that you saw Mrs. MacDonald fill a capsule."

"I didn't see that. Only after Sibyl was dead I knew it must have been that way. I only saw her take the cyanide out of Howard's desk."

"What reason did you have, Mrs. Dexter, for assuming that this package or envelope contained cyanide?"

"I stopped in to see Howard that morning—whenever it was—and he was talking to Sam Osborne about it. Howard said that he didn't want to keep such dangerous stuff around and he wanted Sam to take it away, to keep it somewhere. Sam said he would. But just then Howard was called to the telephone, and while his back was turned, Sam slipped the envelope into the desk drawer, and went out of the room."

"Did you later tell Mr. Fleming about this?"

"No, I didn't. I knew it would worry him, and he's such a frantic worrier. But I spoke to Sam about it, a little later, and he said he'd already taken the stuff away."

She rose, stood with her hands in the pockets of her torn skirt.

"I want to go home now," she said.

"I'm afraid that's not possible, Mrs. Dexter," said Levy. "The District Attorney wants to see you, in his office."

"Not now," she said. "I want to go home. I've got to go home."

"Mrs. Dexter, there is a serious charge pending against you. Illegal possession of narcotics."

"Oh, let me alone! Let me alone," she cried. "Later on, you can hound me and torment me, but now I've got to go *home*."

"Sergeant Crawford will drive you to the District Attorney's office now, Mrs. Dexter."

"I won't go! Not now! I want to go *home*."

"Mrs. Dexter, if you raise any further objections, I shall be obliged to place you under arrest."

"Me?" said Carola. "When you have that murderess here? When—"

"Sergeant!" said Levy, and the young policeman stepped into the room. Then Tilly saw that Pauline and Robert were standing in the little hall hand in hand. Pauline ought to know better! she thought, with indignation. She ought to keep the child away.

"Mrs. Dexter," said Levy.

"No!" said Carola, and then almost at once: "Yes," she said. "I'll go. But I've got to stop off at my own house first."

"Sergeant Crawford has his instructions, Mrs. Dexter."

"I tell you I've got to stop home! I have to—change my clothes. I have to—I've got to!"

"I'm afraid that's impossible, Mrs. Dexter."

"Damn you!" she cried. "I *will* go home!"

She was pitiable and appalling in her desperation. It's that drug she wants, Tilly thought in a sort of wonder. It's horrible, but I'm sorry for her.

"The District Attorney is waiting for you, Mrs. Dexter," said Levy.

She rushed out of the room, her long fair hair floating behind her. In the hall she stopped, staring down at Robert.

"Here!" she said, taking a little package out of her pocket and thrusting it at the child. "Here! Here's a present for you. See how you like it."

"Robert!" cried Tilly, springing to her feet. "Give that to me! At once!"

But he had snatched his hand away from Pauline, and had started up the stairs, with a squeal of excitement. It's that cyanide! Tilly thought.

She nearly caught him at the head of the stairs, but he darted into the bathroom and turned the key; she heard him give a breathless little laugh.

"Open the door, darling," she said pleasantly and calmly.

There was no answer, but she believed she heard a rustle of paper, as if he were unwrapping a package.

Take deep breaths, she told herself. Deep, slow breaths. Don't rattle the knob, don't pound on the door. Don't be so angry at him, so fiercely angry you would like to smash in the door, and grab that package, and hit him, push him, knock him down.

"Open the door, darling," she said again.

There was no answer, no sound but her own loud breathing.

"Open the door, *bébé*," said Pauline's voice behind her. "We go to see if my little dog arrives, no?"

The key turned in the lock, and Tilly pulled the door open. There was a scrap of white tissue paper on the floor, and a bit of string. She unclasped his hands, roughly, but they were empty.

"What was in that package?" she demanded.

"The lady gave it to me!" he protested.

She did push him, back against the wall. She felt in the pocket of his shorts, and brought out what she felt there. It was a ring, an old-fashioned one, a plain gold band in which was set a long oval softly-gleaming opal, circled by tiny diamonds.

"Is that what she gave you?" Tilly asked, and he nodded his head. "You bad, horrible, naughty child!" she cried. "You bad, horrible little thing!

Don't you ever dare to run away again, when I call you."

"Well ... You can keep it, Mommy," said Robert softly.

CHAPTER FIFTEEN

"The ring of poor Madame Fleming ... " said Pauline.

"Yes," Tilly agreed.

"And how did that one come to secure it, I ask you, madame."

"I don't know," Tilly answered.

And I don't care, either, she thought. I'm—I guess I'm tired. Because I don't care—about any of it now.

"You will now telephone, madame?"

"Telephone? To whom?"

"But, madame, to the police! They have gone, the young one, also the Lieutenant. But now you telephone, but, of course, madame. You report about the ring, which that one without any doubt stole from poor Madame Fleming."

"Yes, I'll tell them,"

"But, madame, without delay, I implore you! That one has made frightful accusations against you. Report this ring, and it will be sure that she is a thief, a liar. Who then will believe what she screams? Me, I know very well why she does this."

"Robert, run along to your own room and play," said Tilly.

But he was not going to run; not he. He went off along the hall, with his hands in his pockets, his small dark head bent, tottering as he placed one foot in a straight line before the other.

"I don't know why she hates me so," Tilly said.

"But, madame, I think it is not hatred. I think it is fear."

"You mean she's afraid she might be suspected?"

"No, madame. That I do not think. What motive can she have for this murder? She gains nothing. She loses a good customer for her wicked drugs. No. Me, I understand human nature perfectly. She tells this story that you took the poison from the desk, because she wishes to protect Mr. Fleming."

"You mean she thinks *he* did it?"

"She does not think, that one. She is only in panic. Ah! she says to herself. I have lost my good customer, Madame Fleming. But from Mr. Fleming I can always procure a little money, perhaps even much money. So he must not be molested. She thinks if Mr. Osborne tells the police that Mr. Fleming left this poison in the bureau, that will be bad. For of all persons, he has the most to profit. He— The telephone rings, madame! Shall I answer?"

"No, thanks," said Tilly, and turned and ran down the stairs. It's the police, she thought. They'll want to question me about what Carola said. Perhaps they'll "hold" me. I've read that in the newspapers. "Held for further questioning." That must mean prison. I can't ... I won't.

She went to the telephone in the little hall and took up the receiver.

"Yes?" she said, in a cold, clear voice.

"Mrs. MacDonald?—Abbott speaking."

"What do you want?" she cried, shocked.

"The police have given me permission to take Taylor back to the camp. We're leaving now. And I wanted to say good-bye, Mrs. MacDonald. And to tell you how much—how I appreciate having—it's been a privilege to meet you."

"Oh, thank you," said Tilly.

"Your small son is indeed fortunate, Mrs. MacDonald. Your—er—the influence ..."

"Oh, thank you!" said Tilly again. "Good-bye and good luck, Mr. Abbott!"

And she hung up the instrument. I didn't mean to be rude to him, she thought, but I can't *talk* any more. I don't want to think. I'm tired. I never felt so tired—and so stupid. She crossed the room to the spring-rocker and sat down in it. It's so comfortable, she thought. But I can't rest. I know that. Something will happen. Someone will come, and I'll have to listen. I'll have to talk.

There were footsteps on the staircase. Pauline came down, with Robert behind her.

"Madame ...?" she said, in eager inquiry.

"I can't tell you now," said Tilly. "But you'll hear later, Pauline."

"I understand, madame, but perfectly! A secret of the police. You will report the ring?"

"Yes, I will," said Tilly.

"Now, madame, if you permit ... I go to make some little arrangement in the kitchen—a little ragout of veal—and then, if you permit, I should like to go in my room and rest a little."

"Certainly!" said Tilly. "You must be very tired, Pauline."

"I am tired, madame, and I am sad, for my little dog. But with me, I rest an hour. I spring up, refreshed as at sixteen."

"That's wonderful," said Tilly.

Pauline went into the kitchen with Robert, and Tilly sat in a daze until they returned.

"Now, madame, if I can do something for you, before I rest?" Pauline asked, pushing her hair back from her forehead with a dramatic gesture of fatigue.

"No. No, thanks. Go upstairs and lie down, Pauline," she said, "and Robert and I will bring you a pot of tea."

"Oh! Madame is too good!" Pauline protested.

"No. Go ahead," said Tilly.

"It is too much trouble, madame!"

"No, it isn't," said Tilly. Go on upstairs, and shut up.

Pauline started up the stairs, bending forward, and holding the rail, in what Tilly felt to be an exaggerated exhaustion. Well, let her, if she wants. She's had a hard day. She really is tired. And she seems to think that tea is a sort of medicine.

She put on the kettle, and looked about the unfamiliar little kitchen for a tea pot, a tray, cup, saucer, spoon. Robert climbed on a chair, to examine the shelves in the cupboard.

"Look!" he said. "Look, Mommy! Here's a cup!"

It was a huge old-fashioned white mug with gold lip and handle, and "Grandpa" written on it in gold.

"It's too big, darling."

"No, it *isn't!* She'd *like* it."

"I've got another cup here for Pauline. Get down, Robert, and don't touch the china. You might break something."

"*Look*, Mommy! Look at the little tiny, tiny cup and the little tiny little pitcher! Look!"

"Yes, darling," Tilly said, turning her head. "It's a doll's tea set. Now get down, Robert."

"There's a little *tiny* sugar-bowl with sugar in it. Look!"

"Put the lid back on it, and get down from that chair."

"I want to take this little tiny little sugar-bowl up to Pauline."

"No. Leave it there."

"I *want* to take it up to Pauline! It's *pretty*. It's got flowers on it."

"All right!" said Tilly with a sigh. "Put it on the tray."

"I want to carry it myself!"

"If you promise not to eat any of it, Robert."

"I promise," he said.

Tilly carried the tray and Robert went up the stairs before her, with the sugar-bowl.

"Now, I don't remember which is Pauline's room," she said, confronted by four closed doors.

"*This* one!" said Robert.

Tilly knocked, and Pauline opened the door; she was wearing a very long gray taffeta slip, and over it a knitted bed jacket of pale pink, with a big rosy bow under her chin.

"Ah ... But madame is too good ...!" she cried.

"*I* brought the sugar-bowl," said Robert.

"Then you too are good!" said Pauline.

Tilly put the tray on the table.

"Come, Robert!" she said.

"I think I'll stay here with Pauline."

"No. Pauline wants to rest."

"For a little moment only, *bébé*," said Pauline. "Then I come down, and I prepare your little tea, eh?"

"*I* don't drink tea."

"No, no. You shall have something very nice, eh?"

"All right," said Robert.

Someone had brought his toys here; Tilly waited while he got what he wanted from his room; then they went downstairs together. Tilly sat down in the spring-rocker again, and Robert sat on the floor across the room, and began taking his stone blocks out of their box. He's very clever with them, she thought. Maybe he'll be an architect.

The rocker squeaked softly, the trees rustled, like water. It's very dark here, for only half-past three, she thought. Maybe it's going to rain. Or maybe it's a shadow. It's coming to an end. And then someone will scream.... We have to stay here. We can't get away....

But I hate this little house. Like a witch's house, in a forest ... Hansel and Gretel, in my old picture-book, walking hand in hand through a forest ... And Hansel looked like Robert. No! That's horrible. The witch put him in the oven.... Did Pauline look like a witch, so pale and sharp-nosed, with stringy hair?

"Mommy!" called Robert, pulling her sleeve. "It's too dark. I can't see. Mommy, put the light on! Mommy, *hurry up!*"

She opened her eyes, and it was dark; Robert's face looked white.

"*Hurry up*, Mommy!" he cried, pulling at her sleeve.

She rose in haste, filled with the same urgency that possessed the child. But it was a strange room, and she did not know where a light was. She moved forward, with Robert still clutching her sleeve.

"Where's a lamp, Robert?"

"Here! Here! Hurry up!"

Her outstretched hand touched a table, groped forward, to the smooth cold base of a lamp; she pulled the dangling chain, a pale yellow light blossomed.

"But, Robert ...! Why didn't you call me before, dear? It was too dark to play, wasn't it?"

"I guess I went to sleep," he said, doubtfully.

"Where? On the sofa?"

"No ... I guess, on the floor."

She looked at her wrist watch.

"Heavens! It's twenty past six! We'll go and ask Pauline for your supper."

He ran ahead of her, and pushed open the swing-door, and stopped. Coming behind him, Tilly saw that the kitchen was dark, and it was, she thought, filled with a stifling vapor, a sickening stench. Fire ...? she thought. She felt along the wall for a switch, but found none.

"Hold the door open, Robert," she said, and by the pallid light from the sitting-room, she went into that dark and stifling room. There was a light hanging from the ceiling; she felt for the chain, and pulled it; it made a grating click and no light came. There's got to be a light, she said to herself. I've got to see ... She pulled the chain again, and this time it worked, a feeble little light under a fluted white shade.

Smoke was coming from a pot on the gas-stove; she turned off the burner, and raised the lid, and an ill-smelling puff came out; there was nothing in there but a black, sticky paste. Like witches make, she thought. Stop being so silly. It's the ragout Pauline was making. She must have overslept too. We all fell asleep, Pauline and Robert and I, and it got dark.

That's nothing. I'm sorry Pauline's ragout is spoiled. But it's nothing. It's not important, not serious. She set the pot in the sink; when she turned on the water, there was a fierce hissing, a cloud of steam. That's nothing.

"I'll get you some supper, Robert," she said.

"No, thank you. I'll go and get Pauline."

"No, Robert. Let her alone. She's tired."

"She said she was going to get me something nice."

"I'll get you something nice."

"No, thank you. I want to go up and get Pauline."

"Well, you can't."

"I want to go upstairs to the bathroom."

"No. There's a bathroom down here."

"Why can't I go upstairs?"

"Because I say no. Sit down here, and I'll see what I can find."

"I want to go *upstairs!* I want to see *Pauline!*"

"No!" she cried. "Sit down there and stop bothering me! You're not going upstairs."

"Well, *why?*"

She did not answer him; she could not explain, even to herself, the horrible fear and oppression that weighed upon her. We all went to sleep, and it got dark. And what happened, in the dark? Nearly half-past six, and Pauline's dinner is ruined. Maybe I ought to go upstairs and—wake her up.

But not now. Not yet. I'll give Robert his supper first. Then I'll go up.

But not now. Not yet.

CHAPTER SIXTEEN

It took time to find things, in this unfamiliar place. She laid a checked cloth on the kitchen table; she set out brown bread and butter and honey, and a big glass of milk for him.

"That's nice, isn't it?" she asked.

"Yes, thank you," he answered.

He sat at the table and began to eat, in silence. But he's not being sulky, she thought. Why doesn't he say something?

"Some more bread and butter, Robert?"

"Yes, thank you."

"And more milk?"

"Yes, thank you."

"Don't you feel like talking, Robert?"

"No, thank you."

Let him alone. He's only a child. He can't tell you if he feels ... Feels what? Frightened? Sleepy?

"I'll be back in a moment, Robert. You go on eating."

She went through the dimly-lit sitting-room into the narrow hall, and tried the front door. It was unlatched. Anyone could have pushed it open; anyone could have come into the house. In the dark. But who? Why should I think that anyone came in?

Pauline was so tired that she's overslept. In a few moments I'll go up and wake her. She'll be so upset about her dinner, poor soul.

"There are some nice red apples here, Robert. Would you like one?"

"No, thank you."

"Then—you've finished now. We'll go upstairs and you can have a nice, warm bath."

"Is there anybody else upstairs?"

"Why, no darling. Only Pauline. Who else did you think was there?"

He was silent for a moment, sitting straight in his chair at the table.

"Is Pauline dead?" he asked.

"Robert! Why do you ask that?"

"I went upstairs and I knocked on her door and she didn't answer, and I went in and she looked—all dead."

"When did you go upstairs, Robert?"

"When I was building with my blocks, and you had your eyes closed, so I went upstairs. Will she get well again, Mommy?"

Now I have to go up, Tilly thought. But not Robert.

"You stay here, darling," she said. "I'll be down—"

"No, thank you. I'd rather go with you."

"I'll come down in just a moment, and then I'll tell you a story."

"No! I don't *want* to stay down here alone."

"Robert—," she began, but she could think of no way to appeal to him, no way to reach him in his strange mood.

The door-bell rang. She put her hand to her neck, and stood motionless, frozen in fear.

"That's the door-bell!" said Robert, with an impatient frown.

"Yes. Wait here, darling, just a moment."

But he got down from his chair; he went close behind her. The branch of a tree was scraping back and forth across a screen; it seemed to her that the fumes of the burnt and ruined dinner had made a fog in the little house.

"Why don't you open the door?" Robert demanded, angrily. "Maybe it is the little new dog for Pauline. Open the door, mommy!"

She opened it, only a crack.

"Tilly?" said Howard's voice.

"Oh, *Howard!*" she cried. "Oh, come in, Howard!"

He entered, closing the door after him; he crossed the dim little sitting-room, and turned on another lamp that stood on top of a tall and very narrow bookcase. But this light, too, was feeble, under a lemon-colored shade.

"Tilly!" he said. "I smell smoke!"

"It's nothing. Something that was cooking got burnt."

"Is everything all right here, Tilly?" he asked. "Everything cozy?"

"Howard, I'm worried about Pauline. I wish—"

"Pauline's all dead," said Robert, with a sort of smug satisfaction.

"What's the child mean?" Howard demanded, sharply.

"I don't know. But she hasn't come downstairs yet. And the ragout she was cooking is burnt, ruined."

"She probably fell asleep," said Howard. "If the dinner's spoiled, we'll go to the Inn."

"Howard, I thought if you'd just go up and knock at her door ...?"

"I? Well, see here, Tilly, if she's asleep—tired out—why not let her alone? I'll leave a note—"

"Howard, I want to know. If you'll keep Robert down here, I'll run up—"

"I'm going with you!" cried Robert. "I won't stay here alone."

"Cousin Howard will be with you, Robert. And I'll be back in a minute."

"No! I want to go with you!"

"Howard, can't you—tell him a story, maybe?"

"I cannot," said Howard. "I couldn't undertake to look after such an unmanageable child. And it's not necessary. No reason to disturb Pauline. Come! We'll go along to the Inn—"

"Howard, I can't leave the house until I *know*. Just keep Robert here—even if you have to hold him, even if he's naughty—"

"I'll do nothing of the sort! It's all nonsense."

"Then will you—just go up and knock at her door?"

"I will not, Tilly."

She felt her heart pounding; she forced herself to breathe deeply and quietly; she forced herself to look at Howard.

"Why—won't you go up, Howard?" she asked.

"Dear God in Heaven!" he cried. "Haven't we had enough ...?"

"Then you do think something has happened to Pauline?" she asked.

"No! I do not! Simply, I—that smell of burning—is—is sickening. We'll go to the Inn at once—"

"Not me," said Tilly. "I won't leave this house until I see about Pauline."

"Tilly ... I've had so much—too much. I—you shouldn't ask me—"

"I won't, any more."

She looked at him, and it seemed to her that he was changing before her eyes, that he had changed. He seemed no longer the kindly and pompously courteous Howard; his face, which she had, until now, thought agreeable, but weak, looked strong now, the mouth set, the eyes steady. And it was, she thought, the strength that fear gives. The frightened creature can break bonds, can plot and plan, can fight, or run.

He is the one who profits the most, Pauline had said. If he had desperately needed money, if he had been desperately longing to break his bonds and be free ...?

I don't know ... she thought. But anyhow, he's got to be kept away from Robert.

She moved, to look at the sitting-room door. "If you'll come out into the hall—"

"Why?" he asked, but he followed her, and so did Robert.

She pushed the child back into the room, and turned the key and put it into her pocket. He began to scream, and pound on the door, and it was to her the very sound of a nightmare, her child terrified, abandoned.

"Tilly!" said Howard, catching her by the arm.

"Let me alone!" she cried, jerking away from him.

He caught her arm again, and she pushed him with all her strength, so that he staggered back. It doesn't matter, she thought. Nothing matters—but this.

This has happened before, she thought. In a nightmare. Because I *know*. She knew the steep and narrow little staircase; she knew the feeling of someone standing silent in the hall below, watching her; she knew the darkness and the silence there would be in the upper hall. She felt along the wall, and found a switch, and another dim light came on, to show her four closed doors. I remember which is Pauline's room, she thought. I must knock, I must wait. I must knock again.

There would be no answer. There was no answer. Now you must open the door, and it will be dark in there. It was dark, and close, and there was a queer odor in the air. That's it, she thought. The poison.

A faint light came in from the hall, and she went in, and turned on the lamp by the bedside. Now look at her. Not with horror, not with any fear. This is your fellow-creature, and she is dead, and everyone dies.

She turned away and went down the stairs, and Howard was in the hall, leaning against the door, with his hand over his eyes.

"Call the police, Howard," she said. "Pauline's dead."

She unlocked the door, and Robert flew at her, hitting her furiously.

"I *hate* you!" he cried. "I *hate* you!"

She took his hands and held them together.

"I don't think you do," she said. "Not any more. I had to go away for a little while, darling, but now I'm back."

"I don't *want* you back! You locked me up! You went away!"

She freed his hands and moved away, back to the spring-rocker. Pauline was lying dead upstairs, but the cottage had lost its atmosphere of bewitched horror for Tilly. I'm ready, she said to herself.

Those were the words she found for what she felt now. Robert stood before her for a moment; his face was grimy and tear-stained; the knuckles of one hand were grazed; he was breathing hard, with a sort of snort, the ebb-tide of his weeping. Then he turned his back on her and crossed the room.

He was frightened, she thought, he was terrified. Maybe it's one of those things you read about, things a child never gets over. Maybe he'll have nightmares all his life, about being locked up somewhere, alone.

But it's done. It's happened. And other things will happen to him; he'll be hurt; he'll be frightened again. No matter what I do, I can't protect him—from living. I can just stand by him, and let him feel sure of that.

I can't refuse to listen to people, refuse to answer. I can't get away—with Robert—from horrible and dangerous things. From living. I went up those stairs; I knocked at that door. And I can go on now. I'm ready now.

"Robert," she said, "suppose we go in the little bathroom down here and get your hands and face washed? Then you can lie down on the sofa in here and take a little rest?"

He did not answer; he still stood with his back turned toward her, but when she took his hand, he went with her. His grazed knuckles had bled a little; he winced, and frowned, at the smart of soap on them, but he did not try to pull away.

He'll get over it, she thought. I don't suppose there ever was a child on earth that didn't have things that frightened and hurt it. But we get over things. Even that telegram about Ian. I thought I couldn't bear it, couldn't go on. But we do go on, most of us.

When they went into the sitting-room, Howard was there.

"Levy's coming," he said. "I telephoned. I— My God! What must you think of me, Tilly?"

"I think you're kind and generous," she said. "Here, Robert! Put your head on this pillow and just rest for a while."

The child stretched out, flat on his back, and lay there with his eyes wide open. He's getting sleepy, though, Tilly thought.

"I know how I must look to you," Howard said. "Contemptible, cowardly ... It's all very well. It's true. I—when I found Sibyl like that ... All I could think of was—that I'd be the first one suspected. I mean—the husband ... I mean—the chief one to benefit ... That's why I took that chloral hydrate. As if I'd been poisoned, too ... I had the glass of whiskey in my hand, when I went upstairs, and I put the chloral hydrate in it. That's why I got Osborne not to mention our work—the book, you know—the photographs ... I—I thought that if the police knew we had cyanide ... I—to be frank—I couldn't stand the thought of being dragged into court.... I can see now, that I simply made things worse...."

"Yes," Tilly said. "Do you know—do you think you know who did it, Howard?"

"No ...," he answered. "This may sound like an odd thing to say—may sound heartless, perhaps. But, to tell you the truth, I didn't think much about that. About who was guilty."

I didn't, either, Tilly thought. She said, "And now—Pauline."

"She may not be dead, Tilly. I mean to say, a layman—"

"She's dead."

"Very well!" he said, with another frown. "Natural causes—why not? Overworked herself today—strained her heart—something of that sort. A layman ..."

He let the sentence trail off, and Tilly had nothing she wanted to say to him. Lieutenant Levy is coming, she thought, and he'll find out. That's his business, just as he said, to find the dangerous people and shut them up. To protect the people who aren't dangerous and savage and utterly irresponsible. Someone's killed Pauline, murdered her. I know it. I think I knew it before.

Then a new thought came to her that made her heart jump. She glanced at Howard, saw him standing, with his knuckles pressed against his front teeth, his brows drawn together. Like a frightened animal gnawing at a trap?

He lied before, she thought. He took that—other drug; I've forgotten the name. He didn't think about anything, care about anything but keeping himself out of trouble. Suppose he knew that Sibyl's death was caused by some horrible mistake? Suppose he'd made the mistake himself, by some stupid accident?

Would he let someone else take the blame? I think he would. He's cowardly. And perhaps cowards are dangerous—always dangerous. To everyone. If Pauline knew anything—if he even thought she knew something ...?

Thank God, I don't know anything. Howard's always been kind and generous to me and to Robert. It was kind of him to fix up this cottage for us. But if I did know anything, I'd tell it. No matter what it might lead to. The people who are willing to kill have to be—put away. For the sake of the others. You have to be on one side or the other.

The door-bell rang, and Robert sat up, pale and dazed with sleepiness. "*I'll* go!"

"No!" said Howard, sharply. "Lie down again—"

"Let him go," said Tilly. "It'll be Lieutenant Levy."

But it was Cantrell who entered, with Sam Osborne behind him.

"Sam!" she cried, and tears sprang to her eyes, began to run down her face. "I'm—glad to see you," she said.

He was wearing a gray flannel suit that looked too big for him, a green and blue bow tie that was crooked; he had a ruffled, disturbed look. But— I'm so glad to see him ..., she thought, and could not stop her tears.

"Okay," he said, laying his hand on her shoulder. "Take it easy."

"No," she said. "No ... Pauline ... I don't want to talk with Robert here."

"You don't mean ...?"

"Yes, I do. It's—that. Howard's called the police. Robert, lie down again, won't you?"

"No!" Robert answered, angrily, and fell back on the pillow. The door-bell rang again, but this time he did not stir. As Osborne and Cantrell went out into the hall, Tilly closed the door after them; she heard quiet voices outside, she heard footsteps mounting the stairs, footsteps overhead; a car stopped before the house, the door-bell rang again.

"Tilly!" said Howard.

"Robert's asleep," she whispered.

"Tilly, I—can't stand any more of this. I—I'm afraid I'll have to get a doctor."

"They're sure to have a doctor with them, Howard. When he's finished upstairs—"

"My God, no! No. I'll call up Crowdie. I—all this—the—the whole— *atmosphere* ... It's—my God! All I ever asked for was—peace and quiet—

an orderly life—decency—and dignity—"

Quite a lot to ask, isn't it? Tilly thought. And who was expected to provide it?

"I'm sorry, Howard," she said, and she was truly sorry for him. "Why don't you sit down and smoke a cigarette?"

"Why, yes. Yes. Thanks," he said. "Got to get hold of myself. I suppose they'll be asking more questions. More questions ... Raking up all sorts of—of unnecessary things ... I—we all have things—we all make mistakes.... If the police would stick to the point ... Not go raking up things—"

Let him go on; maybe it did him good. But she ceased to listen to him; she was back in the spring-rocker, and comfortable there, not drowsy, not tired, but ready. It might be a long time, and what was coming would be hard, it would surely be horrible. Very well. You can wait. You can listen, you can answer, you can endure.

Someone was coming down the stairs; someone was telephoning in the hall outside; she could hear the click of the dial, the murmur of a voice, footsteps remounting the stairs. There were footsteps overhead, heavy, and very stout, she thought. Perhaps there was something up there in Pauline's room that would point immediately to the murderer. Perhaps they know already, she thought. Then they won't have to ask questions.

They were coming down, a trampling herd of deliberate steps that shook the wall. Levy opened the door.

"Please!" said Tilly. "Robert's asleep in here. Can't we talk somewhere else?"

"There's the dining room," said Howard. "But it's not quite in order yet."

"All right. Where is it?" asked Levy, with a curtness Tilly had not heard from him before.

"This way," Howard said, and as he went out into the hall, Tilly followed him and closed the door.

"Do you want me, Lieutenant?" she asked.

"Yes," he answered.

Howard had opened a door to an airless and hideous little dining room, the walls papered in dark-red, a dark carpet so padded that it felt like damp grass; there was a round pedestal table in the center and over it a hanging light with a dark-red shade. There were six chairs ranged against the wall; Levy drew one up to the table and sat down, but the others remained standing; the police doctor, the young sergeant, another man in uniform, Cantrell, Sam Osborne, Howard, and Tilly.

"I have some questions to ask you," said Levy, not mild now, not patient. "You are not obliged to answer, but I caution you that evasive, untrue, or incomplete answers will be considered as obstructing the police in the performance of their duty. This woman Pauline Duval has been killed this evening by cyanide poisoning—"

"Suicide!" said Howard. "She was in a bad state—hysterical—"

Levy gave him a glance that silenced him.

"Mrs. MacDonald!" he said. "A chair, Crawford. Sit down, Mrs. Mac-Donald. Are you prepared to answer the questions put to you truthfully and without reservation?"

"Yes," she answered.

"I understand you arrived in this house at approximately half-past two this afternoon. Is that correct?"

"I don't know. I didn't look at the time."

"Very well. We can establish the time later. What persons have been in this house since your arrival here?"

I'll just tell the truth, she thought. About everything.

"Mr. Cantrell and Mrs. Dexter were here before I came," she said. "I saw them leaving. Mr. Osborne came in with me, and later Mr. Fleming came. Then Mrs. Dexter came back, and you found her here. And there was a young man working here; Pietro, they called him."

"Mrs. MacDonald, did anyone else enter this house after your arrival?"

"I don't know."

"You don't know?"

"You see, after I'd taken a tea-tray up to Pauline, we fell asleep, my son and myself. It was dark when I waked up, and the front door wasn't locked."

"You state that you took a tea-tray up to Miss Duval?"

"Yes. She was very tired."

"Crawford?" said Levy, holding out his hand, and the young sergeant stepped forward, holding something wrapped in a handkerchief. Levy set it on the table, and let the handkerchief fall open.

"Do you recognize this exhibit, Mrs. MacDonald?" he asked.

Don't let me be pale! Don't let my heart shake me so! Let me answer.

"Yes. It's a sugar-bowl," she said.

It was the little blue and gold doll's sugar-bowl Robert had carried up-stairs.

"Did you take this sugar-bowl to Miss Duval's room?"

"Yes."

"What was in this sugar-bowl when you took it up to Miss Duval?"

"I—didn't look. I just thought it was sugar."

"How did you know that the bowl wasn't empty?"

"It—didn't feel empty."

"You didn't remove the lid at any time, Mrs. MacDonald?"

"No. I was rather tired myself, and I didn't know where to find things. I just—thought it was sugar."

"Mrs. MacDonald. When you took up the tea-tray—with this sugar-bowl—who was in this house?"

"Just Pauline and Robert and myself."

"Mrs. MacDonald. To your knowledge, did any person or persons enter this house after you had taken up the tea-tray?"

"Mr. Fleming came, but much later."

"Did Mr. Fleming go upstairs?"

"No."

"Mrs. MacDonald, do you suggest that, during the time you state you were asleep, someone entered this house and tampered with the contents of this sugar-bowl?"

"No, I don't 'suggest' anything. I only said that someone could have come in without my hearing."

"But to your knowledge no one had access to this sugar-bowl prior to our arrival?"

"No. Not to my—knowledge."

"You are willing to state, then, that according to your knowledge, this sugar-bowl and its contents are as they were when you took them to Miss Duval?"

"I didn't look in the sugar-bowl. I don't know if somebody else got into the house—"

He lifted the little blue lid by its gold knob.

"Do you recognize the contents of this bowl, Mrs. MacDonald?"

"No. I didn't look in it before."

"This bowl contains cyanide crystals, Mrs. MacDonald."

"I didn't know."

"Mrs. MacDonald, are you prepared to confirm your statement that you took this bowl, without examining its contents, without ascertaining whether or not it was empty, and placed it on a tray, which you then carried up a flight of stairs to Miss Duval's room?"

"I didn't look in it."

I will not let Robert get into this. He looked in it, he said it was sugar, and I let it go. He carried it up. In front of me. Suppose he'd come behind me? He's only five. He might so easily have wanted to take some....

"It seems evident, at present, that Miss Duval believed this to be sugar, and put a certain amount, not yet determined, into a cup of tea. Two or three sips—"

"It's my fault," said Tilly. "I should have looked. It's my fault."

"Can you suggest by what method the cyanide crystals were put into the sugar-bowl, Mrs. MacDonald?"

"No. No, I can't."

"Exactly where did you find this bowl, Mrs. MacDonald?"

"On a shelf in the kitchen cupboard."

"I shall ask you to show me—"

"Wait!" cried Howard, with a sort of gasp. "Wait ...!"

"Wait for what, Mr. Fleming?"

"I put the—the crystals in the bowl. Weeks ago. I —I looked around.... I couldn't find a jar ... So I used that. I—I put it on a shelf in the dark-room we'd fitted up here. I—at the time—there was no one living in the house. I—no one. I—no one used the house. I—I—I assume—full responsibility."

"That's where young Taylor got the stuff, then," said Osborne. "There never was any envelope full of cyanide, addressed to me, in the desk here, or in any other desk."

"I—I—assume responsibility for that, too," said Howard. "For the boy. For what he did. I—"

"I've got some of this responsibility, myself," said Osborne. "The day af-ter Mrs. Fleming's death, I came to search the place—"

"I asked you to," said Howard. "I—I thought that if—if cyanide were found here, there would be—there would be—complications. I—"

"Fleming said there were some cyanide crystals in a blue jar, in the dark-room," Osborne went on. "Naturally, we kept pretty careful track of the stuff, how much we bought, how much we used, and so on. So I looked, all right. Nothing in the dark-room. I looked in both the bathrooms, in the kitchen. Trouble is, I was looking for a blue jar, and I wouldn't call that thing a jar. I probably saw it, because I looked in the kitchen cupboard, but I didn't bother with it. I suppose Taylor put it there, when he'd taken what he wanted."

"I—understood ...," said Howard. "I understood you—"

"I know," said Osborne. "I told you I'd searched the place thoroughly—which was true, in a way, and that I hadn't found any blue jar or any cyanide." He paused for a moment. "When I come to think of it," he said, "I remember a little doll's tea-set. I must have stood six inches from that bowl ..."

"Very well," said Levy, rising. "That's all."

"How do you mean that's all?" asked Osborne, startled.

"I shan't need to ask you any further questions—at the present moment," said Levy. "Or Mrs. MacDonald. Or Mr. Fleming. I'll lay the facts before the Horton County District Attorney, and he'll decide whether or not to make a charge of criminal negligence against any or all of you."

"Not Mrs. MacDonald," said Osborne. "There's absolutely no reason to suspect that she knew what was in that damn bowl."

"There's still less reason to believe that any woman would carry a bowl up a flight of stairs without troubling to see whether or not the bowl was empty, or what it contained. Unless she had accepted the statement of a second person that the bowl contained sugar."

"What 'second person'?" Osborne asked.

Levy glanced at him, and looked away.

"The District Attorney will undoubtedly want to question all three of you, later on," he said. "None of you must leave this vicinity without his authorization."

"I'd like to make a statement," said Cantrell. "Not that I think it's going to help much, but I want to get it off my chest."

For the first time, he seemed handsome to Tilly, straight and stalwart, his ruddy face composed, dignified, a little sad.

"I'm directly responsible for Sibyl's murder," said Cantrell. "I'm not going to deny it. Weeks ago, Carola brought this capsule out of her purse. She told me she'd filled it with cyanide that she'd got hold of when she was watching you and Osborne working on some photographs. She told me she'd fixed up the capsule, carried it with her all the time, so that she could commit suicide if—as she put it—things got worse. She meant, if the time came when she didn't have enough money to buy her cocaine. I didn't believe she had poison in the capsule. She was always talking about suicide, when she needed money. And—" He was silent for a moment. "I'll be candid about it," he said. "I did have doubts about it. But, to tell you the truth, even if I'd been much surer than I ever was, I don't think I'd have taken any steps. I'd talked to four or five doctors about her—and they weren't hopeful. Not one of them. She could have been sent away, for a cure. But there aren't many cures. And—well, you remember what she was like, even three years ago, Howard."

"Yes," Howard said. "I remember. Popular, very pretty. Looked ten or fifteen years younger than now. Yes..."

"As soon as I heard the facts about poor Sibyl," Cantrell said, "I felt pretty sure that this capsule was somehow involved in it, but—"

"But you deliberately withheld this vital information from the police," said Levy.

"It was wrong," said Cantrell. "I admit it. But I didn't want to drag Carola into the thing. She—in her present condition—she couldn't hold her own. She's careless, y' know—to the point of recklessness. Anyone might have stolen that capsule from her purse, or it's equally probable that she might have left it lying around somewhere, anywhere. If anyone else had been accused, I'd have come forward, but in the circumstances ..."

"You did not consider the possibility that Mrs. Dexter might be guilty?"

"Carola?" said Cantrell. "Lord, no! I've known her for years. And anyhow—" He paused, and the color rose in his face. "If I had considered that ... Very well, damn it! I did. But there wasn't any possible motive. I mean—she'd have everything to lose and nothing to gain. And even if she's—well, not quite herself, these days, she wouldn't murder an old friend, for no reason. I've known her for years," he said, again.

That sounds ridiculous, childish, Tilly thought. But I guess we're all like that.

"But you didn't come forward," said Levy. "These two deaths could both have been prevented. But they weren't. If the police had been informed that Mrs. Dexter was in possession of a capsule which she had declared to contain cyanide, the capsule would have been examined, and she would have been put under restraint. Before a murder was committed. If the police had been informed promptly that a blue 'jar' containing cyanide crystals was missing from this house, my men would have made a search. And you can take my word for it that they'd have found it. Before an innocent person was killed."

They were all listening to him, in silence.

"Each one of you four had an idea of 'protecting' someone," he went on. "You withheld information from the police. You protected no one." He put his note-book into his breast pocket. "Think it over," he said.

"Wait," said Tilly. "I meant to tell you this before, but I—I forgot."

She still had the opal ring in her pocket. She brought it out and gave it to Levy.

"Mrs. Dexter gave it to Robert," she said, "just before you took her away this afternoon."

Levy was holding up the ring so that the light shone on it, the tiny diamonds twinkled, brilliant, yet somehow insignificant beside the calm, smooth luster of the opal.

"I don't suppose it's of any importance," Tilly said, apologetically. "Only—I wanted to tell you—everything."

"A beautiful stone," said Levy, contemplating it.

"It's Sibyl's ring ..." said Howard, in a hushed voice. "Belonged to her mother. But Sibyl didn't like to wear it. Bad luck, she used to say."

"Yes," said Levy. "There's an interesting history attached to the opal, and the superstition that it brings bad luck."

He smiled a little, and Tilly was amazed by the change in him, a change that affected all of them in the room. It was as if some intolerable tension were being gently relaxed.

"I'm very glad to get this, Mrs. MacDonald," he said. "It's what you might call the last link in the chain."

From his breast pocket he took out a neat, dark-blue linen wallet, and from it he took a folded paper.

"I found this in Mrs. Dexter's room," he said. "I'll read it to you." He glanced around at them. "'Dearest Carola: I am frightfully sorry not to send you the money as I promised, but I am absolutely out of cash, and I know you never want checks. So I've told Jensen to leave you this little package. You can sell it, or pawn it, or anything you want. Best of luck, darling, and see you soon. As ever, Sibyl.'" He folded the note and replaced it in the wallet. "I didn't, of course, know what had been in the 'little package.' But now I do."

He picked up the ring from the table.

"A beautiful stone," he said, again. "But, in this instance, the cause of a murder."

"What d' you mean?" asked Cantrell, frowning.

"You'll remember Mrs. Dexter's outburst, when the late Mrs. Fleming's will was read, citing her as the recipient of this ring. I suggest that the late Mrs. Fleming sent this ring to Mrs. Dexter, in lieu of the cash she had agreed to pay for her narcotics, and that when she received it, Mrs. Dexter believed it to be a deliberate attempt to bring 'bad luck' upon her. She needed money, but she was afraid to sell the ring, or to keep it. I suggest that her resentment—and her desperate need for money, for drugs—increased to a fury which led her to commit this murder."

"Look here!" said Cantrell. "You're not trying to say that *Carola* did it?"

"That's my belief," said Levy. "It's been fairly obvious for some time. Mrs. Dexter supplied the late Mrs. Fleming with these narcotics. She had free access to any part of the house. She put the capsule into that bottle, and afterwards, she took the bottle away. It was simple. You were all downstairs." He paused for a moment, then went on. "You understand, of course, that the police are not obliged to supply a motive, but, when a case comes to trial, motive is the chief factor with the average jury."

"You can't bring Carola to trial!" said Cantrell. "She's—not responsible."

"The question of an individual's responsibility is a complicated legal matter, Mr. Cantrell."

"You're not going to arrest the poor girl!"

"She's already under arrest," said Levy. "In the State Hospital."

There was a long silence.

"But this ...?" Howard said. "This—about Pauline?"

"So far," said Levy, "I'm prepared to accept this as an accident. Caused by criminal negligence on the part of yourself, Mr. Fleming, of Mr. Osborne, and of Mrs. MacDonald."

He rose.

"Both of these deaths could have been averted," he said, "if all of you—including you, Mr. Cantrell, had had the honesty, the intelligence, and the courage to tell what you knew to the people you pay to protect you."

There was a moment of silence. Then Osborne said, "Is it all right if I drive Mrs. MacDonald and her child to the Inn?"

"I've no objection to that," said Levy. "Provided you all three hold yourselves in readiness for further questioning. Good-night."

He went out of the room with Cantrell, and behind him went the police doctor, the young sergeant, the other man in uniform, all without a word or a glance. The three they had left were silent, Tilly sitting at the table, Osborne and Howard standing, and it was as if they were abandoned, disgraced, stricken.

"I vote we don't start 'thinking things over' tonight," said Osborne. "Ready, Tilly? I'll carry your young hellion out to the car, and maybe he won't wake up."

"But—but . . ," said Howard. "If you'd both come back to—to my house . . .? Gloria'll find something to make us a little snack. I mean—"

"Tilly doesn't want to go back there," said Osborne.

"I don't ... Are you coming back later, Sam?" Howard asked.

"Come along with us to the Inn," said Osborne. "And, for God's sake, don't hem and haw. I want to get Tilly out of here. I'll go upstairs with you while you pack a bag, Tilly."

Pauline's door was closed.

"Is she ...?" Tilly asked.

"Don't be morbid," said Osborne.

He put his arm around her shoulder and drew her close to him; he bent, and kissed her on the temple.

"Hurry up now, and pack," he said. "And don't ask any questions, and don't do any thinking until I tell you to."

"I must say—!" Tilly began.

"No, you mustn't," said Osborne. "Hurry up, and pack."

THE END

Who's Afraid?

by Elisabeth Sanxay Holding

To My Cousin
Mary Louise Cartwright

I

This is life! Susie thought, leaning back in the Pullman chair. She stretched out her long legs and crossed her ankles modestly, she looked with satisfaction at her new shoes. Nice shoes, she thought, and nice feet. Far from small, but narrow. Aristocratic, I dare say.

Mr. Chiswick had put ideas like that into her head. A month ago she had seen his advertisement in a New York newspaper.

> WANTED: *Young lady, with unquestionable social and cultural background. Experience not essential. Write stating qualifications. C. C. Box 907.*

Bogus, she had thought; just another of those things, selling from door to door on commission.

But you never know. She had registered at three agencies, but they had told her July was a bad month, they said there were so many young people just out of college, and indeed she saw them with her own eyes. She had studied those other girls, her competitors, and sometimes she had been depressed. The little cute ones get the breaks, she thought.

She knew better than to make any attempt at cuteness. She was too tall for that, a thin young creature, limber and nonchalant, with a dark, serious, good-humored face. She had dressed as magazine articles advise applicants to dress: she had worn an immaculate white blouse, a black skirt, colorless nail polish; her hair had been neat. She looked all right; but so did practically everybody else.

Only Mr. Chiswick had found her superior. He had liked her letter, and he had arranged an interview, he had told her she was exactly the type he had had in mind. He was perfectly satisfied with her Social Background; a father who was a professor of English in a smallish upstate college, a grandfather who had been mayor of that smallish city. He admired her culture as no one else ever had. She had a good scholastic record, but nothing brilliant, no travel either; she had felt a little nervous when he had given her a list of names to read aloud.

Madame de Maintenon. Madame du Barry. Cleopatra—"There!" he had said. "Now, nine out of ten of the young ladies I've interviewed have pronounced that 'Clear-patra.'" He liked the way she spoke, and he had liked her appearance. "You've got distinction, Miss Alban," he said. She liked that. She liked Mr. Chiswick. Only she was not altogether sure about Gateways.

It was a correspondence course. It offered to the Women of America a system for developing the individual charm that lies dormant in each of you. Through the Three Gateways of the Spiritual, the Physical, and the Mental.

Well, Susie thought, some of those exercises are good, darn good. All that about the care of the skin, and about diet is perfectly sound. And the great women of the past are pretty interesting. It couldn't *hurt* anyone to take the course, and it might help a lot, in some cases.

Let us analyze Charm, one of the folders said. Susie, as was her duty, had seriously studied all the literature of Gateways, but she did not find the Chiswick description of Charm satisfactory. I think he's too fond of the mysterious and the subtle, she thought. Personally, the kind of charm I'd have, if I could, would be a lot more obvious. I'd like to knock them cold. I'd like men to lose their heads completely the moment they set eyes on me.

She sighed. Or even *one* man, she thought. All my beaus have been pretty dingy—and they never seem to have any trouble at all in keeping their heads. Here I am, twenty-one, and there's never been anyone really exciting. I've always picked the right boys to fall in love with, the handsome, debonair ones. But the men who fall for me are very otherwise. Some plump, and several with spectacles. Well, will it be always like that?

No, she said to herself. It won't. I've got the nicest outfit of clothes I've ever had in my life, and I'm going to be traveling around, meeting new people all the time. If I can't get *some* results, I'm hopeless. Or I wonder ... She looked out of the window dreamily. I wonder if I could try the mysterious line myself.... A veil, and mascara? The Egyptian women lengthened their eyes with kohl....

"Pardon me, madam," said a man's voice at her elbow. "Would you care to look at this magazine?"

She had had a glimpse of him before, sitting at the end of the car, a jaunty fellow growing bald, dressed in a brown belted jacket, gray flannel trousers, and brown-and-white sport shoes; he looked, she thought, like a neat, clean tramp.

"Oh, thank you!" she said, taking the magazine he held out. This was done without any thinking, it was pure instinct to be friendly when someone else was friendly. But when he swiveled the empty chair beside her, and sat down facing her, she did begin to think. Maybe I'd better not encourage him.

She opened the magazine and began turning the pages. It was a trade journal devoted to hardware; there were photographs of windows full of tools, photographs of men at dealer's conventions. Well, what's the idea? Susie thought. Is it something subtle, to show me that he's some big hardware man?

"Does it interest you?" he asked.

She glanced up at him, determined not to encourage him. But he had a look that surprised her, a look that was somehow familiar. His underlip was thrust out, his little blue eyes twinkled in his ruddy face. Obviously he thought this was a joke. You can discourage a man if he's trying to flirt, Susie thought, but it's pretty brutal to discourage anybody's jokes. Especially when he's not young.

"Well, maybe it's very instructive," she said.

"It is," he said. "It's good to know that there are thousands of men thinking about hardware, night and day, planning to develop it. Thinking up new ways to display can-openers."

Something familiar about you, she thought, glancing again at him. Have I met you before?

"What's a 'ricer'?" he asked.

"It's a thing you squash potatoes through," she said. "To make those little squiggles, you know."

"Now *that's* it!" he cried. "That's the spoken word." He leaned forward. "If you'd been asked to write a definition of a ricer," he said, "it would have been something like this: A ricer is a kitchen implement by which potatoes are forced through a sieve. Wouldn't it?"

"I guess so," said Susie.

"I'd be willing to bet you can't write a decent letter," he said.

"Well, you'd win," said Susie.

He brought a package of cigarettes out of his pocket. "Confound it!" he said. "I forgot. No smoking in here. Shall we go into the smoker?"

"All right!" Susie said, starting to rise. But she sat back again. After all, she thought, even if he does seem familiar, I don't know anything about him. If it wasn't for Mr. Chiswick, I wouldn't care. I mean he seems like a cheerful little guy, and I'd be willing to talk to him, and no harm done. But Mr. Chiswick was very earnest about appearances. Remember, Miss Alban, he said, that you're representing Gateways not only while you're actually interviewing prospective clients, but *all the time.*

"Well?" said the man. He was standing, looking down at her.

"I don't know about going in a smoking car," said Susie. "I never have."

"Then it's time you did," he said. "You don't want to travel through life in a sissy Pullman."

"I know. But ..."

He brought a wallet out of his breast-pocket, and from that he took a card and handed it to her. Dr. Valentine Jacobs, was engraved on it.

"A doctor?" Susie asked.

"Of philosophy," he said.

"Oh, of course!" she cried. "You're a college professor!"

"You've heard of me?" he asked. "Maybe you've read or seen one of my books?"

"Yes, I probably have," said Susie. I'm certainly not going to tell him he's typical, she thought. Nobody likes to be typical of anything. But that's why he seemed familiar. He's got that special professor's way of being up-to-date. She rose, "I will go in the smoker, thanks," she said.

Not even Mr. Chiswick, she thought, could object to her going with a Ph.D. This is fun, she thought. This is the way traveling ought to be. Meeting new people.

They went through the car, Dr. Jacobs first, jaunty and slight in his belted brown jacket, and the tall young Susie behind him, a pleased look on her serious dark face. They went through a second car, and a third, then he opened the door of the fourth, and they stepped into a gray haze.

"There's a seat," he said, leading the way down the aisle.

There were no other women in here, only men, and they all seemed so subdued and gloomy; the floor was bare and the lights seemed dim. Queer, thought Susie; a ghost train.

"Well, fellow-travelers!" said Dr. Jacobs. He had stopped, and stood resting his hand on the back of a seat where two men were sitting, both of them young, and both good-looking. One of them smiled, and one did not; then the doctor went on to a vacant seat, and waited for Susie to settle herself by the window.

"Two interesting young fellows," he said. "One of them's quite a radical, and the other's a die-hard conservative." He offered her a cigarette, and lit it for her, and one for himself. "It's very instructive—for me," he said. "I continue to learn."

Yes, thought Susie, Father talks like that. I learn from my students, more than they suspect ... I like Dr. Jacobs. He's cozy, and you can see that he likes Youth.

"And do you lean toward the Left?" he asked.

"Well ..." said Susie. She had been asked that question before, and she had an answer. "This is a transition period ..." she began; but he laughed, which was something other professors had not done.

"That's fraudulent," he said.

"I know it," said Susie. "I really haven't any opinions, much."

"You're ..." he said, and stopped, because one of his interesting young fellows had risen and come to his side; a slim fair-haired boy with gray eyes.

"Excuse me!" he said, "but if you'll give me the address of the boarding-house you mentioned in South Fairfield ..." She looked up, and found him looking sidelong at her. They both glanced away.

"Just tell your taxi driver to take you to the Brett house," said Dr. Jacobs.

"I see," said the other. "Thanks ..." He lingered a moment, but nothing more was said. "Well, I think I'll get a breath of fresh air," he said, and went off down the aisle.

"He's the radical," said Dr. Jacobs. "His name is Carroll. He seems to be a very decent sort of young fellow, but of course I don't know anything about him. Would you like to talk to him?"

Susie thought about it.

"That was why he came, of course," said Dr. Jacobs. "He hoped to be introduced to you."

And now, thought Susie, you're just letting me use my own Judgment. You're waiting to see what Youth will do. "I'm going to South Fairfield myself," she said. "Only I'm going to stay at the Fairfield Arms."

"Don't!" said Dr. Jacobs. "Take my advice, and don't. It's one of the most depressing little hostelries I've ever met in a very extensive experience. At Mrs. Brett's you'll get excellent food, a good bed, a big, clean room, and for considerably less money."

"But it's been sort of arranged for me," Susie said. "I'm on a business trip, you know, and I've got a list of what is supposed to be the best hotel in each town."

"The supposition is erroneous for South Fairfield," he said. He did not press the matter, though; they finished their cigarettes chatting affably enough.

"I think I'll go back to the sissy Pullman now," Susie said. "It's pretty thick here."

The doctor escorted her back to her seat, and sat down opposite her. "Would you mind telling me," he asked, "what kind of business trip you're making? It's nothing but rank curiosity on my part...."

"Well, no, I don't mind," said Susie. But she did. She told him in a sketchy fashion about Gateways. "I think," she said, "that any sort of culture is better than none."

The doctor listened; he looked at one of her booklets, and put it into his pocket. He rose. "I hope you'll decide to come to Mrs. Brett's," he said. "But in any case, I'll see you, Miss—?"

"Susie Alban."

"Miss Susie Alban," he repeated. "I'll leave you the magazine, to study."

With a smile he went off, and it was flat and dull without him. If I were a man, Susie thought, I'd wander around in the train like that. Talking to everybody. That Carroll boy was rather attractive. Did he really want to be introduced to me? Did he like my looks when he saw me going past him? Or was he just bored? I'd feel so differently about everything if even one man would be smitten by me at first sight. Of course, it's nice for a man to learn to care for you as he knows you better; but just one sudden, *vio-*

lent conquest would help.

The six or seven people in the car with her were either reading or sleeping. They did not look interesting. She was growing restless and faintly worried. Suppose, she thought, that that Carroll boy is somebody I would have liked, and now I'll never meet him? There must be lots of things like that in life. Your whole future is changed by turning a special corner at a special moment....

I'm going to Mrs. Brett's, she thought.

"South Fairfield!" said the conductor in a confidential tone. "Next stop, South Fairfield!"

He took Susie's two bags out to the platform, and Dr. Jacobs joined her there.

"I think I'd like to go to Mrs. Brett's," she said.

"Excellent!" said he. He descended nimbly to the platform, and helped her down. As the train slid quickly away, young Carroll approached them. "Miss Alban," said the doctor, "this is Richard Carroll—also going to Mrs. Brett's."

Carroll took off his hat, and they looked at each other. "The fellow I met in the smoker is coming too," Carroll said. "Name is Loder."

This Loder was standing a little way off; big, dark, somewhat sullen, but handsome. Carroll made a signal to him, and he came up to them, bag in hand. "We can share a taxi," the doctor said. "Miss Alban, Mr. Loder."

He gave her a dark look, no smile, they all crossed the platform of the sunny little station. "Doctor! Doctor!" cried a voice. A thin man with a neat little straw-colored mustache was hurrying toward them.

"Well, Brett, how are you?" said the doctor.

"We have a new car, y'know, Doctor," said Brett. "So I came to fetch you."

"Excellent!" said the doctor. "And I've brought you three more victims, Brett."

Brett gave a smile like a spasm. "This way, please?" he said, and they went in a little troop. This is fun! Susie thought. The open road, and meeting new people. This is the life!

II

I'll have to get rid of this girl, one of the four men in the car was thinking.

The rich stillness of midsummer lay on the world; the grain was ripe in the fields, the trees marched up the hills, pale-green and emerald-green and yellow-green, here and there a dark spruce and a copper beech, all unstirring against the pure blue sky. It made him sick to look at that un-bounded peace, and to think of his danger.

I could manage Eve, he thought. Eve! God! *what* a name for her! I re-member that book of Bible stories we had when we were children. The An-gel driving Adam and Eve out of Paradise. She had long hair down to her knees, and a little dress made of skins, and she was holding Adam's hand. *My* Eve never had any idea of leaving her snug little garden hand in hand with me. No. She was going to stay right there, and I was to be driven out.

But she liked me, the first moment she saw me. More than liked me. She *loved* me.... She won't admit it. She's too damn respectable and prudent, but I could see.... Even now, if I had money, or prestige. Or anything. Look at the risks she took, coming out to meet me, with that husband of hers, half-crazy anyhow with suspicion.... Even now—if I had anything....

Her letter's in my pocket now. I'm afraid you've misunderstood me.... Bet-ter for us not to meet again. Only, we're going to meet again, Eve darling, and I never misunderstood you. Not for one little minute. You're fright-ened, now, that's all.

"Oh, yes!" said Susie. "I have to send Mr. Chiswick a report every night."

I could be put in jail, the man told himself. I could be locked up like a wild animal. This girl could do that. She could set the pack after me, with one word. I've got to stop her. I can manage Eve, all right; but this girl.... Is she a fool? Or does she know already?

God! In another two weeks, or less, I'd have been all right. I admit I made mistakes, took too many chances. I admit I lost my head—a little—over Eve. But I could have fixed all that. Unless somehow he's found out. Un-less he's sent this girl to spy on me. To get the facts. The evidence. I could be put in jail. I could be locked up.

But I'm not going to be put in jail. If old C. had any facts, he wouldn't have sent the girl. He'd have sent a policeman. So he can't be sure. If he suspects anything, he's sent her to check up, get information. I've got to stop that. I've got to get rid of her.

Is she a fool? Did she say she'd come from Chiswick because she does-n't know anything, or was it a trick? While I'm studying her, is she study-ing me? That friendly air—that could be a good line. But I've got to know—and know quick. And whatever it is, whether she's a fool or not, I've got to stop her.

"Oh, yes!" Susie said, answering a question he had not heard. "I've got the name of at least one prominent woman in every town; and I'm sup-posed to get other names through her."

Why is this other fellow asking her all these questions? What's *his* in-terest? Suppose I ask a question now? Then I'll know. However she answers it, I'll know. Only I've got to take the right tone. Casual ... maybe ... better not ask just now.

But he did ask. "Is your list confidential?"

"Oh, no!" Susie answered. "In fact, I'm supposed to get a line on people before I see them, if possible. Maybe one of you knows the woman I'm going to see here? Her name is Mrs. Person."

There was a silence so complete and so strange that she looked from one face to another.

"Did I drop a brick?" she asked.

Somebody laughed with heartiness. "I wish you luck!" he said. "I suppose you'll be starting off to see Mrs. Person first thing in the morning?"

"Ah reckons Ah will," said Susie.

You won't get there, thought the man. I'll stop you—somehow.

III

The car turned up a gentle hill on the summit of which stood a fine old house, badly in need of repair, with tall white pillars up the front. It was unfenced, no garden, only a wide stretch of grass growing high and rank, and here and there a noble old tree; there was a look of neglect about the place, but it was in no way depressing.

"Queenie'll be a bit surprised," said Brett. "She wasn't expecting anyone but you, Doctor. If you people will make yourselves comfortable on the veranda for a moment ...?"

He stopped the car, and they all descended. On the veranda was a row of rocking-chairs. Susie sat down in one; the doctor sat on one side of her, and the fair-haired Carroll on the other. Loder walked past them to the end of the veranda and stood looking out at the horizon. Insects were chirping in the grass, but that cheerful chorus was part of the golden peace; the shadows of the trees were long, the blue of the sky was paling a little.

I've been in the city so long, Susie thought, I'd almost forgotten how lovely the world is. I'm so glad I came here instead of going to any hotel. I *like* this. I'm so thankful I got this job instead of a job in an office. I wish I could travel for—let's say four years, until I'm twenty-five. Then I'll be ready to get married and settle down.

Suppose nobody very attractive ever wants to marry me? I know the Gateways idea is that every woman can have charm, but I'm not so darn sure about that. And if it was true, and they all found out how to be charming, think of the competition! I honestly could do more, though, about developing a spot of charm in myself. Which would be my quickest way, I wonder? The physical, the mental, or the spiritual? Study Your Self, the course says. Observe how others react to you.

She turned her head quickly toward Carroll to see if he was looking at her. He was not. He was staring straight ahead of him with a tired look on his fine-drawn face. She glanced toward Loder, and he was still gazing at the horizon. Handsome, she thought, contemplating his pale and rather sullen face. I like that sort of haunted, bitter type.

The house door opened and a woman came out; the doctor sprang to his feet.

"My Queen!" he cried, and approaching her, he took her hand and raised it to his lips.

The woman laughed, leaning against the doorway, a slender deep-bosomed young woman in a blue cotton dress, with a blue bandanna tied over her untidy copper-colored hair. She had a wide gamine mouth, a turned-up nose, narrow blue eyes; she was slatternly, she was impudent, and she was fascinating.

"This is Miss Alban, Mrs. Brett," said the doctor. "And the Messieurs Carroll and Loder."

"Which is which?" asked Mrs. Brett, turning her head.

"Oh, you're Mr. Loder?" she said, and her blue eyes looked him up and down. "Well, I hope you'll like it here, Mr. Loder." Then she turned to Susie. "I'll show you your room," she said amiably. "If things aren't so nice you can blame my husband. He had a right to phone up from the station and tell me to expect you." She opened the screen door. "But if there's any way to do things wrong, trust Percy to find it," she said.

She led the way up a broad and beautiful stairway, and opened a door on the floor above. "If you want anything," she said, "just go out in the hall and call me. Dinner'll be kind of late, I'm afraid, but I'll do my best."

She went off, and Susie closed the door. It was a big room, filled with the bright dazzle of the setting sun; the sweet air came in at the open windows; it was bare, very bare, only a little day-bed, a chest of drawers, one chair, one small rag rug on the polished floor, but it was clean, and to Susie, indescribably charming.

This is the life! she said to herself. All these new places and new people. You feel so darn light and carefree, just coming in casually like this for a night or two ... But I probably shouldn't feel so joyous. It's not business-like. I ought to think about my work. They were all stricken when I mentioned Mrs. Person.... Something queer there. Well, I'm sorry, but I *like* there to be something queer.

She strolled up and down the big room, glad to stretch her legs after the journey. Maybe Mrs. Person is evil. The local Lorelei. In that case she won't want our course in how to be charming, but she might give me the name of someone else. Anyhow, I look forward to meeting Mrs. Person. I like a touch of mystery.

She stopped to look at herself in the mirror over the chest of drawers. I'd like either Carroll or Loder to fall for me, she thought. Or both. Nothing serious, but just enough to build me up. The doctor *said* that Carroll wanted to meet me. He may be liking me more than I know. He may have come here simply on my account. They say a woman always knows when a man's attracted, but I don't. I never suspected that Carter boy of being smitten until he began that frightfully embarrassing stammering.

Well, do I like Carroll? I think I like Loder better. More intense. And that's typical of me. I *always* fall for the boys who don't pay any attention to me. This—

A door banged downstairs, and Mrs. Brett's voice came up to her, low and husky but distinct.

"You're a brute!"

"Less of it, if you please," said Brett's voice curtly.

"There's going to be a lot *more* of it," said she. "You're a brute! Four people. *Four* people—for me to cook and scrub for!"

"Queenie!" he said. "Be reasonable—"

"I won't!" she said. "You're not going to make a slave of me, Mr. Percy Fancypants Brett. I won't put up with it, and I don't have to, either. I could walk out on you right here and now; and there's somebody who wouldn't expect me to scrub and slave."

"Very well!" said Brett.

"What do you mean, 'very well'?" she demanded.

"You'll see!" he said.

"Percy—"

"Let me alone!" he said. "I know damned well what you're hinting at, and I've had enough. Stand aside there!"

The door banged again and there was silence.

Pretty sordid, thought Susie. Pretty horrible to think of people tied to each other when they felt like that. I thought Mr. Brett was rather nice; polite and gentle. He's very different from Queenie, better educated, more civilized. But she's an attractive hussy in her way, no doubt about it; and more vital than he. A remarkably ill-suited couple, I should say.

There was a great tramping of feet outside, as if a regiment was coming upstairs.

"Same room you had before, Doctor," said Brett's voice, cheerful now. "Mr. Loder and Mr. Carroll, you can choose between these two to suit yourselves."

"I'll take this one," said Loder, instantly; and a door closed almost with a slam.

"Well, I'll be damned ...!" said Carroll with surprise.

"Seems to be nervous," the doctor observed. Two other doors closed, and then there was a knock at Susie's door. It was Brett with her two bags.

"Everything all right, Miss Alban?" he asked, with a gentle apologetic smile.

"Oh, yes, thank you!" she said.

"I'm just driving down to the village, Miss Alban," he said. "I wondered if you'd like to come along? I could take the road by the lake, and you could see something of the countryside."

"Why, yes, thank you, I'd love it," said Susie.

He seemed to be waiting.

"You mean, right away?" she asked.

"Well y'see, I have a lot of errands to do," he explained.

"All right!" she said, and put on her hat again. They went down the stairs and out of the house to the car that stood in the driveway.

"Complicated," he said, "this business of being an innkeeper. But very interesting. Meet all sorts of people." They sped off down the hill, and Brett kept on talking in a pleasant, but not very entertaining fashion. "Not much going on in South Fairfield," he said. "Prosperous little town, though." He told her the population, the number of churches, he told her about a new bus route. He was driving fast and he kept his eye on the road, so that she did not feel obliged to look at him, or to listen very attentively. She said, "I *see!*" from time to time, and enjoyed the scenery.

They turned into a long straight road, lined with fields behind stone walls, all empty in the golden sunset light, no buildings, no traffic. "Quite lonely," Susie observed.

"Well, y'see," said Brett, in his apologetic way, "it's a new road. People haven't got into the habit of using it much yet. Now, then, here's the lake."

It looked like a flooded meadow, a quiet sheet of water fringed with reeds; it had no beginning, no end, no definite outline, it simply spread out with tongues of still water stretching across the fields. "I see!" said Susie politely. She didn't like this lake, or this road; it seemed to her a melancholy scene. They were coming now to a wood.

"Now, there, just beyond those trees," said Brett. "There's the old road. You can see the roof of the hotel."

That put an idea into her head. "If it's not taking you out of your way, Mr. Brett," she said, "could you stop at the hotel? There might be a message for me, and anyhow I'd like to give them my address in case Mr. Chiswick wanted to reach me."

"Mr. Chiswick ..." Brett said. "Oh, yes! Certainly, Miss Alban." He drove steadily on. "Suppose I leave you there, Miss Alban, while I do my bit of shopping? Might be tiresome for you, stopping at all these shops and so on."

She agreed to that, and he turned into a side street of little wooden houses, each with its front yard and its fence of palings. There was no daylight saving here, and it was twilight now under the fine old trees; here and there a light twinkled in a kitchen window. I wonder ... Susie thought. I wonder if this would be a good time to see people. Better than the morning, maybe. You'd be almost sure to find the women at home   now.

"Does Mrs. Person live near the hotel?" she asked.

He took a long time about answering. "I believe she does," he said at last. "But—" He paused. "If you won't mind my offering advice ...?" he said. "Thing is, I've lived here for some years, and naturally one gets to know something about the natives, what?"

"Oh, yes!" Susie agreed.

"If I were you," he said, "I'd see Mrs. Green tomorrow. President of the Women's Club here. Quite important. Very nice woman. If I were you, I'd skip Mrs. Person."

"Oh, would you?" said Susie. "Why?"

"Waste of time to see her," said Brett, and began telling her how important, how popular Mrs. Green was. "I'll be coming into town tomorrow morning," he said. "I'll be very glad to drive you in, any time you like."

What *is* all this about Mrs. Person, she thought. Everybody seemed queer when I mentioned her, and Mr. Brett obviously doesn't want me to see her. Well, I'm sorry, but that makes me all the more anxious to see her.

They were in the main street of the little town now, and Brett stopped the car before a small, neat building of red brick. South Fairfield Arms, the sign said. "I shan't be long," he said. "Half an hour or so, that's all."

"Oh, I'm in no hurry," said Susie.

The lobby of the South Fairfield Arms was a subdued and forbidding place. In enormous high-backed chairs against the wall, each with a staring light behind it, each within range of a brass spittoon and a brass ashstand, sat four or five men reading newspapers. In a vague and wandering way, she approached the desk.

"Excuse me!" she said to the clerk. "Any mail or message for Miss Alban?"

"Alban?" he replied. "No, madam. Nothing."

"Well, if there should be, will you please send it on, in care of Mr. Brett?"

"Mr. Brett," he said, and wrote it down on a card. Rather a nice-looking boy, Susie thought, if only his hair wasn't so long. He glanced up to see why she lingered.

"I wonder," she said, "if you could tell me where a Mrs. Person lives?"

"Mrs. Alexander Person?" he asked.

"That's it," said Susie.

"Well, about two blocks from here," he said. "You walk straight along in the direction of the Town Hall till you come to Oak Avenue, and it's the first corner on the right."

"Thank you!" she said, and turning away, she recrossed the lobby and went out into the street. It had come into her head that she would go to see Mrs. Person now.

It can't do any harm, she thought. If she's busy, I'll come back tomorrow. I've got some of our literature in my purse, enough to go on with, and I've got some application blanks. It would be pretty nice if I could make a sale now, the very first day. That would certainly impress Mr. Chiswick.

She walked briskly in the cool and pleasant dusk, she came to Oak Avenue and turned the corner. And a completely unexpected and panic fear seized her. She stood still, looking up the quiet tree-lined street of small houses. I—*can't* ... she thought. I can't just walk up to the house and ring the bell. I don't know what to *say* ... I couldn't possibly say that introductory speech. It's awful. "I've been asked to call on you, Mrs. Person, as the outstanding woman of your community—" No! I can't! It's so bogus. Nobody would *let* me go on with that. Nobody would ever dream of buying that course—for seventy-five dollars. It's—

Listen! Get hold of yourself. Mr. Chiswick's paying my expenses and I've got to *try*. I will try. Only the morning is the best time, definitely. This is not a good time. People are getting their dinners. Tomorrow.... No. Now.

She started forward at a snail's pace. I've been asked to call on you, Mrs. Person.... Suppose she's hostile and horrible? All right! Let her be. Probably lots of people will be. I'll have to do this dozens and dozens of times. Here we are.

This was the house on the first corner to the right, but it was a very small and humble house for the outstanding woman of the community. Susie stopped again with her hand on the low gate. There was a dim glow visible through the glass of the door, but otherwise the house was dark. Probably out, thought Susie. She drew a long breath, and pushed open the gate, she walked along the path and up the steps. Her knees felt weak. She rang the bell and waited.

Everyone's out, she thought. Oh, if *only* nobody comes ...! But somebody was coming, stumping along the hall, the door was flying open with a crash, and a frightful little old man stood there, with a pompadour of white hair above a brick-red face, with glittering little blue eyes. He glared at her, and then began to grin slowly.

"Young gal," he remarked. "Young and pretty. Well, my dear?"

"Well, I—does Mrs. Person live here?" Susie asked.

"What's the matter with *Mr.* Person?" he asked gaily. "City gal, ain't you?"

"Well, yes, in a way," said Susie.

He laughed loudly. "Ah!" he said. "That's what I like. A city gal. I like 'em dark, too. Big—black—eyes—mmmmmmmm...."

Is he trying to be funny? Susie thought. Anyhow, I don't like him. She drew back a little. "Well, I'll look in again," she said uncertainly.

"Here! Here! What's your hurry?" he demanded. "If you want to see the missis, why, step right in!"

"No, thank you," said Susie. "I'll come back—"

"Come in! Come in!" he said, coaxingly. "Step in and have a chat—"

"Alexander!" said a low and beautiful voice.

A woman had come into the lighted hall behind him, a slight woman in a limp, dark dress, and black hair pinned in a heavy knot at the nape of her neck.

"Alexander!" she said again, moving forward. "You wanted to see me?" she asked Susie.

"Well ... Mrs. Person?"

"Yes," said the other gravely.

"Well, I've been asked to call on you"— Susie said in an unsteady voice, looking fixed past the old man to Mrs. Person —"as an outstanding woman in your community, Mrs. Person—"

"Yes," said Mrs. Person. "Who asked you to call?"

That was an unorthodox question. "Well," said Susie. "Mr. Chiswick—"

"*Chiswick!*" yelled the old man. "*Chiswick!*"

He came at Susie with his fist raised, his thin old mouth in a tight line, his blue eyes blazing. "Get out!" he screamed. "Get out!"

She turned and ran down the steps, and he stood in the doorway shouting after her. "Your Chiswick ... Tell your blank blank Chiswick to come here himself. Tell the blank blank blank I'm waiting for him...."

Some of the words he used she had never heard, but they were unmistakable, and intolerable; she ran from them as if they were poisoned arrows.

"I'll kill your blank blank Chiswick!" he yelled. "Tell him ..."

The house door closed with a slam, and Susie stopped; she leaned against a tree, sick and shaken.

IV

One of the four men she had met that day was standing on the other side of the street in the shadow of a tree, listening to old Person.

God! he said to himself. How did *he* find out?

"I'll kill your blank blank Chiswick!" yelled old Person.

God! the man cried to himself. Then he was afraid he had cried it aloud, and he looked over his shoulder. The street was deserted, the house behind him was dark. The sound of footsteps made him turn back, and he saw the girl going toward the corner. She looked tall, and very slight in the dark; she went leisurely, and he thought that was because she was satisfied. *She* told old Person, he thought. That's what she went there for.

It shocked him. It's the one thing I never thought of, he said to himself. It's the worst thing she could have done. That damned vindictive old savage ... I'd rather have the police. I'd—well, I'll have the police, too. My God! I only needed two weeks, or less, and I'd have been all right. I'd have been safe. I wasn't even worried, this morning.

A sort of anguish seized him when he thought of this morning. He had eaten his breakfast with relish, he had felt wonderfully well, vigorous, confident, because his plans had been good ones. And then she came....

He started after her, keeping to the strip of grass beside the pavement on his own side of the street. He had nothing definite in his mind, nothing but a feeling that he must not let her out of his sight. Where's she going now? he asked himself. To the police?

He remembered old Person's voice cursing and yelling. That was the first hound baying. But that wasn't enough for her. She wanted the police after him, too. The whole pack, to hound him down. And why? He had never injured her, he had never heard of her, never imagined before today that anyone like her existed. There she was, strolling along, so damned nonchalant. Pleased with herself.

It came into his mind that she was smiling to herself in the shadow, and he hated her. She wants to see me hunted down like an animal, he thought. And he went after her, perfectly silent on the grass. He quickened his steps; his heart quickened, too. There was still nothing definite in his mind, only a curious excitement. He wanted to catch up with her, that was all.

She had almost reached the corner of the deserted street. He wanted to catch up with her before she reached the street light on the corner. So he began to run.

Suddenly there was a clatter of horses' hoofs, and he stopped in terror. The hunt is up. The Four Horsemen ... You don't—you—*can't* be hearing galloping horses.... That's a sound out of a play. Out of a nightmare. The Valkyrie. The witches after Tam o' Shanter. The sheriff's posse after the killer.

She reached the corner. He saw her clearly under the street lamp. So damned nonchalant in her dark suit, her hat on the side of her head. He *knew* she was smiling to herself. Or laughing.

Around the corner came a big, heavy, gray cart horse, ridden by a boy in overalls, who was leading another big gray horse. They went past him with a clatter, and when he turned his head, the girl was out of sight. He went after her, but she had gone into another world, not a tree-lined, deserted street, but a street with little shops, and people, and traffic. She could afford to laugh at him now. She was safe.

She's going to the police, he thought. For God's sake, why doesn't she hurry? Because she was enjoying this; taking her time. Laughing at him. He had to go sauntering along the street on the other side. I've got to make a plan, he thought. When she goes into the police station, I'll ... I'll what? Get a train to New York? Or to Bassville? Or is it safer here? Easier to hide than to run? I need time. I need time to think. I need *time*, I tell you.

She went into the Fairfield Arms.

He stopped where he was, before a very small shop with a newsstand outside it. If she's not going to the police ...? Maybe I'd better wait and see. Only the one thing he could not do was wait. A dreadful sense of urgency possessed him. Wait? he thought. Just hang around and wait until *she's* good and ready to take the next step? I won't!

Someone coughed, and he turned his head to find a man standing at his shoulder, staring at him. He took some pennies out of his pocket and picked up a newspaper, and turned back along the street.

I'll see Eve, he thought. And you're going to keep me out of this, my dear Eve. You can keep that damned old savage quiet, if you try. And you're going to try. If I can shut him up, I've got a chance. No matter what that girl does.

That sense of excitement came back to him. I've got a chance, he thought. I'm not a fool. I can deal with this if I keep my head. I don't have to be hunted.

He lit a cigarette, and he smiled to see how steady his hand was.

V

Susie sat in one of the high-backed chairs against the wall waiting for Mr. Brett. Don't be silly! she told herself. In work like this, I'm sure to run across *some* unpleasant people. This was really nothing—all in the day's work. When you analyze it, what was it but a nasty old man swearing? I don't understand though, why the very mention of Mr. Chiswick's name started him off.

She thought of Mr. Chiswick, thin, elderly, with his pince-nez, and his trim little gray beard; Mr. Chiswick, so polite and correct. Nobody could call *him* names like that, she thought. Unless the old man was crazy. That seemed rather probable when you think how he behaved the moment I got there.

She sighed and glanced again at the clock. Mr. Brett was very late. Well, she thought, I certainly can't go back to see Mrs. Person, ever. I'll have to see this Mrs. Green tomorrow. I wonder if I ought to put all this in my report to Mr. Chiswick? Tell him how the old man made threats. I don't know.... Maybe it isn't important. I *am* silly, to be so upset. Only there was something about that old man—something pretty horrible.

She moved restlessly, and then an idea came into her head, and she rose and went to the desk.

"Do you know Mr. Brett by sight?" she asked the clerk.

"Yes. madam," he said, coldly.

"Well, when Mr. Brett comes in, will you please tell him that I've decided to walk back."

"Very well, madam," he said.

"And can you tell me how to get to that new road by the lake?"

He looked as if this were almost more than he could bear.

"You go straight along to Oak Street," he said, "and you take the first turning to the right—"

"Oh, by Mrs. Person's house?"

"Yes," he said. "Right next to that house you will see the entrance to Woodmont Park. You can go straight through there to the New Road."

"Thank you!" said Susie.

She was very reluctant to go near that house again, but she despised the reluctance. I need a good brisk walk in the fresh air, she thought. I haven't had any exercise all day. I haven't had very much to eat, either, she thought, as she set forth. Just a sandwich and a cup of coffee before I got on the train. I hope Mrs. Brett is a good cook.

Oak Street looked better now, there were more lights in the houses. It's just an ordinary street, she said to herself. And probably what happened was ordinary, too. I wonder how I ought to report that interview? As a failure? I wonder if an experienced and very good salesman could have coped? Or would it have been hopeless for anyone? I wish it hadn't happened the very first place I went. It sort of undermines your self-confidence. If this Mrs. Green is hostile ...

There were lights in the Person house, lights upstairs, and as she turned the corner, she saw a very bright light in the back of the house, shining out over the grass. Very quiet neighborhood, she thought, not even a dog barking. I wish I had a nice cheerful dog along with me. Now, where's the park?

It was not at all hard to find. Half-way along the block there was a signboard with a glaring light over it.

WOODMONT PARK DEVELOPMENT
CHOICE HOME SITES. LAKE SHORE LOTS
IMPROVEMENTS

APPLY TO A. PERSON. SOLE AGENT

Beside the sign was the entrance to a macadam road lined with woodland, but straight and broad and well-lit; she could see the roofs of houses ahead. It's not lonely, she thought. The lights were strung on a wire, and each one made a bright circle among the leaves, with massed darkness behind. Quite a thick wood, she thought.

The houses had no lights in them, and as she came abreast of them, she saw that they were empty and unfinished. She saw the stone walls of a foundation like a ruin. The trees rustled with an unceasing sound. Very quiet neighbors, she thought, going a little quicker. I hope there aren't any owls. I—wouldn't like it if an owl started to hoot.

The road was downhill now, and the lights, she thought, were farther apart. She thought that she could see through the rustling branches, the pale gleam of water below her. The lake, she told herself and remembered how it had looked, spreading out formless and still over the meadows. Well, then I must be getting near the New Road.

She stumbled over something, and looked down. It was a foot in a white sock and black shoe.

Someone was lying among the trees at the side of the road. Someone hurt? Someone—more than hurt? I'll go and get a policeman—I'll go—

She stopped herself. You can't run away. You have to see ... She moved closer, but it was dark in the shadow of the trees. "Is there—anything wrong?" she asked aloud.

No answer. She opened her purse, and took out a book of matches; she struck one, and bent down. She had a glimpse of old Person's scarlet face and staring blue eyes; then she dropped the match, and stumbled backward.

He's dead, she thought. *Don't run.* That's a horrible thing to do. He's dead.... I'll have to get somebody. But I won't run. I'll walk. The trees were making a strange sound—as if they were rushing after her. Don't look back. Just go ahead, quietly.

But there was another sound, a soft crackling. She had to look back over her shoulder, and she saw a little pile of leaves blazing at the foot of a tree. I did that, when I dropped the match, she thought. She had started the fire, and she would have to put it out. She had to go back.

It was a small blaze. But it was only a few inches from old Person, and that made her give a sob like a gasp. She trampled out the blazing leaves in a sort of frenzy in her desperate haste to get away.

Then almost at her shoulder, a voice spoke. She sprang away from that dark form, she knocked her shoulder against a tree, and leaned back with no strength left in her.

"It's me," said the voice. "Charles Loder. Anything wrong?"

She could not speak for a moment, so overwhelming was her relief.

"Yes," she said. "Yes. It's something.... It's a man. Right—there. He's—dead."

"I've got a flashlight here," said Loder. "I'll take a look."

She closed her eyes, so as not to see that figure again. But with her eyes closed, she saw even more vividly that scarlet face, and the staring blue eyes.

"Dead drunk," said Loder, in a moment. "Let's get going."

"Drunk?" she repeated, still with her eyes closed. "Do you honestly think so?"

"Sure of it!" said Loder. "Let's go."

He took her arm, and she opened her eyes and moved forward mechanically.

"Oh, but not that way!" she said. "We've got to go back to the village and get help."

"He doesn't need any help," said Loder.

"We can't just leave him there."

"Why not? It's a nice mild night."

"His wife might worry...."

"Maybe she's used to it," said Loder. "He doesn't look like anyone you'd miss very much."

He tried to draw her away, gently enough, but she stood still.

"I think—we ought to do something about him," she said. She spoke in a nice, reasonable way, but her teeth were chattering.

"I think you'd better come along to the house and get your dinner," he said. "Come *on*, you poor kid."

His voice was very gentle; when she did not move, he put his arm around her shoulders. "Come on, Susie!" he said. "We'll go along the road a little way, and then we'll sit down and have a smoke until you're—rested."

"That's a good idea," she said.

He kept his arm around her shoulders, and it was a comfort to her. He was young and friendly and kind, and she liked him. They started down the hill under the rustling trees; she drew a deep breath and felt steadier.

"It was sort of startling to come across him like that," she said. "And I'd already had trouble with him."

"Trouble?" asked Loder.

"I went to see his daughter, or his wife, or whatever she is," Susie said, "and he opened the door. He flew into a frightful rage, and yelled at me."

"But what about?"

I guess I'd better not tell that, she thought. It's not right to talk about Mr. Chiswick's affairs. "Goodness knows!" she said. "I suppose he was drunk then, or anyhow beginning to be."

It was reassuring to think that old Person had been drunk, so that what he said didn't count. She was beginning to feel cheerful again. They went on down the hill, and there beyond the trees was the lake. They stopped, looking at it, a pale sheet of water stretching out over the fields, perfectly still.

"If it is a lake …" Susie said, half to herself. "It looks like the Deluge. It hasn't any banks."

"There's a little path here," he said. "Let's go along it for a way, and see what it's like."

"Let's not," she said.

"Come on, Susie," said Loder. "We'll find some place to sit down and have a smoke."

She liked Loder, and he was, she thought, being as nice as he could be. But she didn't want to go in among those dark trees, or any nearer to the lake.

"We'd better—" she began, and stopped at the sound of whistling. Brisk and lively whistling that was coming nearer; it was the Priests' March from Aïda, pepped up.

"Look here, Susie!" said Loder, almost in a whisper. "Let's…. Come on, Susie! I want to talk to you."

He tried to pull her toward the wood. "No!" she said. "No, thanks. I want to see…."

"Susie!" he said with a certain urgency. "Please—" Footsteps rang out, two figures appeared at the top of the hill, marching in step to the brisk whistling.

"Susie!" said Loder. "Don't say *anything*. To *anybody*."

"Why not?" she said, startled and uneasy.

"Because it might lead to a lot of trouble," he said. "Villages like this often have very strict laws about drunkenness. If the police pick up that fellow, and they know you've seen him, you'd have to go to court as a witness. You might have to stay here for days. The whole thing would be in the newspapers. It wouldn't do your business any good."

"They couldn't—"

"The old Blue Laws," he said. "It's against the law to get drunk, and it's a criminal offense not to report it, if you see a drunk."

"I honestly don't think—"

The two figures were marching smartly down on them. "Then keep quiet on my account," said Loder. "*I* don't want any trouble with the police."

The two figures passed under a light, and Susie recognized the doctor with young Carroll.

"Hello!" she called, very glad to see them.

Loder let go of her arm; he got out a cigarette and lit it. "*Hal*-lo!" cried the doctor. "It's never Miss Alban. Well! Well! And who's this? Loder? *Al-*

lons, mes enfants!"

He was in high spirits, in very high spirits; and it did not seem to trouble him that the two young men were completely silent. He took Susie's arm, and began to sing. "*Glo-ry and love-to-the men of old....*

"Sing!" he urged her. "I can't," said Susie, and he went on alone in a surprisingly good tenor voice. He started one song after another. "*Mine eyes have seen the glory....*" All along the road by the lake, and on to the highway. Then he started *Sambre et Meuse*, in French, excellent French. When he stopped for breath, Susie said politely: "You have an awfully good accent."

"Why not?" he said. "I was in France three years."

"Oh, were you? Studying?"

"Oh, no!" he said. "Killing."

He made a lunge with an imaginary bayonet. "*Comma çi!*" he said. "*Comme ça!*"

"Don't!" cried Susie.

He laughed cheerfully, and began singing again. "*There'll be a hot time—in the old town—tonight.*" All the way up the hill, up the steps of the veranda; he was still caroling when Percy Brett opened the door for them.

VI

It was half-past seven when they all sat down at the table.

"Seven o'clock is the regular time," said Queenie Brett. "But I didn't know there'd be four extra, so I had to send Percy to the village to get some things, and the car broke down." She paused. "Anyhow, that's Percy's story," she said.

She had put on a long dress of black lace with a big, white artificial flower on one shoulder; her coppery hair was done high on her head; black mascara made her long blue eyes strangely vivid. Hussy, thought one of the four men at the table. But she can cook.

And I can eat, he thought. I'm not even nervous. My hand's perfectly steady now. I've got a good appetite. It's damn queer, but I feel—better now.

Well, he thought, that's natural. I mean I've proved that I can think fast and act. I admit that I was nervous before. But when the time came, I was absolutely cool and collected. I didn't make a single mistake. And no matter what happens in the future, I know that I can deal with it. I like the way that hussy cooks. I'm hungry. I didn't know I was like this.

Nobody here knows it. They think I'm an ordinary, commonplace man.... If they had any idea ... He put his napkin to his lips to hide a grin.

I didn't mean to smile, he thought. I'm not callous. I wouldn't have done that if I hadn't been driven to it. Hounded. I had to defend myself; and I did.

Eve will know what's happened. It'll do her good. She'll be frightened. She certainly never thought I had it in me to—defend myself that way. It'll be a lesson for her. She's treated me like a dog—but she won't in the future. I don't need to worry about Eve. *She'll* never say a word, naturally. But she'll know. I'll go to see her tomorrow, and it'll be very different. You won't be quite so condescending now, my dear Eve. You never dreamed I was like this.

Yes. I feel better. My worries aren't over, not by a damned sight. But I can cope with them later. This is a breathing-space, and I need it. A good dinner, and a good night's sleep, and then I'll be ready for whatever happens. It's a mistake to try and make long-range plans. You have to be guided by circumstances. You have to be flexible. What happened today, for instance, was completely unexpected, but when it happened, I was able to handle it. I seem to have the type of mind that works best in an emergency. The thing for me to do is to get a good night's sleep, and wait.

"And how do you like South Fairfield, Miss Alban?" asked Queenie.

"Well, I haven't had a chance to see much of it," Susie answered.

He glanced up at the sound of her slow and amiable voice. Yes, he thought, you're still here. And I may have to do something about you later on. But not now. *You're* not dangerous. You're simply a fool. A colossal fool. You don't know anything. If you'd ever suspected anything, you wouldn't have gone home *that* way. Alone, in the dark. No, he thought, I was mistaken. I'll have to watch her, in case she finds out anything, or suspects anything later on. But I don't have to bother about her now. I'll get out of here early tomorrow, and settle things in Stonebridge. All I need is twenty-four hours' start ahead of her. She can't do me any harm here.

"It's a beautiful town, so Percy tells me," said Queenie. "Not as big as New York, maybe, but better. More trees, and more caterpillars. We've got everything here. There's the Palace Theatre, only twenty-five cents to see a picture a year old, and so cut it don't make sense. We've got Society, too. We've got the grand Madame Alexander Person. I suppose you'll be seeing her bright and early in the morning?"

"Well, no," said Susie. "I guess I'll change my plans a little. I'm going to take an early morning train to Stonebridge—"

God! the man cried to himself. That was the one thing he had not expected; the one thing that must not happen. Here! he thought. Take it easy. It's only chance. It doesn't mean anything. She's just a fool.

But he had to be sure.

"I used to know somebody in Stonebridge," he said. "A Mrs. Burke. I wonder if she's on the list of your prospects?"

"No," she said. "It's Mrs. Malter I'm going to see there."

All that vigor and confidence, that sense of well-being drained out of him; he felt collapsed. But he sat straight in his chair, and he thought, he hoped, that his face did not betray him. This could not be chance. This was—what? A threat?

It must be a threat. And he would have to meet it. There was to be no breathing-space. No good night's sleep. Back came that horrible feeling of urgency and haste, that swirling confusion in his head. He had to make a plan now, instantly. While he sat here at the table.

He couldn't rest, even for a few hours. Because he was hounded. And if one of the snarling pack was silenced, others were coming on; God knew how many others. A silent and invisible pack, to hunt him down and destroy him.

He had to look at Susie again, and this time she smiled. He had never seen anything so horrible as that smile of hers, slow, subtle, triumphant. She's enjoying herself, he thought. She wants me to know she's going to Esther's. She thinks I can't stop her.

She knows what's happened here. Maybe other people know now. The police. A cold sweat came out on him and that physical nausea returned. He wanted to push back his chair and go. Run. *Run....*

Take-it-easy. You can't run.

"It's hot in here, isn't it?" said Queenie.

She was looking at him. He was afraid to wipe his forehead. She noticed everything; that damned hussy....

"Let's go into the other room," said Queenie. "And maybe we could have a game of poker."

"I don't know how to play poker," said Susie.

I do, he thought. I've always been lucky. Look at the whole thing that way. Like a poker game. Bluff. Watch her. Be ready. What if she does know what's happened? She can't prove anything. Nobody could. I didn't make any mistakes. Not a single one.

My brain's beginning to work again, he thought. I'll find a way to stop her from going to Esther. I'll find a way to stop her from smiling like that.

VII

When dinner was finished, they went, all except Queenie, into the next room which was in every way a Front Parlor, a big handsome room, but filled with shiny furniture upholstered in a sickly green, and lit only by a chandelier in the ceiling.

Brett brought in a box of chips and two decks of cards, he set up a folding table in the center of the room. "Let's see," he said. "Five of us—"

"Thanks, but I'll just watch," said Susie.

"Oh, no!" said Dr. Jacobs. "You must sit in."

"I don't know how—"

"I'll teach you," he said.

"Well, thanks," said Susie, "but I don't think I will. Not tonight, thanks."

"Oh, come on!" said the doctor, and took her arm. Somehow, she did not like that. "No, thanks!" she said.

Then he tried to pull her toward the table. Just as Charles Loder had wanted to pull her back from the road by the lake. "*No!*" she said, trying to free her arm.

The doctor began to laugh, silently; his shoulders were shaking, his mouth was stretched wide, it seemed to her as if he were panting like a dog. She looked at him with a strange uneasiness.

"Let me go!" she said, sharply.

He released her arm at once, and he stopped that laughing. "Please join us!" he said. "I'll stake you to a dollar's worth of chips, just for the pleasure of your company."

A phrase was running in her head, picked up Heaven knows where. Certainly it was not advice that her parents or her teachers would have thought necessary to give her. Never play cards with strangers. It seemed to her of singular importance.

"No, thank you!" she said very distinctly.

There was a complete silence. And it occurred to her, for the first time, that she was the only woman among four men. Well, what of it? She asked herself. But her uneasiness was growing again. The doctor stood at her shoulder, not stirring or speaking. She glanced at Brett who was bending over the card table, and she thought he was watching her through his blond lashes. In haste she turned her head to look for Charles Loder, the one she liked best, the one who had been kind and nice. He was sitting on the sofa with his legs stretched out and his arms folded; she smiled at him but he stared back at her with a dark unwinking stare.

They were strangers, and she was alone. She knew nothing about them, and she could guess little or nothing. They were not only strange, but they seemed hostile. "I think I'll go upstairs ..." she said and turned toward the door.

Carroll was standing there, and *he* smiled in a way that touched her. He looked tired, a little shabby in his gray suit; but so young, so understandable, so nice.

"Will you stay and look on for a while?" he said. "You might bring me luck—and I need it."

"All right!" she said.

"Now then!" said the doctor. "Loder?"

Loder didn't answer; he sat there with his arms folded, staring straight ahead of him.

"Hey, *Loder!*" said the doctor, and he came to with a start. "Yes?" he said, "What?"

"Are you sitting in this game?" the doctor asked.

"Why not?" said Loder, rising.

He had been nice in that park; he had put his arm around her, he had spoken in a very kind and friendly way. But now he was queer. Susie sat down on the sofa as the four men took their places at the card table, and she thought that the doctor and Brett were queer, too. Maybe that's just because I'm tired, she thought. My first working day—if you can call it work.... I hope it isn't a sample of how things are going to be. I hope I'll never come across anyone else like that old man. But I've got to put him out of my head. He was drunk, that's all. That's why he yelled those things about Mr. Chiswick. He just seized on that name. Mr. Chiswick told me this was entirely new territory.

Of course, she thought, frowning, it's possible that the old man had met Mr. Chiswick somewhere. They might have met in New York. It might have been years ago, and Mr. Chiswick may not have been so nice then as he is now. Maybe he's *not* nice now. I'll kill Chiswick, the old man said, and he meant it. He meant he wanted to. People do kill people. When I first came across the old man lying there by the road I thought he'd been killed. I thought ... I've got to stop thinking about him, lying there, staring. He's probably home in bed now, with his eyes closed. It's morbid, to keep on thinking about him. I must be tired—only I'm certainly not sleepy. I might try to take an interest in this poker game. It's probably a typical scene. Typical of traveling salesmen. Only the doctor's not a traveling salesman. I don't know why he's here. I don't know whether Richard Carroll and Charles Loder are salesmen, either.

She looked at Carroll's thin, tired young face, and he seemed to feel it, for he glanced at her and smiled again. She looked at Loder, and as he took no notice, she stared at him. His face in profile was very handsome but with something ominous in the straight black brows, the out-thrust underlip, even the quick way he moved his smooth dark head. He looked like a fighter, she thought.

It was a very quiet game. Someone would say—Pass—Raise you one—Raise you two.... Not very interesting, she thought. "I'll see you, Brett!" said the doctor. There was complete silence while he and Brett looked at each other. Then they laid down their cards, and Brett raked in all the chips.

Carroll shuffled the pack with virtuosity, and dealt a new hand. Loder took his up, glanced at it and laid it down. "I'm out!" he said, and pushing back his chair, he rose and came over to the sofa. "Cigarette?" he asked.

"Thanks!" said Susie.

He bent and lit it for her, and remained standing before her. "Sit down?" she suggested, but he didn't answer. That seemed to be a habit of his. He lit a cigarette for himself and went back to the table; he sat there, pale, dark and somber.

"All right! It's yours, Brett," said young Carroll; and again Brett raked in all the chips. "I guess that's finished me. I'm too hard up to lose any more."

"I'll stake you," said the doctor.

"Thanks," said Carroll, "but I guess my luck's out tonight."

He came and sat down by Susie. "I didn't bring you luck then," she said.

"It wasn't that," he said, "but—" He lowered his voice. "The doctor's—a bit high," he said. "I never like that, in a game."

"High?" Susie said. "You mean that's a way he has of playing?"

"Don't you know what 'high' means?" asked Carroll, surprised.

"Oh, that?" she said. "You mean you think he's been drinking?"

"Who's been drinking?" asked the doctor, turning round in his chair, and as Susie's face grew hot, he began to laugh again. "That's set me thinking," he said. "If you've got a drop of anything in the house, Brett ...?"

"Beer, Doctor," said Brett.

"Then—" the doctor began, when the doorbell rang, and Brett pushed back his chair. But footsteps were already going along the hall, so he waited.

"Well, for the love of Pete!" said Queenie's voice from the hall. "And what do *you* want?"

"I want to see Mr. Percy Brett," said a man's voice.

"Why?" Queenie asked. "What about?"

"Ask Mr. Brett to step out here, if you please," said the man's voice.

"I won't," said Queenie. "I won't have cops coming here, spoiling my business."

"A cop ..." said the doctor in an undertone.

"Get Mr. Brett out here, or I'll go in and get him," said the man.

Brett rose, and went into the hall.

"Well, Sergeant?" he said in his pleasant voice. "What can I do for you?"

"I'll have to ask you to come along to the station, Mr. Brett."

"He will not!" said Queenie. "What *about?*"

"Now, Mrs. Brett—" said the sergeant.

"Queenie ..." said Brett. "Why do you want me, Sergeant?"

"Captain Catelli wants to ask you some questions," said the sergeant.

"What *about?*" cried Queenie. "You've got to tell him what about. This is America, and you're not going to pull him in—"

"Wants to ask you a few questions," said the sergeant, "in re this here accident to Mr. Person."

"What accident?" asked Brett.

"That's what we want to find out," said the sergeant. "Now, Mr. Brett ..."

"Don't you go, Percy!" said Queenie.

"I'm perfectly willing to answer questions," said Brett.

The doctor moved to the doorway, and Susie followed him.

"Mr. Person's accident serious?" the doctor asked.

The sergeant looked at him calmly. A blond man, he was, portly and erect.

"A fatal accident," he said.

"My God!" cried Queenie. "Murdered—"

She checked herself, and there was a complete silence. Looking over the doctor's shoulder, Susie saw how very white Brett was. He was looking at his wife, and she looked at him, her lips parted.

"I just thought that ..." she said, "because he was so unpopular.... I just thought that maybe somebody ..."

"Perfectly natural," said the doctor. "The sight of a policeman puts ideas like that in anyone's head."

"Yes, that was it," said Queenie.

There was another silence. "Well, Mr. Brett—" the sergeant began.

"Are you arresting Mr. Brett?" asked the doctor.

"Nope," said the calm sergeant. "Captain Catelli wants to ask him some questions."

"I don't know whether it's a legal requirement," said the doctor, in an affable, apologetic way, "but it's customary, isn't it, to give a witness some information as to what he's being questioned about?"

"I'm not trying to put anything over," said the sergeant. "Not on nobody. Old—that is, Alexander Person was killed this afternoon between around five-thirty and seven; and the Captain wants to know where Brett was at that time."

"Excuse me!" said Susie, and everyone turned to look at her. "Was ... is it all right for you to tell me how Mr. Person was killed?"

"Knifed," said the sergeant.

She had to go on. She had to know.

"Was he—did it happen in his own house?"

"Nope," said the sergeant. "By the roadside."

Then he was dead when I found him, she thought. He was murdered when I saw him there. Murdered. Knifed. With his eyes open.... She felt a little sick for a moment; she waited for that to pass, and then she turned back into the sitting-room to Loder. He stood near the table, and he looked at her, a dark narrow look. Someone outside closed the door into the hall.

"Look here!" she said, going close to him and speaking very low. "We've got to tell about finding—"

"*Sit down!*" he said, and almost pushed her onto the sofa. "Don't say *one word!*" he whispered. "I'll explain later."

"But—"

He was looking down at her, still with that dark, narrow glance. "If you say *anything*," he told her, scarcely moving his lips, "you'll ruin two innocent lives."

He turned on his heel, and walked off into the dining-room, and she sat on the sofa, paralyzed. I'm the one who found the body, she thought. It's a serious thing, to keep that from the police. Even if my telling did get some innocent people into trouble.... And I have only Charles Loder's word for that.

A new thought came to her that made her eyes widen. But did he know *then?* she thought. He had a flashlight. He could see better than I. He bent over him and had a good look. Then he said, "dead drunk," and he told me that tale about Blue Laws. I don't know why I believed him—except that he seemed young and nice, and there weren't any reasons for suspicions. But if he did know....

And where did he come from, anyway? I was stamping out the fire, and he was there. I didn't see him on the road. I didn't hear him until he spoke. It was so dark under the trees ... I couldn't have seen him if he'd been there all the time.

It was horrible to think of that. Horrible to imagine Charles Loder standing there in the dark, under the rustling trees.... "Knifed?" she said to herself. That could be done in silence.

"You look pale," said Carroll. "Don't you feel well?"

"I'm all right," she answered.

"I'm sorry you're so upset," he said. "You didn't know the man, did you?"

"No," she answered. "Only—"

Charles Loder was coming back with a glass of water. "Like some whiskey?" he asked. She shook her head and took a sip of water, and glanced up cautiously at Loder. Oh, no, she thought. *He's* not a murderer.

I know that. Maybe it's instinct, or intuition, but anyhow I *know* it. She gave a long sigh, and he stood smiling down at her; they smiled at each other.

The door opened and the doctor came in holding Queenie by the arm. She was as white as paper, but she was smiling in a dazed, almost idiotic way; she sat down on the sofa beside Susie, and turned the smile on her. Then in came the sergeant walking proudly, his back curved in, his front curved out, his head a little on one side.

"A few little questions ..." he said, persuasively.

The doctor seated himself on the arm of the sofa beside Susie.

"Where's Mr. Brett?" she whispered.

"They took him to the station," he murmured. "But don't worry. Don't worry about anything." He laid his arm along the back of the sofa behind her shoulders.

"Been having a little game, I see," said the sergeant, looking down at the cards on the table, with a sly smile on his pink-and-white face. He's the first policeman I've ever seen inside a house, thought Susie, and studied his profile, a rather sharp nose, a short upper lip. Like an Easter rabbit, she thought. I hope he's stupid. Because I'm nervous, or something.

"Now, miss!" he said. "Just a few questions."

No! she thought, in a panic. I haven't made up my mind yet whether to tell, or not ... I need a little time ... I'm not ready ...

Name? Age? Address? Occupation? She answered in a vague and hesitant way, and he wrote down the answers in a note-book.

"Now, Miss Alban," he said. "I understand you were in town this afternoon. If you'll give me an account of your movements between five-thirty and seven ...?"

"Well," she said, "Mr. Brett drove me in to the hotel."

"Yes?"

I'm not going to make up a lot of lies. I can't. I won't. What "innocent lives" could be ruined? I don't believe that. I *hate* this! I *hate* this!

"Mr. Brett drove you to the hotel," said the sergeant. "And then—?"

"I walked around."

"Around where?"

"I don't know."

"Take it easy," said the doctor, and his hand was on her shoulder with a firm and steady pressure. "The clerk at the hotel—"

"Here now!" said the sergeant. "That'll do, Doctor."

Thank you, Doctor! Susie cried in her heart. Of course, the hotel clerk would tell, or had already told, how she had asked the way to Mrs. Person's house. And he would tell how he had later told her the way home—through Woodmont Park. I *can't* lie, even if I wanted to, she thought.

"I don't remember the names of the streets," she said. "I went to call on Mrs. Person, to sell her one of our courses, but I didn't get a chance to talk to her."

"See anybody at the house?"

"An old man opened the door."

"Did you have a talk with him?"

"Well, not exactly," said Susie. "He was—disagreeable. He told me to go away."

"In what you would call an abusive way?"

"Yes," she said. "He yelled at me."

"Did he threaten you, miss?"

"No," she said.

"Did you see Mrs. Person again when you went back to the house?"

"I didn't go back to the house."

"You didn't go back to Oak Street?"

"Yes, but not to the house."

"You went through Woodmont Development on your way home?"

Now it's come! she thought. I'm sorry, but I'm not going to lie. "Yes," she said.

"What time was that, miss?"

"I don't know. But it was dark."

"Now, after Mr. Brett left you at the hotel—when was the next time you saw him?"

"When we got back here. He opened the door for us."

"Did you meet anybody you know in Woodmont Development?"

"Yes," she said, and again she felt the pressure of the doctor's hand on her shoulder. "Mr. Loder, and Mr. Carroll, and Dr. Jacobs."

And now he'll ask me—

"Thank you," said the sergeant, and he turned to Carroll. He had finished with her.

Richard Carroll. Age, twenty-six. Address, River Turrets Hotel, New York City. Occupation?

"Salesman," said Carroll.

"What's your line, Mr. Carroll?"

"I can't see how that matters," said Carroll, briefly.

"I don't, either," said Queenie, suddenly. "I don't see why you have to come here and pick on my guests."

"Now, then, Mrs. Brett ..."

"What do you think this is?" Queenie demanded. "A special excursion from New York, to bump off old Person? And if you think *they* did it, why did you go and pull in Percy?"

"That's enough, Mrs. Brett," said he.

"It's a damned sight too much, if you ask me," said Queenie. "You live here, and *you* ought to know who's the likeliest one to knife old Person."

"You'll have to leave the room, if you won't keep still," said the sergeant.

She laughed. It was a clear and a pretty laugh, wonderfully insolent. The sergeant's face reddened.

"*I* know who killed old Person with a knife," she said.

"You'd better be careful what you say—" he began.

"Want to make something of it?" said Queenie. "Because I don't care. I'll say it to anybody."

"Any more interruptions, and out you go," said the sergeant.

"Really?" said Queenie, resting three fingers elegantly on the crown of her tawny head.

There was something magnificent about her, something in her defiance that changed the very air. So that they no longer seemed like puppets, helpless before an impersonal force. They were people now. And the sergeant, still red, turned back to Carroll.

"I'm a salesman," said Carroll.

"If we want more information on that later," said the sergeant, "we know how to get it. Now let me have an account of your movements between five-thirty and seven."

"I drove into town in a taxi with Doctor Jacobs and Loder. We went to the hotel and had a drink, and then I went out and took a walk. I don't know where I walked, and I don't know what time I started or what time I got back to the hotel."

"All right! Who did you meet when you took a walk?"

"Nobody I knew."

"Ever been here before, Mr. Carroll?"

"Yes."

"When?"

"Two or three months ago."

"Still being a salesman?"

"Yes."

They were frankly hostile, curt and wary. Carroll's tired young face was tense, and somehow happy as if he enjoyed this.

"When you went back to the hotel, who was there?"

"Doctor Jacobs. We had another drink."

"Mr. Loder there?"

"I don't know. The bar was crowded. I didn't see him; but that doesn't mean he wasn't there."

"And then?"

"And then we walked home."

"Your name, Mr. Loder?"

"Charles Loder. Age twenty-two."

"Occupation?"

"I'm on a holiday," said Charles.

"What's your occupation when you're not on a holiday?"

"I'm an author."

"Mean you write books?"

"Short stories," said Charles.

"Address?"

Charles lit a cigarette.

"I'm not settled anywhere," he said. "I move around, looking for material."

"Where's your mail sent to?"

Suddenly Charles changed his manner; his brusque and almost sullen air turned to a confidential bonhomie.

"That depends on who's writing to me, and where I happen to be," he said.

"I've got to put down some address," said the sergeant.

"Well, what's the matter with this place?" asked Charles. "I've got a room here and a bag."

"Do you want to give this house as your address?" asked the sergeant.

"Why not?" said Charles, airily.

"It's up to you," said the sergeant, and wrote in his book. "Now, about this afternoon?"

"I drove into town with Doctor Jacobs and Carroll. We went to the hotel and had a drink. Then Carroll said he was going to take a walk, and after a while I thought I'd do the same. So I went out, and I walked around."

"At what time, and where?"

"I didn't notice the time," said Charles with a brilliant smile. "You don't, you know. I simply went out and walked. And when I came to the Park, I strolled into it. I didn't keep to the road. I like to walk on grass. It feels nice. I strolled around under the trees, and when I caught a glimpse of water, why, I went in that direction. When I got to the lake, there was Miss Alban just coming from the direction of the highway."

A mistake! Susie cried to herself. That's just dragged in by the heels. The whole way he's talking is a mistake. The way he's smiling. Why is he telling these lies? I don't *like* it. I want to tell the truth and get it over with. I suppose it does make plenty of trouble and bother, to be the one who found a body. They might keep me here. They certainly would ask questions. Hundreds of questions. It would probably be in the newspapers. All right! That would be better than feeling like this. Even being falsely accused would be better than feeling like this.

Charles Loder was going on in a garrulous and utterly unconvincing way. About how he and Miss Alban had sat down and had a smoke. I want to tell the truth! she cried in her heart. It was as if she were enmeshed in a spider's web, bound by something fragile, almost intangible. She could break free by a word; but she could not say that word. Because, if I do, she thought, I'll get him in trouble.

How much trouble and how serious? I don't know, she thought, but I can't do it without warning him. She looked at him lying, she watched him smiling with that unconvincing bonhomie, and the strangest pity filled her.

"All right!" said the sergeant.

But nothing could still Loder's volubility. "We were chatting about this and that," he said, "when we heard somebody whistling, and along came Doctor Jacobs and Carroll."

"*All right!*" said the sergeant. "That's all I want."

He closed his note-book and put it back into his pocket. "Don't you want my pedigree?" asked the doctor.

"Why, no, thanks, doctor," said the sergeant.

"Are we free to come and go as we please?" the doctor asked.

"I'll let you know," said the sergeant.

"What I want to know is, what you're doing with Percy," said Queenie.

"If he can give account of himself, he'll be home in a little while," said the sergeant.

"Well, he probably can't," said Queenie. "He's got that English way— sort of mixed up. He's stubborn, too, stubborn as a mule. It would be pie for you smart cops to frame him. But you're not going to do it. I'll get a lawyer, and I'll turn your police department inside out. Percy wouldn't hurt a fly."

"That's for Captain Catelli to say," the sergeant answered.

"No, it isn't," said Queenie. "Frank Catelli better let Percy go, or I'll tell how he made passes at me at the Columbus Day Outing."

"You'd better look out what you say," the sergeant warned her, with a looked of shocked amazement.

"Then you tell Frank Catelli to send Percy right straight home," said she. "Or I'll tear the whole town wide open."

She was superb. The sergeant looked at her sternly, but he could not face those blazing, steady blue eyes. "If anybody—" he began, when the telephone rang. Queenie sprang up, but the sergeant moved fast; he reached the telephone in the hall.

"Yes ... Yes ..." he said. "Dorfer speaking. Yes ... Yes ... Why ...? Yes ... *Yes*, I'm starting now.... Yes, I've got two men here.... Yes ... Right!"

He stayed in the hall, and Queenie went out after him. "Was that any news about Percy?" she demanded.

"Yes," he said, looking past her. "You can pack a bag for your husband if you like, and I'll take it."

"What d'you mean?"

"They're holding him."

"For what?" she asked.

"It seems he's been charged," said the sergeant, and after a brief pause, "with the murder of Alexander Person."

Queenie leaned back against the wall, and closed her eyes. There was no defiance in her now. In a moment she opened her eyes again and moved toward the stairs.

VIII

Susie was left with the doctor and Carroll and Loder in the sitting-room with the harsh overhead light.

Perhaps if I told about finding Mr. Person, it would make a difference, she thought. But she had no way of knowing whether it would be a favorable or a disastrous influence. Or who might profit, or who might suffer. She had a respect for the law, for truth and order, and discipline. But for the first time in her life she thought of the processes of the law not as an impersonal working of justice; but a hunt. Powerful, inexorable forces moving upon a terrified and helpless creature. If you see dogs after a rabbit, you don't think about the damage rabbits do to the fields, she thought.

"Try this," said the doctor. He was standing before her with a glass. "What is it?" she asked. "Water," he said. "Tinged with whiskey. Merely tinged."

"No, thank you," she said.

"Take a little," said Carroll, sitting down beside her. "You look pale."

"No, thank you," she said again.

"It'll help you," said Carroll.

"No, it won't!" said Loder. "Will you come into the dining-room for a moment, Susie?"

She rose. "The sergeant is still in the hall," said the doctor. "I'd strongly advise you against any little private conferences."

"To hell with him!" said Loder. "Come along, Susie!"

Carroll rose, too. "Susie," he said very low. "For God's sake, be careful. You're getting into deep water. You don't realize...."

"Meaning?" said Loder.

"You know what I mean," said Carroll, briefly. He crossed the room and closed the door. "You're using the girl as a shield. She doesn't realize—"

"Come, come!" said the doctor, hastily. "Sit down everybody. This won't do!"

"I want to speak to you, Susie," said Loder.

"There's no reason why I shouldn't speak to him," said Susie to Carroll and the doctor. Because there was something about Charles Loder that alarmed her. She went toward the dining-room, and he followed her. There was no door, only an arch with ugly green curtains drawn back on a rod; they stood at the far end of the room, by the big sideboard in full view of the other two, but out of hearing if they spoke quietly. Charles picked up a red china lobster that was hollowed out to make an ash tray; he stared at it with a frown.

"Yes?" Susie suggested after a moment.

He remained silent and downcast. And she noticed how long and how thick his black lashes were; he was so very handsome that he was almost theatrical. And she noticed how nervous he was, turning the scarlet lobster over and over in his thin, strong hands.

"Yes?" she said again, gently. Sorry for him, unreasonably, almost unbearably sorry for him. He's only a boy, she thought, and he's so sort of blundering....

"Susie," he said, looking at her. "I love you so darn much—I don't know what to do."

She looked toward him in stunned silence.

"It hit me like a ton of bricks," he said. "As soon as I saw you on the train. You came along into the smoker with the doctor. You looked so gay and brave.... You looked so happy.... You looked so sweet. That's why I got out here. I thought ..." He got a pack of cigarettes out of his pocket, he took one out, and dropped it on the floor, and kicked it with the toe of his shoe. "I thought that if I felt like that, possibly you did, too. I—mean. I thought that maybe it was—one of those mutual things."

"Well," she said, and began to cry. She quickly turned her back to the archway.

"I mean ..." he said. "I know we only met a few hours ago, but I mean—when it happens like this ... I mean, I *know* you. I know exactly what you're like. I mean—" His mouth twitched. "I'd trust my life to you," he said. "Maybe you'll marry me."

"Well, Charles," she said. "You see ... this is pretty unexpected...."

"Is it?" he said. "I thought it was pretty obvious."

She shook her head and dried her eyes.

"Could you give me any idea how you feel about me?" he asked.

She shook her head again, not able to speak.

"Well," he said, "if you can't, you can't."

He moved away. When she looked up, to say something, or at least to smile, he was going through the archway into the sitting-room. The sergeant stood there looking straight at her, and she felt her face grow hot. It's none of your business, she said in her heart. Maybe her talk with Loder was not his business but everything else was. As she entered the sitting-room, Queenie came running down the stairs and appeared in the door-way. She had changed her clothes; she wore a dark suit and a green straw hat like a large halo at the back of her head; in her white-gloved hands she carried two suitcases.

"I'm ready!" she said.

"Sorry," he said, "but you can't come."

"I will come!" she said. "I don't believe it's the law for you to take a man out of his own house and lock him up in jail, and not let anybody see him."

"He can see his lawyer,"

"He hasn't got any lawyer. I can see him. I'm going to see him. I just want to stand out in the hall and say hello to him."

"You can't come," said the sergeant. "You can see him tomorrow, if you get a permit, but not now."

Queenie was defeated. "I can ring him up, can't I?" she asked, suddenly gentle and winning.

"No," said the sergeant.

"Let's go upstairs," said Susie. "Let's have a nice cozy chat together."

For a moment, Queenie did not answer; then she set the bags down on the floor. "Take this to Percy, then," she said to the sergeant. "And I hope that one of these days you get treated just the way you've treated Percy and me."

"I'm doing what I'm paid to do," said he.

"I wish to Gawd I could get paid for treating *you* the way I'd like," said Queenie, and turned to Susie, and took her arm. They went up the stairs together.

"Let's sit in your room," said Queenie. "It drives me crazy to go in our room and see all Percy's th-things.... Oh, Gawd! I wonder *why* you do mean things—to people you love?"

She closed the door and stood against it; her eyes were glistening with tears, her coppery hair glittered, she looked strange, resplendent, and in-finitely touching. "All of this is my fault," she said.

"I don't think it could be," said Susie, "Won't you sit down and have a smoke?"

"I've got to talk," said Queenie. "It's—I feel as if my heart'd burst. You're a woman. *You* know how I feel. I've been so mean to Percy ... picking on him, and goading him ... I let that old bastard hang around here...."

"What old bastard?" Susie asked.

"Old Person. I let him give me a watch. And Percy took it and threw it on the floor and put his heel on it, and just scrunched it.... Then he put it in an envelope and sent it back to old Person. I was *glad* he did it. Only I pretended ... I kept at Percy all the time—about not having a fur coat, and all.... Oh, Gawd! I'd give my eye-teeth now, if I could get him back. If I could only, only go and tell him what a lot I love him...."

"Do sit down, Queenie," said Susie, and put her arm around her. "Try to take it easy, won't you?"

"Yes, but when I think of him locked up in a cell.... And he doesn't *know* how I love him."

"Yes, he does," said Susie. "And you'll see him tomorrow."

"He not the kind of person they—ought to put in jail," said Queenie, weeping. "He's so fastidious. Little things mean such a lot to him. Suppose they don't give him those bags? Maybe they won't even let him have a smoke. Maybe they're still asking him questions. One of those bright lights in his eyes, and not even a glass of water."

"They won't do that," said Susie. "Come on, darling. Sit down. That's the way. Now! You'll be more comfortable without your hat. Here's a cigarette. I'll light it for you."

"Listen, Miss—"

"Susie."

"Listen, Susie. If this was an accident ... I mean, not done on purpose ... if I could tell them how I'd sort of goaded Percy...? If I told them how that old bastard used to hang around the back door...? I could go and tell Catelli right now."

"Yes, and you might do all the harm in the world," said Susie. "I know it's hard, but you've got to wait. You've got to keep quiet until you know what's the best thing to say."

"Percy wouldn't ever use a knife," said Queenie. "Only sometimes the cops say things like that for a trap. I mean they'd say it was a knife, so that somebody would look surprised."

They sat side by side on the bed, and Queenie was smoking now, and growing quieter.

"One time, in New York," she said, "a, girl friend of mine got in trouble with the cops. She hadn't done a thing. Only this fellow she knew, a playboy he was, a millionaire, he committed suicide in her place. She wasn't even home. She was out with another fellow, and when they came back, she couldn't get in, because the door was locked on the inside. But that didn't help her any. The cops had her down at headquarters, day after day. They dug up things—everything."

She was silent for a while.

"They could do that to me, too," she said. "Not that I'd care. I never did anything to worry about. Only Percy'd hate it like poison. He doesn't like anyone to know I used to be a hostess in a dance hall, and a lot of things like that. I don't mind people knowing. I'm glad I did a lot of different things. Only I wish I'd had more education. More culture. I thought maybe I'd take piano lessons, or French, maybe. Only twenty-eight is too old to start, maybe."

"Lord, no!" said Susie. "Mr. Chiswick told me about people who started our course, who were fifty and older."

"I've heard about Gateways," said Queenie.

"From whom?"

"Oh ... around," said Queenie. "Hooey, isn't it?"

"I don't think so," said Susie, in a tone that would have upset Mr. Chiswick badly. "I think there are good things in it. If you'd like to look at the literature ...?"

Queenie said that she would, and Susie brought her the elegant brochure with the pictures of Madame Recamier, Du Barry, Cleopatra, Ninon de Lenclos and, strangely enough, Mata Hari. The Three Gateways to Enduring Charm. The Spiritual, the Mental, the Physical.

"The Mental is what I mean," said Queenie, deeply interested. "Now here, where it says how to develop poise and learn the art of conversation ..."

She read, turning the pages, frowning a little. "Listen!" she said. "If I took this course, do you think I could get to be—sort of more like Percy? You know what I mean."

Mr. Chiswick's instructions provided an answer to that question. But Susie said, reluctantly, unhappily, "I don't know."

"I could try," said Queenie. "I'd sort of like to."

"It's seventy-five dollars," said Susie.

"Well, it says you only have to pay ten dollars down," said Queenie.

She wanted the course. She would have it. She filled in the application, and she gave Susie a ten-dollar bill.

"I feel better," she said. "Now, if they keep Percy for a while, I can be sort of improving all the time. I always got on all right with men, only it was like it says here. Physical. You got to have more than that to keep a man...." She turned back to a certain page, and read aloud, "'The French call the sheer physical loveliness of youth, *beauté du diable*. Pronounced bow-tay doo dee-a-bel. Beauty of or from the devil. And, indeed it can be that, a sudden and devouring flame, that flickers out into ashes if there is not behind it the alabaster lamp of the Spirit, shining steadfast and glorious.' That's true."

She went off to her room then, calm and fortified, with all the sample lessons Susie had. Susie lit another cigarette and went to the window; she stood looking out at the sweet summer night, thinking over this strange day. She thought about old Person; she thought, with a shiver, of the lake.

But she thought about Charles Loder more than about anything else. She had, in these few hours, come face to face with murder, with violence. She was confronted with the ethical problem of Gateways in a stark form. She had felt the thrill of adventure, the confusion of doubt, she had known fear.

But she thought more about Charles Loder and his words, I love you....

IX

Susie undressed in a daze. Famous firsts, she said to herself. The first time I've even seen a dead person. The first time I've ever been questioned by the police. I've made my first sale today. And I've had my first proposal.

She got into bed, and turned out the light. It was good to be in bed in the breezy dark. I'll sleep well tonight, she thought. Then suddenly she remembered the report she should have written to Mr. Chiswick, and she turned on the light and sat up, worried and displeased with herself.

Too late to mail it tonight, she thought, but anyhow, I'll write it. Her fountain pen was feeble, but she began with élan. "I have sold a course to Mrs. Percy Brett, and received a ten-dollar deposit." All right! But shall I put in any of the other things? Mr. Brett being in jail, for instance? No, I'm not mixed up in this, thanks to Charles, and I'd better not say anything.

How was it that Charles felt like that, as soon as he saw me? Here I've been, all these years, and nobody else ever felt like that. I know I'm not hideous. I have nice eyes. Nice legs and feet and hands. But he said, I love you so darn much.... It makes you cry to think of that. He said he came here just for me.... It makes you want to be rather gentle and lovely....

All right, but I'm taking Mr. Chiswick's money. I've got to remember that. He asked me to write every night and tell what I'd done, and where I'm going. I suppose I'm going on tomorrow to Stonebridge. Why not? I mean I've got to. Well ... I don't suppose he'll come along. That would be a little too much to expect. Of course, if he's an author, he can go anywhere he wants, he can work as well one place as another. But he won't go following me all around.

It would be—rather sweet. In a way. But maybe he thinks I don't want him. I wonder if I was discouraging? I wonder if I *want* to be discouraging? I'm not in love with him. I do know that. But I like to have him around. I like him to say I love you so darn much.... It's a pretty wonderful thing. It makes you feel like crying.

But Mr. Chiswick isn't paying me to sit here, weeping, "I am sorry I haven't got more names here in South Fairfield; but I was unable to interview Mrs. Person." Yes, and his instructions about that had been definite. Always give the reason, if you fail to see a prospect. Susie thought about that. "And I will not be able to try Mrs. Person again, on account of domestic trouble," she wrote. She addressed an envelope, put the letter into it, and got back into bed. I'm terribly sorry for Queenie Brett, she thought. And I'm sorry for Percy. But on the whole, I'm sort of happy. And she fell asleep.

She waked in a sterner mood. This whole thing has been upsetting, she thought. Exciting, and so on. But now I've got to think about my work. It was a brisk, cool day; a good day for traveling, she thought. But I won't be likely to meet three more people as interesting as the doctor and Richard and Charles.

She found Queenie in the kitchen, cooking and singing. "I'm not going to let this get me down," Queenie said. "They'll have to let me see Percy today. And all the spare time I've got, I'm going to be studying that sample lesson. The one about that Greek woman."

She stood by the stove with her hands on her hips; a creature warm and glowing with life, clean in her green cotton dress as a growing plant.

"I used to think culture was hooey," she said. "And maybe, when you're real young, you don't need it. But I'm twenty-eight, now. If I'm going to keep Percy, I've got to be more sort of subtle. That's where that damned Eve is smart."

"What damned Eve?" asked Susie.

"Person. Gawd! *If* you could see the way men fall for her! When I first came here, I thought she was a joke. That long hair, and no make-up, so old-fashioned. But then Percy talked about her. He used to meet her—just by the merest chawnce, don't you know. And he'd tell me how he'd seen her in the drug store, or somewhere, and how remarkable she was. And then, one time when there was a dance for the Veterans, I met her. I watched her working. I hated her—I guess because Percy admired her so much. But what I ought to do is, try to be more like her."

"Is she cultured?" asked Susie.

"Yes," said Queenie. "Speaks French, and plays the piano, and everything."

"She didn't pick out a very attractive husband."

"He's one of the richest men in South Fairfield," said Queenie. "Mean and stingy as they come. He wouldn't even let her have a girl to help in the house, or a car, or anything. But he was twenty-five years older than her, and she's one of the patient kind." She paused. "D'you know," she said, "I sort of liked that old billy-goat."

"Did you?" said Susie, interested.

"Yes, I did," said Queenie. "He was a bad old man, all right, and he was a terrible landlord. He wouldn't do a thing for you; and if you were a week back in the rent, he'd raise Cain. But there was something about him ... *I* don't know ... Percy couldn't stand him, but Percy's very fastidious. I used to sort of like talking to him sometimes. He'd come and sit on the back steps and have a cup of coffee and a cruller I'd been baking, and—well, he made you laugh. He was—I don't know the word for it, exactly, except that he liked being alive. And he didn't give a hoot about anyone. Independent, he was."

She turned her head and looked out through the screen door at the back steps, where old Person had used to sit. "I'm sorry he's dead," she added, simply.

Susie was quiet for a while, impressed by that honest requiem. After a moment: "Can you tell me about trains to Stonebridge?" she asked.

"But you're not going today?" Queenie asked startled.

"I've got to."

"But Doc said you were going to wait, and go with him."

"What did he mean by that?" asked Susie.

"He said he was going to buy a car, and drive you. He said you'd be here two or three days."

"That must have been a joke," said Susie. "Anyhow, I've got to go this morning."

"I'll miss you," said Queenie. "I wanted to get to know you better. I like you."

Susie liked her. Moreover, she felt she had learned a great deal from Queenie. The knowledge was not yet sorted out, not yet digested; only she knew that she had met someone who knew more than she did. They breakfasted alone together in the kitchen, an excellent breakfast, and Queenie brought out a timetable.

"There's a train at eight-fifty," she said. "I'll drive you to the station, if you've really got to go. Only I wish you could've stayed until Percy got out."

"I'll call you up tonight from Stonebridge," said Susie.

"What I'm going to do today," said Queenie, "is find out what they've got on Percy. He told me he was held up that afternoon by engine trouble. But you never know. He might have been hanging around Eve's house. And if the cops have found out how he threatened old Person ... It wouldn't be hard to find out. One time when they met in Schulte's garage, Percy went at him. Told him he'd shoot him if he found him around here. It didn't mean a thing, and Percy hasn't even got a gun, but it's just the kind of thing Frank Catelli would like. He thinks he knows all about psychology. He's got it into his head that Percy's dangerous. He told me so once."

"Dangerous?" Susie repeated.

"Yes, some sort of psychological way. Frank Catelli's stubborn, and he's got funny ideas," said Queenie. "Only he's kind of smart with psychology."

She sighed, and finished her coffee. "Well ..." she said. "Doc said he'd lend me some money, if I needed it, to get Percy out of this."

"When ...?" Susie began, and checked herself.

"Mean, when did I get a chance to see Doc?" said Queenie with a smile. "When I came out of your room last night, he was hanging around in the hall. We went down and had a drink, and a chat. Funny guy, he is, isn't he?"

"I don't know much about him," said Susie.

"Well, he seems to know plenty about you," said Queenie. She pushed back her chair. "I'll get the car," she said. "You better step on it, Susie, if you want to make the eight-fifty."

While Susie packed her bags, she left the door into the hall open. She thought if there were any people around, they could see her. They could say good-by. But all other doors were closed. Nobody came.

I suppose I could have taken a later train, she thought. But after all, I've got to think of my work. I'd have liked to stay here a while longer, to see how things came out. I'd have liked to say good-by to the doctor and Richard Carroll. And Charles. But it can't be done.

She took her bags downstairs, and Queenie was waiting for her.

"It's a lovely day," Queenie said. "I only wish Percy was out in it. I've been mean to him about living in the country. He just loves it. But I never would admit there was anything nice about it."

She started the car; the windows were all open, and the fresh air blew her bright hair; her face in profile was grave, and very handsome.

"I'll be at the Jefferson Hotel," Susie said. "In case anyone wants to reach me."

"Doc will," said Queenie. "He's crazy about you."

"No, he isn't," said Susie.

"He certainly is," said Queenie. "You ought to hear him. He's nice, and I think he's got plenty of money. But, Gawd! To marry for money is about the worst thing.... Well, here we are...."

She drew up to the station which was almost deserted.

"You got about six minutes," said Queenie. "I'll wait with you."

Susie went in to buy a ticket, and the sergeant was there.

"Good morning!" he said.

"Good morning!" said Susie, and would have gone past him to the ticket office, but he moved into her path.

"Just a minute," he said. "Do you mind telling me your middle name, miss?"

"Why, no," she said. "It's Louise."

She moved sideways, but so did he.

"I'm sorry, miss," he said. "But I'll have to ask you to come along with me."

"Where to?" she cried.

"Captain Catelli wants to see you."

"But I'm going on business ..."

"You can explain that to Captain Catelli," said he. "This way, please."

"But, *why?*"

"Listen, Susie," said Queenie. "Don't argue. You go along with Buck. And just you remember you got friends here. If they try to frame you, don't worry."

"This way!" said the sergeant, again, and Susie went with him, to a little sedan, with a policeman in uniform sitting at the wheel.

She got into the car, her hands like ice, her heart like lead. If they ask me about Mr. Person...? she thought. I don't *want* to lie. But if they ask me—if I tell them the truth about finding him, and if Charles sticks to that story be made up, he might get into serious trouble. Oh, if only I could talk to him first! Because if I tell the truth ... about Charles being suddenly there ...

It may not be that at all, she told herself. The sergeant asked my middle name. It may be just something for their record. The thing is, to keep cool. "Ruin two innocent lives," Charles said. He had some good reason for not telling the truth....

Some good reason—or some bad reason? What if he knew who killed old Person? No! He wouldn't have let them arrest Percy Brett. Unless Percy did it and Charles knows. Oh, if I only knew what was going on! I suppose what I ought to do is, to think of truth and justice, and not care about consequences. I would, if I could only let Charles know. But how can I, now? I'll have to put them off somehow.

The car stopped before a big old wooden house in a back street. A tree-lined street, and a fancy house with scroll-work and bay windows, so that the sign over the portico, which said POLICE STATION, seemed very unsuitable. They entered a hall, and went into a room at the right, a large high-ceilinged room with a bay window and a fireplace, and there at a desk sat a neat grave man with a little black mustache. "Here she is, Chief," said the sergeant.

"Good!" said Catelli. "Sit down, Miss Alban."

She sat down on a kitchen chair, directly opposite to him, and the sergeant stood beside her. A shaft of sunlight came in at the window, and dust shimmered in it; she thought that the room smelled of dust. Captain Catelli was very quiet; he was very serious.

"What is your complete name, Miss Alban?" he asked.

"Susan Louise Alban."

"Then your initials are S. L. A.?"

"Yes, they are," she answered, more and more alarmed. He opened a drawer of the desk and brought something out; he leaned forward, and opening his hand, revealed a little watered sick pouch.

"Ever seen this before?" he asked, his brown eyes fixed upon her face.

"Well ... yes," she answered.

Of course, she had seen it. It was a strange little thing, made for her last Christmas by rich, stingy Aunt Myra. There was a powder puff inside it, too hard to use, and her initials were embroidered on the back of it. But she could not remember having taken it with her anywhere, ever.

"Is it yours, Miss Alban?"

"Well, it *seems* to be," she said. "But I don't know where it could have come from."

"You don't?" he said.

What did it signify? "Well," she said, "it might have got in with some letters—I mean, I brought a letter from my aunt along to answer when I had some spare time, and it might have got in with that."

"When did you last see this—?" He did not know what to call it, and neither did Susie. "This article," he said.

"I don't *remember* seeing it since last Christmas," she said. "Maybe it isn't mine."

He turned it over, and there were the initials S. L. A.

"Do you identify this as your property, Miss Alban?" he asked.

She felt a confusion that was worse than fear. She could not imagine what this meant. Where this was leading. Suddenly she remembered what the doctor had said last night.

"I think you ought to tell me—why you're asking me these questions," she said.

"Not at all," said Captain Catelli. "I'm asking you whether or not you identify this as your property."

"Well," she said, feeling her way, "I don't think I have to answer."

"You couldn't find a worse line to take," said he. "I'm asking you a simple question that any respectable citizen would be willing to answer—frankly and freely. Is this—this article yours, or is it not?"

"For all I know," said Susie, "this could be a trap. I want to know where you found it."

He was silent for a long time, and that also was a trap, she thought. Maybe he thought she would break down.

"This was found," said Captain Catelli, "under a heap of partially burnt leaves. Approximately one yard from the body of the deceased."

"Oh, I *see!*" she said. "That's a queer accident. I struck a match, and I didn't put it out properly, and it set fire to some leaves. I suppose I pulled this—article out of my purse when I got out the matches."

"Why did you strike a match, Miss Alban?"

"To get a light," she said, coolly enough.

"Why did you want a light?"

"For a cigarette," said she.

And now she had done it. Now she had crossed the Rubicon. She had told a lie. But I can get out of it later, after I've seen Charles, she thought. As long as I don't go any further.

"What did you see when you struck this match?"

"Nothing much," she said.

"Miss Alban," he said, "this is a very serious matter. This is a case of murder, and it is your duty to assist the police to the best of your ability. I want a free and honest account of what you saw when you struck that match."

If I say I saw old Person...? And just walked off? I can't do that. And I won't say Charles was there. He told that lie, about my coming from the main road. They'll want to know why he said that. And why did he, anyhow? Was it to help me, to keep me from getting mixed up in this? If I knew—if I only knew. If I could only speak to him for five minutes ... if I only had a little *time.*...

"Come, now!" said Catelli.

All your life you are trained not to say indiscreet or injurious things. If you know something to somebody's disadvantage, you are supposed to keep quiet about it. And now I'm to tell everything, without knowing what harm it could do. Well, I won't, she thought. I'm not going to tell a lot of lies, and I'm not going to tell the truth until I know what it's all about.

"Come," said Catelli, "I'm waiting."

She sat with her lashes lowered, and a vague, gentle, young-girl look on her face.

"I haven't any more to say," she answered.

"Miss Alban, this article was found within a few feet of the body. When were you there? And what time did you light this fire?"

"I only lit it by accident."

"At what time?"

"I'm sorry, but I don't know what time."

"You left the hotel for the second time at approximately ten minutes past six."

"Did I?" she murmured.

"You aren't doing yourself any good by these evasions," said he. "I'm going to ask you a direct question, and I expect a straight answer. What were you burning up in that fire?"

"Nothing!" she said, amazed. "Honestly, nothing. I dropped the match, and it set fire to some leaves. It was an accident."

"Miss Alban," he said, "we've found charred paper among those leaves."

"I didn't burn any papers. I—give you my word I didn't."

"We found this—article lying beside the leaves. And we found ..." He paused. "A portion of an envelope, with your name on it."

"Well, then, it fell out of my purse. It was an accident."

"Mr. Loder said last night that he saw you coming toward the lake from the direction of the New Road. How did you get there?"

"I don't know. Anyhow, it doesn't—it can't matter. I didn't have *anything* to do with—what happened. I never was here until yesterday. I don't know *anything*."

"Do you want to make a statement?" he asked.

"Well—about what?"

"Do you wish to give a statement of your movements after arriving at the Fairfield Arms?"

"I have. I've told you ..."

"As soon as you reached the hotel," said Captain Catelli, "you asked for directions to Mrs. Person's house. I have a witness to the fact that you quarreled violently with Mr. Person—"

"I didn't quarrel with him."

"We have the evidence of the article and the envelope to show that you were on the scene of the murder at a certain time. We've got to have an explanation, Miss Alban." He paused again. "And it's got to be good," he said.

"Well ..." she said. "I didn't quarrel with Mr. Person. I didn't burn anything, unless it was by accident. I don't know anything about the—murder. That all I can say."

"Then we'll have to hold you, Miss Alban."

"Wh-what does that mean?" she said.

"We'll have to hold you as a material witness."

"You mean—in prison?"

"That's exactly what I mean," said Captain Catelli.

X

This isn't serious, she said to herself. It's ... it's pretty horrible, but it's not serious. I mean I can get out of this any time I want, by telling the truth. It's not like being falsely accused, and not being able to explain. It's because I don't want to explain. Just yet.

"This way," said the sergeant, and she went with him out of the house and down the steps and along a path beside the house. It all looked so cozy, with shrubs and green grass. Behind the house stood a square cement building, whitewashed, like a garage. Only that it had barred windows.

"Is this—where I'm going?" she asked.

"County jail," said he.

"Can I telephone to anybody?"

"One call," said he.

"Can I make it now?"

"Yep," he said. "Who's it to?"

"Do I have to say?"

"Yep."

"Can't it be private?"

"Nope."

"Then I'll wait a little while," she said. Because this had to be thought out. I can't ring up Charles, she thought. That would look much too queer. A man I only met yesterday. It would drag him into it right away. I've got to let him know, of course, but it will have to be done more intelligently. We'll both have to tell the whole story. Only I want him to be warned.

The sergeant was unlocking the door of the square, little, white building. This is a jail, she thought. Once you get in you—can't see anybody. You can't even know what's going on. Suppose they built up an elaborate case against me? That's nonsense. Charles wouldn't let them. He's sure to find out in a little while, even if I don't call him up. And then he'll get me out.

There was another door directly behind the first door. It's a jail. It's—suppose it gets in the newspapers? What will poor Father and Mother think? And Mr. Chiswick? No! *This won't do.* I don't want to get Charles in any trouble, but I've got to think of my family. This won't do!

"I'll make the call now, please," she said.

"Okay!" said the sergeant. "Who's it to?"

"Mrs. Brett."

"Well," he said. "I suppose that's all right. But if I was you, I'd get hold of a lawyer."

"I don't need a lawyer," said Susie. "I haven't done anything."

"I've heard that one before," said the sergeant.

They were in a sort of office, with nothing in it but a desk and one chair; whitewashed walls and bare floor. And a barred window. It was light, it was airy, but it was horrible. Horrible because it wasn't human. It was a place where you were shut up, locked in, and left. Nobody cared....

"There's your telephone," said the sergeant. "Brett's number is 907."

She sat down at the desk and dialed the number, and in a moment Queenie's warm contralto voice answered, "Hello!"

"It's Susie. They—they're holding me."

"For Gawd's sake! They still got you there?" asked Queenie, understanding without any explanation.

"Yes," Susie said.

"What's the charge?"

"I'm a material witness, they say."

"Listen," said Queenie. "I know you can't say anything much. You answer, yes or no; I'll understand. Have they got anything on you, Susie?"

"Well ... in a way," said Susie. "It's complicated. And, of course, I'm a stranger here, and I don't know anybody. Will you please tell the others. The doctor, and Richard Carroll, and Charles Loder?"

"Loder's gone."

"Gone?" Susie said.

"Yes. He came to the station in a taxi, just after the sergeant took you away. I told him; he said he was sorry. But he said he had to get the train."

"Do you know where he went?" Susie asked.

"I didn't ask him. I was upset, with the sergeant taking you away like that. I came right home, and I told Doc and he said, not to worry. He said they wouldn't hold you."

Susie was silent.

"Listen, darling," said Queenie. "Don't worry. Just take it easy. Doc will fix it."

"Thank you," said Susie. She could not go on.

"You take it easy, darling," Queenie said again. "Doc's on the war-path. He'll get you out. Don't worry."

"Thank you," said Susie.

"Did you happen to hear anything about Percy?" Queenie asked.

"No," said Susie. "I'm sorry." She hung up the receiver.

The sergeant was waiting. He led her out of the office to a corridor lined with four doors with little square gratings in them. He unlocked the one at the end, Susie entered it, and he went out, and locked the door after him. She stood looking at the door; after a minute she went to look out through the grating. She couldn't see anything.

Suppose I wanted something. Suppose I felt sick...? Well, I'm not sick. I'm young and healthy. This is nothing. I won't be here long. There was a cot, a wash-basin, and a shelf; there was a window, barred, and so high she could not see out of it. She sat down on the cot.

I shan't be here long. Take it easy. Only—I don't know exactly what to *do* ... I'm locked in. If I called, I guess nobody would hear. But I'm not going to call. It's perfectly clean here. There's plenty of air. I don't really feel as if—I was smothering. Take it easy.

Charles has gone. He knows the sergeant brought me here to ask me questions, and still he went away. Without a word. He got me into this. He stopped me from telling the truth. And then he just went away. So that now if I do tell, he can't be here to back me up.

He said I love you so darn much. And then he left me in this jail. All right!

I guess he said he loved me, just to keep me quiet. That happens. You read about things like that. You read about men who make love to women and then get all their savings. Things like that. Women believe them. I believed him. I liked him. I tried to help him out of trouble. And he just went off and left me holding the bag. I guess I'm just one of those women. Those fools.

But if I liked him—why not have faith in him? When I remember how he looked, and how he talked—I *can't* think he's mean and cowardly and hateful. Why should I think that? Why shouldn't I give him the benefit of the doubt? I liked him. Maybe it was an instinct. And your instincts—are right.... I don't care if I'm crying. Nobody can see me or hear me. I feel like crying. I'm in jail....

After a while they'll ask me questions again. And this time I'll tell the truth. I've got to. I can't—get convicted and really sent to prison. I'm afraid—if they get really serious.... I'm afraid I'll have to say that Charles was there. Beside the body. It will look bad for him. But he can get out of it. Because he didn't do that. I *absolutely* know that. He'd no more stick a knife in anyone than I would. He had some reason for going away. It—wasn't—because he was afraid.

I think I'd feel better if I walked up and down. Only—it's awfully *small*. It's awfully quiet here ... Of course, after a while somebody will come and bring me something to eat. They never just leave people....

This is pretty bad. This is worse than you'd think. But I can take it. It's not like really being in prison. There are other people now—this minute—locked in cells—and they know it's going to be for ages. Some of them—for life. For *life*.... We shouldn't do that to people. Shut them up for life ... think of it....

I haven't thought enough about anything. I've just gone around enjoying myself. Glad to be alive. I had the whole world to go around in. And now I'm in jail. I want to get *out*. I don't know what—to do with myself. I want to get *out*. If I call...? If I bang on the door...? I'll tell them the whole story now, and they'll let me out.... I've *got* to get out.... I can't stand—being shut up.

Listen. Take it easy. I'm not a coward. I *can* stand this. I can have a little dignity and pride. I can sit down and think. I can think about—something. Not myself. About books I've read. I can think about Gateways.... There was that list of French phrases that cultured women must know. *Qui vivra, verra*.... I don't care if I'm crying. That's all right, as long as nobody can see you.... If they don't let me out pretty soon, Father will do something. Mother ... Mother, I want you....

"That's only natural. Even soldiers—called for their mothers. When they were wounded ... I do wish—Mother were here. When you're locked up like this you feel—as if everybody'd forgotten you. But Mother and Father would never forget me.... It's only—for a little while....

If I go on walking up and down, I'll get tired enough to go to sleep. That will make the time go.... Charles asked me to marry him. The only kind of marriage I'd ever want would be like Mother and Father. That loyalty. That—that kindness.... Charles went off and left me ...

It hurts to cry so much. It hurts your ribs. I think I'll try a cigarette.... If you're really in prison, you can't have cigarettes ... An envelope with my name on it? I must have pulled it out with the—article.... Poor Aunt Myra! I wonder what name she had for that thing? Of course, it does look bad, finding that article and the envelope, right there. They couldn't think I killed Mr. Person. But they might think I knew who did it ... accessory after the fact ... You go to prison for that.

Am I an accessory after the fact? Am I helping the murderer? Where did Charles come from? I don't know. But I know he didn't kill Mr. Person with a knife. Not Charles. He's—too young. He's not the type. I'd know. Something would tell me if I met a murderer.... Murder. It's a horrible thing, to be locked up. But what is it like to kill? To take somebody's life? Old Person liked to sit on the back steps in the sun. The sun is still here; but he's dead.

What are some more of those phrases? *Revenons à nos moutons* ... Queenie will be learning them. Queenie loves Percy. Really loves him. But she can be hateful to him. It's not like Mother and Father. It's a different way of loving. And maybe Charles—cares about me—in another way ... or maybe—I'm only a *fool*....

XI

My God! What a fool she is! thought one of the four men, with a sort of delight. I didn't realize what a fool she was. Things aren't so good for me just now. I'm in a spot, just now. But I can get out of it as long as she keeps this up.

As long as she doesn't get to Stonebridge for a couple of days, I'll be all right. She's the only one who could really have made trouble for me. Serious trouble. But now she's done for herself. Nothing she says now will carry any weight.

They'll let her go in a few days. Her people will hear about this, in the course of time. Highly respectable people. And the girl's highly respectable. They're the easiest to handle. I remember that respectable girl on the ship. Thirtyish—a very good job. A good background. But she'd have thrown it all away—chucked everything, if I'd gone a little further. I didn't because

I'm not a cad. There's no harm in a little flirting, a few compliments, a little love-making. But I've never treated a woman badly. I never will.

As long as little Susie can't get to Stonebridge in time to spoil things for me, I'll never bother with her again. I have nothing against her personally. I rather like her, in fact. Only, when I thought she was meddling in my affairs ...

She was, too. That was undoubtedly what she came here for. To spy on me. To get me locked up. But now she's locked up, herself. Women ... my God! Women will believe *anything*. You can't lay it on too thick. Except Eve. She didn't believe anything.

But Eve won't do any talking now. She can't. She's got to mourn now. For Alexander. She can't give even a hint about me. How she loves her respectability! The Duchess of South Fairfield, Queenie calls her. Poor Queenie! She's attractive enough. She can get all the men she wants. But she'd never know how to exploit a man, like Eve. How to get everything, and give nothing.

When I've got my little affair in Stonebridge cleared up, maybe I'll blackmail Eve. She's a wealthy widow now. Anyhow, she's going to pay me back that money I gave her. All of it—with interest. God! When I think of the risk I took ...! Even now ...

But I'm fairly safe now, as long as young Susie's locked up. That was a bad moment when she said she was going to Stonebridge to see Esther. As long as I can get there first, I'll be all right. I can manage Esther. But if Susie had started today, I'd have had to stop her.

It's queer, he thought. You don't care. No nightmares, no cold sweats. After all, it's the most natural thing in the world. Instinctive and natural as eating, to get rid of someone who threatens you. They suspect me, but that's nothing. They've no proof. There never will be any. I did the thing quickly and neatly; humanely. I'm not cruel. If I'd had to get rid of Susie, I'd have done it decently.

It's queer what confidence it gives you, to know that you can protect yourself. I've been inclined to be a little shy and lacking in self-confidence, up to now. But now that's finished. It was foolish, very foolish, for me to get into this mess. I did it for Eve, of course. And it was the worst way to behave, with a woman like her. The more generous, the more chivalrous you are toward her, the more domineering she is. But she'll be very different now. She'll be afraid of me now. Gentler. A little cringing, maybe.

It made him smile, to think of that. And when he thought of Susie, he nearly laughed aloud. If Susie had any suspicion ... he thought. Susie thinks I'm nice. She liked me from the very beginning. But if she knew I'd thought seriously of wringing her neck ... Nice little neck ... I'm rather fond of Susie. As if I were a king, and she were one of my subjects. Power of life and death....

Eve, too. By—God! Eve, too. I could wring her neck. And she *knows* it! She knows now what I'm capable of. When I see her she'll be so damned frightened.... The tables are turned now, my dear Eve. I'm the master now. Because I'm afraid of nothing. Nothing! There's only one little detail to clear up. I've got to see Esther Malter, and arrange it so that she'll never talk. After that, I'm free. It was foolish to get into this mess. But the way I'm handling it isn't foolish.

I never knew I had it in me to act with this decision. I've killed a man, and it doesn't bother me one bit. I slept well, last night. In spite of worrying about Susie. I'll never worry again, because now I know. Now I know how to cope with any problems that come up. I've never felt so well. I could lick my weight in wild cats. I heard Queenie say that once. Poor Queenie … handsome wench....

And Susie sat on the cot, with the clean, peaceful exhaustion that can come after tears. It was as if everything were finished, all feeling, all thought. She leaned her head against the wall, not caring how long she sat here, or what happened. A pleasant breeze blew in and stirred her hair. Her ribs felt a little sore, so she breathed gently. Her eyes felt sandy, so she closed them.

Then someone was at the door, rattling with the key. The door opened and the sergeant was there.

"Okay!" he said. "You can go."

"How do you mean, go?" she asked, dazed.

"Sign the book, and go," he said.

"Go—anywhere I want?"

"That's it."

"Well, why? What's happened?"

"Captain doesn't need you, that's what."

"But why?"

"You don't have to worry about that," said the sergeant. "You can take your train and go anywhere you want."

He spoke, she thought, with a sort of calm triumph, and it worried her.

"Well, doesn't anyone want to ask me any more questions?"

"Nope," said he. "Come along now, Miss. I've got work to do."

"I don't understand it!" she cried.

"No," said he. "I guess you don't."

XII

Queenie was there, sitting in the bare, dusty room, alone. Bareheaded, in the fresh green cotton dress, she looked strangely domestic.

"They rang me up and said they were letting you out," she explained. "So I came. I just wondered if you happened to hear anything about Percy?"

"I'm sorry," said Susie.

"Well," Queenie said, "Doc's got me a lawyer, and he'll be here any minute. The Doc says they've *got* to let me see Percy."

They went out into the sunny street together. It was very strange, to be free. To walk along under the trees with Queenie.

"Doc's sending this lawyer," said Queenie. "And he said, tell you he'd be seeing you. He's certainly crazy about you."

"I think you're mistaken," said Susie.

"Here we are!" said Queenie, stopping beside the car. "The sergeant carried out your bags. You won't mind if I sort of hurry you, will you, Susie? I hate to be away from the house on account of the lawyer ringing up, or maybe Percy."

"Of course not," Susie assured her.

"You'll have about half an hour to wait at the station," said Queenie. "But I bought a magazine for you to read."

"I'll call you up this evening from Stonebridge. I hope by that time you'll have good news."

"They've got him framed," said Queenie. "That's why they're acting this way. Trying to keep anyone from seeing him. Not telling him what they've got against him. But this lawyer is smart. He'll get Percy out. And then I'll go for Frank Catelli bald-headed."

They drew up to the station—for the second time that day. Susie looked at her watch. "Only eleven-thirty," she said.

"The time must seem terribly long, shut up in jail," said Queenie. She took Susie's hand, and leaning forward, kissed her on the cheek. "I *hope* I'll see you again soon," she said. "I like you, Susie."

"I like you!" said Susie, fervently. "Now, you go along, Queenie. I know how you feel about being away. Good luck, Queenie!"

"Good luck to you!" said Queenie. "I'll work hard on the course, too. Maybe the next time you see me you won't know me."

Susie sat on a bench on the platform; and it was all so very strange. And sad. I feel as if they were old friends, she thought. Queenie, and the doctor, and Richard Carroll. And probably I'll never see any of them again. I suppose this was just an episode. Charles, too.

Maybe I'll meet other men like that. Men who'll make love to me and not mean a thing. Or maybe mean something disgraceful. I never thought of *that* with Charles. It's certainly a thing that happens often enough. Men talk about marriage to lead girls on. Queenie thinks the doctor is smitten with me. Could I possibly be that type, the type it spoke about in Gateways? "The woman who, consciously or unconsciously, awakens lust in men...."

It was a curious and completely novel idea. It could lead to a lot of complications, she thought, traveling around and having men feel like that as soon as they see you. Of course, it would be hateful, and as it says in Gateways, it's nothing but a misfortune for a woman, and you have to learn to make a different kind of impression if you want any true and lasting happiness. But it *would* be dramatic. Suppose I met someone on the train—

I ought to be ashamed of myself. I am. And it's not true, either. I'd certainly have noticed it before this. The real explanation probably is, that when you're traveling you meet men who are at loose ends, and they make love *pour passer le temps*. If I'm any good, I'll stop thinking about love and what not, and keep my mind on my job.

It's been a queer beginning, but now it's all over. From now on, it'll be humdrum. And if any other men try to make passes, I hope I'll have some sense and dignity. The train was coming now, and she rose. And if she was sad and troubled about many things, still there was in her heart the sense of adventure. Of going on to a new place.

She had not got a Pullman seat for the ride of two hours; she got into the day coach and sat down. And waited. Stupid! she said to herself. There's nothing to wait for. Nothing is going to happen.

"First call for luncheon in the dining car!" called a porter.

I guess I'll eat now, thought Susie. And while she went through three cars, while she stood looking for a vacant table, she was waiting for something to happen. She had lunch and went back to her place. There was an old lady, knitting. There were two girls—college types, reading. There was a bald man, asleep. They won't let you in the Club Car without a Pullman ticket, she thought; and I haven't the nerve to go into the smoker, all alone. Anyhow, it's only a little while longer.

I hope Percy's home by this time. Do they really frame people? I wasn't framed. I really looked very suspicious, what with the article and the envelope; and being evasive. I wonder why they suddenly let me out. They *must* have found out something.

Something about Charles? Or have they arrested somebody else? Well, suppose—? A new idea came to her, that turned her cold with dismay.

Suppose that if I'd told the truth, it would have cleared Percy?

That, she thought, was possible. If she told the police that she had found old Person dead, it would establish a time; and that might be the one essential fact for Brett. I know now what it is like to be in prison, even for a few hours. Am I letting Percy Brett go through that, letting poor Queenie suffer, because I've concealed important evidence? It was a mistake. It's always a mistake to lie. It always hurts someone; if not other people, then yourself. I'm going to set this straight. If Charles hasn't done anything stupid, or wrong, it can't do him any serious harm. And if he has, let him pay for it.

I have done something stupid and wrong, she thought; and I'll have to pay. I'll have to go back and tell Captain Catelli. Maybe I'll have to be locked up again. Is it perjury to tell a lie, if you're not under oath? I don't know. But I hate lies. I'll certainly lose my job. Maybe it will get in the newspapers, and Mother and Father will see it. They'd be sweet and dear about it, but it would hurt them horribly. She had a vision of her father sitting at the breakfast table. "What a tangled web we weave," he would quote, "when first we practice to deceive." Or something like that. He's so good and kind.

I owe something to Mr. Chiswick, though, she thought. After all, he pays my expenses; and I can't use all my time for this personal thing. I'll go and see Mrs. Malter, and I'll try and get an order from her. And then I'll go back. I'll tell Captain Catelli the whole thing. If it makes trouble for Charles, I'll be sorry but that can't be helped.

I'll be sorry if I have to be locked up again. Well, I won't think about that. I'll concentrate on making a sale. If this is the end of my job, and my traveling, all right. I'll try to make it a good end.

"Stonebridge!" said a conductor, in a brief, cold way. "Stonebridge, next stop! Stonebridge."

He took her bags from her out to the platform; the train came to a stop at a nice station with flower-beds. The conductor took her bags down the steps; when she thanked him, he raised his eyebrows as if amazed, and got back on his train that glided away.

Susie picked up the bags and moved toward the two or three waiting taxis.

"Miss Alban?" a voice asked.

It was a compact, burly man, with a very crooked nose who spoke, a queer-looking man, she thought, with yellow shoes, and a straw hat, and bow tie.

"Well ... yes ..." she said.

"Leave me carry your bags," he said.

But she kept hold of them. "Are you from the hotel?" she asked. Although how could he be, when she had forgotten to wire for a reservation?

"No," he said. "No. I'm just an acquaintance like."

"How do you know who I am?"

"A little boid told me," he said.

This was disturbing. "Never mind, thank you!" she said briefly, and moved forward. So did he.

"I'm an operative," he whispered.

"What?" she asked. "What's—that?"

"An operative!" he replied in a more explosive whisper. "I bin told to keep an eye on you."

She set the bags down, and he instantly picked them up.

"Do you mean you're some kind of policeman?" she asked.

"No, miss," he said. "Private operative."

"But then why—? But then who said to keep an eye on me?"

"That's confidential," he said. "It's for your protection, see?"

"Well, I don't need any protection, thank you," she said, uneasy and puzzled. "If you'll put those bags down, please—"

For she did not like his face, with the nose all on one side and the deep-set little greenish eyes. She wanted to get away from him.

"Listen, miss," he said earnestly, "this party is paying me to protect you."

"What's the party's name?"

"Confidential," he said again.

"Well, it's a mistake," said she. "I don't *want* to be protected."

"Listen, sister," he said, "this is serious. You're in a spot. You got an enemy."

"You're mistaken," she said. "I've got to be going along, now—"

"Sister," he said. "Please co-operate! This is serious. There's someone that's in a hurry to get rid of you."

It was sheer fantasy to hear these words on a sunny afternoon in this cheerful little station with flower-beds. She looked at him with a faint frown, and there was a look of distress on his ugly mug that made her a little sorry for him.

"Honestly, you're mistaken," she said, more kindly.

"Listen, sister!" he said. "Were you locked up without being charged?"

"Well ..."

"Yes—or no?" he demanded. "Were you locked up without no charge being brought against you? The answer is, yes. All right. Were you framed with some phoney evidence? Yes, or no?"

"No."

"No?"

"I mean, I don't think so."

"Well then, this party does think so; and this party's engaged me to see it don't happen again. That, or worse."

"But, you see—" said Susie with her customary politeness. "Nobody's mentioned this to me. And if I don't know who you are—"

Setting down one bag, he took a card out of his pocket. Hobart Minck was printed on it, and in the lower left-hand corner: Bridges' Agency. Registered. And an address on Lower Broadway.

"Just co-operate!" he pleaded. "I got no one here to relieve me."

"Well, co-operate how?"

"Just keep me informed where you're going," he said. "Let me know any unusual letters or phone calls or any strange visitors. And here's the chief thing. Don't take no taxi or private conveyance whatever without letting me know."

"I'll have to think it over," Susie said. "You see, I'm here on business—"

"I won't interfere with your business, sister. Just tell me where you're going now. And when you're going out, tell me where you're going. I'll be sort of hanging around the hotel you're at."

She reflected seriously.

"No," she said, at last. "I'm sorry, but I can't possibly do that. I can't imagine who told you to do this, but it's either a mistake or some kind of joke. I haven't any enemies. I'm not in any danger."

"Okay!" said Hobart Minck, somberly. "I'll just put your bags in a taxi for you."

"Then what will you do?" she asked.

"I'll do my job," he said. "You'll just make it harder for me, that's all."

He set off with the bags and put them into a taxi; he stood by while she got in, and said, "Hotel Jefferson" to the driver. As they drove away, she looked back, and she saw Hobart Minck standing there in his blue suit, and his straw hat, and his yellow shoes, and fear came over her. It was Hobart Minck himself she was afraid of; she kept her eyes fixed upon his face until the cab turned the corner.

Then they were in a pleasant tree-lined street; she saw a young woman in a summer dress driving in a car with three little children, she saw a small boy with a dog, she saw a baker's shop with cakes in the window. This was real; and Hobart Minck was a fantasy.

The Hotel Jefferson was attractive; the lobby was furnished in modern style with low blue leather chairs and sofas; there was a cheerful atmosphere.

"Room and private bath, three fifty, and up," said the desk clerk.

"How about one for four dollars?" asked Susie. Because Mr. Chiswick has said it was not advisable to take the cheapest accommodation. "Front!" said the desk. "Show the lady six-o-nine. Will you sign the register, please?"

She filled out the card, and she felt a little important. A business woman, she thought. The room itself was very nice indeed, and she was pleased at finding a corkscrew set in the bathroom door. That's a cute idea, she thought. She looked out of the window at the street that was bright and animated as a scene in a musical comedy.

But then she remembered what lay behind her; and before her. I'll go right away and try to see Mrs. Malter, she thought. I'll try to sell her. And then I'll go back and tell Captain Catelli the whole thing. It may get Percy out. Or it may not. But the thing is to be honest and straightforward, and not try to figure out the consequences. Like Father says. Hew to the line; let the chips fall where they will.

But suppose the doctor or his lawyer has already got Percy out, and nobody else has been arrested? Or suppose they've caught the real murderer by this time? Then I'd just be an imbecile to go back. Good Lord! What a confusing business this is! And there shouldn't be any confusion. There ought to be just simply a right thing to do, or a wrong thing.

Well, it isn't like that. Anyhow, now I'll get on with the job. She washed and brushed her hair, she put on a clean blouse of blue linen, she put her big, square purse under her arm, and went out of the room. I've been asked to call upon you, Mrs. Malter, as an outstanding woman in your community.

I don't think that's so hot. Mr. Chiswick says that the whole sales talk was gone over by a psychiatrist. Mebbe so, but even at that, could there be one approach that was right for every type? When I see Mrs. Malter— if I ever do—something better might come into my head.

The elevator came, and she got into it. Mr. Chiswick's got women sorted out into three types, she thought. I think there ought to be different approaches. I might work that up a little. Now, for the Queenie type, for instance.... The elevator stopped and she got out. And standing in the lobby was Hobart Minck.

She stood still, startled, worried, and a little angry. He gave no sign of recognizing her. He was smoking a cigarette; he glanced casually at her and then looked away. I won't have this, she thought. I'm not going to be followed everywhere by Hobart Minck. Who ever hired him, anyhow? The doctor, out of kindness? Or could it be Charles?

Or is the whole thing a lie? she thought. Hobart Minck inspired no confidence in her. He may be a crook, she thought. The only thing is, why should a crook bother with me? I'm not rich or important. Nobody'd get up a plot about me.

She went past Hobart Minck to the desk, and in a low voice she asked the clerk if he could direct her to Mrs. Henry Malter's house. She spoke too low; the polite clerk could not hear, and she was obliged to ask again a little louder. Oh, yes! He could, and did tell her. Mrs. Malter lived a little outside the town, in the Breezy Point section. You could go by bus. By taxi? Oh, fifteen minutes, maybe ten.

Mr. Chiswick had said taxis when possible. "And try," he had said, "to produce an appearance of leisure. Make your call seem personal, rather than business-like." She went out of the hotel, and a taxi stood there; she got into it and off they set. They turned the corner, they crossed a bridge over the railway tracks, they were going good and fast. She looked out through the rear window, and she could see no one following.

When I get back to the hotel, she thought, I'll ring up Queenie. And if Percy's still in jail, I'll go back. I'll have to, even if it means jail again. But in the meantime I can hope for the best. I can hope the case is solved, and Percy's home.

Several times she looked out through the window in the back of the cab, but she did not see Hobart Minck. I wish I never would see him again, she thought. It worries me, having him around. It—almost frightens me. I dare say that's foolish, because who on earth would have any plots against me? But I don't *like* him. And I don't want anyone following me.

"Here you are!" said the taxi driver. "Will I wait?"

"How much for waiting?" she asked, looking up and down the empty country road.

"Two dollars per hour," said he.

"That's out," said Susie. She paid the sum which he told her was customary and proper for this trip, and off he went, leaving her standing before a rather foreign-looking wall, painted a pale yellow. She pushed open the arched door and went along a path toward the house, which was also foreign-looking, long and low with a terrace before it, and a trellis upon which vines were trained. Her knees felt weak; she frowned at this and rang the bell, and a thickset little maid in yellow chambray and ruffled cap and apron opened the door.

"Is Mrs. Malter at home?" Susie asked.

"I'll see, ma'am," said the maid, and presented a little silver tray. This was a contretemps. The only cards Susie had were business cards, and the theory of the thing was not to mention business or Gateways, until there had been a little introduction, all about culture.

"Oh ... just say it's Miss Alban, please," she said.

The maid thought the less of her for having no cards, but she ushered her into a drawing-room, and left her. It was a nice room, airy and gay, bright with flowers, although very arty, and she saw hammered brass and Japanese prints, and a pretty quaint fireplace, and ash-trays purloined from Paris restaurants.

I ought to be able to get a line on Mrs. Malter from this room and the house and the maid, Susie thought. But I can't. She's apparently been to

Europe; and maybe she's already got enough culture.

"Yes?" said a low, cultured voice.

A woman had entered the room, a stout lady of middle age, well-corseted, in a dark green chiffon garment that was not quite a dress or quite a negligee. She had a fine head of hair, of somewhat suspicious auburn; she had a haughty bearing, standing straight on her tiny feet in high-heeled sandals.

Oh, Gawd! thought Susie. I wish I was Queenie.

"I've been asked to call on you, Mrs. Malter," she said, quickly, "as the outstanding woman of your community. I think that if you can spare me a few moment of your time, you could give me some information—"

"I don't think I have the pleasure of your acquaintance," said Mrs. Malter, coldly.

"May I talk to you for a few minutes?" Susie asked, with a winning smile. "I think you'll be interested—"

"It's not likely," said Mrs. Malter.

I *quit!* thought Susie. I will *not* do this again. But now that I'm here ...

"I should imagine," she said, in a serious tone, "that there are a good many women in your community, Mrs. Malter, who ought to be interested in what I have to say. The ones who are *not* traveled and cultured."

"Yes, there are," said Mrs. Malter. "What is it? Books?"

"No," Susie answered, encouraged. "It's a course for self-development."

"Physical culture?" asked Mrs. Malter, with a spark of interest.

"Yes," said Susie. "That's included. There are eight lessons on care of the skin and hair, diet, figure, flexing—"

"What's that?" asked Mrs. Malter.

"It's an individual method for improving contours."

"Sit down, won't you?" said Mrs. Malter, but still not smiling, and Susie did sit down, and from her purse brought out a sample lesson.

The Figure.

"But—!" cried Mrs. Malter. "*This* is the Three Gateways!"

"Yes, it is," said Susie, surprised. "Have you heard of it?"

"Of course! Mr. Chiswick was here himself a few months ago."

"Mr. Chiswick ...?" Susie repeated, staring at her.

"He explained that the course wasn't quite ready then," Mrs. Maher went on, "but he told me that when it *was*, he would come back, in person."

Susie was astounded. Never did Mr. Chiswick mention making any such call; on the contrary, he had given her to understand that he had never been in this part of the country, had never set eyes on any of these Prospects.

"It's odd that he didn't tell you he'd been here," said Mrs. Malter.

"You—you *saw* Mr. Chiswick?" Susie asked.

"*Saw* him?" said Mrs. Malter. "Naturally I saw him. He came here twice. On his horse."

"No ...!" said Susie. It was not possible to imagine Mr. Chiswick on a horse.

"Why do you say 'no'?" Mrs. Malter demanded.

But Susie neglected to answer. She was thinking hard.

Mrs. Malter was also thinking; there was a prolonged silence.

"Kindly describe Mr. Chiswick," said Mrs. Malter.

"Certainly," said Susie. "He's quite thin, with a gray mustache—"

Mrs. Malter rose.

"You're an impostor!" she said. "And I suspected it from the first. I knew there was something queer about you."

Susie had risen, too.

"There's some mistake—" she began.

"Yes. There is," said Mrs. Malter. "And the mistake was for you to come to *me*. I don't make mistakes in judging people. I knew as soon as I saw you. I could tell by your eyes."

The whole thing was so fantastic that Susie felt like laughing.

"I can easily prove—" she began again.

"You march yourself right straight out of this house!" said Mrs. Malter.

This was not funny. Susie put the literature back into her purse. "I'm going to find out—"

"You march yourself right straight *out* of here!" said Mrs. Malter. "And if I hear of you trying any of your tricks on anyone else in Stonebridge, I'll have you locked up."

Susie was slow to anger; she was friendly, easygoing, always more inclined to walk away from unpleasant people than to dispute with them. But Mrs. Malter's words, and her tone, were intolerable.

"That's nonsense!" she said, briefly.

"Is it, indeed?" said Mrs. Malter. "You won't think it is nonsense if I set the police after you, you imposter!"

"As far as that goes," said Susie, very white, very cool, "I think I'll go to the police myself. About you. I think I'll sue you for libel."

"I never heard such impudence! Out you go! Marie! *Marie!*"

"Yes, madam?" said the maid, appearing with curious quickness.

"Put this person out!" said Mrs. Malter.

"I'm going," said Susie. "But I'll be back."

She opened the door and went out onto the terrace.

"Marie!" called Mrs. Malter. "Never let this person set foot in the house again! She's a *swindler!*"

"You'll hear from me," said Susie.

She went along the path slowly; she opened the gate and went out into the road. She did not know where she was, or how to get back to the town; she set off at random. In the course of time she was sure to come to a filling station, a shop, some place where she could make enquiries; find a taxi or a bus. She kept to the side of the road; well away from the cars that sped past; and she was still walking slowly, absorbed in her own grim anger.

A car slowed up beside her.

"Hop in!" said Hobart Minck.

XIII

He sat at the wheel of a little coupe; his straw hat was pushed back on his head, and his curly hair was matted and damp on his forehead; his face was flushed.

"No, thanks!" said Susie. "I feel like walking."

"I know what that dame said to you," he remarked.

"Do you?" said Susie, and began to walk. But he drove along with the utmost slowness beside her.

"'A swindler,' she called you," Hobart Minck went on. "And then you said to her, you said, 'You'll hear from me.'"

"That's right," said Susie, keeping her head turned away.

"Listen!" he said. "Why not let me handle this? I can fix her. Look at the experience I've had! Every kind of crook. Every kind."

"She's not a crook," said Susie, briefly.

"I know that. Just a mere doop is what she is. But somebody's soitenly been putting ideas in her head. You been framed again, sister."

"I don't think so," said Susie. "And, anyhow, I don't feel much like talking about it, thanks."

"*If* you'd only co-operate!" he cried. "Here I am, getting paid to help you, and you won't let me do a thing. Why is it you haven't got confidence in me? Want to see credentials? I got plenty. Want to ring up the Agency in N'York?"

"Thank you," said Susie, "but there's nothing you can do for me."

"I can give you a lift back to the hotel. I can do that, anyhow."

"Look here!" she said. "I don't want to be rude, but I'd like to be let alone. I have a lot of things to think over, and I feel like walking. By myself."

"There's one thing is obvious," said he. "You haven't got confidence in me. It's the first time I was ever put on a job like this, when the party I was protecting didn't have confidence in me."

Well, it's true, Susie thought. I wouldn't get in that car with you for a hundred dollars. I don't know whether it's an instinct or just a notion; but that's the way I feel. I don't trust you, and I don't like you.

She was not prepared to say that to his face though, so she said nothing.

"*Won't* you get in?" he asked.

"*No, thanks!*" she said with energy.

"All right! All right!" said he, and drove off.

And she forgot him in a moment. She thought, very steadfastly, about Mrs. Malter, and what she could do to her. She's going to eat those words, she thought. I'll make her take back what she said, if it's the last thing I do. I never felt like this before. So vindictive. It's sort of nice to feel as mad as this. I could walk for hours and not be tired, as long as I think about Mrs. Malter. Put this person out! Maybe it's funny, but I don't feel like laughing.

As soon as I get back to the hotel, I'm going to call Mr. Chiswick. And he'll have to call up that Malter woman. He'll have to tell her that I'm the right one. The accredited representative of Gateways. There must really have been an impostor here before me, pretending to be Mr. Chiswick. All right! That's *his* headache. He can tell the police, or do whatever he wants about it. But first, I've got to make that Malter woman see that she's nothing but—a mere droop. I'd love to bring a libel suit against her. Calling the maid to put me out—calling me a swindler.

The road went on and on; nothing but private houses and lawns and gardens. But Susie was satisfied to go on walking. She turned a corner at random, and she came to a garage. A taxi had just come in there, for gas; she got into it and drove to the hotel; she lit a cigarette and leaned back, planning exactly what she would say on the telephone to Mr. Chiswick. It's his duty to back me up, she thought. If I'm insulted and turned out of places where he's sent me.... He's got to tell this Malter woman that I'm his representative....

The taxi stopped before the hotel, she paid the driver and got out and went into the lobby still absorbed in her plans for revenge. She went to the desk to get her key.

"Hello, Susie!" said Charles Loder.

He was standing there, smiling. And when she looked at him, the tide of her anger rose and rose, and swept over him.

"Nice, seeing you," she observed, equably. "You certainly got out of South Fairfield at the right time."

"I had to go on business," he said.

"*I* had to stay," she said. "In jail."

"Susie," he said. "You look—you look like the devil—"

"And that's just how I feel," said she.

"I mean—you're as white as a ghost," he said. "Look here, Susie. Come and have a drink—"

She was seized by a peculiar and dreadful feeling of breathlessness, as if that anger were throttling her. "That's a cute little idea," she said, "only I'm afraid I don't feel—very friendly just now. Maybe I'm just a little bit sick and tired—of what's been happening...."

"Susie," he said. "Come and sit down."

"Oh, I've been sitting down such a lot today, thanks," she said. "In jail, to begin with."

She thought of all that had happened. Old Person had yelled at her. Captain Catelli had suspected her of Heaven knew what, had locked her up in a cell. Mrs. Malter had put her out of the house. She had come out into the world yesterday, friendly and good-humored, to meet with this reception. And Charles Loder was the worst of all. He had betrayed her, utterly.

He was speaking, but she did not hear him. She put her hand to her throat, because of that unbearable feeling of suffocation; she looked at him blankly, and turned away. He moved so that he faced her.

"I was going back to South Fairfield," he said. "Only when I rang up, Queenie said you'd gone here. So I came. It's—the way I told you last night ... I'll go wherever you go."

"Stop!" she cried in a sort of horror.

She had not really looked at Charles yet; she did now. He himself was pale, his eyes were narrowed, his mouth was set in a tense line.

"I won't stop," he said. "Come and sit down somewhere, and listen to me."

"I think I listened to you once too often," she said, not very steadily. "You asked me not to tell the police—and I didn't."

"This is no place to talk—"

"This is the place where I'm going to talk," she said. They were both speaking in low voices; there was nobody near enough to hear them. "I didn't tell—and I went to jail for it. And you ran away."

"I knew you weren't in serious trouble—"

"It was serious to me," she said. "I'm ashamed of it. I was a fool—worse than a fool—not to tell the truth to the police right from the start. I don't like telling lies, and I'm not going to tell any more. I'm glad you're here, so that I can warn you. I'm going to tell Captain Catelli now."

"Look here!" he said. "No."

"I've warned you," she said. "So that you can run away again."

He didn't like that. He looked as if she had hit him.

"Susie," he said. "Just one minute.... Susie, haven't you any faith in me?"

"That's a rather strange thing to ask."

"Can't you tell?" he went on. "Don't you *know* I'm not a cheap cowardly rat, who'd just run off, and leave you in a spot?"

"You did! That's what you did do."

"I went home. I hadn't any money. I had to get some."

That was not a convincing reason. And yet he did not seem to her like a cheap, cowardly rat. He seemed to her like somebody young, and blundering—and honest. I'm not going to be a fool again, she thought.

"All right!" she said. "Now you're back. And you can come with me to Captain Catelli, and tell him the whole thing."

"What's the sense of that?" he demanded.

"Percy Brett's in prison," she said. "Maybe if we tell—"

"That won't help Brett."

"How do you know?" she asked.

"How could it, if they've got a case against Brett? What we have to tell couldn't make any difference."

"It could. It might establish a time, or something. Anyhow—" She paused. "Anyhow it's what I want to do. It's what I've got to do. We'll take the next train back to South Fairfield."

"Susie," he said. "I want to do whatever you say. But ... Susie, let's talk it over first. Come up to my room—"

"No."

"Your room, then," he said. "Let's talk it over, dear. Darling. Susie, you know how I feel—"

"I'm sorry ..." she said, and turned away. Because she wasn't *that* much of a fool. It's the same technique, she thought. He made love to me before, to keep me quiet. That time it worked. This time—it doesn't. I'm sorry.

"I'm sorry," she said again. "But—no. I'm going to call up Captain Catelli now."

She could not say any more; she shook her head.

"Susie," he said, "if you tell Catelli, you'll get me in a hell of a lot of trouble."

She stood before him, sick at heart.

"You want me to tell lies—to help you out?" she asked.

"There's no need to tell any lies. Just—drop it, that's all."

"Miss Alban! Paging Miss Alban! Miss Alban!" a boy began calling.

"Here!" said Susie.

"Telephone, Miss Alban."

She looked up at Charles; one quick glance. He was handsome, something likeable in him, something touching. But he wasn't admirable, he wasn't straightforward. He wasn't any hero. Then she moved away, she followed the boy to a telephone booth. She went in it, and closed the door halfway.

"Miss Alban?" said a mellifluous voice, vaguely familiar. "Oh, Miss Alban, this is Esther Malter. I—really must apologize for being so hasty.... I just wondered, Miss Alban, if you couldn't come to dinner tonight?"

Susie stared at the telephone with the bridge of her nose wrinkled, her lips parted.

"I'll send the car for you," Mrs. Malter went on. "Would six o'clock suit you? Then we can have cocktails before dinner, and talk about Gateways."

"Well ....." Susie said.

"Please!" Mrs. Malter said, cajolingly. "I'm so interested in Gateways."

"Thank you!" said Susie. "I'll come then, Mrs. Malter."

For that was undoubtedly her duty. She owed it to Mr. Chiswick. I don't understand this, she thought. I can't imagine what's made her change her mind. But I don't feel like thinking about it now. I don't feel like thinking about anything too much. Too many things are happening, too fast. I guess I'll take a nap until six o'clock. I guess I'm pretty tired.

XIV

One of the four men she had met yesterday saw her in the telephone booth, and heard her say, "I'll come, Mrs. Malter."

He was frightened to feel his teeth chattering; when he clenched them, the muscles in his cheeks twitched. He went out of the hotel, and along the street, looking for a place to get a drink. A place to be alone.

I mustn't walk too fast, he thought. But when he walked slowly, he thought that was more conspicuous. They notice strangers in a little one-horse place like this. I need a drink. A drink will steady my nerves, and then I can think.

This is serious. This is—this could be—dangerous. This needs strong nerves and a clear head. Only it's been a bad day.... I feel—pretty well shot to pieces.... They're after me now, all right. They're almost up with me. I wish to God I could find a bar somewhere.... I don't like to ask anyone. It would look queer, to come out of a hotel with a bar in it, and to wander around looking for another bar. I have to be careful what I do.

They're almost up with me now. The whole pack. And this time it's not just prison. It's— What do they do in this state? Hang you? A black bag over your head...? Get hold of yourself! This won't do. Nobody knows about *that*. Only, if they get me for the other thing, they'll start thinking.... Asking questions. You wouldn't think that just being asked questions was so bad. It's a sort of torture.

Don't they have any places in this damned town where you can get a drink? I'm sick; that's what it is. Flu? Something I've eaten? God, if I do really get sick ... if I have to go to a hospital ... Suppose I got delirious...? I'm *not* sick. Tired, that's all. Worn out. I've been through hell. And when I heard that girl say, "I'll come, Mrs. Malter...." Esther rang her up. *Sent* for her. What in God's name does that mean?

I was afraid she'd seen Esther already. But if she hasn't…? If she hasn't, I can stop her. Somehow. I can think of a way. I've *got* to think of a way.

He saw a bar now, on a corner. Henry's Cafe and Gardens. He opened a door and entered a room with little zinc-topped tables and green-slatted chairs. There was nobody here but the bartender.

"Double Scotch, straight," he said.

"Soda on the side?" the bartender asked.

"No. Yes. No," he answered quickly. That frightened him. That was queer. "Plain water," he said with a smile. When he got his drink he carried it to a table and sat down and lit a cigarette. I've got to think of a way to stop that damned girl, he thought. And stop her for good. He sipped his whiskey. As soon as I get one thing settled, *she* comes along and makes some new complication. Again and again. I'm sick of it. I'm going to—

He swallowed half the drink. All right! he said to himself. I'm going to kill her.

All the horrible nervousness, the chattering of his teeth, the trembling indecision left him at once, the instant he put that thought plainly to himself. I'm going to kill her. I've had enough of this. I don't care whether she knows what she's doing or not. She's a nuisance to me. A danger to me.

The question is, how I'll do it. Some way that will look like an accident…. I might take her for a drive. He laughed to himself. Take her for a ride, he thought. She said "six o'clock" to Esther. All right! *I'll* be there at six o'-clock, and *I'll* drive her—

"How's about a drink?" said a voice, and with a violent start he looked up, to see a man standing before him, a villainous-looking fellow with a crooked nose and a thin mouth.

"No!" said the man at the table, curtly.

"You could be polite, couldn't you?" said the man with the crooked nose, greatly aggrieved. "I didn't ask you any favors, did I? What I did say was, how's about a drink?"

"All right! No thanks, then."

"I only thought," said the man with the crooked nose, "that you looked like a stranger here, same as me. If there's one thing I don't like, it's to have a drink alone. It's not good psychology, either."

Oh, get the hell out of here! the man at the table cried in his heart. Not aloud, though. He mustn't get into any sort of row. He mustn't lose his temper.

"Thanks," he said. "I'm just leaving, though."

"There's time for a quick one," said the man with the crooked nose. "This is on me, mister. My name is Minck."

The damn fool's been drinking, thought the other. I can't afford to argue with him now. Not now. Only I need this time—to think....

"My name is—Parsons," he said.

"Well, I'm pleased to meet you, Mr. Parsons," said Minck, and sat down at the table. "I saw you around up to the hotel. What's yours?"

"Scotch," said Mr. Parsons in a sort of despair. "But it will have to be a quick one."

"Two Scotches, brother," said Hobart Minck to the bartender. He lit a cigarette. "I'm noivous," he remarked. "I don't mind saying so. I just come off the kind of a job I don't like."

"What's that?" asked Mr. Parsons, one hand clenched in his pocket.

"Well, it's got to do with a strike," Minck explained. "Up in one of them mill towns. You take chances, in work like that, and the pay is lousy. Fellow I know got his arm broke on him in two places, only last week it was."

The bartender brought over the drinks.

"Is it—police work?" asked Mr. Parsons.

"Private work," said Hobart Minck.

"Just in connection with—strikes?"

"No. It's varied like," Hobart Minck explained. "I do about everything—" He raised his glass. "Here's to crime!" he said.

Mr. Parsons smiled and drank that toast. But he was worried about himself now, seriously worried. I'm going crazy, he thought. This is what it must be like. I'm—going to pieces.... I can't stand this one more minute.

"I do anything I get paid for," said Hobart Minck, with a sigh. "What a life! What a life!"

"Are you here on a job?" Mr. Parsons asked, for the sake of saying something.

"Sort of," said Minck. "But I think it's a phoney."

"A phoney?"

"Don't you know English?" asked Minck, troubled.

"Yes, yes! I understand the word. But I mean—what's phoney in this job of yours?"

"I don't talk about woik I'm hired for," said Minck. "No matter how lousy the pay is. What I say, I'll do, and I keep my mouth shut."

It's damned nonsense to think that everything's got something to do with my affairs, Parsons thought, that's what crazy people think. Delusions of persecution.

"I just re-marked, I thought it was a phoney," Minck went on. "And I wish I had a bigger job on hand, and more pay. I *have* done bigger jobs, all right. You'd be surprised."

"Now you must have a drink on me," said Mr. Parsons.

"And then I'll have to be going." He paused. "I have an engagement," he said.

"If you ever come across anyone who wants anything done by somebody that knows what it's all about, and that can keep quiet," said Minck, "think of me. Anything at all, if the pay is right."

"I will," said Parsons, and told the bartender to bring them two more. That's four for me, he thought. But it hasn't helped me. If I could have been let alone, to think things out ... It's too much, having this drunken gargoyle forcing himself on me.... Only I can't afford to have a row.

"Anything whatsoever," said Hobart Minck.

It seemed to Mr. Parsons that his voice sounded strange. He glanced at him; he met those deep-set little eyes looking straight at him. A cold shiver ran up his spine.

"I'll remember," he said, forcing himself to smile. "Sh-shadowing, for instance?"

"That's a fancy name for it," said Minck. "Not much used. And it's work that there is not much money in."

What are you getting at? Parsons thought. He was cold all over now, and that was a strange thing, after three whiskeys. The man can't mean ...

But when he looked at Hobart Minck, he thought he might mean anything.

"You're—practically the same as a policeman, I suppose," he said.

Minck smiled, with his lips tight together.

"You'd be surprised, Mr. Parsons," he said.

What did he mean? How much or how little? There are people like that. People who can be hired ... What does he mean?

He glanced at Minck, and there was a glitter in his little eyes that was horrible. My God! he cried to himself. This man's a criminal! A murderer. That's what he means. A hired killer. I've got to get away from him. I'm sitting here drinking with a criminal.

That put him in a rage. What right has this damned criminal to come forcing himself on me? I'm not going to put up with it. Only I can't afford to have a row.

He gulped down his drink, and rose.

"It's late ..." he said. "Sorry, but I'll have to be going."

"Oh, I'll be seeing you," said Hobart Minck. "So long, Mr. Parker!"

No, you won't! thought Mr. Parsons. Anything—anything at all would be better than getting into the clutches of a fellow like that. No. I'll look after my own affairs. There's no time left for thinking. I've got to act, and act at once. Susie's not going to Esther Malter's. I'm going to take Susie for a ride.

He thought he was sure of a way back to the hotel. But he erred. He lost himself. He was not cold any longer, but hot and sweating, hurrying up and down strange streets, stared at by strange people. Everybody looked hostile. That's the way it is, too, he thought. You have to fight your battles alone in the world, and if you slip, if you're down, even for a moment, the whole pack is on you. There's not one soul who'd help me now. Not one.

He was completely lost now, and he stood still, wiping his forehead. He would have to ask directions. He would have to accost one of these hostile strangers. All right! If the world was against him, he was against it. He was cornered, and he would fight.

Six o'clock, Susie said. I've got to get back to the hotel before six, and stop her. I mean, stop her for good and all. If I'd done that before, it wouldn't be like this now. No time for thinking. I'll offer to drive her. I'll get her into a car; and then an idea will come to me.

He stopped a workman and asked how to get to the hotel. He was nearer than he thought, and that was a good thing, for it was near on six o'clock. I wish there was a mirror somewhere, he thought. I hope I look all right. He straightened his tie, and wiped his face again. He did not want to walk too quickly now, as if he were in a hurry.

He entered the lobby; and there she was, coming out of the elevator. She didn't even turn her head; she walked straight past him, tall, cool, arrogant. She *was* arrogant. He hated her so. He wished he could choke her.

She went out into the street, and he had to follow her.

"Susie," he said, but she did not hear him. A chauffeur in uniform was holding open the door of a car, and she got into it.

He stood in the street and watched the car drive off. It was Esther's car; he recognized it. Esther would turn against him now, like all the rest. He didn't have one friend. Not one soul in the whole world, he could trust. He was harried, hunted, sick with fatigue and misery.

It's her fault, he thought, all of it. I'd never have done what I did in South Fairfield, if it hadn't been for her.

What he had done in South Fairfield could never be undone. He would never be free from it. Never be safe again. And it had been utterly useless.

Her fault, he thought. She's going to pay for it. By God! Even if I have to hang, I'll finish her.

He could not live in the world, if that tall, cool, arrogant girl went sauntering around, free.

XV

Mrs. Malter was inordinately hospitable. She took Susie upstairs to leave her hat and coat in a bedroom.

"What a sweetly pretty blouse!" she said.

She herself wore a black dinner gown with a broad green sash, her henna hair was done high on her head; she had green sandals on her tiny feet. It was not a becoming outfit, and the eager hospitality of her manner was not becoming either.

And yet, instead of enjoying her victory, the girl felt sorry for Mrs. Malter. Someone's said something, or done something to her, she thought. I'd certainly like to know what it was, but I can't ask her. Mrs. Malter tripped across the room and opened a door, and turned a switch to illuminate a pink and white bathroom.

"What a pretty bathroom!" said Susie.

"This is my guest room," Mrs. Malter said. "My cousin is coming tonight.... Would you like to try some of this face powder? It's something *quite* new."

Susie said she would, and sat down at the dressing-table.

"Your—friend, Mr. Minck, came in and explained," said Mrs. Malter. Susie turned round and stared at her.

"He explained," Mrs. Malter repeated.

"Well ... what did he explain?" asked Susie, cautiously.

"He told me who you were," said Mrs. Malter.

"Well, but who am—" Susie began, and stopped herself in time.

"He told me about your connections," Mrs. Malter went on. "My dear, if you'd only *mentioned* the Ambassador and the Commissioner ... You do understand, don't you, that I have to be careful? With my husband president of the bank, and altogether so prominent in Stonebridge; I do have to be just a weeny bit suspicious.... But now, of course, I see what a mistake I made." She laughed a little. "We were simply talking at cross-purposes, weren't we? I mean, *you* were talking about *one* Mr. Chiswick; and I was talking about the *other*."

Two Mr. Chiswicks, Susie thought? I'd better go slow. I don't understand this at all. I don't see why this Hobart Minck got into it. Or why Mrs. Malter, or anybody else, would believe what *he* said. The Ambassador and the Commissioner ... What's the idea? Why did he tell her all these lies, and why did she believe him?

She took a little powder puff from a big glass jar, and put some of Mrs. Malter's powder on her face. It was a pinkish powder that did not go with her olive skin. But I'm sorry for her, she thought. She's frightened.

"Are you ready, my dear?" asked Mrs. Malter. "Henry's mixing cocktails...." She laughed again. "Imagine!" she said. "Henry actually took lessons from a bartender! But he says that if a thing is worth doing at all, it's worth doing well."

Henry doesn't sound very exciting, thought Susie. I'd much rather have stayed home. I have a lot of things to think out. But this is business. My job is to get Mrs. Malter to buy a Gateways course. I'm sorry if Hobart Minck has intimidated her, or blackmailed her, or whatever he has done, but if I'm going to be a business woman, I can't be squeamish. Business means competition. The law of the jungle. Kill or be killed.

I don't like that. That's exaggerated. She followed the stout erect figure of Mrs. Malter down the stairs and into the drawing-room, and there Henry Malter was presented to her. "This is Miss Alban, Henry." As if she were very choice.

Henry was a square, sturdy man, growing bald; he had a solemn round face and a deep voice. "Very pleased, Miss Alban," he said. "You'll try one of my cocktails? In times like these, we all need a little relaxation."

He picked up a big silver shaker from a table and began shaking it; like a baby with a rattle, thought Susie.

"If the pound is pegged ..." he said. "A good deal depends upon that. D'you agree?"

"Well, yes," said Susie.

"We're watching the fluctuations with considerable anxiety," he continued. "As a man was saying to me just the other day, a man who knows what he is talking about, too—the modern war is fought behind the lines, as well as on the battlefields."

"Henry, *don't* talk about the war!" said Mrs. Malter. "It's too distressing."

"We might just as well face things," said Henry Malter. "I was reading an article the other day. It mentioned what the author called an 'ostrich-complex.' Very well put, I thought. He said that too many of us put our heads in the sand—figuratively speaking, of course. His meaning was—"

He had now finished with the giant rattle, and he poured out foaming drinks while he explained fully, very fully, what the author had meant by an ostrich-complex. He then offered Susie a cigarette, and he told her about exchanges, and how the war was affecting the market and several ways in which it might affect it in the future.

I shouldn't take a cocktail, thought Susie. I'm pretty sleepy already, and it will make me worse. But the time for refusing had passed, and she had to accept it. The maid brought a tray of very interesting canapés, and Susie took two of them; she enjoyed the cocktail, and listened to Mr. Malter; and there was no doubt that she was growing drowsy.

I mustn't! she told herself. I'm here on business. But, how queer—when you think that only this morning I was locked up in prison. And a *very* little while ago, Mrs. Malter was calling me a swindler. .

"If you have any foreign investments ...?" said Mr. Malter.

"Well, no," said Susie, "I haven't."

"Or commitments?" said he.

"No," she said. "No—commitments, either."

He sat down to enjoy his drink and his cigarette, also his conversation. But Mrs. Malter had other ideas.

"I think we can get some Wagner on the radio, now," she said. "I *adore* Wagner, don't you?"

"Well, not *very* much," said Susie.

Mrs. Malter looked disappointed, but Mr. Malter looked pleased. "Six-forty-five," he observed, looking at his watch. "We could just get the end of Gramma's Rocking Chair."

"Henry, nobody wants to hear that."

"On the contrary," he said, "by actual checkup, they have eighty thousand—"

All right! thought Susie. If you get Gramma's Rocking Chair, it's the end of me. She forced down a yawn that made her throat ache and brought tears to her eyes. I'm tired, she thought. And sort of blue. I'll be glad to get away from here tomorrow. Away from Hobart Minck. And Charles Loder. I'm sorry I couldn't say good-by to the doctor and Richard Carroll. Maybe I'd have liked Richard Carroll if I'd got to know him.

Mr. Malter was busy at the grand tall radio of black wood, richly carved. Howls and screams came. "Static!" he explained; perhaps in case she thought it was witches. "There's a thunderstorm hovering around."

"Miss Alban will have another cocktail, Henry," said his wife.

Susie said, No, thank you, but nobody paid any attention to that. She got her glass filled, and Mr. Malter returned to the radio. Peep-peep-peep-peep, came an intolerably high note.

"Henry, stop!" cried Mrs. Malter. "There's the door bell."

He would not stop; with a passionate concentration he went on. Crack! Crack! Crack! Peep-peep-peep.... Something snarled, something whined, something cracked, something banged. And in the midst of this infernal noise, Mrs. Person came into the room.

She stood just inside the doorway, looking at Susie. She was all in black; she looked tall, thin, pale, and passionate, like the Belle Dame sans Merci.

"Henry!" cried Mrs. Malter in a rage. "Here's Eve!"

He turned off the radio immediately; he grew red with embarrassment.

"Eve ..." he said in a hushed voice, and went toward her, holding out his hand. She took it, unsmiling. "Come and sit down," he said.

"Eve wants to go upstairs first," said Mrs. Malter, and she took Eve Person's arm and led her out of the room.

"Tragic ..." Mr. Malter said to Susie in a low voice.

"Yes," Susie agreed.

"Her husband, y'know," he went on. "Only yesterday. She's a cousin of m'wife's, and she rang up. Said she'd like to stay here for a day or two. Until the inquest. She said the publicity—newspapers, and so on ... Well, you can understand *that*." He sat down beside Susie. "These tabloids have got up some sensational yarn about his being murdered. There's not a word of truth in it."

"Are you—sure there isn't?"

"Certainly!" he said. "How could there be? Mrs. Person's a cousin of m'wife's. Old Person owned a good deal of property in South Fairfield. I've been there in his house, a dozen times."

I know how you feel, thought Susie. You just think it's some other kind of people who get murdered. Not the people you know.

"What probably happened *is*," said Mr. Malter, "a stroke. Person was well on to seventy, or more and—" He stopped. "He smoked too much," he said, putting the thing politely and kindly. "It'll all blow over. But it's very unfortunate for Eve. She's an extraordinarily reserved woman. Dignified. Quiet. Old-fashioned, m'wife calls her. But in *my* opinion, if we had more of these so-called old-fashioned women today, the world would be a better place."

He looked rather severely at Susie, and took another sip of his cocktail.

"Eve doesn't drink, doesn't smoke. Doesn't play cards. Her interests, she told me once, lie in her home. Very musical, too. Sings and plays, and so on. A remarkable woman."

"I see," said Susie.

That stopped the conversation; and before either of them had found anything else to say, Mrs. Malter returned still holding her cousin by the arm.

"Eve, dear, this is little Miss Alban," said Mrs. Malter. "She's just passing through Stonebridge...."

"How do you do?" said Eve, in her low, beautiful voice.

Beautiful altogether, when you studied her. Beautiful rich mouth, dark arched brows, black hair smooth and shining. And that's a beautiful dress! Susie thought, surprised. Eve held out her hand, and as Susie took it, she felt a little piece of paper being pressed into her palm.

She gave a start but she mastered it. She kept her fingers closed over the paper, and when they were all sitting down, she opened her purse and took out a handkerchief, and put the paper inside.

"How are you feeling, Eve?" asked Mr. Malter, gravely.

"I hardly know, Henry," she said. "The whole thing is such a nightmare."

"Naturally," he said. "Yes. Naturally. But Time—the great healer...."

"The police are doing absolutely nothing," she went on. "They arrested a man, but they let him go this morning."

"Try not to think about it, Eve," he said, obviously shocked that she was able to speak about it.

"Nonsense!" said Mrs. Malter. "It's the best thing in the world for Eve to talk about it; and not *repress* anything. It's repression that leads to breakdowns. Eve, my dear, I think you're so *right*."

"Dinner is served, madam," said the maid; and they all went into a dining-room that looked somewhat like a torture chamber of the Spanish Inquisition. Four pale green candles burned in tall silver holders on a heavy black refectory table covered by a lace runner; about it stood four black chairs with towering backs; on the giant sideboard an electric chafing-dish glowed.

A bad silence came. And, through a gap in the heavy green curtains that hung over the window, Susie saw a flash of lightning in the sky.

"I'm *so* glad you came here, Eve," said Mrs. Malter.

"Thank you," said Eve. "I had to get away from South Fairfield. It was ghastly." She took a little soup. "And I wanted to see about the cottages here," she said.

"Er—in what way, Eve?" asked Mr. Malter.

"There's only been one of them rented this season," she said. "People wanted to look at them; but they all said the furnishings were too shabby and miserable. Alexander had his own ideas about that. He insisted that the furniture was quite good enough. But I'd like to see for myself."

"Well. Yes. Later, of course."

"It's June already," said Eve. "Almost too late; if they're not put in order, and rented immediately, they'll stand empty all summer."

"You're quite right, Eve," said Mrs. Malter. "It's much, much better to find something to do now, in a time like this. It takes your mind off—other things."

"Yes," said Eve, going on with her soup.

It was a good enough dinner, and Susie was hungry. But impatience consumed her. What *could* she write me a note about? she asked herself. If I could only read it.... Poor Queenie hates her ... but Queenie wouldn't be very subtle about judging people. Why did she write a note to me? And when, and how?

I must say I like things like this. Mystery, and adventure. I like to be *in* things. I'm frantic to read that note. Suppose it's something appalling? "I know that you murdered my husband." She glanced at Eve Person, and she had a vision of Eve in court, in her beautifully-cut black dress, pointing her finger at Susie. "I accuse her—"

That's just plumb silly, Susie told herself. Things like that don't happen in courts. Anyhow, she wouldn't write a note to me about it. She'd go to the police. No. Maybe she wants me to help her find the murderer. Or maybe—I'll have to quit this. I'm getting too excited. I can feel my cheeks simply burning. Maybe the cocktails were extra strong. Or maybe it's because I was tired. Everyone says you feel drinks much more if you're tired.

No, I'm not tired now! I could do anything, go anywhere. I want to know who killed Mr. Person. So they let Percy go? If I'd told them the truth about finding Mr. Person, would it have made any difference? Charles Loder ... never mind about Charles Loder. I don't feel like thinking about him.

But if he's the one? How would I feel about helping to get him hanged? I wouldn't do it. I may be a fool. Just like those women you read about. It may be just because he's handsome. They say men juries hardly ever convict a beautiful woman. Well, if I was on a jury, I'd hate to convict Charles Loder. If I saw him standing there in the dock.... All right! Maybe that's quite base; but that's the way I am.

Don't let the note be about Charles Loder! she cried in her heart.

"Shall we have our coffee in the drawing-room?" said Mrs. Malter's cultured voice, and they all rose. I wish I could think of something clever. Some way to read that note now, Susie thought. I might say I wanted to go upstairs, and powder my nose. But that wouldn't be very clever, I must say. Slightly vulgar. I've got to sit here and listen to Mr. Malter tell about pegging the pound. I don't know what that means; but Eve does. Or anyhow she looks as if she did. Well, I'll drink all the coffee I can, so that I can think...

Mr. Malter talked.

"Miss Alban," said Mrs. Malter with benevolence. "I was thinking perhaps Eve would like to see your little Gateways books, and so on."

"No, thank you," said Eve. "Not tonight."

There was a rumble of distant thunder; and Susie in desperation took advantage of it.

"Will you mind if I go?" she said. "I'm nervous about thunderstorms. I'd like to get home before it breaks."

"Oh, not at all!" said Mrs. Malter. "I'll send for the car at once."

Susie said she would take a taxi; but both the Malters rejected the idea. Mr. Malter rang up the garage; and Mrs. Malter went upstairs with Susie.

"You must come again tomorrow; and let me see all your little books," she said.

"Thank you," said Susie. Then with a dazzling smile, she went into the pink bathroom, and closed the door and locked it, and took the note out of her purse.

I will manage to get away from here at eleven, and will come to your hotel. Will you slip out quietly and meet me on the corner by the drug store, at about eleven-fifteen? There is something you ought to know. I don't want to frighten you; but it is very dangerous for you not to know.

Eve Person.

Mrs. Malter escorted her down the stairs, and into the drawing-room. Mr. Malter shook hands, and so did Mrs. Person. And Susie looked at her; their eyes met.

"Au revoir!" Susie said. She was sure Eve understood.

XVI

You're in danger, Susie told herself, leaning back comfortably in the Malters' fine car.

She wanted to take this in a cool, intelligent way. She wanted to grasp the situation; to consider it quietly. But what she really felt was an excitement that was rather agreeable.

Now, look here! she told herself. There's been a murder committed, and I was mixed up in it, in a way. There's this Hobart Minck thing, and the two Mr. Chiswicks—a lot of very queer things. Mrs. Person wouldn't have written me a note like that for nothing. This is serious.

But she did not, and could not feel serious. She felt almost violently alive in every inch of her tall young body. She felt able to cope with danger. Once I know who it is, she thought. Or *what* it is. Of course, I'll be sensible. Not take any foolish risks.

Only it was in her nature to take foolish risks. She had done so in the past. Beneath her amiable and easy-going air there was a considerable recklessness that sprang partly from sheer youth and health and partly from her immense zest in life. She liked things to happen. She remembered how, only a few years ago, she had dared herself to go into Uncle James' field, where the bull was. She had planned it out, she had kept close to the fence, and when the bull advanced in her direction, she climbed over in time.

And she remembered making up her mind to beat a squall, in her canoe, up at the lake. Well, she had done it. Just done it. She remembered how she had climbed out of the attic window at home, with a rope. Just to see if you could do it.

All these things were done alone, and never talked about afterward to anyone. She was, in a way, a little ashamed of them. It's one thing to take chances to save somebody's life, or for a cause, she thought, but to run risks—just for the hell of it ... nothing admirable in *that*....

But still she looked forward with an undeniable thrill to meeting Eve Person, to hearing about this danger.

They were in the town now, and a new worry seized her. Should I give the chauffeur a tip? she thought. I read in that etiquette book that you tip servants if you spend a week-end in somebody's house. This chauffeur's driven me both ways. Is it the customary thing to give something? Well, how much ...?

Mother and Father never taught me about that sort of thing. I don't believe they know. They never spend week-ends anywhere. If they visit, it's somebody in the family. Of course, we have people visiting us. Professors and what not, lots of them foreigners. I bet you they don't leave tips for Katie. We're nearly there, now. Should I give him something or not?

She looked at the back of his head, a lean and reddish neck, short, light hair under his cap. Put yourself in his place, she thought. That's always a good rule. All right, then! I'd like a dollar. The hotel was now in sight; she opened her purse in haste and got out a dollar. The car stopped, the chauffeur sprang down and held open the door for her, and she handed him the dollar, with a nervous smile.

"Thank you, miss!" he said and touched his cap. No telling by his tone or his face whether he was pleased, surprised, or disappointed. Or maybe he thinks it's a five, she thought, and hastened into the lobby and toward the elevator.

"Susie!" said a voice.

It was Dr. Jacobs, coming out of the bar, holding out both hands.

"Hello!" she said, and she was delighted to see him. So neat and clean in his brown belted suit and a purple tie, his ruddy face beaming.

"We just missed you," he said. "I wanted to get up a little dinner party, but when I called your room, they told me you'd gone out."

"But what are you doing here?" she asked.

"You embarrass me," he said. "You'd think I'd know better, at my age, wouldn't you? But I came here—because you're here. How are you, anyhow, after your incarceration?"

"Do you know why they let me go?" she asked.

"I do," he said. "I'm happy to say I had a hand in that. I went to see Catelli, and I told him who you were."

"But I'm not anybody. I mean not anybody special."

"You belong to the Brahmin caste," he said. "Your father's a professor. Your uncle's a mayor. You have an aunt who is the widow of a highly esteemed clergyman."

"But how on earth do you know all that?"

"I made it my business to know," he said. "I was interested in you directly. I saw you on the train. And after we'd chatted for a while, I was still more interested."

"I'd love to know why," she said, half apologetically.

"I wonder whether you'd understand, if I told you ...?" he said. "It's that look you have, that air of adventure, of faith in life. Of being ready and able to take what comes." He paused. "I've met so many young people lately," he said, "who wanted to be safe. Trying to plan how to be safe up to the age of sixty-five and after. I don't think you're very much interested in being safe."

"Well, that may be stupidness," she said.

"It may," he said. "Or it may be something else. However ... will you have a glass of brandy or port or a liqueur?"

"Thanks, ever so much, but I've had cocktails."

"Lemonade, then," he said. "That's full of vitamins. We can sit down over here in a corner."

"Well, thanks ... the only thing is, I can't stay long, I—have to write a letter."

"Go when it suits you," he said. "Now! Here we are."

They sat down in two big leather chairs; and he leaned forward, his hands on his knees.

"There's one disturbing feature," he said. "Young Carroll is here, too."

"Oh ...!" said Susie. "Well ...?"

"We came together," the doctor went on, "in a car he bought second-hand. As I couldn't stop his coming, I thought I might as well accept his invitation."

"Why did you want to stop him, Doctor?"

"No idea?" he asked.

"No ..." she said, after a moment's thought.

"Young Carroll's interest in you is becoming—a little excessive," said the doctor.

The color rose in her olive cheeks.

"But—even at that," she said.

"Susie," said the doctor, "I advise you to avoid that young man—like poison."

"But *why?*" she cried, startled.

"Here he comes," said the doctor, and leaned back in his chair with a sigh.

Susie watched Richard Carroll as he crossed the lobby, and she saw nothing sinister about him. A slim, good-looking boy, a little tired, a little shabby in that gray suit, but with a nice smile.

"Would I be in the way?" he asked.

"Yes," said Dr. Jacobs.

"I'm only staying five minutes, then," said Carroll. "I just want to ask you how you are, Susie."

"I'm fine, thank you!" she answered.

He lit a cigarette and sat down on the arm of another chair.

"I had to come out this way on business," he said. "And I thought—"

He couldn't seem to get any further. There was a complete silence.

"It seems like a nice town," Susie observed.

"*I* thought so," said Richard.

The doctor leaned forward and beckoned to a waiter inside the bar. "A lemonade for you, Susie!" he said. "Mine's a rye. And how about you, young Carroll?"

"Er—nothing, thank you, sir."

The doctor took a cigarette from his pocket. "Match?" he asked Carroll. Carroll handed him a book, and it was empty.

"I've got some," said Susie, and took them out of her purse.

If the doctor was serious about Richard Carroll, she thought, he wouldn't invite him to have a drink. Was it one of his jokes, to advise me to avoid him—like poison? Professors, as she well knew, were rather fond of jokes about romance. Her father himself said things like, "Why not put this unfortunate youth out of his misery?" and so on. She glanced sidelong at Richard, and caught him looking at her; they both looked hastily away.

So you take an excessive interest in me, do you? she thought. Pretty interesting—if true. Pretty interesting if Richard Carroll *and* Charles Loder both came here on my account. And the doctor, too. But it's strange, when you think I've lived twenty-one years without causing a ripple.... Have I got much more attractive all of a sudden? Or is it because I never met my type of man before? Or am I just a conceited idiot? Well, time will show.

Time! she said to herself. I've got to keep track of the time. I mustn't be late meeting Eve. And it's going to be hard now, with the doctor and Richard here. If I say I'm going to the drug store, one of them will offer to come along. I'd better go up to my room, and then perhaps they'll go back to the bar. If they don't...? I wonder if there's any other way of getting out. There must be. Only, how can I find out? It would be very suspicious and disreputable to ask at the desk at this time of night. This needs thinking about.

She was glad that her two companions were silent. She glanced at her wrist-watch. Ten-forty. But it could be wrong. She moved in her chair, and looked around a pillar, to consult the clock over the desk. And there was Hobart Minck standing there.

He looked back at her with a blank, unsmiling regard. And a little chill ran through her. She began to drink the lemonade, which had just come, in such haste that she choked.

"My dear child!" said the doctor, rising, and hitting her between the shoulders. "Relax! Relax the diaphragm...."

She choked until tears came to her eyes. She got out her handkerchief and dried them. "I'm sorry," she said, "but I just remembered—about—a letter I've got to write. A report. I'll ... Thanks, ever so much, Doctor." She rose. "I'll be seeing you both tomorrow?" she said.

"Yes," said Richard, briefly. He walked with her to the elevator. "I've got this little car now," he said. "I can take you around tomorrow."

"Well, won't you be busy?" she asked.

"Not very," he said. "I—would you like to take a drive now? I mean, get a breath of air before you turn in? It's quite a nice car."

"Thank you," she said, gently, "but I can't, tonight."

"Good night, Susie," he said. "Sleep well."

He smiled, an unhappy, tired smile, and she smiled back at him. Then she got into the elevator. Excessively interested in me? That's rather touching—if it's true. I rather like him. He may be much nicer than Charles Loder. In fact, I haven't any reason at all for thinking Charles Loder is nice. On the contrary. I have plenty of reason for disliking him. *What* is there to say in favor of Charles Loder, except that he's so darn good-looking?

The elevator stopped at her floor, and as she got out, she ceased to think of Charles Loder or Richard Carroll. She had to think of some way to get out of the hotel unobserved, and not only by the doctor and Carroll, but by Hobart Minck.

And if he's here on purpose to watch me, it won't be easy, she thought. It gives you a very uncomfortable feeling to be watched. I don't like Hobart Minck. He worries me. He complicates things. If I go out, he may simply walk out after me. I've got to find out if there's another entrance. Let's see ... shall I call up the desk, and ask?

She rejected that. The clerk might be heard answering her, or he might think it was so strange that he himself would send somebody to watch her. Shall I ask the elevator boy? she thought. I don't like to. It will seem so—leering and queer. No ... the night-maid?

She called the desk, and asked for the night-maid to be sent to her room; then she sat down to wait. It was eleven-fifteen, wasn't it? she thought; and opened her purse to re-read the note.

The note was not there.

It's got to be there, she told herself. She turned the pocketbook upside down, emptying everything out onto the bed. She felt in all the compartments. She felt in the pockets of her jacket. The note was not there.

Now, think! she told herself, exactly what have I done? I opened the pocket-book in the car, to get out that dollar. I opened it in the lobby to get out matches, and again to get out a latchkey. I could have pulled it out any of those three times, and dropped it, without noticing.

Anyhow, it's gone. I hope it doesn't matter much. I hope it won't make any trouble for Mrs. Person. It's—unfortunate ... it's worrying....

There was a knock at the door; the night-maid had come before Susie was prepared.

"Yes, miss?" said the maid, stout and comely in black and white.

"You'll understand," said Susie in an earnest and confidential way. "I want to make a telephone call—and *not* in the hotel. I was going to run out to the drug store—but then these people I know came. And they're sitting in the lobby. I can't go out by myself. And they'd tease me so...."

The night-maid smiled benevolently.

"Is there any way I can get out without going through the lobby?" Susie asked.

"Yes, miss," said the maid. "You can go out the service entrance. Only there's a storm coming up."

"Oh, it's only a step," said Susie. "Will you tell me how to find the service entrance?"

"Yes, miss," said the maid. Certainly she saw nothing amiss with Susie; she seemed in no way suspicious, or leering. "They *say* the operators don't ever listen in ..." she observed, smiling again.

"I know," said Susie. "But you know how it is."

The maid was not only completely trusting; she was pleased with what she no doubt believed to be a romantic episode. She looked up and down the corridor. "This way, miss!" she whispered. "You can take the service elevator, if four flights is too much...."

Susie said four flights were nothing. "You just go straight down, miss," said the maid, "and then there's a little hall, like. It's where the timekeeper sits, daytimes, but he won't be there now. You go out that door, and it leads you in an alley, like. And right up at the corner you'll see the drug store!"

Dimly lit these stairs were, and on the first landing Susie nearly stepped on a tray of glasses. There was a small window here, and through it she saw a white streak of lightning; she heard the mutter of thunder. On the next landing she stubbed her toe against a bucket. It was very quiet here, and there was a moldy smell. If a waiter, or another maid, met me...? she thought. Well, what of it? Nothing illegal about coming down the backstairs, is there?

She saw by her watch that she was going to be too early. If it starts to rain, I'll wait inside the drug store, she thought. She had reached the ground floor now, and the hall was before her. She suddenly wanted to run. Because she imagined that Hobart Minck might appear. But she forced herself to go at the reasonable pace; she opened a door and stepped into the alley. A flash of lightning revealed no sinister figure; the thunder was drawing closer, but no rain fell yet. She could see the bright lights of the drug store only a few yards distant. I can even lurk here in the alley until Mrs. Person comes, she thought. It's lucky I'm not nervous about anything much, except Minck. If I only didn't imagine that he was coming right along behind me....

She reached the end of the alley, and it was disconcerting to see three youths standing outside the drug store, smoking. Well, I've got twenty minutes to wait, she thought. Maybe they'll go away by that time. She leaned against the wall of the hotel in the shadow, and she looked back down the alley to see if anyone were coming. Only a cat.

Another flash of lightning, another crash of thunder, very close now; and a raindrop fell on her face, cold and heavy. The three youths yelled, "Hey, come on, fellers ...! Hey ...!" They started off up the street and a little convertible coupe came along, and drew up at the curb; the door was opened.

Susie came out of the alley, peering at the car with a frown, and Eve Person looked out. Susie ran across the pavement and got in beside her.

"I came early on account of this storm," Eve said. "I don't like thunderstorms."

"Do you want to come into the hotel?" Susie asked. "I know how to get in by a side entrance."

"No," Eve said, "there's somebody there I—don't like. I meant to ask you to come to my cottage; but we can't now."

"Why?"

"There are too many trees. It wouldn't be safe in a thunderstorm; I'll drive to the corner of the boulevard, and we can talk there."

The rain was coming down hard now, drumming on the roof of the car; lightning glared in at the windows, the thunder was very loud.

"These damned storms get on my nerves," Eve said unsteadily.

"I'll drive, if you like," said Susie.

"I would like," said Eve. She stopped the car, and they changed places. "Straight ahead for eight or nine blocks."

A quivering sword of lightning seemed to stand on end across the road, a crash of thunder came, and Eve seized her arm.

"Don't!" cried Susie, as the car skidded a little.

"I'm sorry ..." said Eve, and drew away, and kept silent until they came to a broad boulevard where the rain swept along in a sheet, silvery, across the blurred lights.

"Shall I stop here?" Susie asked.

"Yes," Eve said. She gave a violent start as the thunder crashed again. "They're doing an autopsy tonight," she said. "Now."

Susie's spirit rebelled against this; she closed her lips stubbornly.

"It's ghastly!" Eve cried, as the lightning flashed in at the windows. "It's like hell!"

"You're making it ghastly," said Susie briefly. "If you'll pull yourself together—"

"I had to go and identify him. He—stared at me."

"Would you like a cigarette?" asked Susie.

"Yes," Eve said.

They remained silent for a time. Susie slouched down in the seat, looking straight before her, trying not to think about old Person. Long-haul trucks came by at intervals, going slowly on the wet road, huge, impersonal, like giant beasts on a trail.

"Well?" Susie said. "Let's have our talk."

"What I told you is true," said Eve. "You *are* in danger."

You didn't bring me here to tell me that, thought Susie. You're afraid, yourself.

"Did you see Percy Brett today?" Eve asked.

"Today? No."

"He's here," said Eve. "I saw him on the street. Frank Catelli let him go on purpose— What's that?"

"The roof seems to be leaking badly," said Susie. Drops of rain were falling on the crown of her head, sometimes one struck her hand.

"I wish to God I had a drink!" said Eve.

"I thought you never drank or smoked."

Eve was silent for a while. "I'm cold," she said.

The rain was leaking in faster; Susie felt it on her shoulders now, she heard it patter on the leather seat.

"Is Percy Brett the one you think is dangerous?" she asked.

"You don't know about Percy," said Eve, and her teeth were chattering; Susie could feel how she shivered.

"Look here!" she said. "We can't stay here and get soaked. Where is your cottage?"

"No! We'd have to go through a wood. It's too dangerous under the trees—with this lightning."

"Tell me how to get there," said Susie. "Then you can close your eyes."

"All right," Eve agreed, after a moment. "It's the first turn to the right, straight ahead. There's a road—a lane, and the cottage is at the end."

She took off her coat and put it over her head. They put something black over you when you're going to be hanged, Susie thought, and was angry at herself for thinking that. She started the car, and for a while drove along beside a truck. She saw the driver with another man beside him, both of them young, sitting together up there, as if in a dimly lit house. It made her feel lonely.

There was a street light at the entrance to the road, but the road itself was dark, black under the trees; the wheels slipped and churned in mud. All Susie's attention was concentrated on driving, upon getting away from the rain and the dark. Under the headlights the muddy road glistened like a brown river; the lightning came and made the leaves a vivid green, tossing in the wind. Eve was quiet, shivering, with the black coat over her head.

"Here's a house!" said Susie. "If it's the right one ...?"

Eve slipped back the coat. "That's my house," she said, and at a crash of thunder grasped Susie's arm again.

"Give me the key," said Susie. "I'll unlock the door, and you can make a dash for it."

"No," Eve said, and sat there holding Susie's arm.

"Oh, let's get on with it!" said Susie. "We're getting soaked here."

"All right!" Eve said, and got out of the car. Susie followed her, running up a sort of boardwalk that led from the street to the house. Eve got out a bunch of keys, but as the lightning flashed, she dropped the bunch with a scream.

"They attract lightning," she said.

Susie bent and picked them up, and tried one in the lock, and then another; the fourth one fitted, and she opened the door upon darkness and a smell of mold. Eve went past her and turned a switch, a light came on and Eve closed the door.

They were in a wretched little sitting-room with rotting cocoanut matting on the floor, a couch bed with a flaming red cover, two old rocking chairs, and in the center of the room, a rickety square table. The shades were drawn down, and they might have been down for years, keeping out all air and light.

"This is what Alexander advertised as a 'Summer cottage furnished. Ready for occupancy,'" said Eve. "I haven't seen this house for three years. He wouldn't let me come. He wouldn't give me the train fare. He never would let me have a car."

But you've got a car, thought Susie. And you know how to drive it.

"He wouldn't let me have *anything*," Eve went on in a low voice. "No money. No clothes. No friends. For twelve years ... think of it! The twelve best years of my life, given to that horrible drunken—"

"He's dead," Susie interrupted, sternly.

"Everybody has to die," said Eve. And sat down in one of the rocking chairs. "It was an easy way to die. He bled to death, the doctor told me. He just lay there."

"Look here!" said Susie. "I don't like this."

"I want to talk," said Eve. "I haven't said an honest word to anyone for twelve years. And now—" She paused. "Now I've come to the breaking-point," she said. "This evening, with Esther and Henry ... I had to get away from them, or I'd have screamed at them, sworn at them. I told them I'd feel better—alone, in one of the little houses Alexander had built himself.... They seemed to think that was quite natural. So I took my bag—I'd never unpacked it anyhow—and got out of their damned house...."

"Yes ..." said Susie. "Do you mind if I open one of the windows a little? It's stuffy in here."

"Go ahead!" said Eve.

Susie tried to pull up one of the shades; but almost as she touched it, the whole thing fell down upon her. She let it lie on the floor, and opened the window a little; rain blew in, but a stream of cool, clean air came too. Eve had put on her black coat, and buttoned it up to her chin; she had taken off her hat, and rested her dark head against the back of the chair.

"Nobody knows what my life has been like," she said. "I've never had anyone to talk to."

Susie lit a cigarette, still standing.

"I don't want to seem unsympathetic, or anything," she said. "Only it's late, and I'm pretty wet. If you'd mind telling me about the—the danger you mentioned...."

Eve smiled faintly.

"Yes," she said. "Naturally you're interested in yourself, not me."

Susie flushed a little; but she let that pass. As a matter of fact, she thought, all I want is to get away from here. I suppose she has had a bad time of it, but—all right! I can't seem to feel very sorry for her.

"You *are* in danger," Eve went on. "But, of course, you must have known you were taking certain risks in coming to South Fairfield."

"No, I didn't," said Susie.

"Can't we talk with some sort of honesty?" asked Eve, with impatience. "You must have known there was a risk in coming to track down a criminal."

"*I?*" Susie said, staring at her.

"You've been rather clever," said Eve. "That bluff about being arrested, and put in jail. But you've made mistakes, and some of them are serious. They could be *very* serious."

Susie was speechless, and motionless, waiting for more.

"I can help you a lot," Eve said. "If you'll help me. I have money now. Quite a lot of money. I'm willing to pay quite a lot to keep this Chiswick thing quiet."

"What—Chiswick thing?"

"I wish you wouldn't act like such a fool!" said Eve. "We can help each other, if you'll be frank and a little bit decent. After all, *you're* responsible for Alexander's death."

Susie sat down on the couch that sagged and creaked beneath her. Now I'm going to know, she thought. For a long time she had been aware of ugly and menacing things submerged beneath the surface; and the first faint intimation had come when she had first mentioned Eve Person's name, in the car, driving to the Bretts'. Now she was going to know. She was going to see those things beneath the surface.

I'll have to be careful, she thought; I mustn't let her suspect that I don't know anything.

"Do you really consider me responsible?" she asked.

"You—" Eve began, and stopped. "*What's that?*" she said in a whisper.

"Nothing! The thunder," said Susie.

But it sounded very like a step on the veranda. Eve was staring at the blank window; she turned her head to look, too. There was a knock at the door.

Eve got up and came to her. "Be quiet!" she whispered. "Don't answer!"

There was another knock. "Go upstairs!" Eve said, close to her ear. "Lock yourself in one of the rooms, I'll—"

Susie shook her head.

"For God's sake, *go!*" said Eve, seizing her by the shoulders. "Don't you realize ...?"

There was a rap on the windowpane now. There was a man standing out there, with his collar turned up, and his sodden hat brim turned down; his face looked unnaturally white and unfamiliar.

"Who's that?" asked Susie, jumping to her feet.

"It's me," answered Richard Carroll's voice.

"You can't come in ..." said Eve, unsteadily.

He began to push up the sash.

"No!" she cried. "You can't! Susie! Susie! Run for your life!"

"Susie," he said, "stay where you are."

He had a revolver in his hand, and he kept it aimed at Eve, as he climbed over the sill. He was drenched, and he came with a cloud of rain behind him.

"Susie," he said, "don't be frightened. I've come to get you out of this."

"Susie," said Eve. "He's going to *murder* you!"

He gave a sigh, as if he were almost exhausted.

"What shall I do with her, Susie?" he asked. "After all, it's up to you. Shall we take her along to the police, or just leave her?"

"Why ...?" Susie said. "What—has she done?"

"Susie!" Eve cried. "Listen to me!"

Susie turned to her. And Eve disintegrated before her eyes. Her beauty and her grace vanished; she sat down on the couch with her hands clasped between her knees and her shoulders hunched; she looked ungainly, defeated, somehow battered.

"Yes," said Susie, "I'm listening."

"Nothing to say," said Eve. "Let me alone."

"Someone's got to explain," said Susie, briefly.

There was a moment's silence.

"I'm afraid you walked into a trap," said Richard, reluctantly. "I don't want to upset you, but we'd better get out quick, Susie, while there's still time."

But Susie hesitated, looking at that defeated and most miserable woman.

"Eve ...?" she said. "If you have anything to say—anything at all ...?"

"I haven't," said Eve. "Let me alone."

Still Susie couldn't bring herself to go.

"Eve," she said, "if you'll just tell me.... Was this—a trap?"

Eve looked up at her, and laughed.

Susie turned away from her, cold and sick.

XVII

"We've got to hurry," said Richard.

"Why?" Susie asked.

"Before—somebody else comes. I don't want to upset you; but we've got to hurry."

"All right!" she said, after a moment. "Have you got a car?"

"Just down the road."

In the doorway, she looked back, and Eve was still sitting there in that hunched, ungainly attitude, defeated, guilty. Guilty of Heaven knew what; but it was a burden that crushed her. "Come!" Richard said, and he opened the door. The thunder was trailing away, the lightning flickered on the horizon, but the rain still fell steadily.

"Sorry to have to go through this rain," he said. "Can you run?"

"Sure I can run," she said, briefly.

He took her arm, and they ran together down the boardwalk, past Eve's car, and along the muddy road to a little sedan.

"Here we are!" he said, opening the door.

She did not want to get into that car with him. She did not trust him; she could not trust anybody now.

"Please!" he urged.

"I'd like to drive, if you don't mind," she said.

"Certainly. But don't you want me to turn the car for you?"

"I can do it, thank you."

It was hard to turn the car in that narrow road lined with trees, with the wheels slipping in the mud. But the difficulty of it did her good; it did her good to be in control of a car again.

"Now," she said, when they were started back down the lane. "Now, please tell me. Please explain."

"No," he said.

She turned her head, startled, but she could not see his face in the dark.

"I hope you'll never find out," he said.

"I will," she said.

"Not from me," he said.

"How did you know where I was?" she asked.

"I'll tell you that," he said. "A telegram came for you, and I heard the desk-clerk calling your room. I was in the lobby, you know. He called for five minutes, and there wasn't any answer. I heard him say to the messenger boy, 'That's queer. She sent for the night-maid just a little while ago.' Then he signed for the telegram, and the boy left. I was worried about you."

"Why?"

"For a lot of reasons," he said. "I didn't know what the devil you could be doing out in a storm like this. So I called Mrs. Malter's house. I knew you'd been there to dinner—"

"*How* did you know that?"

"I made it my business to know," he said. "I've been worried about you for quite a while. I asked for Miss Alban, and Mrs. Malter didn't understand me. She said—'Mrs. Person? She's gone to stay in one of her little cottages.' So I went after you."

"Why?"

"I'm not going to tell you, Susie. You're out of that house safely; and that's all that matters."

"No," she said. "I'm going to know it *all*."

They had reached the boulevard now, and the feeling of horror and isolation was leaving her. There were trucks going along, and now and then a private car speeding through the rain.

"It was nice of you to come," she said, without any great animation.

"I did something else you may not think was nice," he said. "Before I thought of ringing up Mrs. Malter, I got a copy of that telegram that came for you."

"How did you do that?"

"I went into a little restaurant, and got the waitress to call the telegraph office and say there seemed to be a mistake in the thing, and would they read it back. They did, and I wrote it down. It was a night-letter from your Mr. Chiswick."

"What did it say?"

"I've got the copy here, if you'd like to stop the car, or let me drive ..."

"I'll stop, thanks," she said, and he turned on the light in the roof.

ALBAN HOTEL JEFFERSON
SERIOUSLY DISTURBED REPORTS OF IMPOSTER
PLEASE LEAVE STONEBRIDGE IMMEDIATELY ON NO
ACCOUNT REMAIN THERE OVERNIGHT WILL MEET
YOU EARLY TOMORROW MORNING GENEVA HOTEL
BASSVILLE IF POSSIBLE AVOID ANSWERING ANY QUES-
TIONS UNTIL CONFERENCE
VICTOR CHISWICK

This surprised her and disconcerted her.

"I don't intend to leave Stonebridge until I know what it's all about," she said.

"Suit yourself," said Richards "You'll have a visit from the police tonight, if you stay."

"How do you know I will?"

"Because I'll send for them," he said.

She glanced at him, and his face was grim.

"Well, why?" she asked, more mildly.

"Because I'm going to see that you're protected," he said. "You're the most stubborn, pig-headed girl I ever came across, and I won't trust you out of my sight, unless you have a cop outside your door."

"Nothing could be safer than a hotel like that."

"You may think so. I don't."

"If you'll be reasonable ..." she said. "If you'll tell me *who's* dangerous...."

"No," he said. "It wouldn't do any good. You wouldn't believe me."

"And *why* should anyone want to do me any harm?"

He did not answer at all, and he did not look at her. He sat with his arms folded and a perfectly blank look on his face.

"I should think you could understand how I feel," she said.

There was no response to that. She waited; thinking hard.

"Well?" said Richard. "Which is it? Are you going to drive to the station and get a train to Bassville? Or are you going back to the hotel—to wait for the police?"

"Neither!" she said, with spirit.

"I see!" he said. "You're going to stay here all night. Very good!"

She really did not know what to do. If it weren't for Mr. Chiswick, she thought, I'd rather see the police right away and get it over with even if I had to be locked up again. But if he wants to talk to me first ... I suppose he has to protect his business.... How did he hear about the impostor, I wonder? I don't know *anything*. If I did, if I had a few facts, I could decide.

She looked up at Carroll, and it seemed to her she was treating him rather badly. He had worried about her. He had come to save her from a trap— or what he believed was a trap. I could be nicer to him, she thought. Only ... she frowned to herself and the thought that came into her mind. I don't trust him, she thought. I just didn't like the looks of him when he came climbing in at the window with that gun.

He did not have that look now, that haggard and even desperate look. He was a good-looking boy, his clear-featured face was intelligent. Maybe he's right ... she thought. Maybe I am being simply pig-headed. I wish there was somebody else to consult.

She said that aloud.

"Suppose we talk it over with Doctor Jacobs?"

He looked straight at her then.

"Did you read what your Mr. Chiswick said?" he asked. "Hasn't it occurred to you that this impostor could be someone you've met?"

"It couldn't be Doctor Jacobs. Not possibly."

"D'you think you know, by instinct?" he asked. "D'you think you're such a good judge of human nature? Or d'you think that maybe you've made a few mistakes? About Eve Person. And others."

"You think I ought to go to Bassville?"

"I've stopped thinking," he said. "It's obvious you think I'm some sort of dangerous character. I don't know why, but you do. You'd better get rid of me. I'll get out here, if you like."

"That's silly."

"I'm silly, all right," he said. "I'm a fool. I was a fool to come here after you. I was a fool—to get out at South Fairfield. Now I quit. I'll get the police to keep an eye on you, and I'll drop out."

Why am I treating him like this? she asked herself. What on earth have I got against him? Maybe he's just saved my life.

Pig-headed, stupid, confused. She thought of that scene, of Richard climbing in at the window of Eve's cottage; of Eve's horrible laugh. I don't know ... she said to herself. Perhaps the one thing to think of is Mr. Chiswick. I'm working for him, taking his money. He tells me to leave here, and go to Bassville. *That* ought to be clear enough.

"I'll go to Bassville," she said.

"Good!" he said, his face lighting. "Do you know the way to the station?"

"I can't go without my bags."

"Can you get them without being seen?" he asked.

"Why? Do you think he might be hanging around?" she asked, quickly. It was a trap.

"Sure to be," said Richard.

"Do you think he'd try to stop me?"

"Certainly not. But he'd follow you. If you can't get your bags without being seen, you'd better go without them."

"I can get them out of the side entrance," she said, and started the car. "How long does it take to get to Bassville?"

"About three hours by train," he said. "Don't drive up to the hotel, Susie. Get out a couple of blocks— Look here. If you're not afraid I might steal them, I can go in and get your bags. It would be a lot better that way."

"Thank you," she said. Then she felt that she was not half nice enough. "Thank you, Richard!" she said.

He turned out the light, and she started the car; they drove on along the boulevard in the steady rain. She was thinking; or rather she was trying to think. About the impostor, about Eve, about old Person. About Doctor Jacobs and Charles Loder.

What's the matter with me? she cried in her heart. I keep on trusting Charles Loder when there are real, definite things against him. And I go on not trusting Richard Carroll, when there's nothing against him. Maybe it's because I'm tired. Very tired.

She reached the corner of the main street, and turned off the boulevard. "Better wait here," Richard said.

"You'll have five blocks in the rain."

"I guess I can bear it," he said with a smile. "Got your room-key?"

She gave it to him, and he got out; she watched him walk off quickly down the empty street, and she remembered his smile, boyish and gentle. She cried a little, from fatigue and distress and a certain remorse. She lit a cigarette to quiet herself.

She remembered sitting in almost this very spot, in Eve's car with Eve beside her, trembling, her head covered with the black coat. I don't know what she's done, or what she meant to do; but I'm sorry for her. Even if she meant to do something horrible to me, I'm sorry for her. I never saw anyone so wretched in all my life. She said, "He's going to murder you ..." Well, he had a good chance. We were all alone in that dark lane, and he had a gun.

She finished the cigarette, watching the empty, rainswept street for Richard. She glanced at her wrist-watch. Five minutes to twelve. She leaned back and closed her eyes, not sleepy, but tired and depressed as she had never been before. I always knew there was evil in the world, she thought. But I hadn't come across it. Murder. *That's* what I'm not going to think about.

The thunder was growing louder, the flashing lightning more brilliant. The storm's coming back, she thought. I wonder if Eve's alone in that ghastly little house. Or if somebody else has come. Who else...? Charles Loder said he came here on my account. Will he pop up again in Bassville? And the doctor?

Richard's taking a long time, she thought. I'll have another cigarette.

She didn't want it. Her throat felt dry. But she lit one, doggedly. It was a measure of time. If he hasn't come when I've finished this, she thought, what? I don't know. Drive along to the hotel? Something may have happened to him.

The storm was prowling closer. It's a bore! she thought. The cigarette was done; her watch said twelve-twenty-seven. At half-past, I'm going to the hotel, she thought.

At half-past twelve she started the car, and drove down the street very slowly, giving Richard every chance to appear. I'll wait outside that drug store, she thought. I won't go in—yet.

She came abreast of the hotel, and there standing on the steps under the lighted portico, stood Hobart Minck, smoking a cigar. She accelerated, shot past, turned a corner, and drove back to her previous waiting-place. That's why Richard can't come, she thought.

Because Hobart Minck was on the watch. At half-past twelve, there he stood, square and burly. As if he never would, never could be tired. I don't exactly know what to do, she thought. If Minck stands there all night...? Richard won't want to go past him with my bags. Mr. Chiswick wanted me to go to Bassville tonight. I'd go now, if I could let Richard know some way. If I leave his car at the railway station, he'd be almost sure to get it, wouldn't he? He'd understand what I'd done. I think I'll have to do that.

A dazzling sheet of lightning lit up the scene, and she saw Richard coming, not up the main street, but down the boulevard, carrying three bags, one of them under his arm. She opened the door of the car, and he got in.

"I had to come around another way," he explained. "Somebody was watching in the front of the hotel."

"The one's who's following me?" she said. "The dangerous one?"

It was another trap, and he fell into it. Not knowing, of course, that she had driven past the hotel, and had seen who had waited there.

"Yes," he said, briefly. "Well, anyhow here we are. I left money in your room to cover your bill."

"Oh, thanks!" she said. "I hadn't thought of that."

"And I did the same for myself," he said. "Because I'm going to Bassville, too. You needn't see me, or speak to me, if you don't want to. I'll sit in the smoker. Only—" He paused. "I can't let you go alone," he said.

You *are* nice! she thought. Nobody's ever been nicer to me. He was putting aside all his own business, his own affairs; devoting himself entirely to her. Doing everything he could.

"I'm glad you're coming, Richard," she said. "We can have a nice talk on the train."

She couldn't see in the dark, but she imagined he smiled again.

"Which way to the station?" she asked, and he told her; they got there within five minutes. "What about your car?" she asked.

"I'll lock it, and leave it here," he said. Ready to leave his car, anything and everything, to go with her.

They went into the station and the ticket window was closed; there was no one around. "I'll find someone," he said. "There's an owl-diner across the road."

If he gets a bad cold from all this running around in the rain, Susie thought, I'll be responsible for it. Suppose he gets pneumonia? She sat on a bench in the waiting-room, and presently he came back.

"Next train at four-fifty," he said, and sat down beside her. He stretched out his legs and stared at his shoes that were wet and muddy.

"That's quite a wait," said Susie.

"That doesn't matter," he said. "As long as this fellow doesn't find us here."

"What could he do?"

"He'd get me locked up," said Richard, "and he'd arrange to take you back to South Fairfield. You're wanted there. But—"

"But what?"

"Susie," he said, "don't go with him. Don't go anywhere with him. No matter what happens. Make a row. Make a scene. Insist on being taken to the police station *here*. Never mind if he has a warrant. Don't go any-where with him."

"Is it—really dangerous?"

"I'll shoot him, *if* I get the chance," said Richard, and put his hand in his pocket.

"No!" cried Susie.

"I'd enjoy it," said Richard. "Only he's no fool. He's not likely to come alone, and he's absolutely certain not to come unarmed. If I could think of a way to get him alone somewhere; off guard—"

"Don't think of things like that," said Susie. "The thing to do is to go to the police, Richard. Tell them what you know."

"I can't," he said. "Well ... try to get some sleep now, Susie."

Sleep? she thought. While you sit there with a gun, and ideas like that in your head? She sat still beside him, and the storm broke overhead. The thunder came crashing and rolling, the rain was dashing against the win-dows. You could never hear anyone, if anyone came now. She turned her head to face the window. If I saw Hobart Minck looking in, I'd scream, she thought.

Or if that door opened—very slowly...?

Not one o'clock yet. Four hours to wait. It's not possible! she said to herself, and turned from the window to Richard.

"Can we drive to Bassville?"

"Yes," he said, looking up. "But I didn't think you'd want to."

The color rose in her cheeks. "Let's go," she said.

She was ashamed of the suspicion she had felt toward this boy who had done nothing at all to merit suspicion. He had helped her in every way he could, he had been signally patient with her obstinacy, her perfect plain distrust. Here he sat tired, drenched, all in her service, with his hand in his pocket where he had the gun he was ready to use—in her service.

"Sure," he said. "Would you rather take the car by yourself?"

She shook her head, and bit her lip.

"My feelings wouldn't be hurt," he said. "I know how it is. I mean you must be so damned nervous and upset...."

She shook her head again. "Let's go," she managed to say.

They went out again into a raging storm; they got into the car again.

"Do you know the way, Richard?" she asked.

"No, I'll have to ask, later on," he said. "But I know you take the boulevard in the beginning."

Again they passed that corner where she had sat with Eve, where she had sat alone waiting for Richard. I hope I'll never see it again, she thought. I hope I go on with my life after this.

He drove into the teeth of the rushing wind; the rain streamed across the windshield, the lights they passed were blurred and sad.

"How far is it by road, Richard?"

"I don't know, Susie. I'll ask later."

He drove fast. Very fast for this weather. The lightning seemed to run ahead of them, glaring out across the road; the thunder seemed to roll along over their heads. It had grown cold, Susie thought; she shivered.

"We'll stop somewhere and get some hot coffee," he said. "After we're well away from Stonebridge."

He drove fast. The car made a rushing sound. I'm cold, Susie thought. Like Eve. Very well; the night won't last forever. The morning will come, and I'll be in a plain, ordinary hotel. I'll be talking to nice matter-of-fact Mr. Chiswick. This will be over.

It was an endless boulevard. They went on and on, and still it stretched before them, straight and almost always empty. There were marshes on both sides where the lightning showed the reeds and rank grass.

"Want me to drive for a while, Richard?" she asked.

"Not unless you especially want to," he answered. "I like this."

They were running out of the storm, only the rain was always there.

Richard's shoulder touched hers, bony and hard beneath his thick damp coat; she heard him whistling very softly.

"I'm glad you're whistling," she said.

"It's because we're getting away from Stonebridge," he said.

On and on. Before them was a violent dazzle of lights, a big filling station, with a sort of café beside it; loud music was coming from it. And the lights and the loud music were forlorn in the rain without a car or a human creature anywhere in sight.

"I think I'll stop here," Richard said. "I'll get directions—a road-map if I can. And we'll have some coffee and hot dogs."

As he drove the car into the circular driveway, a man in a raincoat came out. "That restaurant open?" Richard asked.

"Brother," said the man, "we've lost the key."

"I'll leave you there, then," said Richard. "Order me something, will you? Anything! I need gas, and I want to have a look at the oil."

He stopped the car at the foot of the steps, and Susie ran up them and into a vast room with a bare floor with tables ranged around it. There was one blue-jowled waiter standing beside a phonograph. "Five cents more music," he observed.

"It can rest," said Susie, and sat down at a table. "We'd like two pots of coffee, please—"

"No pots."

"Well, two cups then, to start with. Have you got any hot dogs?"

"Hot dogs, Western sandwiches, Ham. Har' boiled eggs. Anything!" he said. "Except no cold dogs."

She laughed out of politeness, and that pleased him. "I'll give you another tune," he said. "On the house."

A rhumba began, incredibly loud, gay, insolent. When the hot coffee came, and Susie began to sip hers, her spirit stirred, her cold heart warmed a little.

After all, she thought, some day when I look back on this, I'll think it was pretty exciting. Half-past two in the morning, sitting here—I don't know where. Escaping from Hobart Minck. With Richard.

"Another cup of coffee, please," she called.

"Absolutely!" said the waiter.

Richard came in then, and sat down at the table with her.

"I've got full directions," he said. "But I'm afraid we won't get to Bassville much before five."

"Well, we can take turns driving and sleeping," said Susie.

They had more and more coffee, hot dogs, sandwiches and doughnuts.

"Ready?" asked Richard.

"Yes," Susie said, and yawned.

"Poor kid!" said Richard. "You sleep for a couple of hours."

"If you'll promise to wake me in an hour and a half."

"I promise," he said.

It was nice in the car with the rain pattering outside; she felt drowsy and peaceful after the hot drink and the food. Richard drove faster than ever, but he was a good driver. They shot past an old barn; she saw the dark swell of hills against the horizon; they went clattering across a bridge.

"Promise to call me?" she said again, with a yawn.

"I promise."

I will go to sleep then, she thought. I can hardly keep my eyes open. I'll move the bags, so that I can be more comfortable. She leaned forward to shift the bags, and they weren't there.

"Richard!" she said. "My bags are gone!"

"They can't be," he said.

She switched on the light, and he slowed down. There was only one bag in the car, and that was not hers.

"My bags are gone!" she said. "We'll have to go back."

"We can't go back, Susie."

"But I can't lose all my clothes! And all my Gateways literature!"

"I'm darn sorry, Susie, but we can't go back. It's too much of a risk. Put the light out, will you? I can't drive."

"But somebody at the filling station must have taken my bags! And why not yours?"

"I don't know," he said. "I'm very sorry."

On and on in the rain, driving fast.

"But it is queer ..." Susie said.

XVIII

Queer? thought Richard Carroll Chiswick, smiling to himself in the dark. You'd think it was a damned sight queerer if you knew where your bags were. In the marsh behind the filling station, jammed down into the mud there. They've disappeared.

And you've disappeared, Susie. You went out of the Hotel Jefferson, and you never came back. If anybody saw you when you left, they saw you with Eve. And Eve is not talking. No. You've just disappeared; bag and baggage.

That stop at the filling station was all right. Nobody saw me with my hat off except that waiter. It would be my word against his, and I'll have a good enough alibi. I paid my bill and checked out of the Jefferson soon after dinner. And tomorrow I'll be in my room in New York. Nobody can prove I wasn't there all night. Nobody can prove I drove North, a little way. We must be passing Stonebridge now. Not on the way to Bassville.

Eve was wonderful. What a woman! Beneath all that high-minded dignity—what a woman! She knew, all right. She knew where her little friend Susie was going. And she let me take her.

That was a bad moment, when she called that out. He's going to murder you. If she'd said it once more, Susie'd have believed her. But she didn't say it once more. She shut up. She let me take Susie for a ride.

An immense exultation flooded him, a sense of glorious power. I've got myself out of this, he thought. The rest is easy. The other time wasn't planned. I had to act on the spur of the moment. But, even at that, it was done without a single mistake. Nobody connected me with it at all. Except Eve, and Eve isn't talking. This is much easier, because I've had a little time to plan.

I'll get this over with, and then I'm free. Eve will help me out. She's rich now. I can pay Uncle Victor this money I was able to clean up on his racket. I only got a few hundred, after taking all that risk. If I pay him back, he'd keep quiet. For the sake of the family name.

The family name! It's enough to make a cat laugh. If I hadn't been able to pay him back, he'd have junked the family name fast enough. He'd have seen me in jail, for a few hundred dollars. Damned old hypocrite! He'd probably have said that a few years in prison would do me all the good in the world. Look at the way he talked about my going back to college! I went to college from that rather second-rate boarding school. I didn't know the ropes, naturally. I didn't know how to get in with the right crowd. Coming from a school like that. I didn't even know who the right people were. And just because I flunked, that first year, he wouldn't give me another chance. I was only nineteen, and he made me take a job as an officeboy.

I've never had a break. I've never had anything. My dear Uncle Victor likes to talk as if he saved me from the horrors of an orphan asylum. I'd have been better off in an asylum, instead of those second-rate schools where everyone had more money than me.

Now I'll have money. I don't want much. Just enough to make a start. I'll drive down to Mexico; and later, Eve can join me. I've never really traveled, never seen very much. Mexico ... Some place by the sea ... blue sea and a hot sun ... I'm chilled to the bone.

Asleep now, are you, Susie? Leaning against me, sound asleep while I do all the work. My God! What I've been through with that girl! I'm worn out. For a moment, I thought she knew. Out there in Eve's cottage, the way she looked at me.... And afterwards when she said she wanted to drive ... for a while, I felt like giving up. I thought I'd quit—run away.

But I didn't! I kept on, and in the end, I won. God, it was hard! Making up answers to her questions, thinking up reasons.... The thing that worried me the most was, how I *looked*. I've felt like that before. I didn't know whether I was grinning from ear to ear. I tried not to, but then my face felt stiff. Queer. I was afraid she'd see.

I've been through hell these last two days. And it's all her fault. She evidently doesn't know, even now, who this "impostor" was, but she must have been sent to find out. That telegram from Uncle Victor.... She's a fool; but she would have found out before long. Eve would have given it away, without meaning to. Eve thought she knew, and she was going to bribe her. That was another bad moment, standing on that veranda in the rain, hearing Eve start to talk.

I haven't had anything *but* bad moments. That time with Minck. Thank God, I didn't take up Minck's offer to do this job for me. If I had, I'd be in his power. He would blackmail me—anyhow. But I've done it myself, and I'm free.

Well, I haven't actually done it yet. It's not finished. There's still a lot of bother and annoyance. That's because she's so damned stubborn. This, for instance, this stretch of road would be just about perfect. Only I know I couldn't make her get out of the car, and walk a little way. Well after all ... He grinned. I've got to admit that would seem a little phoney to anyone. Let's take a little stroll in the woods, at half-past three in the pouring rain.... No, I'll have to stick to my original plan. I'll have to be patient. My big fault is impatience.

But if I *could* do it now ... I've never fired a gun, but if I put it up to her head, it couldn't fail. Right now. This moment. Out of the question. I can't do it in the car. There mustn't be any traces—of anything—in the car.... No. I've got to be patient and follow out my original plan. It's the only way to get her out of the car. We're nearly there now ... It ought to be all over inside an hour; and in two hours I'll be home in bed.

But it's this last hour that's so hard. After all I've been through ... Now I'll have to start all the wheedling and lying and answering questions all over again when I'm so tired ... If she makes any trouble I'll have to use the gun. I don't want to. I have a sort of dread of that noise.... I've always hated noise and violence.

It's all her fault. If she hadn't come out to South Fairfield to hunt me down ... I never wanted to do any harm to anyone. Only, all my life, I've been treated like a dog. Everyone against me. Except Eve. *She's* stood by me all through this. She's been loyal. She knows what happened to her husband, and she knows what was going to happen to Susie. But she shut up.

We ought to be just about coming to the place now ... If I remember correctly, that is. I generally do. I have a remarkable sense of direction—locality—whatever it is. Let's see ... I turn here ... hell of a road this is. It'll wake her up—and then I've got to start.

The car stubbed against something, a root or a stone, went over it with a tremendous jolt, skidded a little in the mud.

"Oh, Lord!" said Susie. "What's that?"

"I'm afraid we're lost," he said.

She sat up straight.

"I must have taken the wrong turn," he said. "Well, I won't try to turn here and go back. Better to go ahead, and see …"

"I'll drive now, Richard."

"No. Let's wait a while. This worries me. I want to get you to Bassville."

"What time is it, Richard?"

"I don't know."

"This road might be a dead end, Richard."

I can't help laughing at that, he thought. A dead end. "Yes, Susie, it might be."

They skidded again in the mud, and nearly ran into a tree.

"This is the worst road I ever struck," she said.

"Never mind," he said. "It can't last forever."

But he was beginning to be worried now. More than worried. Suppose I've made a mistake? he thought. Suppose this is the wrong road? It'll be light in an hour and a half …

And he thought, suppose the daylight came and found him still with Susie. Miles and miles from Bassville. Somewhere on the outskirts of New York. Then she'd know, he thought. Then it would be too late.

If I don't strike that other road in ten minutes, he thought, I'll have to use the gun. I'll ask her to get out and hold a flashlight for me while I look at the tires. Then I'll leave her here. The way I planned was better, but this would do.

His wrist-watch had radium hands, and he could keep track of the ten minutes. I'm—nervous, he thought. I hate the idea of a gun. That noise … I don't see how I could have made a mistake like this. I always remember a route … I tried to plan this thing very carefully.

Eight minutes, and nine minutes, and ten minutes. He stopped the car.

"I think I felt the left rear tire go," he said. "I'm sorry, Susie, but would you mind holding the flashlight for me while I check?"

"I don't mind," she said.

He opened the door of the car, and they got out into the chilly, steady downpour. It was entirely dark here. It was very quiet. The rain made a hissing sound, the wet leaves stirred. He turned on his flashlight and handed it to Susie; the clear narrow beam showed the narrow road like a stream of lava. He put his hand in his pocket.

"I hear a brook somewhere," Susie observed.

He stood still.

"A brook?" he repeated.

"Yes. Don't you hear it? It sounds pretty."

He looked at the tire.

"It's okay," he said. "I'm sorry I got you out in the rain for nothing."

"Oh, it doesn't matter," she said, cheerfully, and they got back into the car. "You'd better let me drive, Richard. You must be dead tired."

"I'll wait till we got off this stretch of road," he said. "Then we'll see ..."

For if there was a brook, it was the right road. He remembered that brook, running through the woods, the clear water under the bare February trees, a bright blue sky. He had strolled along beside it, and he had felt happy.

If I could go back! he thought with a sudden anguish.

But he could never go back. He had to go forward. It's her fault! he said to himself.

XIX

It's nearly over, Susie thought. It will be daylight soon, and this will be over. I'll be in a little hotel room and take a hot bath. My bags...! I haven't anything, not even a pair of stockings, or a toothbrush.... I don't really care; I only want it to be day again, and this to be over.

All her drowsiness was gone and all sense of fatigue. What she felt was an almost intolerable impatience, a desperate longing to be out of this shadowy nightmare and into the daylight world again. It's been raining for so long ... she thought. It's been confused and horrible for so long.

"Can't I drive now, Richard?" she asked.

"Wait a minute," he said. "I see a house there. I'm going to ask them how to get to Bassville."

"You can't wake them up at this hour!"

"Why not? I'm sick and tired of this!"

"Well, there might be a farmer with a shotgun," said Susie, "or a dog."

"I'll take a chance," he said. "Wait here, will you, Susie?"

I've spent plenty of time tonight waiting in cars, she thought. I wish I could get out. I'd rather walk miles in the rain and the mud than sit shut up like this any more. She opened the car window and the rain blew into her face. Let it! I'm burning with—I don't know what—impatience—something.... I never felt like this before. So on edge....

She could see Richard walking quickly across an unfenced lawn; then he turned the corner of the house. Going around to the back door, she thought. It seems like rather a lot of nerve, to wake people up at this hour, just to ask directions. I couldn't have done it. I'd just go on and on until I got somewhere.

It was a big house, or it looked big against the rainy sky. It looked enormous. She waited to hear a dog bark, a window open, a voice call. But there was nothing but the steady hiss of the rain on the ground, the patter on the roof of the car, the purling of that brook.

Maybe it's an empty house, and then we'll have to go on. But this road looks better. Even if we're lost, we'll get somewhere. And the daylight will come soon. I never longed for the daylight so much. I never felt like this before. So restless, and so—sad.

Sad—about Eve. I don't know why. Except that I know she's done some dreadful thing, and never can forget it. Sad about Charles Loder. I'll admit it. I wanted him to be different. It's good to feel the rain. My face is burning, but my hands are cold. Richard's been gone a long time, hasn't he? Only everything seems a long time tonight. It's been dark so very, very long....

Now she saw Richard coming back, slender and light-footed, across the lawn. He came up to the open window.

"I've gone completely wrong," he said. "Miles out of our way. It would take us four hours at least to reach Bassville."

"Well," she said. "Let's get started."

"This place happens to be a tourist camp; and I've taken two cabins from the woman in charge."

"No! Let's go on!"

"There's no sense in that, Susie. We'd better get a few hours' sleep and a wash. I told the woman to call us at six. We'll have breakfast, and then start."

"Let's not," she said.

"Susie," he said, "I'm sorry but I'm just about all in."

"Oh, I'm sorry!" she cried. "Are you ill, d'you think?"

"Only tired," he said. "I've been under a pretty heavy strain. I'll tell you tomorrow."

"I'm sorry...."

"I'm through," he said. "A couple of hours' sleep in a decent bed will set me up. I'm afraid you'll have to take another walk in the rain, Susie. The cabins are down there where those trees are."

"I'll drive as near as we can go."

"No. The woman asked me not to. It wakes up the people in the other cabins. I'll leave the car here."

"But we needn't make any noise."

"Look here!" he said. "If you *only* wouldn't argue so about every little thing. You don't realize how hard you make everything. I told the woman I'd leave the car here. Why d'you have to *argue?*"

"All right, Richard," she said.

He reached into the car, and got out his bag. Then he turned out the lights, and the world was very dark.

"Where's your flashlight?" Susie asked.

"Don't want to burn it out, we may need it," he said, taking her by the arm. "Never mind! I can see pretty well in the dark. Come on!"

"Not so fast, Richard!"

"Sorry!" he said.

They went along a drive toward a grove of trees, and she could see a line of cabins. Looking back over her shoulder, she could see that big house all in darkness. The woman must have gone back to her bed, she thought. I wish there were a light somewhere.

Richard stopped before the first cabin; he stood still for a while, and then he knocked.

"Why are you doing that?" she asked, surprised.

"The woman forgot to tell me which two cabins were ours," he whispered, and waited again. Then he put the key in the lock and turned it, and opened the door. They stood side by side in the dark; she heard him breathing quickly.

"Where's the light?" she asked.

A switch clicked, but no light came. "Bulb must be burned out," he said. "Never mind. I have a flashlight here in my pocket."

A little silver circle of light shone out; he stood the flashlight on the chest of drawers, and the bright circle was on the ceiling, ringed with black.

"Can't you ask the woman in the house for a bulb, Richard?" she said.

"I can't bother her *now*, Susie. It's too late. You can manage with this, can't you?"

"I guess so."

"Keep the shades down, Susie," he said. "Sometimes there are tramps around these places."

"I'll remember," she said.

"Got everything you want now, Susie?"

Glancing at him, she saw how ill and feverish he looked; and she answered with a certain gentleness:

"But I haven't anything, Richard. Can you lend me a pair of pajamas?"

He didn't answer; he stood leaning against the closed door staring beyond her.

"I'm sorry," he said, after a moment. "I haven't any pajamas or dressing-gown along with me. Nothing much but some shoes, and some books and ..." He paused again for a long time. "I've got a sweater," he said, suddenly. "It's a good warm one."

He knelt beside his bag, and opened it; he brought out a gray sweater and re-locked the bag. "This will keep you warm," he said. "You'll be all right now."

"Where's your cabin, Richard?"

"Oh, probably the next one. I'll try the key. Good night, Susie."

"Good night, Richard! Sleep well!"

He went out with his bag, and Susie went to the door to lock it. The key was not there. She opened the door to see if it were on the outside. It was not.

In the middle of the road, outlined against the sky, Richard was standing with his back turned to her. Standing there in the rain. As if he were waiting. Then she knew.

All fear left her. Her strong young body, her brain, her nerves, fused together into a perfect unity. She was entirely matter-of-fact. This was a problem.

She closed the door, silently.

He's waiting to kill me, she thought. Waiting until my light goes out. Eve warned me. There have been plenty of warnings. My bags ... I didn't take the warnings, and here we are. Now, let's see ... If I could get to the car? If I could get it started before he could reach me? No. He has a gun.

Is that big house empty? If only I knew that...! If I could get into it anyhow ... I think that's what I'll try to do.

She lifted the shade and opened the window. It was a very small window, but big enough. She climbed out of it, and ran a little way to the grove of pines. It was dark there, but the trees were far apart. He could find me here easily, she thought.

He was still standing there in the middle of the drive, but he was facing toward the cabins now. I've got to get behind him somehow, she thought. Only there's such a wide space there to cross; the road and then the lawn. If he saw me, even if I were near the house, he would shoot. If these weren't pine trees, I could climb up one.... She went back a little, and looked up at the branches, but the rain made her close her eyes. She dried them with her sleeve; and looked up again at Richard.

He held a lighted flashlight in his hand now. If he comes looking for me here with that, she thought, he'll find me at once. Isn't there anywhere to hide?

She looked around her, not in any panic, only with a tingling alertness. This is a bad spot, she thought. Let's see ... Then she thought of something. She ran down the hill, and climbed in at the window again, a little bothered by the rattling noise the shade made. She pulled the little white chest of drawers out from the wall and across to the door. I hope he doesn't hear this, she thought. Because then he'd come straight around to the window. Maybe he's there now. Maybe, when I climb out, he'll be standing there.

I've got to try, anyhow. I'll look—carefully. If I don't see him, I'll have to take a chance. She pushed the shade aside cautiously and looked out. The light from the window showed nothing but an empty square of ground, with the rain falling steadily. He could be standing in among the trees, she thought. He could come suddenly around the corner of the cabin.

I've got to chance it, that's all, she thought. But it was a bad moment, running up the little slope to the trees. They weren't much good, but it helps to feel something at your back. He was still there in the driveway, and as she watched him, she heard him sneeze. But he's a human being! she thought. How can it be like this?

Only it was like this. He swung the flashlight in a circle close to the ground; the beam came down to the trees. She moved backward; she could hear the pleasant purling of the brook. A few steps brought her to the edge of the grass, and beyond that lay a field, flat and empty and vast. No cover there, no chance at all.

Then, just beyond the field, she saw the lights of a swiftly moving car. She almost cried, to see it. There was a highway there; and she could not get to it. There was the world; and she was held here in a nightmare, with only herself and Richard. That big house was in darkness.

But we're on a road here, she thought. It's unlighted and deserted now, but this is a tourist camp, and cars must pass by sometimes. If I could hide in the car…? The car and the house were almost equally distant from the grove of pines, and to reach either, she would have to get behind Richard, and she would have to run across an open space. There might be someone in the house, she thought. Someone asleep, who'd help me. There might be a telephone in there.

But if it was an empty house…? Well, even then, it's so big I might be able to hide. Lock myself in a room. I could break a window to get in. With a stone. She bent and groped on the ground for a stone; she found one, cold, slimy with moss. She wiped it off on her skirt. I'd be glad to get into the house with a roof over my head. And doors. She tried to put the stone into her jacket pocket; it was too big, but she jammed it in, tearing the flap. Mr. Person was killed with a knife, she thought. A knife would be better. You'd have more chance to fight, or to get away. But a gun … I don't know how far his gun can shoot …

He was coming. Coming very slowly. Waiting for my light to go out? she thought. What will he do? Go first to the door? If he goes behind the cabins to the window first, that—won't be so good. He'll be very close to me there. He'll have to go past me. And if he swings that flashlight around again, he'll see me here.

I'm going to run for the car, she thought. Not the house. If the shutters were closed, I couldn't get in. I'll hide in the car—if I can get there. He's coming.... She stood among the trees, her heart beating furiously. He was coming slowly in the rain, his head bent, hands in his pockets. He said he could see well in the dark....

He had almost reached the row of cabins. Will he turn and come this way? So—close to me? Or will he go on to the door?

He went on past the corner. The moment he was out of sight behind the cabin, she left the shelter of the trees and began to run. The flat, empty space stretched before her interminably. She ran, ran fast, but she made no progress. She never got any nearer to the dark bulk of the car. Is he running after me? I wouldn't know. I couldn't hear him on the wet grass. Or will a shot come...?

I am running fast ... but not getting anywhere ... and I—can't breathe. He's coming after me.... I hear him—running ... Suddenly the car was there, just before her. She slipped in the muddy road and fell, and got up, ran to the far side of the car and tried to open the door. The car was locked.

She sat down on the running-board to get her breath. I can't stay here. I'm not—going to sit here—and wait—to be shot ... I'll get under the car— when I hear him coming. Only—I couldn't hear him—in the rain. He may be—almost here now ... but you don't want to be shot—lying—in the mud, under the car ... If I can stop breathing—so hard—I could listen.... If my heart wouldn't beat so loud—right in my ears, I could hear better....

Is he coming? Could I—crawl along the road to that lane? Too far. No cover. I'm going to get up on the roof of the car. He might never think of looking there.

The stone fell out of her torn pocket as she rose and she felt in the mud for it and put it back. Somehow it was important. I'll have to get up on the hood; and if he's looking he'll see me. But I've got to chance it.

Then she saw the headlights of a car, coming from the main road. She made a queer sound, a sob, or a gasp. She sat down on the running-board again, because she could not stand. She waited.... It was really coming, some sort of light truck; the headlights streamed along the road. She sprang up and shouted:

"Stop! Stop!"

The car was abreast of her. "Stop!" she cried with all her might. "Let me—get in!"

A flashlight was turned full on her face for an instant. Then the truck went on. "Stop! *Please!*" she cried.

The red tail-light vanished around the bend. And the shot she had been waiting for crashed out, so near, so shattering. Her hands flew to her ears; she leaned back against the hood of the car. There was a great roaring in her ears; she could see nothing.

But the roaring ebbed away, and looking up, she saw Richard standing in the road facing her. Nowhere to run now, nowhere to hide. Nothing to do but wait. She put her hands behind her on the hood, to steady herself, and now she heard him crying in the dark.

Crying? she thought. Is he sorry...? Or is he—crazy? Could I speak to him? If he'd answer, if he'd speak, he *couldn't* do this.... Only it was hard to speak. She tried once, and no sound came. She moistened her lips.

"Richard ...?" she said, faintly.

"Shut up!" he shouted.

She looked horrible, bent over that way backward. Is she dying? he thought. I shot her. Why isn't she dead? I can't—this can't go on. This is awful.... I never fired a gun before in my life. It's—too loud. It—it makes me nervous.... I'm cold.... I'm *sick*. I left her in there; and she got out.... This is—is awful. Running around in the dark and the rain—and she *won't* die ... She's been torturing me—for days. Playing with me, like a cat with a mouse. It's—too much. If she speaks again, I'll shoot. I'll *finish* her.

"Richard . . ?" she said, in the same tone of strange, faraway wonder.

He raised the revolver and fired again. She went down in the mud.

Now I'm going to get out of this place, he told himself. She can stay where she is. My bag's here in the car, that's a good thing. He brought out his keys to open the car. And she was getting up! She was trying to pull herself up. She *wasn't* dead.

He got out the knife he had in his belt. He had carried a knife since he was twelve and used to play Indians. It was in every way better than a gun. A gun didn't kill. That was obvious.

A brilliant light came streaming into his face. He looked up, because he thought it came from the sky. But it was the headlights of a car, coming closer to him. He had to move a little. If that dying thing in the mud would keep quiet, the car would go past....

The car stopped, the door opened, and a man got out.

"Charles!" said Susie. "Stop! He's got a gun!"

She saw Charles Loder raise his head like a deer, looking for her. Then he found her.

"Don't!" she said.

But he came straight toward her until a shot stopped him, and he fell. He lay face down and he did not stir.

Susie let go. She dropped down into a spiraling blackness, went sliding round and round, down and down.

XX

She opened her eyes, and there was nothing but the dark and the rain. She felt sick and dizzy, and she closed her eyes again, listening to the patter of the rain that had been going on for ever and ever. She tried to sink down into that blackness again where there was no feeling and no thinking.

But you can't do that. The numbness was going. She tried to open her eyes again. And she was in a car with her head on a man's shoulder. What man? What car? Going where?

She was afraid to stir. Before her she saw a windshield wiper, moving with a click; the headlights showed a muddy road lined with trees. All as it had been before. A nightmare that did not end when she awoke. *What man?*

Charles was shot, she told herself. He was lying there, face down in the road. And there was nobody else but— A paralyzing terror ran through her. This is Richard Carroll beside me, she thought. I've got to begin again. This numb and frozen creature would have to stir, to think, to struggle. For an instant, temptation seized her; the temptation to give up, to perish rather than struggle.

But she was too strong and too sound for that. She drew a deep breath, and raised her head.

"Take it easy," said Hobart Minck's voice.

So, it's you, she thought. The man she had been afraid of, the man she had tried to escape.

"Is Charles—was Mr. Loder shot?" she asked.

"Well, he's not dead yet," said Minck. "You better lean back, and re-lax."

"Where are we going?"

"I'm taking you to Doctor Jacobs," said Minck. "That's what I'm being paid to do."

"But why?"

"He hired me to keep an eye on you," said Minck, grimly. "But it seems I slipped up. Now I'm taking you back to him and I quit."

"Did you—just leave Charles Loder there?"

"Mister Charles Loder is not my headache," said Minck. "If he feels like walking right up to the muzzle of a gun, that's his business."

"Where—what happened to Richard Carroll?"

"He's all right," said Minck. "You better take it easy now, and not talk."

"I've got to talk," she said.

"Well, I haven't got to answer," said Minck.

"Are we nearly there?"

"Nearly where?"

"Wherever we're going."

"Thirty-forty minutes," said Minck. "If we don't have any trouble."

She was silent for a moment, trying to steady herself. "Can't you—stop a car—and sent somebody back—to see about Charles Loder?"

"I'm in a hurry," said Minck. "I want to get finished with this job. It's the worst job I ever had. I never had anybody who treated me like you have. Absolutely no confidence in me whatsoever. All right! Look what it led to."

"I—didn't know ..."

"I told you," said Minck. "I told you I was hired to protect you. I soitenly did everything I could. I 'phoned up Mr. Chiswick in New York, and I got him to wire you to quit. I went out of my *way* to be helpful. I went to this Mrs. Malter, and I fixed her up so's she'd ask you to come back. That hadn't any object whatsoever but to kind of make you feel good."

"Yes, you did."

"I did. And what is the result?"

"Why did Doctor Jacobs get you?"

"One thing is, he knows me, and he's got confidence in me. When they locked you up, he calls me in New York. There is a situation here that soitenly smells, he says. There is this girl will not give the police a straightforward account of her actions, he says, and that has got to mean she's covering somebody. Come up, and keep an eye on her for a while, he says, because she's young, and hasn't got much sense—much experience."

The fear of sudden death had left her; all fear for herself. Minck was hostile, but she was no longer afraid of him. She was thinking of Charles Loder lying face downward in the road.

"Will you let me telephone—about Charles Loder?" she asked. "Please ... I won't take long. I won't—even say where I am ... Just to—send help ..."

"When I hand you over safe to the Doc," said Minck, "like I'm being paid to do, all right. You can do whatever you like. Just now I'm in a hurry."

Thirty or forty minutes ...

"Didn't you even arrest Richard Carroll?"

"I'm not a policeman," said Minck. "I'm a private operative."

"He—tried to kill me," she said.

"I could of told you he'd do that," said Minck. "I knew it. I had a talk with him this afternoon. Only it did not occur to me that you'd sneak out of the hotel and go for a ride with him."

"I didn't know. I *couldn't* know. Even now.... Why should he want to—?"

"You'd be probably better off if you'd relax, and take it easy," said Minck, "but if you will talk, all right. He got this idea of killing you because he thought you were going to make trouble for him."

"But how could I?"

"His name," said Minck, "is Chiswick."

"Chiswick?" she cried.

"Nephew of your boss, Mr. Victor Chiswick. It seems Uncle Victor brought him up, gave him everything—"

"That's a lie!" said Richard's voice just behind her.

"Shut up!" said Minck.

"That's a lie!" Richard said again. "He's always treated me like a dog. He wouldn't give me—"

"Either shut up," said Minck, "or I'll stop the car a minute, and shut you up."

Susie turned around in the seat to face him. But he was only a shadow in the dark. A shadow so horrible that she felt it hard to breathe.

"Take it easy," said Minck. "He's tied up good. He can't hurt you."

But she sat sideways in the seat, for she could not turn her back upon that shadow.

"It seems our friend Richard Chiswick wasn't getting as much as he wanted. So, before Uncle Victor has got this proposition ready, Richard gets hold of some of the little books and the list of people to visit and all, and goes out on the road, same route you had, of course, and sells the courses, and puts the money in his own pocket. His idea is, that when the thing is ready to sell, Uncle Victor will ask him to do it. Only Uncle Victor gets a-hold of you, instead, without telling our friend Richard. He got a shock when he found that out. When he heard you were going straight to Mrs. Person, where he'd already been, and cleaned up."

"Trying to make out that I'm a thief?" said Richard with a laugh.

"No," said Minck. "Oh, no! Only saying you stole."

"It's a damned lie! I had every reason to think my uncle was going to give me the job of selling Gateways. He practically promised it to me. It was simply a matter of collecting the money a little earlier."

"Well, don't talk any more," said Minck. "This young lady don't want to hear you."

They went on in silence for a while, in the everlasting rain and darkness.

"Eve betrayed me," said Richard, suddenly. "It must have been Eve."

"It was a mean, low-down trick, wasn't it?" said Minck. "If she'd kept quiet, you'd have got away with this. Maybe. Only she told Brett."

"Why Brett?" he asked, sharply.

"Well, maybe because Brett was there on the spot. He went out to this little cottage of hers to see her; and he was mad. Mad that he'd been locked up, and Mrs. Person never said a woid to get him out. Course, they never should've locked him up, is my opinion. No case. However, he was plenty mad, and I guess Mrs. Person was just about ready to talk, anyway. She felt sort of upset about letting you go with Carroll."

"She betrayed me," said Richard again.

"That's it," said Minck. "Now shut up!"

"Let him go on!" Susie whispered in Minck's ear, and she felt him shrug his heavy shoulders.

"She told you where to find me," Richard went on. "It couldn't have been anyone else. Very well. She'll be sorry for that. Damned sorry."

"Oh, I don't know," said Minck. "I don't think you're going to do such a lot of harm in the future."

"Don't you? Eve won't like what I'll tell the police."

"Women are funny," said Minck. "It seems she was brooding over the little trip you were taking with Miss Alban. Upset about it, she was. So she told Brett, and he came to the hotel, and told me."

"What *was*—that place?" Susie asked.

"It was a tourist camp a while ago," said Minck. "And it seems young Chiswick stopped there one time, and he heard they were closing up. Too out-of-the-way. So it seemed to him a good idea for him to steal the key to one of the cabins. He thought it would be a nice quiet place to go back to some day. Mrs. Person knew about his having that key, and she thought it would be a likely place to find you."

There was another silence.

"Mrs. Person knew other things, too," said Richard.

"Nope," said Minck.

"Yes," said Richard, "she knew what—happened to her husband."

"Nope," said Minck, again.

"You mean she's trying to deny it?" said Richard. "She won't get away with that. By God! I'll see that she doesn't. I went to see her to explain about selling Gateways a little in advance; and that damned old savage threatened me. Said he'd kill me. He followed me into Woodmore Park. He attacked me. He tried to kill me."

"And with what?" asked Minck.

"With a gun."

"And you took his gun off him."

"Person was insane. Insane with jealousy. He happened to catch sight of me when I was here the first time—talking to Eve in the Park. And when he saw me the second time ... I tell you he *followed* me. He tried to kill me, I tell you!"

"This is not getting you nowhere," said Minck. "Person was an old man, and he was drunk. And what's more, he got the knife in his back."

"He threatened to kill me, Susie!" His voice sounded eager and boyish in the dark. "You heard him threaten me, Susie."

"Thinking of calling Miss Alban as a witness in your defense?" asked Minck, slowly. "That's pretty good."

"Why not?" said Richard. "I didn't do her any harm. I never touched her. She came with me of her own free will. You'll have to admit that, Susie. I can prove it. We stopped at a restaurant and had something to eat together. Does that look as if I was kidnapping her? Susie, you haven't—there isn't *anything* against me."

"What about Charles?" Susie said.

There was another silence. She thought of Charles lying in the rain. I called out to him, and he came ... she thought.

"Susie," said Richard, "you've made a big mistake about Loder. He was a crook. And that can be proved. I happened to see inside his suitcase, and it was half full of silver spoons and forks; all sorts of silver. Susie, remember he was the one who got you in jail—and then he ran away and left you there. Susie, they'll examine his bag now, and they'll see all that silver. Susie, he was a crook."

She listened to him in stunned amazement. In an instant he went on again, in the same eager, quick way.

"You *really* haven't anything against me, Susie! I never did you any harm. Susie, be fair about it. I—we got on very well together."

She listened, staring at him in the dark.

"Susie!" cried Richard. "For God's sake, be fair! Don't let anyone turn you against me. Don't—"

"This is where you have to shut up," said Minck, and stopped the car.

"I don't care what you do!" said Richard.

"You might, though," said Minck.

"Please!" said Susie. "Please, Mr. Minck, let's go on."

"But he makes me sick," Minck explained. He started the car again.

"Susie," Richard went on, "if you'll stand by me, I can get out of this, Susie, you don't want to see me—accused of—of something I didn't do...."

She turned away, and the eager loud voice stopped.

"Listen, sister," said Minck. "Take it easy and don't cry." He patted her arm. "You had a kind of a wild night, and you ought to rest."

"What about me?" cried Richard. "What d'you think this is like for *me?* Susie, remember that—that I'm young. I've been decently brought up. I can't *stand*—being shut up—being locked up—like a wild animal.... You'll tell them, won't you, Susie, that I didn't do any harm?"

She made no answer, and he stopped; and she heard him breathing hard.

"Women are soitenly funny," said Minck. "Now, take my wife."

"Have you a wife, Mr. Minck?"

"Yes, why wouldn't I? I got two little boys, too," he said with dignity.

"I may not be any Clark Gable, but there was never anybody else that took the—abhorrence to me that you did."

"I'm sorry, Mr. Minck."

"Think nothing of it," he said, kindly. "Only—"

"Susie," Richard began, "for God's sake say you'll stand by me! Eve's turned against me—my uncle—everyone. I haven't a friend on earth. If *you* —"

"*Shut up!*" bellowed Minck. "And I mean it. If I hear another word out of you, I'll shut you up, and in a pretty rough-and-ready kind of way, too."

"Susie! He's taking me to the police station! Susie, for God's sake stand by me. Help me!"

They were driving up to the old house where she had seen Captain Catelli. Two green lights burned outside it, looking big and blurred in the rain. Minck blew the horn loudly.

"Susie!" said Richard "You *can't* let this happen to me! Susie!"

"Take him away," said Minck. "I'll be back in a while. He's the one who did in old Person. Here's the knife. I saw him drop it."

"You better come in and see the Captain," said one of the men.

"I'll be back in half an hour," said Minck. "I'll be back by the time you wake up your Captain, and he gets around here. Just hold this baby; and hold him good. He's about the lowest skunk I ever met."

"Susie! Susie!"

She heard that voice calling until they turned the corner.

"Listen, sister," said Minck. "Pull yourself together now, that's a good girl. The woist is over. Of course, you'll have to answer questions and all, but you'll get a little rest before that."

"All right. I'll try," she said.

But they were going up the drive to the Bretts' house now. The rain still fell, but the sky had grown lighter. She remembered driving up here for the first time, and it was infinitely remote. It was like a bright little picture from childhood. And she had been so happy, so excited, sitting in the car with Brett and the doctor. And Charles, and Richard. It was only yesterday, she thought. But there was an abyss between yesterday and today; and there was no bridge back.

"Come, now, sister!" said Minck.

He got out of the car, and helped her out. Her legs were shaking, as if she had not used them for weeks; she was glad that he held her arm as they mounted the steps. He rang the bell, and somebody came running along the hall.

"For Gawd's sake!" said Queenie's voice. "Come in, you poor kid, and—"

She gave a strange little sound like a squawk.

"It's nothing," said Minck in a tone of displeasure. "Once she gets rested up, she'll be all right."

Susie turned toward the mirror in the hall; and she saw a ghastly little face streaked with mud, wet hair plastered around the forehead and temple, huge, sunken dark eyes.

"Susie!" cried Charles from somewhere. He caught her in his arms, and she held him tight.

"Oh, Charles! Oh, Charles!" she cried. "But I thought—"

"Come in and sit down," he said. "You must be tired."

She looked up at his pale and desperate face; and she began to laugh.

"Stop that!" said Queenie, sharply. "Here! You come upstairs, and get yourself washed and fixed up. Stop that, Susie!" She tried to stop, but she could not banish the wide and wavering smile on her face, she could not stop her shoulders from shaking.

Queenie led her upstairs, sat her in a chair, and brought her a drink. "Stop that now, while I run a bath for you," she said. "A nice hot bath, and I'll put my good bath-salts in it. Drink that whiskey."

The bath was run, fragrant with perfume. An entire outfit of clothes was set out for her, underclothes, very fancy, a pink taffeta house coat, black satin mules. She stayed in the hot bath a very long time, and she was crying. She washed her hair, still crying; she put on the outfit, and by that time she felt warm and much quieter.

Queenie was waiting in the hall for her. "Minck wants to see you," she said. "In here."

Minck was standing in one of the neat and empty bedrooms, and she was surprised to see that it was daylight there. A gray and rainy daylight; but the night was over. He closed the door.

"One thing I want to say," he said in a low tone. "That gun that young Chiswick took off of old Person ... loaded with blank cartridges, that was."

"But—"

"I knew it," he said, "hoid it from Mrs. Person. Seems that the old man always loaded it with blanks. To scare dogs and cats, and so on. That's why I let Loder get out of the car alone, and walk right up to that gun."

"But he fell—"

"That's just what happened. He stumbled on a rock, and he fell. What I want you to remember is, Loder *didn't* know," said Hobart Minck. "He thought he was facing the real thing."

"But, Mr. Minck ..."

"I'm tough," said Hobart Minck. "You got to be, in a job like mine. But I got a whole lot of sympathy for romance. I feel sorry for that guy."

"For Charles?"

"Yes," he said. "Why, it was pitiful, the way he did everything wrong.

Making you keep still about old Person, so you wouldn't get in trouble. This about saying he was an author. He thought that would make him interesting. The truth is, he's the son of Hamly Loder, the silver-plate manufacturer. Millionaire. But that poor guy doesn't think it's interesting to have a millionaire father."

"Well, I don't know if it is," said Susie.

Minck compressed his lips and shook his head.

"I see," he said. "Well, you're romantic, too. However, this poor guy was traveling for his father, and he was not supposed to get off at South Fairfield at all. He was supposed to go right on to Boston, where there was money waiting for him. Instead of which, he gets off the train when you get off, and he doesn't have any money. He rings up his old man in New York to wire some, so that he can get a beauteous damsel out of jail, and the old man does not see it. So the poor young guy goes in to New York and he gets some money. All for your sake."

There was a knock on the door.

"Breakfast is ready!" called Queenie.

"Good enough!" Minck called back. And he said to Susie out of the corner of his mouth, "Just remember he didn't know it was going to be a blank cartridge."

"Yes, I will," said Susie.

There was the doctor waiting for her in the dining-room, and Percy and Queenie and Charles. They all sat down at the table, Minck with them. Queenie brought in eggs and bacon, and griddle cakes with maple syrup, and beautiful, strong, clear coffee.

"Susie," said Charles, sitting beside her. "Try to eat a little, won't you— dear?"

Yesterday she might have laughed. She might have told him she was almost frantically hungry all of a sudden.

But today she thought that wasn't what he wanted from her. She raised her eyes to his face, and for the first time in her life, she knew how pretty she was.

"I'll try, Charles," she said, gently.

THE END

Elisabeth Sanxay Holding Bibliography
(1889-1955)

NOVELS

Invincible Minnie (1920)
Rosaleen Among the Artists (1921)
Angelica (1921)
The Unlit Lamp (1922)
The Shoals of Honour (1926)
The Silk Purse (1928)
Miasma (1929)
Dark Power (1930)
The Death Wish (1934)
The Unfinished Crime (1935)
The Strange Crime in Bermuda (1937)
The Obstinate Murderer [aka No Harm Intended] (1938)
Who's Afraid [aka Trial by Murder] (1940)
The Girl Who Had to Die (1940)
Speak of the Devil [aka Hostess to Murder] (1941)
Kill Joy [aka Murder is a Kill-Joy] (1942)
Lady Killer (1942)
The Old Battle-Ax (1943)
Net of Cobwebs (1945)
The Innocent Mrs. Duff (1946)
The Blank Wall (1947)
Miss Kelly (1947)
Too Many Bottles [aka The Party Was the Pay-Off] (1950)
The Virgin Huntress (1951)
Widow's Mite (1953)

STORIES

Patrick on the Mountain (*The Smart Set*, July 1920)
The Problem that Perplexed Nicholson (*The Smart Set*, Aug 1920)
Marie's View of It (*The Century Magazine*, Dec 1920)
Mollie: The Ideal Nurse (*The Century Magazine*, Jan 1921)
Angelica (*Munsey's*, May-Oct 1921)
The Married Man (*Munsey's*, Dec 1921)
The Foreign Woman (*Munsey's*, July 1922)
Hanging's Too Good for Him (*Munsey's*, Sept 1922)
Like a Leopard (*Munsey's*, Nov 1922)
Lost Luck (*The Bookman*, Dec 1922)
The Girl He Picked Up at Coney (*Metropolitan Magazine*, Feb/Mar 1923)
The Aforementioned Infant (*Munsey's*, Mar 1923)
It Seemed Reasonable (*Munsey's*, Apr 1923)
Old Dog Tray (*Munsey's*, May 1923)
The Matador (*Munsey's*, June 1923)
A Hesitating Cinderella (*Munsey's*, July 1923)
The Postponed Wedding (*Munsey's*, Aug 1923)
With Unbowed Head (*The Century Magazine*, Aug 1923)
This is Life (*The Nation*, Aug 15 1923)

The Marquis of Carabas
(*Munsey's,* Sept 1923)
Out of the Woods (*Munsey's,* Oct
1923)
Benedicta (*Munsey's,* Dec 1923)
Nickie and Pem (*Munsey's,* Feb
1924)
His Remarkable Future
(*Munsey's,* Apr 1924)
His Own People (*Munsey's,* July
1924)
Who Is This Impossible Person?
(*Munsey's,* Aug 1924)
Ye Gods and Little Fishes (*The
American Magazine,* Aug 1924)
Mr. Martin Swallows the Anchor
(*Munsey's,* Sept 1924)
Too French (*Munsey's,* Jan 1925)
The Good Little Pal (*Munsey's,*
Apr 1925)
Flowers for Miss Riordan
(*Munsey's,* May 1925)
Sometimes Things Do Happen
(*Munsey's,* June 1925)
Miss What's-Her-Name
(*Munsey's,* July 1925)
The Long Night (*Ladies Home
Journal,* Sept 1925)
The Wonderful Little Woman
(*Munsey's,* Sept 1925)
As Patrick Henry Said (*Munsey's,*
Oct 1925)
The Worst Joke in the World
(*Munsey's,* Nov 1925)
As Is (*Munsey's,* Dec 1925)
That's Not Love (*Munsey's,* Jan
1926)
Rosalie Gets Out of the Cage (*The
American Magazine,* Feb 1926)
The Thing Beyond Reason
(*Munsey's,* Feb 1926)

Dogs Always Know (*Munsey's,*
Mar 1926)
Highfalutin' (*Munsey's,* Apr 1926)
Bonnie Wee Thing (*Munsey's,*
May 1926)
Vanity (*Munsey's,* Jun 1926)
The Compromising Letter
(*Munsey's,* July 1926)
Miss Cigale (*Munsey's,* Aug 1926)
Blotted Out (*Munsey's,* Sept 1926)
Human Nature Unmasked
(*Munsey's,* Oct 1926)
Home Fires (*Munsey's,* Dec 1926)
The Grateful Lunella (*The
American Magazine,* May 1927)
The Old Ways (*Munsey's,* July
1927)
By the Light of Day (*Munsey's,*
Aug 1927)
For Granted (*Munsey's,* Nov
1927)
Incompatibility (*Munsey's,* Dec
1927)
One Misty Night, (*The American
Magazine,* Feb 1928)
Derelict (*Munsey's,* Mar 1928)
Half an Hour Late (*Woman's
Home Companion,* Mar 1928)
This Road Is Closed (*The
American Magazine,* Apr 1928)
Inches and Ells (*Munsey's,* June
1928)
It Is a Two-Edged Sword
(*McCall's,* June 1928)
Too Late (*Liberty,* July 21 1928)
Outside the Door (*The Elks
Magazine,* Oct 1928)
Hard as Nails (*Liberty,* Oct 20
1928)
Important Things (*Liberty,* Nov
17 1928)

A Dinner Date (*The American Magazine*, Jan 1929)

Vera's Superior Smile (*Pictorial Review*, Jan 1929)

Saving Up (*Liberty*, Jan 5 1929)

Flow and Ebb (*Liberty*, Jan 26 1929)

Without Benefit of Police (*Complete Stories*, Feb 1929)

The Sin of Angels (*The American Magazine*, Apr 1929)

Dare-Devil (*The American Magazine*, June 1929)

Little Deeds of Kindness (*Liberty*, July 6 1929)

Broken Faith (*The American Magazine*, Oct 1929; *Cassell's Magazine of Fiction*, July 1930)

Carline (*Liberty*, Oct 12, 1929)

Rose-Leaves (*Liberty*, Jan 18 1930)

The Chain of Death (*Liberty*, May 24, May 31, Jun 7, Jun 14, Jun 21 1930)

The Girl in Armor (*Street & Smith's Detective Story Magazine*, Aug 8 1931)

It's All Right for Men (*Liberty*, Oct 10 1931)

Brides of Crime (*Street & Smith's Detective Story Magazine*, Nov 7, 1931)

The Preposterous Mrs. Manders (*Woman's Home Companion*, Mar 1932)

Hound's Bay (*Street & Smith's Detective Story Magazine*, Mar 26 1932)

If It Hadn't Been for Laurel (*Liberty*, Jan 28 1933)

A Man Can Take It (*Collier's Weekly*, May 12 1934)

The Green Bathtub (*Collier's Weekly*, June 16 1934)

The Last Night (*The Passing Show*, July 14 1934)

All She Could Get (*Collier's Weekly*, Sept 15 1934)

"I Could Brighten Your Life!" (*The American Magazine*, Jan 1935)

The Bride Comes Home (*Cosmopolitan*, Feb 1935)

The Root of Evil (*Collier's Weekly*, Apr 27 1935)

Nobody Would Listen (*Mystery*, Aug 1935)

Somebody's Cynthia (*Collier's Weekly*, Aug 3 1935; *The Passing Show*, Nov 2 1935)

You Never Can Tell (*Collier's Weekly*, Dec 14 1935; *Grit*, June 1936)

Unscathed (*Ladies Home Journal*, Jan 1936)

Lost (*Redbook*, Feb 1936)

Cross Purposes (*Collier's Weekly*, May 30, 1936)

Can Do! (*Pictorial Review*, July 1936)

Scandal (*Woman's Home Companion*, July 1936)

Night Life (*Redbook*, Sept 1936)

Third Act (*Pictorial Review*, Apr 1937)

Drifting (*McCall's*, May 1937)

Wedding Day (*Cosmopolitan*, Sept 1937)

The Nicest Little Lunch (*Cosmopolitan*, Nov 1937)

Echo of a Careless Voice (*McCall's*, Jan 1938)

Illusion (*Good Housekeeping*, Aug 1938)

They Take It So Lightly!
(*Cosmopolitan*, Oct 1938)

Two Passes for the Show (*Liberty*,
Nov 5 1938)

So Sort of Proud (*Good
Housekeeping*, Mar 1939)

Money Can't Buy It (*Liberty*, Aug
5 1939)

Open That Door (*Liberty*, Aug 26
1939)

Blonde on a Boat (*The American
Magazine*, Dec 1939)

Late Date (*Cosmopolitan*, May
1940)

Proposal (*McCall's*, May 1940)

On Yonder Lea (*Good
Housekeeping*, Aug 1940)

Tropical Secretary (*The American
Magazine*, Feb 1941)

Tomorrow's Not Soon Enough
(*McCall's*, Mar 1941)

What It Takes (*Grit*, Mar 9 1941)

Loved I Not Honor More
(*Liberty*, Apr 12 1941)

The Fearful Night (*The American
Magazine*, June 1941; expanded
to *The Obstinate Murderer*)

Another Baby (*Woman's Home
Companion*, Nov 1941)

Not Goodbye But Au Revoir
(*McCall's*, Oct 1942)

The Kiskadee Bird
(*Cosmopolitan*, 1944)

The Old Battle-Ax (1943;
abridged, *Liberty*, Mar 18 1944)

Bait for a Killer (*Collier's Weekly*,
Sep 30 1944, as "The Blue
Envelope"; *The Saint Mystery
Magazine*, Mar 1959; *The Saint
Detective Magazine* [Australia],
Nov 1959; *The Saint Mystery
Magazine* [UK], Oct 1960)

The Unbelievable Baroness (*The
American Magazine*, 1945)

The Net of Cobwebs (*Collier's
Weekly*, Jan 6, 13 & 20, 1945)

Funny Kind of Love (as by
Elizabeth Saxanay Holding,
*Boston Sunday Globe
Magazine*, Nov 11 1945)

Farewell to a Corpse (*Mystery
Book Magazine*, Oct 1946)

"Be Careful, Mrs. Williams"
(*Cosmopolitan*, July 1947)

The Stranger in the Car (*American
Magazine*, July 1949)

People Do Fall Downstairs (*Ellery
Queen's Mystery Magazine*, Aug
1947; *Ellery Queen's Mystery
Magazine* [Australia], Aug
1949)

Friday, the Nineteenth (*The
Magazine of Fantasy and
Science Fiction*, Summer 1950)

Farewell, Big Sister (*Ellery
Queen's Mystery Magazine*, July
1952; hardboiled satire)

The Death Wish (*Cosmopolitan*,
Feb 1953)

Most Audacious Crime (*Nero
Wolfe Mystery Magazine*, Jan
1954)

Shadow of Wings (*The Magazine
of Fantasy and Science Fiction*,
July 1954)

Glitter of Diamonds (*Ellery
Queen's Mystery Magazine*, Mar
1955; *Ellery Queen's Mystery
Magazine* [Australia], May
1955)

The Strange Children (*The
Magazine of Fantasy and
Science Fiction*, Aug 1955)

Very, Very Dark Mink (*The Saint Detective Magazine*, Dec 1956; *The Saint Detective Magazine* [UK], Oct 1957)

The Darling Doctor (*Alfred Hitchcock's Mystery Magazine*, Mar 1957)

Game for Four Players (*Alfred Hitchcock's Mystery Magazine*, June 1958)

The Blank Wall (*Alfred Hitchcock Presents: My Favorites in Suspense*, 1959)

Suspense Classics from the Godmother of Noir...

Elisabeth Sanxay Holding

978-0-9667848-7-9
Lady Killer / Miasma $19.95
Murder is suspected aboard a cruise ship to the Caribbean, and a young doctor falls into a miasma of doubt when he agrees to become medical assistant in a house of mystery.

978-0-9667848-9-3
The Death Wish / Net of Cobwebs $19.95
Poor Mr. Delancey is pulled into a murderous affair when he comes to the aid of a friend, and a merchant seaman suffering from battle trauma becomes the first suspect when Aunt Evie is found murdered.

978-0-9749438-5-5
Strange Crime in Bermuda / Too Many Bottles $19.95
An intriguing tale of a sudden disappearance on a Caribbean island, and a mysterious death by pills, which could have been accidental—or murder.

978-1-933586-16-8
The Old Battle Ax / Dark Power $19.95
Mrs. Herriott spins a web of deception when her sister is found dead on the sidewalk, and a woman's vision of a family reunion is quickly shattered by feelings of dread when she answers her uncle's invitation to visit.

978-1-933586-41-0
The Unfinished Crime / The Girl Who Had to Die $19.95
Branscombe tries to control everyone around him with such a web of deceit that he is the one finally caught up in its tangled skein. Jocelyn is convinced she is going to be murdered, so naturally everyone suspects young Killian when she is pushed off the cruise ship.

978-1-933586-71-7
Speak of the Devil / The Obstinate Murderer $17.95
Murder stalks the halls at a Caribbean resort hotel, and an aging alcoholic is called in to solve a murder that hasn't happened yet. "Strongly recommended."—*Baltimore Sun.*

978-1-933586-97-7
Kill Joy / The Virgin Huntress $17.95
A young lady finds trouble when she follows her employer to a house where death seems to stalk its every visitor; and a young man tries to stay one step ahead of the huntress who tries to uncover his questionable past. "Unbearable suspense."—*St. Louis Post-Dispatch*

Two novels in each trade paperback edition from:

Stark House Press
1315 H Street, Eureka, CA 95501
griffinskye3@sbcglobal.net
www.StarkHousePress.com

Available from your local bookstore, or order direct with check or via our website.

www.ingramcontent.com/pod-product-compliance
Lightning Source LLC
Chambersburg PA
CBHW071752190726
48292CB00003B/956